PRAISE FOR

The Dream Lover

"Exuberant . . . The pages fly." —*The New York Times Book Review*

"Exquisitely captivating . . . [George] Sand's story is so timely and modern in an era when gender and sexual roles are upended daily."
—*USA Today*

"Fantastic . . . a provocative and dazzling portrait . . . Berg tells a terrific story, while simultaneously exploring sexuality, art, and the difficult personal choices women artists in particular made—then and now—in order to succeed. . . . The book, imagistic and perfectly paced, full of dialogue that clips along, is a reader's dream."
—*The Boston Globe*

"[An] absorbing new work of historical fiction [and] an armchair traveler's delight. Berg rolls out the wonders of nineteenth-century Paris in cinematic bursts that capture its light, its street life, its people and sounds. [*The Dream Lover* is] an illuminating portrait of a magnificent woman whose story is enriched by the delicate brush strokes of Berg's colorful imagination." —*Chicago Tribune*

"Elizabeth Berg weaves an enchanting novel about the real life of George Sand." —*Us Weekly*

"The book opens a window on Sand's unconventional life and an exciting era for the arts in Paris." —*Richmond Times-Dispatch*

"*The Dream Lover* is the novelization of author George Sand's life that you didn't know you absolutely needed." —*Bustle*

"Lavishly described . . . Elizabeth Berg uses her own skill as a writer to graphically present the reader with a clear picture of a brilliant, yet flawed woman." —Fredericksburg *Free Lance-Star*

"Meticulously researched . . . Berg illuminates [Sand's] courage and contradictions in luxuriant detail." —*San Jose Mercury News*

"Berg offers vivid, sensual detail and a sensitive portrayal of the yearning and vulnerability behind Sand's bold persona."

—*Publishers Weekly*

"[V]ivid . . . Berg sets off on a project that's part biography, part George Sand fantasy, alternating between scenes from Aurore's fairy-tale childhood and tales of her adult affairs—her brilliant career, her difficult family life, her struggles with femininity and the limitations of femaleness, her complicated sexuality and, above all, her many, many whirlwind romances." —*Kirkus Reviews*

"[A] beautiful, imaginative re-creation . . . Berg's years-long immersion in the writings of and about Sand has resulted in a remarkable channeling of Sand's voice."

—*Library Journal* (starred review)

"Regardless of whether or not readers were familiar with Sand before reading *The Dream Lover,* they undoubtedly will be fascinated by this singular woman's life." —*Bookreporter*

"[Berg's] subject is exciting and on-trend: George Sand, the nineteenth-century French writer whose insightful novels took readers by storm, and whose cross-dressing persona and many love affairs scandalized contemporary society . . . lived by her own rules, and her imagined voice—warm, sincere and wise—is wonderfully disarming. . . . Berg's descriptive skills are remarkable throughout."

—*Booklist*

"Instantly inviting . . . Berg honors [Sand's] life and loves on each page as she delves so deeply into this unforgettable woman."

—*Everyday eBook*

"Elizabeth Berg is both tender and unflinching as she explores the heart of the enigmatic writer George Sand. Her lyrical prose caused me to pause and savor the words; her penetrating insights made sense of a cross-dressing writer as notorious for her romantic conquests as her brilliant novels. Sand is captivating in *The Dream Lover*. With an eloquence of the heart worthy of her subject, Elizabeth Berg gives us a very human portrait of a nineteenth-century legend who dared to live and speak freely."

—Nancy Horan, *New York Times* bestselling author of *Loving Frank* and *Under the Wide and Starry Sky*

"*The Dream Lover*—what a bold, insightful, and enticing novel. And how vigorously Elizabeth Berg brings us the iconoclastic life of George Sand. Berg writes with such intimacy and compassion that I think she must have some shared ancestral DNA with Sand. I savored every page."

—Frances Mayes, *New York Times* bestselling author of *Under the Tuscan Sun* and *Under Magnolia*

"Elizabeth Berg's *The Dream Lover,* which explores, through the eyes of George Sand, what artistic life means for women, is a delightful departure into a very different world, a wonderful challenge the author has taken on and met full tilt. The scintillating cityscape of Paris comes alive for us here, complete with writers and painters and musicians, priests and rogues and noblemen, all revealed in their glory, their passion, and their very human failings."

—Chitra Divakaruni, author of
Oleander Girl and *The Mistress of Spices*

"*The Dream Lover,* a historical novel at once expansively researched yet intimately imagined, may seem like a radical departure for this beloved author. Yet the more I read, the clearer it became: we are in *quintessential* Berg territory. Indeed, George Sand may be the ultimate Berg heroine. "A life not lived in truth," Berg writes, "is a life forfeited." In this latest work, Elizabeth Berg has poured her own great gifts and her own great heart into the story of a woman determined to refuse any such forfeiture, no matter the cost."

—Leah Hager Cohen, author of
No Book but the World and *The Grief of Others*

"*The Dream Lover* is the dream match of writer to subject, Elizabeth Berg animating George Sand so vividly that you feel the Frenchwoman speaking directly to you. Infamous for her eccentricities and her passions, Sand is shown to be a touching figure, a woman needing to love and be loved, a writer needing to be read and understood. Bravo to Berg for pushing aside decades and decades of misunderstanding to reveal so compelling a story, and so human a heart."

—Robin Black, author of *Life Drawing*
and *If I Loved You, I Would Tell You This*

"What a rich, heartbreaking, triumphant novel Elizabeth Berg has written! I recommend reading it with a highlighter in hand so you can mark the insights about love and life and being a woman that are on every page so you can reread and savor them. George Sand was a remarkable woman; Elizabeth Berg is one of our finest storytellers. I can't think of a better match of subject and writer."

—Ann Hood, author of
The Knitting Circle and *The Obituary Writer*

"In *The Dream Lover,* Elizabeth Berg brings George Sand to life as never before: meet the brilliant, impulsive, haunted, and yet fearlessly honest woman whom no one in her lifetime ever forgot. Berg's language sings as she channels the untamed spirit of a nineteenth century writer who lived by her own rules. We *recognize* her voice. George Sand was a modern woman, someone who might feel ahead of her time even now. By sharing Sand's multifaceted dreams, Berg enriches and deepens our own. This book, like George Sand, sparkles."

—Blue Balliett, *New York Times*
bestselling author of *Chasing Vermeer*

"*The Dream Lover* is more than just a rich, affecting portrait of George Sand, a brilliant woman in a man's world who has to fight to become the artist she was meant to be. With its births and deaths and love affairs and revolutions, it's an opera. Elizabeth Berg has gone back in time and written a dense, full-fledged nineteenth-century novel."—Stewart O'Nan, author of *West of Sunset*

BY ELIZABETH BERG

The Dream Lover

Tapestry of Fortunes

Once Upon a Time, There Was You

The Last Time I Saw You

Home Safe

The Day I Ate Whatever I Wanted (stories)

Dream When You're Feeling Blue

The Handmaid and the Carpenter

We Are All Welcome Here

The Year of Pleasures

The Art of Mending

Say When

True to Form

Ordinary Life: Stories

Never Change

Open House

Escaping into the Open: The Art of Writing True

Until the Real Thing Comes Along

What We Keep

Joy School

The Pull of the Moon

Range of Motion

Talk Before Sleep

Durable Goods

Family Traditions

THE DREAM LOVER

Dream Lover
BALLANTINE BOOKS
New York

THE *Dream Lover*

A NOVEL

ELIZABETH BERG

The Dream Lover is a work of historical fiction. Apart from the well-known actual people, events, and locales that figure in the narrative, all names, characters, places, and incidents are the products of the author's imagination or are used fictitiously. Any resemblance to current events or locales, or to living persons, is entirely coincidental.

2016 Ballantine Books Trade Paperback Edition

Published in the United States by Ballantine Books, an imprint of Random House, a division of Penguin Random House LLC, New York.

Ballantine Books and the House colophon are registered trademarks of Penguin Random House LLC.

Random House Reader's Circle & Design is a registered trademark of Penguin Random House LLC.

Originally published in hardcover in the United States by Random House, an imprint and division of Penguin Random House LLC, in 2015.

Grateful acknowledgment is made to HarperCollins Publishers for permission to reprint excerpts from *Leila: The Life of George Sand* by Andre Maurois, translated from the French by Gerald Hopkins, copyright © 1953 by Andre Maurois and copyright renewed 1981 by Gerald Maurois. Reprinted by permission of HarperCollins Publishers.

Library of Congress Cataloging-in-Publication Data
Berg, Elizabeth.
The dream lover: a novel/Elizabeth Berg.
pages cm
ISBN 978-0-345-53380-7
ebook ISBN 978-0-679-64470-5
1. Sand, George, 1804–1876—Fiction. I. Title.
PS3552.E6996D73 2014
813'.54—dc23 2014043629

Printed in the United States of America on acid-free paper

randomhousebooks.com
randomhousereaderscircle.com

4689753

Book design by Barbara M. Bachman

TO MY DAUGHTER,

Jennifer Sarene Berg

The finest female genius of any country or age.

–Elizabeth Barrett Browning

She is beyond doubt or comparison the strongest woman and the most astonishingly gifted.

–Franz Liszt

When my submission has been claimed, no longer in the name of love and friendship but by reason of some right or power, I have drawn upon the strength that is buried in my nature, I have straightened my shoulders and thrown off the yoke. I alone know the latent force hidden within me. I alone know how much I grieve and suffer and love.

–George Sand

THE DREAM LOVER

PROLOGUE

April 1873

COUNTRY ESTATE AT NOHANT

CENTRAL FRANCE

IN THE DINING ROOM, THE MEN ARE EATING ROSES. THE SMALL BOUquet I placed at the table's center will soon be naked stems. A wreath of cigar smoke hangs in the air above my guests' heads, moving ever upward toward the Venetian glass chandelier, where the pink and turquoise colors will give in further to the dimming of their clarity.

The men—Gustave Flaubert, Ivan Turgenev, Alexandre Dumas fils, and my darling son, Maurice—are pushed back in their velvet chairs, sated; and the conversation has gone languorous. But not for long! Soon we will be dancing, singing, playing at charades, and making a great deal of noise, though Gustave will no doubt sulk and complain that we have too quickly turned our attentions away from literature, his raison d'être. The rest of us—Ivan especially—greatly enjoy the kind of raucousness that takes us back to the easy pleasures of childhood. I love doing my work and the reverie it requires, but too much contemplation turns to melancholy, and gaiety must then come to the rescue.

Before we begin our evening's amusements, our puppet show and readings and bagatelles, I have sought the out-of-doors and a temporary reprieve from my role as hostess. I stand now in a mantilla of shade, beneath a tree here so long its mere presence dwarfs the idle happenings or musings of those who seek out its shelter.

The light is amber, the air still; the daylilies have folded in on themselves. Soon the hooded blue of dusk will fall, followed by the darkness of night and the sky writing of the stars, indecipherable to us mortals, despite our attempts to force narrative upon them.

I sense the beginning of my end. At random moments I find myself in sudden need of an intense privacy. Then I excuse myself from my own table, from the trilling conversation in the bookshop, from the darkened theater or the street market, with its bins of fish and chard. I stand somewhere alone to calm myself, to draw breaths past the knot in my chest. I lose focus of my surroundings in order to accommodate a more compelling vision in which I undress my life, searching for the vital place, the beating heart of what I most truly was and am.

I am in agreement with Goethe, who said that every day one ought to "hear a little song, read a good poem, see a fine picture, and if it were possible, to speak a few reasonable words." I would add to this the need to love. Without it, the rest is dust.

January 1831

NOHANT

OUTSIDE, I HEARD THE CRUNCH OF GRAVEL AS THE HORSES PULLED into the driveway. I moved to the window and saw the driver climb down to open the carriage door, then stand aside to wait for me. The morning sky was a dull gray, leaking pale yellow light here and there; thick clouds hung low. I picked up the small bag I had packed; I was not taking much. Later, after I had moved from the pied-à-terre on Rue de Seine that my half brother was reluctantly lending me and into my own place, I would send for my things.

The horses' breath rose up in the air as nearly solid-looking columns of white, and the driver in his heavy coat shivered. *I must go,* I thought, and took one last look around the bedroom, disallowing myself any sense of sorrow.

I descended the winding staircase. It was so oddly quiet, the children—seven-year-old Maurice and two-year-old Solange—off with the servants, no sounds coming from the halls or the drawing room or the dining room or even the kitchen. It was as though the house were holding its breath. I missed my children already, though my husband, Casimir, and I had arranged to alternate caring for them.

When I opened the front door to go out, I saw Casimir, standing coatless on the porch. I raised my chin and moved quickly past him. He kept his arms crossed and made no move to touch me. The driver hesitated, looking to my husband for direction. Casimir nodded brusquely, and the driver put out his hand to help me into the carriage.

Once I was settled, I tightened my gloves and leaned my head out the window to speak to Casimir. "You should go inside. You must be cold."

"I am not." But clearly he was.

"Well, then. Au revoir."

"You will write to me immediately upon your arrival in Paris," Casimir said.

I nodded, then faced forward and rapped on the wall of the carriage to let the driver know I was ready to go. The vehicle lurched forward, as did I. There was in it a moment of indignity, nearly comedic—a feeling that I had lost my balance. But I had not.

We rolled slowly through the gates of the estate, and then the driver turned the carriage onto the main road, made a clicking sound, and the horses began a rapid trot. When we passed the cemetery that lay directly to our right, I looked over at the graves of my father and my grandmother. I thought about the ways in which one is shaped, starting from birth and even before, into the person one becomes. One cannot stand isolated from those who came before him, and fate decrees that there are many other things over which one has no control. Yet if one has courage and resolve, there are ways to make changes in one's life.

I pushed my hand into my valise to rest it upon the manuscript I had tucked in there—a novel I had completed, called *Aimée,* which I intended to show to a publisher with whom I had a connection through a mutual friend. I would need to find a way to support myself, for the allowance of 250 francs a month that Casimir would be giving me would not go far in a city where I had been told one needed at least 25,000 a year to live. I had inherited most of the money we had, as well as the house here at Nohant, but the law stipulated that my husband controlled both.

A light snow began to fall, then rapidly intensified. I kept my hand upon the pages, closed my eyes, and gave myself over to my thoughts. Into my head came the sounds of violin music, my father playing on the day I was born.

My father's name was Maurice Dupin. His great-grandfather was Augustus II, king of Poland; and his grandfather was Maurice de Koenigsmark, later called the Maréchal de Saxe when he was the most exalted field marshal in Napoleon's army. This *maréchal* was renowned not only for his cunning and bravery upon the battlefield but for a particular kind of bonhomie he demonstrated in war. For instance, he commonly arranged for women and theater for himself and his men to enjoy after a good day of battle—never, he believed, would they appreciate such things more. All of France knew his name.

And so it was in my father's blood, his great love of the military, and he joined the army in 1798, when he was twenty years old, never mind his mother twisting her handkerchief. Two years later, he was transferred to Milan, Italy, as an aide-de-camp, and it was there that he met my mother.

She was Antoinette-Sophie-Victoire Delaborde, called Sophie, a courtesan currently living with a general who'd been smitten by her great beauty, her passion, and her gaiety. As was my father. He stole her away from the general, apparently with little ill will, for he was later promoted.

In many letters written to his mother at this time, my father spoke of his love for his fine mistress, and my grandmother worried and fretted, frightened to death that her son might marry someone so far beneath him. She knew that my mother was four years older than Maurice and of a lower class, born to a poor man who sold songbirds on the quays of the Seine, and that in addition to working as a camp follower, she had a young daughter. It was not the match my grandmother had in mind for her beloved son.

There was in this no small measure of hypocrisy. My grandmother may have had illustrious aristocrats in her family, but she came from a long line of illegitimate births, including her father's. And she herself was illegitimate—her mother, ironically, was a courtesan who had captured the Maréchal de Saxe's attention.

My father went on to distinguish himself in battle, as his grandfather had, but then he was captured by the enemy and held for two months as a prisoner of war. In May 1801, after his release, he returned home to my grandmother at Nohant. His normally buoyant personality had changed; he had about him an air of melancholy. One would expect such a change after a man is subjected to the ills of imprisonment—vile treatment, near starvation, and only straw upon the ground for a bed. Add to this the mental distress of my father coming to understand that he was perhaps not destined always to be lucky, as he had often told his mother—he was as vulnerable as anyone else. But what beleaguered my father most in those days was the thought that he would have to choose between two women, both of whom he loved.

My grandmother had been my father's only parent since, when he was nine years old, his father died, leaving the little family enough of a fortune that my grandmother had a comfortable yearly income. In 1793, when the eleven months of the Reign of Terror began and the ruling Jacobins were ordering mass executions by guillotine in order to compel obedience to the state, she had fled her apartment in Paris and bought a peaceful country estate 150 miles south of the city. It was in the Berry region, a gently hilly, largely agricultural area of central France, and the estate lay just outside the little village of Nohant-Vic, population 272. Nohant was situated between the larger towns of Châteauroux and La Châtre.

The house itself, done in the style of Louis XVI, was commodious without being ostentatious. It had once been the site of a fourteenth-century feudal castle, and the bell tower still stood, its dusty, tile-lined belfry serving as a gathering place for doves. On the estate's acreage were the smaller houses of peasants, tenant farmers who worked the land. With its fields, expansive gardens, acres of forests, and the Indre River running through it, it was a beautiful place in which to grow up.

In the absence of his own father, my father displayed toward his mother the protective attitude that is understandable in such situations. Their correspondence to each other revealed a mutual affection and appreciation as well as a deep level of trust; and oftentimes the language my father used in expressing his longing to see his mother bordered more than a little on the romantic.

But Sophie! Literally from the time my father first saw her, he was obsessed with her. He had had plenty of opportunities to delight in the charms of highborn, beautiful, and cultured women. Sophie offered something different, something more. He—and many others, I might add—found her irresistible. The more time he spent with her, the more his love intensified.

After he'd been released from prison, my father had gone to see Sophie in Paris. At that time, she was again living with a general, but she begged my father to take her with him when he went back to Nohant. Because he was at that point a penniless soldier (he did not then or ever like to rely upon his mother for his support), she even offered to lend him money to fund the trip. My father's response was that my mother should think carefully and without his influence about whether she truly wanted to be with him, leaving behind a man who kept her in a manner most comfortable. My father's charm would not buy bread.

It took almost no time for my mother to make her decision: she elected to throw in her lot with my father, the man she truly loved. And so the two of them set out for Nohant.

My father had a plan: rather than introducing the two women

right away, he would set Sophie up three miles away in La Châtre, at an inn called the Tête Noire. When the time was right, he would make the introduction.

After he spent a few days at Nohant, my father began disappearing for long stretches of time, telling his mother he was visiting relatives. But she suspected he was seeing a woman and finally confronted her son.

My father admitted that it was Sophie he was seeing, that he was keeping her at the inn. He said, "She has sacrificed everything in order to be with me. I am full of gratitude toward her, full of joy that she has chosen to be by my side."

My grandmother's feelings were hardly the same. Bosom heaving, lace cockade trembling at the top of her head, she told her son that she refused to meet Sophie. She berated him for the scandal such a woman's presence would cause and requested that he immediately send Sophie back to Paris, without him.

"For so many long days and nights I turned away food, I could not sleep, for worry about you," she told him. "I rejoiced that when you came home on leave you would be with me until you had to return to the service. Now even when you are with me, you are not; your thoughts are always with her. Please, I beg you, send her away; give yourself time to think carefully about your future!"

My father's response was uncharacteristically strident. "You ask me to turn her away as though she were a vulgar mistress, when I tell you over and over again that in fact I adore her! Was it not you who made me an acolyte of Jean-Jacques Rousseau, who said that we are all born good and capable of self-improvement? Have you not all your life taught me to appreciate the noble attributes of people regardless of their class?"

My grandmother only stared at him, helpless to explain the difference between what is in a mother's head and what is in her heart.

They went round and round, each wounded, each hoping the other would come to understand their version of the irrefutable truth. The dinner table, once gay with stories and laughter, was now all but silent, the clinking of silverware and the murmur of the servants the only sounds.

It was Jean-François Deschartres who finally resolved the issue in a bold move, one that came with dire consequences.

Deschartres was my father's tutor. He was a secularized cleric, having studied for the priesthood without being ordained, and he was under my grandmother's employ. He was inordinately devoted to both my father and her.

He was an odd man, very thin and tall, pale of skin and eye. He kept his tonsured hairstyle, and he favored wearing knee breeches and stockings and yellow gaiters. In cold weather, he always wore the same ancient brown coat. He had a stutter that was more pronounced when he was nervous, and he was occasionally excitable in the way of an old woman. He had, too, an air of perpetual distractibility, as though he held the Almighty in one hand and you in the other and could never quite decide to whom he should give his complete attention.

But Deschartres was also highly intelligent, an expert in teaching a great variety of subjects. He had no understanding of love or passion, however. He looked upon such emotions as something that must be tolerated in his fellow human beings, a kind of tic of personality he felt fortunate not to be burdened by.

Hearing the arguments between my father and my grandmother must have distressed Deschartres greatly; he had never before seen them behave toward each other in this way. And so early one morning, while the rest of the household was asleep, he went to see Sophie. He intended to persuade her, for the good of all, to leave immediately.

He picked a bouquet of flowers before he left, and on the ride over, he practiced in his mind what he would say to her. When he got to the inn, he quickly climbed the stairs to her room and knocked at the door.

No response.

He knocked again, loudly now, and heard a low voice, sweet in tone, say, "Maurice?"

"It is I, François Deschartres, Maurice's tutor." He felt a sudden rush of blood to his head, an outbreak of perspiration. He wiped his upper lip and leaned forward to speak authoritatively into the crack of the door. "I have come with an important message for you." He put his ear to the crack to listen for her response and heard Sophie walk quickly across the floor. There were sounds of rapid dressing, and then she flung open the door.

Upon seeing her, Deschartres was at first speechless: she had been sleeping, and there was a soft pink flush to the cheeks of her heart-shaped face. Her eyes were wide and dark and very beautiful, direct in their gaze. She was barefoot, and her black hair was not done up but loose around her face, cascading over her shoulders. Her bosom was ample, her waist narrow, and she had about her an air of sultry grace.

He asked if he might come in.

"Bien sûr," she said, most pleasantly, and stepped aside to let him pass. She was very small in stature, and it must have given even dry-souled Deschartres pause to think about delivering such a stern directive to one so tiny.

He offered her the bouquet, and she took it without looking at it. "Has something happened?"

"Only this," Deschartres said. "Your presence here has made for a great rift in the relationship between Maurice and his mother, whom, as you must know, he loves more than any person on earth. Every day they argue bitterly, and I can tell you most assuredly that this is not their way; they have always been unusually close. I have come to ask you to go back to Paris. Maurice says you love him; what better way can you prove it than to spare him the terrible pain you are now causing him? Give him distance, give him time, do not subject him any longer to such terrible strain, especially when he has so recently been freed from prison. Surely, without any need for elaboration, you can see that you are not meant for each other. He is in need of peace and care and quiet. Now, if you will kindly collect your things, I shall arrange—"

"Out of my sight, you fool!" Sophie cried, flinging the bouquet to the floor. "Go back to kissing the withered feet of your benefactress! Do not spoil Maurice's and my happiness with such a ridiculous demand. Do you imagine that I do not know what Maurice needs now? You may rest assured it is not his mother!"

And then, small as she was, she forced Deschartres from the room, slamming and locking the door after him.

An outraged Deschartres knocked again and again, to no avail. Finally, he said, "Have it your way, then, ignorant girl! You leave me with no choice but to call upon the authorities. Then we shall see how long you stay here spinning your web! You are a common prostitute, rightfully worthless in the eyes of respectable people, and you do not belong here!"

"I'll leave this pedestrian place all right," Sophie shouted. "And I'll take Maurice with me, you'll see! You have no idea how much he loves me. Every day, he begs me to marry him! I'll take him with me and we will never return!"

The flustered tutor did go to the police, then to the mayor, and to them he made a most dramatic case for evicting the dangerous interloper holed up at the inn who would not listen to reason and go away from a place where she was not wanted. She was causing trouble of the most terrible kind. She was torturing the soul of a decorated officer in the army of Napoleon, a newly released prisoner of war, and this officer's mother, Madame Dupin, was a gentlewoman and a saint, as surely they knew. Madame was deeply distressed by this interloper's presence and was spending her days in tears and anguish. Who knew how long her health could withstand such an assault? The wench must be made to leave immediately. Surely some reason for forcing her away could be found. She did not have papers, say; or if she did have papers, something was wrong with them. They must find a way, even if she needed to be imprisoned!

In his heart, I am certain that Deschartres thought he was doing the right thing. He believed Maurice would come to see the wisdom in exiling someone who was an irritant and a distraction and who was, besides, far beneath his station. Once Sophie was gone, Maurice would understand why she had had to leave. All of this would be no more difficult than the days when Deschartres had to force the loudly protesting young Maurice to bed, only to see the boy, once his head hit the pillow, fall asleep immediately.

But when the excited police arrived and demanded that my mother let them in, they found only what looked like a weeping angel, a lovely figure in a white dress, barefoot and seemingly defenseless. Those men were susceptible to my mother's charms in a way that Deschartres could not be, and they ended up expressing not outrage but pity for her. Upon gentle questioning, my mother told the authorities the truth: she had met Maurice in Italy and they had fallen in love. She had left a wealthy general for him, a poor lieutenant; she had listened to her heart and chosen love over riches and comfort. Was this a crime?

Deschartres, who was waiting outside, agreed to leave only when he was told that the police would persuade my mother to go back to Paris that very day.

Deschartres had just left when my father came galloping up, having learned that his tutor had gone to castigate his true love. Everyone knows this simple truth of the heart: Nothing will bring lovers closer together than people trying to keep them apart. And so my father rushed to Sophie's defense. He leapt off his steed, raced up the steps to her room, and embraced her. He tenderly dried her tears, kissed her forehead, her cheeks, her mouth, and the palms of her hands. He begged her to forgive the behavior of his family, whom he now disavowed. He told her to take the coach back to Paris, promising that he would soon follow her there.

Back at Nohant, a breathless and red-faced Deschartres, nearly choking on his self-righteousness, had been telling my grandmother that she was more than justified in having serious doubts about my father's lover. "She is the lowest kind of commoner," he said, pacing back and forth in the dining room. "She is uncouth and selfish, totally without proper upbringing, and you are correct in thinking that the sooner Maurice is separated from her, the better. He cannot think straight around her; she clouds his reason, but he is of course in every way too good for her!"

Into this scene came my father, panting and wild-eyed. When Deschartres started to speak, my father turned his back to him, ignoring him, and stood close to his mother to tell her that he must get away from Deschartres immediately or he would throttle him at the least. My father would go and visit friends in Châteauroux for a few days to clear his head; when he came back, all would be calmer and they could talk.

"But now you leave me yet again," my grandmother said, weeping. "How it hurts me for you to go away when all I want in the world is to have you nearby!"

My father could engage in fearsome battles with his sword, he rode on when cannonballs were whizzing by him, he could withstand being wounded or made a prisoner of war, but never could he bear his mother's tears.

His heart softened and he embraced her, kissed the top of her head and rocked her side to side, saying, "Now, Mother, dear Mother, you know that we are all beside ourselves! Let me go for a brief visit and have some time to think. Do not concern yourself with Sophie! Perhaps she will go to Paris and console herself in the arms of another man and I will be shown to be the fool that you suggest I am. But let me go away now, and give me your blessing; I shall soon return to you and even to that reprobate Deschartres in a much better frame of mind."

My father knew very well he could not stay angry at Deschartres, for above all else, they loved each other. The tutor had helped raise the little boy, and the boy's mind and spirit were enriched by the odd soul who taught him arts and sciences and took him for long walks in and around Nohant, oftentimes carrying him home, asleep on his shoulder.

My father did go to visit friends, and from there he sent my grandmother a long letter of appeal, which contained these words: "Some women are, to use Deschartres's vocabulary, mere wenches and harlots. I do not like them or seek them out. I am neither libertine enough to waste my powers, nor wealthy enough to keep women of that sort. But never could these vile words be applied to a woman of feeling. Love purifies everything." Nonetheless, he assured his mother that marriage was not on his mind, nor on Sophie's.

After a few days, he returned to the house at Nohant. There he had a tearful reconciliation with Deschartres, who was standing morosely outside arguing with the gardener about the placement of lettuce seedlings. Soon afterward, though, my father went to Paris and stayed there, first on one pretext, then on another. My grandmother suspected correctly that his real reason for being there was to see Sophie. Finally, he returned to Nohant and, while he was there, seemed to make an honest effort to forget Sophie.

It was to no avail. The heart is a small muscle with tremendous strength; it will have its way. Eventually, my father went back to Paris and Sophie. When he became active again in the army, she followed him from camp to camp.

A week before I was born, Sophie decided that she wanted her child to be both legitimate and born on Parisian soil. And so my father was given leave to return to the city, where he and my mother were married in a civil ceremony. My grandmother was not told of this at the time; indeed, she was not told for two years. My father did try, at first: he traveled to Nohant the day after the ceremony to make the announcement, and it must have happened that his nervousness showed. My grandmother must then have suspected the reason for his visit, and before he could utter a word that would make real her deepest fear, she began to weep, saying that my father, by his involvement with a woman of whom she could not approve, had shown that he no longer loved her. Rather than inform her of his marriage to the woman he adored, my father reassured my grandmother of his love for her.

July 1804

RUE MESLAY

PARIS

ON THE DAY OF MY BIRTH, MY FATHER WAS PLAYING HIS BELOVED VIOLIN at a party given for my mother's newly engaged sister, my aunt Lucie. My mother, resplendent in a ruffled pink silk dress and matching shoes with pearls at the center of their bows, was dancing a quadrille. She excused herself suddenly and repaired to a nearby bedroom overlooking the garden, where she gave birth to me, reportedly without a sound and also very quickly. It was Lucie who attended my birth, a consequence of my mother having latched onto my aunt's arm at the moment she realized it was time.

I have imagined the scene of my birth many times. Both my parents and my aunt told me about it, and, along with the details they provided, over the years I lavishly added my own. I saw it unfolding thusly:

I opened my eyes in murky warmth, aware of a squeezing sensation that grew in intensity from all sides and finally thrust me down a narrow passage of flesh and out into a bright light, against which I closed my eyes and wailed. A single spindle of saliva broke as I opened my mouth. There was crust in one eye. I was transferred from one set of arms into another. I heard the lilting voices of women.

After she ensured that mother and baby were stable, Lucie went back to the party to tell my father the news. She made her way through the revelers and approached the small group of musicians, who stood with my father in the corner of the room. She laid her hand on Maurice's arm, stopping his playing. The other musicians stopped playing as well, and the crowd grew abruptly silent. Lucie said into the stillness, "Come, Maurice, you have a daughter." This announcement was greeted with a great burst of applause.

"She will be fortunate," my aunt told the guests, over her shoulder, as she led my father to the bedroom. "For she was born in the time of roses, to the sounds of music." Now the crowd laughed, and then the music began again. I turned my head toward the sound, drawn to music then as I ever would be.

And then there was my father, holding me in his arms. His tears fell on my forehead, and his long forefinger gently wiped them away; but I, still in possession of the short-lasting but infinite wisdom that is ours in the womb, felt his great joy as well. I was given the name Amantine-Lucile-Aurore, and my father said, "We shall call her Aurore, after my mother, who does not bless her now but, in time, will."

Surely it tore at his heart to hold me that day, an infant whose weight barely registered in his arms, knowing that his mother would condemn his marriage and, by extension, me. He pulled me closer and rocked me side to side, crooning.

A writer has a most fertile mind, or he is no writer at all. He has an imagination that soars when given the most meager starts: a wet blade of grass, croissant crumbs on a plate, the sight of a woman hurriedly crossing a street. And in the way that the fiction a writer produces can assume a truth of its own, these details of my birth seem less story to me than memory.

AFTER I WAS BORN, my father felt there was no more hiding from my grandmother; now he would need to tell her of both his marriage and the birth of his daughter.

My grandmother's position was always this: she could forgive one's circumstances at birth. After that, though, came the life one chose to fashion for oneself. She herself, for example, despite being born illegitimate, had conducted herself properly, married well, lived a life of great dignity, and never gave cause for criticism or scorn. She had plans to raise her own (legitimate!) child, my father, in the same way. She could and did turn a blind eye to her son's dalliances: he had fathered a son with a girl in the village outside Nohant. My grandmother doted on the boy, called Hippolyte, and contributed money to help raise him after he was put in the care of a peasant woman next door to the estate. But to give him the name Dupin, to consider him in any way an heir to her fortune? Certainly not! His last name was Chatiron, after his mother. Whom her son most emphatically did not marry.

My father argued that Sophie's life experiences had not permitted her to make the same choices as my grandmother and reminded her that Sophie was legitimate, as was her daughter, Caroline. But my grandmother persisted in her complete disregard for Sophie, as well as in her belief that the differences between her and Maurice were too great to sanction a relationship between them. It could not last. It was not proper. My father was an aristocrat: kind, deep-feeling, optimistic, and intelligent. He was also a brilliant artist and gifted in his knowledge of languages and of literature. He was very much sought after to sit at the tables of many important and influential people, for he was a most charming and witty conversationalist. He loved music perhaps most of all, and he was widely praised for both his singing and his violin playing. He acted impulsively, but with the kind of courage and trust that can make rash decisions seem like good ones, even well-considered ones. He loved—and, I daresay, lived for—the beauty in life. He found it everywhere, and he was as glad to give it as to receive it.

My mother was mercurial, a beautiful, dark-complected bohemian with a dramatic way of expressing herself, whatever her mood. She had been cast out of her home in her early teens to work as a dancer in a theater in the hope that she would find a "protector." She was strong and practical and had, as well, an air of mystery and magic about her; she was one of those charismatic beings who draw the eyes and ears of everyone in the room. Most of all, she was well aware of the uses and power of passion—my father alluded obliquely but clearly to skills she possessed that turned strong men into weak-kneed devotees.

Never mind my grandmother's concerns about such a mismatch. I learned in time to use each side of my family for my own particular advantage.

I AM SORRY TO SAY that in the end, my father lacked the courage to tell my grandmother about his marriage, but he did write to her of my birth. He told her my name was Aurore, after her, in an effort to win whatever goodwill that might bring. But my grandmother had heard rumors of my parents' marriage, and she wrote to the mayor of the Fifth Arrondissement of Paris, where they had supposedly exchanged vows, with the request that he confirm the union, which he did. Soon afterward, she went to the city and set about trying unsuccessfully to have the marriage annulled. She would not stop in her quest to force my parents apart. After her husband's death, she had turned all her hopes and attentions to her only son. For him to marry a woman like my mother ruined her plans, so carefully conceived and meant to serve as comfort to her in her old age.

But there was something else, too, something of which she may not have been consciously aware: there is always trouble of the worst sort when a widow effectively remarries and the man she weds is her son.

When my father heard that his mother was in Paris, he concocted a plan of his own. He brought me to her apartment building and conspired with the concierge to find a way for my grandmother to see me.

The concierge came to my grandmother's apartment to show off "her" granddaughter. "Look at her; I can hardly bear to put her down!" she said, then offered me to my grandmother to hold. When I was in her lap and my grandmother saw my eyes, so like my father's—large, black, and with the softness of velvet—she understood that it was her own granddaughter she was holding. "Who brought her here?" she demanded. The tone of her voice caused me to burst into tears.

The instinct to protect children that lies in the breast of most mothers took hold, and the concierge stepped forward with her arms outstretched. *"Ah là là,"* she said, "give her back to me. I can see she is not wanted here."

She started to lift me from my grandmother's lap, but my grandmother only held on to me more tightly. She raised me to her shoulder and, sighing, began to pat my back. "Poor little mite," she said, "none of this is your doing. There now, stop your crying; you are safe with me.

"Who brought her here?" she asked again, albeit more gently.

The concierge raised her fingers nervously to her mouth, then clasped her hands before herself. She spoke rapidly, saying, "If you please, madame, it was your son, Monsieur Maurice, who waits downstairs. We thought if only you held the child, you would—"

"Maurice!" my grandmother cried and, with a great deal of emotion, called for my father to be brought up to her. They embraced and wept, my small body between them, but in the end my grandmother would not agree to meet Sophie or to bless the marriage. All she could manage was to take a ruby ring from her hand and press it into my own; she wanted the ring to be given to my mother.

Thus my grandmother made a conciliatory move toward my mother, but with a mediator in between: me. Just like my father, I was caught in the middle.

January 1831

RUE DE SEINE

PARIS

IN THE PREDAWN DIMNESS, I LAY IN BED, TRYING TO PINPOINT THE start of the events that had led to my being here in Paris, on my own. I had no husband, no children with me; it was just I, my valise in the corner of the bedroom not fully unpacked, and my footsteps echoing in the apartment whenever I moved about. The noises outside, even at this early hour—carriages bumping over cobblestones, the night cleaners finishing picking up garbage, the cynical laughter of prostitutes on their way home—did nothing to penetrate the quiet around me.

In many ways, it was a political revolution that had led to my personal rebellion. In the summer of 1830, all of us at Nohant had yearned for news about the neighborhood uprisings in Paris that took place during the July Revolution. There was a great deal of hatred for Charles X, and young resisters armed with not much more than paving bricks had attempted to force the king's abdication. I had worried about my mother and other relatives living in Paris, of course; but I had also worried about those young laborers I had never met yet fully sympathized with: factory workers and students who put their lives on the line for their beliefs. They were not alone in reviling the Bourbon Restoration; Charles X was maligned not only by the poorest people on the street but also by the wealthiest in their well-appointed mansions.

On July 26, in the midst of a heat wave, workers who had been barred from the factories took to the streets. More than forty journalists from eleven newspapers signed protests against Charles X, and for seventy-two hours there was bloody and chaotic fighting, which left six hundred dead and two hundred wounded. The next month saw the abdication of Charles X; and then Louis-Philippe, whose nickname was "Citizen King," came back to Paris from London, where he had been in exile.

The ones who brought this news to us at Nohant were a group of young men, students who lived now in Paris but were originally from our Berry district. They returned home now and then, and when they did, they often gathered or stayed at our house. I welcomed them because they caught us up on the news, but also because they were stimulating company, a welcome relief from the usual tedium my husband, Casimir, and I fell into when we were by ourselves.

One day, I went to the nearby Château du Coudray to visit my friends Charles Duvernet and Alphonse Fleury, whom we called "the Gaul." With them was a man seven years my junior whom I had not met before, a nineteen-year-old recent law graduate from La Châtre named Jules Sandeau. He had an endearingly shy demeanor. I asked if he went hunting with my friends, and he flushed, answering, "I'm afraid I don't care for loud noises. The truth is, I'm a lazy sort of romantic dreamer whose greatest pleasure is to read and to make up my own stories."

I found him very handsome. He had a pink-and-white complexion and thick, curly blond hair. His build was rather slight, the kind I preferred, and his confession that he was a "romantic dreamer" did nothing but make me more interested in him.

I told him I had been talking with my other friends about the recent revolution in Paris and had asked them if a new republic had been declared. They hadn't been sure, and I asked if Jules knew. He did not. I mounted my horse to set off for La Châtre in search of news. Before I rode off, however, I invited Jules to come to dinner at my house the next day and told him to bring the others.

At that dinner, I read a letter to my guests that I had just received from my children's tutor, who was now in Paris. There had indeed been a new republic declared.

Soon afterward, my husband, Casimir, joined the National Guard. I worried about this, I told Jules and my other friends when

I saw them a few days later. I worried about my husband and my mother and my aunt Lucie, who had had a job associated with the previous regime.

Jules shrugged. "When the blood is on fire, there is no room for reason. The citizens will defend themselves." Later, though, we took a walk by the river, and his approach was more gentle. "I know they will be safe," he told me.

"How do you know?" It was getting dark outside; I could hardly see his face.

"Because I want them to be. For you." He looked about, then moved closer to me and offered his arm. "We should go back."

I didn't want to go back. Suddenly, I wanted to stay out all night with this young man. My attraction to him had grown stronger in the days since we'd met. He knew literature and politics and history. Though he had studied law, he wanted to become a writer, as did I, and we spent hours talking about our methods and habits in writing stories. In spite of my being so much older than he, I saw that he was equally drawn to me.

Not much more time passed before I fell in love with Jules, and I told him so. He confessed that he felt the same, and finally we gave in to temptation.

There was at Nohant a kind of summer house I had created. It was away from the main house and one could get to it without going through the village, so it was in that respect a very private place. Jules and I met there a few times and indulged ourselves not only in lovemaking but in the sweet talk and tender foolishness all lovers enjoy.

I felt no guilt about this. Like my father, I believed that love purified everything. The only thing wrong in making love was being intimate with one you in fact did not love.

I had no love for my husband. And for almost two years, I had been sleeping in my own room, apart from him. Not long after we were married, I had become aware that he regularly bestowed his affections on others, including our housemaids. In addition to that, because of a secret I would very soon uncover, I would be vindicated in my belief that his feelings toward me resembled hatred more than love.

Divorce had been abolished by Napoleon, and as long as the law still gave husbands the right to manage their wives' money and assets, I had no thought that I would get an equitable separation, one with a settlement that would allow me and the children to live apart from Casimir. For a long time, I had been trying to make the best of things, at considerable cost to my health.

I felt I'd been drowning, and now love had thrown me a rope. I could refuse it and slowly die or take it and live.

Before Jules left the country to go back to Paris, he begged me to join him there. With tears in my eyes, I said I wished I could, but surely he understood that I could not.

But now here I was, in Paris.

I went to the window of my half brother's apartment. Morning had broken, and the city was alive with movement and color and sound. I wanted to gobble up everything: the people bustling down the sidewalks, many with dogs as sophisticated-looking as they, the pink-gray light, the tall brick buildings near me and the rounded domes in the distance, the Seine, the stores, the street vendors, the cafés with their beautiful gilt-framed mirrors, the magnificent churches, the gardens with their marble statues, the streets crowded with carriages and coaches and bicycles, the elegant gas streetlamps. I wanted to know everything, do everything, I wanted to leave my provincialism far behind and be part of a city of eight hundred thousand that was growing exponentially. I wanted to immerse myself in a life of writing, the life of an artist. I wanted to be like the bohemians, who cared nothing for the opinions of others. They dressed as they pleased and lived as they saw fit and honored their own ways of thinking. They did what made sense to them, rather than following the restrictive and sometimes ridiculous mandates of the bourgeois.

Equally, I wanted to be in the arms of my lover, into whose

rented room I would soon be moving, unbeknownst to my husband. Hippolyte's apartment would serve only as a place to receive mail until I found an apartment for Jules and me. I was seeking a building with a concierge who would announce visitors, and with a back door that would accommodate a quick getaway, should my husband happen to appear without advance notice.

I dressed quickly, stuffed the heel of a loaf of bread into my mouth, and put on my coat. I was going to buy men's boots, which were solidly constructed and had iron heels that would not wear down. I had been slipping and sliding on the icy streets. The delicate shoes I'd come here with had cracked almost immediately after my arrival, and I'd found myself tripping in the clumsy overshoes I had bought to replace them. I needed to feel secure on my feet because I wanted to know every part of the city, to walk it from one end to the other until it was as familiar to me as Nohant was. I would buy boots, and then I would make arrangements to meet with the novelist who would help me publish my book.

January 1805

PARIS

BY THE TIME I WAS SIX MONTHS OLD, RUMOR AND INNUENDO ABOUT my parents' misalliance was more than my grandmother could bear. People were condemning my father for marrying so far below his station, not in small part because of my grandmother's disapproval of it. But they were condemning of my grandmother as well, for not supporting her son now that the deed was done. Finally, she agreed to attend a religious ceremony for my parents' marriage, followed by a small and uncomfortably quiet supper. She would recognize the marriage, if not her daughter-in-law.

In many respects, it was nearly impossible for her to become close to my mother; their personalities were so very different. Whereas my grandmother could not so much as put up an umbrella without following an unwritten law, my mother lived by her own rules. And she did not suffer fools, no matter what their station in life. She felt that in some respects she was superior to aristocrats. "Look at my hand," she once said. "Do you see how my veins are larger than those nobles'? My blood is redder, too; I have more stamina than they could ever dream of!"

This seemed true. Whereas my grandmother seemed incapable of walking more than a few feet, my mother rarely went to bed before one, and she was up at six, working. She did all her own cooking, sewing, and cleaning. If my grandmother had tried to emulate her for even one day, it would have been the death of her.

Sophie did not enjoy long dinners, evenings out, glittering society balls, or many other things that upper-class people did or aspired to do. What she liked best was being at home, in the company of someone whose heart was sincere, someone she could trust and who could trust her enough to let her be herself absolutely. There was a person whose beliefs were very much like hers, and that person was my father. Despite what my grandmother thought, my parents were exceedingly well matched.

Soon after my birth, my father went back to his duties as an officer in the army. When I was around two years old, my mother joined him at a camp in Montreuil. Seven-year-old Caroline, the daughter born to my mother before my father and she met, and I lived then with my aunt Lucie and her daughter, Clotilde, in a village called Chaillot.

I remember how Caroline and I rode in creaking baskets on either side of a donkey my aunt occasionally rented from a neighbor. She used the beast to carry carrots and cabbages to the market at Les Halles. I remember how I loved both the peace of the country and the garden especially; but I was equally taken by the vibrancy of Paris. Though they were opposites, even as a child, I wanted both.

May 1808

RUE DE LA GRANGE-BATELIÈRE

PARIS

AT THE AGE OF THREE, MY FATHER WAS OFF TO WAR AND I WAS BACK in Paris, living with my mother in a small garret apartment. My half sister, Caroline, was for the most part away at school. To keep me from running all over the place, my mother fashioned a makeshift playpen from four rush-backed chairs. In the center of the space she put an unlit foot warmer for me to sit on, but I rarely sat. Mostly, I leaned my foreams casually on the seats and chatted on and on, like a grandiloquent patron in a barroom.

It was really here that I began my profession as *conteuse.* Then, as later, I started with not much, something more feeling than idea, an image or a thought or even a question that flew into my head and perched there. After that, there came quite naturally some sentence followed by another and then another, each building upon the last. I did not think about what should come; I only spoke out what was quite suddenly *there.* I made what would otherwise have been long, boring hours enjoyable by offering to myself and anyone who cared to listen another place to be, a place as real to me as the chair walls that surrounded me.

My stories satisfied me, if not my exasperated mother, who called them *romans interminables.* We stayed in the kitchen together for hours on end, the sun shining through the narrow window or rain pattering against it, she with her sleeves rolled up to make her stews and chicken livers, her plum tarts. While she labored, she sang in a beautiful, pure voice. So it was that I learned early on the satisfying combination of food and music and literature. And though my mother was often impatient with my lack of quiet, she was also sometimes drawn into my stories enough to put down her knife, wipe off her hands, and pull me onto her lap, where she then listened to me more closely, and sometimes laughed and kissed me. And so I also learned early the seductive power of words.

Ah, Maman. In later years, when we tore at each other, I kept in mind those kitchen tableaux, times when I sat at her feet and watched as she gamely made soup of bits of onion and potato peels and scant grindings of pepper because she had not budgeted our food allowance properly. She often spent too much money on theater tickets so that we might go out of our grim surroundings and lose ourselves to the glory of the stage. We needed to have something to do besides go to daily Mass. Though I couldn't have articulated it at the time, I wasn't sure I saw the point of Mass, anyway: it seemed to me that my mother was as inclined to feel the spirit of God in the beauty of nature or the kindness of friends as much as when a largely indifferent priest placed a white host in her mouth.

My mother told me Bible stories, or stories about herself and her sister, my aunt Lucie, playing dress-up in clothes given to them by the old woman who lived next door, or stories about her father taming his little birds before he sold them, teaching them to sit on his finger, then making smacking noises so that the birds would kiss him. He showed his daughters how to do this; they laughed at the odd feeling of the birds' beaks pulling gently at their lips and at the sight of the tiny purplish tongues.

There were many nights when my mother fell into bed and wept quietly with longing for her husband fighting in Napoleon's Peninsular War. After he was transferred from cold and rainy Prussia to Spain, he was promoted to major and stationed at the palace of the deposed prince of Asturias in Madrid, to serve under Joachim Murat, marshal of the empire and imperial lieutenant to Spain.

There, the weather was fine and the women beautiful. And Sophie's husband was beautiful, especially in uniform, with his gold epaulets and shiny sword, the sabretache that featured an eagle embroidered out of seed pearls. He had a white woolen cape with gold buttons and braiding and a matching pelisse with black fur, which he wore tossed over the shoulder. His trousers were purple with a gold lace overlay. He had red Moroccan leather boots with the seams done just so, and he wore an eighteen-inch yellow plume on his velvet-trimmed shako. He wrote to my mother of his own magnificence in uniform, though it was done in such a charming way one would never accuse him of immodesty: he gave the credit to the clothes and not the person.

So, yes, he was handsome and well-mannered and witty and cultured and easily seduced, as she well knew. Never mind that he wrote to her words meant to be reassuring and romantic: "I've had only one ambition since I met you, namely to make up to you for the injustices of society and destiny, to assure you of an honorable life, and to shelter you from unhappiness. Nothing is worth more to me than the modest chamber of my dear wife. Nothing is equal in my eyes to her lovely dark hair, her beautiful eyes, her white teeth, her graceful figure, her little prunella shoes." Beautiful words, to be sure. But she was here in Paris, in a drafty garret apartment with me, and he was there, with other women with lovely dark hair.

Finally there came a day when she stood leaning against the

window jamb, looking out, then turned and announced quite suddenly that we were going to join him—she knew of another army wife who was going that day to be with her husband, and there was room in the coach, which was soon departing. My mother was almost eight months pregnant with my brother then, and the two-week journey would be arduous if not dangerous for her; but when she was determined, she could part the seas.

Hastily, she packed a bag and then held out a hand to me.

"But, Maman."

"What is it?" she asked, impatient as always, one foot quite literally out the door. I pointed to the table, where she had put out carrots to slice for pot-au-feu, and where she had poured herself a glass of red wine.

She shrugged. "Never mind that. Come quickly! Now!"

"First I must find my doll," I said, for even then my maternal instincts ran high. But she grabbed my arm and pulled me out the door.

I wept most bitterly as we made our way down the stairs—what would become of my Véronique, when I was not there to care for her? How could I go to sleep without my doll beside me? My mother was unmoved. She kept saying, "There is no room!" But I believe she meant there was no time.

WE TRAVELED IN GREAT discomfort to Spain, crammed together in a carriage that bumped and strained along the roads. When we descended into the valley of Asturias, the temperature was exceedingly hot; my mother fanned herself and me uselessly. Everywhere there were signs of wartime desperation: a severe shortage of food, ruts in the road, the gaunt and despairing faces of the people we passed, a burnt smell in the air. At the inns where we stayed, we were sometimes served roasted pigeons for dinner, and that was considered a luxury. When I could, I slept on a table my mother padded with cushions from the coach.

Finally, we arrived at the palace in Madrid where my father was stationed. His quarters were above those of his commander. There was not the usual staff to care for the large and beautiful rooms in which we stayed; they were nearly as dirty as the coach in which we had ridden. But people who love each other and are together make a home, and so although we were not in our apartment in Paris, we were nonetheless content.

Despite the lack of cleanliness, we were surrounded by luxury: silver cutlery, gilt and brocade furniture, high ceilings, mirrored doors, and heavy draperies. Huge oil paintings hung on the walls, the subjects seeming to take haughty note of our presence; and the Oriental carpets that lay on the floors were easily the size of our entire apartment in Paris.

One afternoon not long after we arrived, I was told to go out onto the balcony to play, and the French doors were locked behind me. I amused myself for some time with the magnificent dolls belonging to the infanta that had been left behind. Then I sat daydreaming, and I'm sure that on my face was the look of slack-mouthed "stupidity" my mother and others accused me of when I took my flights of fancy. Eventually, though, I wanted in. It was hot; I was bored; I was in need of a drink of water. I knocked at the glass many times, then called out. Finally, the door was opened to me.

When I came in and my eyes adjusted to the light, I saw my mother lying on a chaise in the corner of the room. She was pale and still, her eyes closed. At first I thought she was dead, and I began to cry. But then she opened her eyes and signaled for me to come to her. In her arms was a bundle, and I walked over slowly to inspect it. My mother turned back the edge of a blanket to reveal a baby, his eyes and his fists squeezed tightly shut. I touched the whorl of hair at the top of his head, then moved my fingers to the place where you could see his heart beating.

"*Gentle!*" my mother said, her eyes flashing.

She loosened the blanket to reveal more of my baby brother. "Pretend you are a feather when you touch him," she told me.

My brother took in a shuddering breath, and it made for a peculiar stirring in me. I gently stroked his hand, traced the curling cartilage of his ear, peered at the sucking blister he had already developed at the middle of his upper lip.

"His name is Louis," my mother said.

The baby opened his eyes and turned toward me. There was something wrong. His irises were a very pale blue, and the pupils seemed made of glass. He appeared unable to see. I looked up at my mother.

"Soon we are going home," she said.

Very well then, I thought. Louis would be fixed, and I could now attend to getting a drink of water and to settling myself in my father's lap, my back against his buttons, my small hand tucked within his. We would have dinner and he would do his napkin puppet tricks for me; and soon we would be home.

As it happened, my mother was right. In July, we learned that my father's commander was being transferred to Naples. My father would be given several weeks of leave and would then join him there.

MY MOTHER AND I were once again put into a carriage, this time with a two-week-old baby. My father rode at the head of the departing entourage astride his Andalusian horse, aptly named Leopardo the Untamable. That animal was forever tossing his head, pulling left, then right at the reins, high-stepping and shying at movements at the side of the road. It was a point of pride for my father to be in the saddle and in command of Leopardo. He even managed to control the beast when they came across a snake that lay across the entire width of a narrow mountain road. My father dismounted, cut the snake in half, remounted, and we went on.

The journey home was far more difficult than the journey to Madrid had been. It was blisteringly hot. The only things to eat were raw onions and lemons and sunflower seeds. We saw scorched earth and gutted-out buildings, and smelled the decomposing bodies of the victims of war on the roadsides. There were clouds of flies around the dead, vultures circling overhead. On one occasion, the carriage lurched dramatically, side to side and up and down, and there was an odd crunching sound as we rolled over the obstacle. My stomach knew what it was, but my child's brain, seeking reassurance, made me ask my mother, "What was that?"

"Nothing," she said.

"What did we just roll over?"

"Tree branches," she said, but the tears that shone in her eyes told me what I suspected: it was a body we had run over, someone who had once been alive and now was being broken further by people escaping what he could not.

My father journeyed to the back of the line to check on us when he could, and despite the appalling conditions around us, he was in high spirits. We were going to Nohant. He had written his mother to tell her we were coming; he was certain she would receive us now. However hard her heart had been toward us in the past, surely she would not turn away from his wife with a newborn, nor from me, her four-year-old granddaughter, who had grown so thin and whose eyes were now enormous in her face. Surely she would welcome me even though my hair crawled with lice and I had numerous scabs from the scabies I'd contracted. And of course my father knew his mother would not be able to turn him away; she had missed him with an ache she had described to him in a letter as "a dagger in my heart which turns constantly, reminding me of its presence and your absence." It had been too long: she would embrace him and his family; she would welcome them all with tears of joy, he knew it.

When we got to the Basque foothills, the weather was cooler and the land green again. We lodged at inns and slept on beds with sheets; we ate decent food again, even little cakes. I was bathed and treated with sulfur powder—covered with a paste of it and made to ingest it as well. It had a disgusting smell, against which I was given a bouquet of roses into which to dip my nose for relief.

Early into our journey we had lost our carriage in service to the wounded and had been riding in a farm wagon stuffed with baggage and soldiers who had gotten ill, just as we had: we were all feverish and dehydrated and miserable. My mother begged my father to obtain a boat to take us up the coast to Bordeaux, thinking that the sea air would be good for us. He was able to rent a sloop, and he found a carriage as well, which he tied up on board. We sailed without incident until we reached the estuary of the Gironde, where, just off the shore, the boat hit a rock and began to take on water. While my mother carried on hysterically, my father used a shawl to fashion a sling, into which he intended to put his children. "Don't worry," he said. "I'll secure them to my back, and I'll hold you under one arm and swim with the other." He swung his sword to cut loose our carriage—we could not lose our only means of land transportation. As it happened, he had no need to use the sling or to swim; we were at the last minute rescued just offshore. My father went back into the water for our carriage and all our belongings, much against my mother's wishes, who did not feel it was worth the risk. As for me, I saved my bouquet: withered, drooping, but still roses.

Our terrible journey ended on July 21. We rode through the village of Nohant, with its little stone church and tall elms, then on through the gates of my grandmother's estate, where she waited for us.

January 1831

PARIS

THE SIXTY-TWO-YEAR-OLD NOVELIST WITH WHOM I WAS TO SPEAK about my novel was named Auguste-Hilarion Kératry. He was from the Berry region, and our meeting had been arranged by a mutual friend who was also from there. The meeting took place on a very cold morning. I had elected to wear my best dress, which was not nearly warm enough. I stood shivering on his doorstep until I was let in by his maid and then escorted to, of all places, his bedchamber!

It was clear that Kératry had just arisen and hastily dressed himself. On his bed, a woman who looked to be my age reclined under a silky pink comforter—his wife, I gathered; I had heard that his wife was very young. I nodded awkwardly to her; she nodded back; and then Kératry and I took our places opposite each other at a desk at the side of the room.

After we'd exchanged a few pleasantries, Kératry said, "Well, then, shall we?"

Nervously, I pulled my manuscript out. I had not known how many pages to bring, and so I had brought them all. My hope was that he would listen to me read several pages out loud, comment positively, then ask to keep the rest to read himself. After a few days, perhaps he would let me know what publisher he had given my work to. And after that, I hoped, I would be called into the publisher's office to be given my advance.

I began reading in a soft voice, and Kératry boomed out, "Louder, I can't hear a single word!"

I read louder, aware of the fact that not only he but his wife was listening. I could not bear to look up at either of them.

I had just started the fourth page when I heard Kératry clear his throat in a way that was not necessity but statement. And then I did look up.

His expression was pained. He put the tips of his fingers together, stared off into space for a moment, then turned to me to say, "Well. This, my dear, is my advice to you: Make babies, not books."

I nearly gasped. I was so overwhelmed with humiliation I didn't know what to do. But then I recalled how this author whom I was asking to judge my work had written a book I had found ridiculous. It was about a priest who violates a woman he believes to be dead.

I put my pages back into the bag with great care. Then I stood and said, "I thank you most sincerely for your time. As for your advice, if you think it is so good, I suggest you follow it yourself."

I walked out, my head high.

At the first café I came to, though, I sat dejected at a table near a window, my chin in my hands, and watched the people passing by. I thought about the life I had begun to build here: the friends with whom I had pooled resources so that we could rent a warm room in which to read, the modest dinners we shared in one another's apartments. I loved the theaters and museums, the literary and political events we went to. I enjoyed, as well, the ambience provided by things we could not directly participate in: ballrooms with glittering chandeliers, fine restaurants whose posted menus set our mouths to watering, two opera houses. Most of all, I loved my routine of taking my coffee every day in a café across the street, where I was able to indulge in that greatest pleasure and necessity for one who wants to write: observation.

Despite this embarrassing setback, I had never felt so alive and happy. I would not give up. There were other people I could ask to read my work, and perhaps one of them would help me. I would not go back now. I could not.

July 1808

NOHANT

I WAS FOUR WHEN OUR LITTLE FAMILY, HAVING LEFT SPAIN, ARRIVED at my grandmother's house at Nohant. I had heard my parents speak about my grandmother, sometimes when they knew I was listening and sometimes not. Even when they were saying innocuous or kind things about her, I heard with a child's perception the feeling behind the words. Furthermore, I had heard my mother talk to her sister about the witch who tortured her son because of his love for another woman. I believed that my grandmother was essentially an enemy to us, a presence to be wary of, if not feared.

But here was my father, embracing a diminutive, ivory-complected woman who could not stop smiling. He lifted her off the ground in his enthusiasm, and her little feet dangled in a way that struck me as humorous, though I was careful not to laugh. She had on a brown dress that ignored the empire waistline of the times in favor of a dropped waist, and on top of her head was a little silk cap. She wore a blond wig with a small tuft at the crown, and her face was quite lovely: large eyes, high forehead, straight nose, and a Cupid's bow mouth.

The carrying-on between mother and son lasted for some time, and I heard many variations of expressions for incredulity and joy that we were all finally here. My grandmother at long last separated herself from her son and embraced my mother. Then she bent to kiss the forehead of little Louis, who lay sleeping in my mother's arms. "Poor thing, you are exhausted, I know," she told my mother, and before my mother could answer, she was whisked away to be cared for by the servants.

Next my grandmother turned to me, and despite her small stature, she seemed very tall and imposing. I stood still and held my breath. She took my face between her hands and said, "You, I myself will care for." She grasped my hand and began to lead me off, to where I had no idea. I looked back at my father, and he smiled and nodded, so I let her take me to her chambers. After we passed through the anteroom and into her bedroom, she laid me down on what looked like a kind of chariot. I had never seen the likes of it, not even in the palace where we had stayed in Madrid. It was a high four-poster bed with feathered cornices and double-scalloped curtains. There was a down mattress, and sinking into it made me feel as though I were in a nest. There were lace pillows everywhere, more than I could count.

Just after I had been put into the bed, a tall, thin man came into the room and marched straight to my side. "Aurore, is it?" he asked.

I nodded.

"Very well. Now then, I am Deschartres, and among my many roles here I serve as physician. I am going to examine you." This he did immediately and quickly, and if not brusquely, then not gently, either. Afterward, he confirmed that I had scabies. "We shall not tell the servants," he said to my grandmother, who hovered anxiously nearby. "She is almost through it. The baby is infected as well, and of course he is also blind."

My grandmother gasped, and Deschartres said, "My dear madame, forgive me if I surprise you with this news, but surely you saw that his pupils are crystalline? He is otherwise quite unhealthy as well: listless in manner and quite underweight; he will bear watching." He pointed at me. "This one will recover in days, if not hours. And now if you have no further need of me . . . ?"

My grandmother nodded, and Deschartres left the room. I could sense that he had not meant to be cruel in telling my grandmother—and me—the things he had. It was simply the unalterable truth: unfortunate but upon us; and so it had to be borne.

My grandmother stood still for a moment, collecting herself. Then she came to sit beside me. "Tell me, child, do you think you can sleep for a bit?"

I nodded.

She fussed with the bed coverings and then left the room: a rustle of silk, the light fall of her footsteps, the residue of her scent, which was then and always vetiver. I heard her pull the door shut, and I took in an enormous breath, then let it go.

At first, exhausted though I was, I could not sleep. Every time I closed my eyes, I felt the rhythm of the carriage and saw again the slow blur of the scenery we had passed, those times I was aware of it, anyway: the villages and fields, the forests, rivers, and churches, the cemeteries with tilting headstones. We had encountered travelers walking on the road who moved to the side to let us pass, staring—peasants, mostly, with their aprons and kerchiefs, but sometimes soldiers, too. Most of the time, I had ridden with my eyes closed, drained of energy and very nearly of feeling, a nonreactive sack of blood and bones; and my poor little brother was even worse off. Every now and then I would hear my mother or father call, "Aurore!" as though from a great distance away. I would open my eyes and look at them; it seemed that was all they wanted, to know that I had heard them. I would keep my eyes open a bit more, my head lolling on my neck, then close them again.

After so long a time on the road, my surroundings here seemed impossibly luxurious. I lay still in the middle of the bed and dared not move for fear it was a dream and would disappear, the bed and the large flowers on the Persian cloth that covered the walls, the finely carved furniture, the high, multipaned windows, the trompe l'oeils in colors of blue and yellow and rose and cream.

It was so cool in that room, and the breeze carried the perfume of flowers. There were no soldiers bumping along in a cart with us, their knees bent high so that they could rest their heads upon them; there was no white-hot sun raising blisters on our flesh; there was no whine of mosquitoes or neighing of weary horses or groan of wooden axles or sounds of distant cannon fire reverberating in one's chest. Instead I heard the call and repeat of the birds, the dim clatter of the kitchen staff preparing a meal. All around me was peace and beauty and a blessed sense of safety. I tried to relax into it, but in a corner of my mind I kept the memory of the one whose bones we had run over in service of our getting here.

Eventually, I did fall asleep, though not for long. I was roused by a boy of about nine years old, a big boy with thick black hair and full red cheeks, thrusting a ragged bouquet into my face. "Here, girl, these are for you," he said.

I raised my eyes to my grandmother, who stood with her hand on the boy's shoulder. "This is Hippolyte, who has come to meet you, and whose manners I daresay need improving!" She did not tell me at the time, but this was my half brother, from my father's relationship with the peasant girl.

"Do you want to come outside to play?" Hippolyte asked. He blinked once, twice, then reached his finger up to dig inside his nose.

"Ah là là!" my grandmother said, tsking, and yanked his hand down from his face. She asked me, "What do you think, my dear? Would you like to go outside?"

I nodded, and within the space of a few minutes, Hippolyte and I were out in the beautiful day, the sky nearing sapphire in its depth of blue, clouds moving slowly, nearly hypnotically, above us. I saw acres of black earth, tall trees, and many varieties of flowers, both wild and cultivated. I stood staring at the star-shaped grass-of-Parnassus, which had delicate, veinlike etchings on each petal, until Hippolyte pulled on my arm, impatient to take me elsewhere.

There was a large vegetable garden, a vine arbor, and thick-trunked walnut trees, whose gentle deterioration only added to their great beauty. There were enclaves of little houses where peasants lived, and Hippolyte showed me his, only a few steps away from my grandmother's house.

The Indre River ran through the land, and Hippolyte brought me to it. He told me he caught fish there with his bare hands. When I looked askance at him, he said, "It is true; I shall show you someday. And then we shall make a fire and cook the poor fellow! I shall pick my teeth with his bones!"

He looked with satisfaction at my face, hoping, I think, that he would see fear. But I was only intrigued and eager to catch a fish myself.

"And now we shall play war," Hippolyte said, picking up a long stick that I thought would serve as a sword. "I shall be Napoleon."

"No," I said. I had had quite enough of war.

"Very well—then I shall be a dog, as I was in a previous life. You will be a cat, and I shall chase you." He tilted his chin to the sky and barked, then waved his hand imperiously, giving me a head start. "You must run with your tail straight in the air and your back arched. You must be very afraid. You might spit at me a little."

I considered this, then said, "I shall be a dog as well."

"Don't be silly. Only boys can be dogs. Girls are cats."

I stood taller and spoke with great authority: "I am a dog because that is what I want to be, never mind that I am a girl! We shall find a squirrel to be a cat."

After about half an hour, I came back inside. My grandmother was playing the harpsichord in the drawing room, and I stood shyly at the threshold of the room, watching her. When she saw me there, she called me over to sit beside her on the bench. "Do you play?" she asked. I shook my head. "Never mind," she said. "You will learn. For now, just listen."

I sat still, listening, enraptured. After a while, I slid off the bench and lay on the floor beneath the instrument so that I could feel completely enveloped by the music. I closed my eyes and soon fell asleep. I was awakened by my father's laughter as he gently pulled at my ankles, then stood me up. "You must offer your apologies to your grandmother for being inattentive to her wonderful performance!"

"No apology is necessary," my grandmother said. "She is still tired, and anyway, you used to do the same thing, Maurice, you used to lie there in that same spot to listen—do you remember?"

He looked down at me, smiling, a light in his black eyes. "Are you feeling better, little cabbage?" He put his hand to my forehead. "No fever!"

"I am cured!" I said.

Not so for my baby brother, who mostly lay in my mother's lap, crying in a reedy wail so very different from the robust cries I'd heard from him before. He was like a little animal in a trap who despaired of any help arriving, whose only solace was to make sound out of his suffering.

That night, I awakened in my grandmother's bedroom. I was for a moment completely disoriented. Then I remembered where I was and tried to be glad of my soft bed, to appreciate the beauty of the bright stars I could see out the window. But I missed the presence of my parents. I tiptoed to their room and stood watching as they slept, my mother with my father's arm about her, my baby brother silent in his cradle nearby. I tiptoed over to my brother's cradle and started to lie down on the floor beside him. My mother sat up in bed.

"Aurore!" she whispered.

"Yes, Maman."

"What are you doing here?"

I didn't answer, merely hung my head.

"Come here," she said.

When I got to the bed, she moved over to make room for me. I climbed under the covers and nestled close to her. "There," she said. "Better?"

"Better."

From that night on, I let myself be put to bed in my grandmother's room, then snuck into my parents' bed. Downstairs, my grandmother slept on a bed made up for her in an otherwise empty space that my father dreamed of turning into a billiards parlor. She would not have approved of my sleeping in my parents' bed. She herself had lived a life largely devoid of passion or even touch. She reportedly had never had relations with her first husband, who died quite suddenly very early in their marriage. She adored her second husband, my father's father, whom she married when she was just over thirty and he sixty-two, but naturally he was more like a father to her—he even asked her to call him "Papa." My grandmother, ever on the side of being coddled and cared for, only too readily acquiesced. In addition to that, she was a rationalist, closer to Deschartres in that respect than to her quite romantic and sentimental son. So the kind of natural warmth and openness that was for my parents second nature was to my grandmother something both foreign and distasteful.

But for me, sleeping with my parents was blissful. Oftentimes, before I drifted off, I heard my parents talking about their hopes for my father to quit the military in favor of staying home and pursuing music and theater. I would try to imagine what that would be like. To be able to see both my father and my mother every day!

My mother was in much better spirits when my father was with us, and at those times I suffered far fewer slaps and admonishments from her. As for my father, he never was anything but gentle and loving with me; he had not been shown the rough examples for child rearing that my mother had.

Sometimes my parents lay in bed and talked about me. They praised my intelligence and my inquisitiveness, the way that I charmed my grandmother, even my occasionally imperious attitude toward Hippolyte and the other children from the village with whom we played. My parents also enjoyed it immensely when I irritated Deschartres, fond as my father was of him.

Lying in bed with my parents, I naturally heard, as well, their worries about my brother, but when they started talking about Louis failing, I let myself fall asleep. There was nothing I could do about it.

February 1831

QUAI DES GRANDS-AUGUSTINS

PARIS

I STOOD LOOKING OUT AT THE CITY FROM THE ROOM THAT JULES and I were sharing. The view was of the Pont Neuf, the towers of Notre Dame, the rows of little houses on the Île de la Cité. But I was not really seeing any of those beautiful things. My arms were tightly crossed, and my foot tapped against the floor so relentlessly I feared the neighbors below might complain. The sky was dark, full of rapidly moving clouds, and I was as unsettled as the weather.

I had just finished reading a letter I had picked up at my half brother's apartment, one he had written to me. In it, he told me that the most admirable thing I had done in my life was to have given birth to Maurice, and that my son loved me with all his heart. Hippolyte warned me that staying away from Maurice for such long intervals would test that love, and it was likely that it would soon go away entirely.

When I had left Nohant, two-year-old Solange had been reassured by the fact that her father was there, and by my telling her that I would see her soon. Maurice, at seven, was more anxious, and I had finally made him smile by promising him that I would send him a uniform just like the policemen in Paris wore. Then, when I watched him walk away from me that morning, my heart ached so hard I nearly canceled my plans.

But I had come to see that a life not lived in truth is a life forfeited. I believed that what I intended to do for myself in Paris was ultimately better for all of us than my staying home and trying to pretend that I was content sewing and cooking and overseeing dinner parties, all the while turning a blind eye to my husband's cruelty and betrayals.

Had I had known what passion would be born in me around

living the life of an artist, had I known what absorption and dedication it would require, I might never have married and had children. But I had married. I had borne children. One could not retract the birth of a child or the love for them that came with it. Now I needed to think of the best way to manage all of our needs.

If letters from the children's tutor and even from Casimir could be believed, Maurice and Solange were not suffering at all but thriving. Hadn't my own life served as evidence that the love one had for one's mother could survive her absence?

In contrast to my mother, I wrote to my children every day. But letters did not pull a blanket up higher before a good-night kiss, or listen to progress in reading, or ferret out hiding places in a game of hide-and-seek, or soothe the fears brought on by a nightmare.

Hippolyte's letter, in which he had, as usual, felt so free to criticize me, burned in my hand.

Did he ever tell Casimir that his frequent absences from our children—his vaguely described "business trips"—would threaten their love of him? I knew the answer to that: of course not. It was men's privilege and pleasure to travel away from home whenever they wanted to, so long as they could afford it (and sometimes when they could not). It seemed a woman never had a good enough reason to leave her post. It was another part of the great hypocrisy that existed between men and women that was held as a natural law. But it was not a natural law; it was man-made.

I would stay with the plan Casimir and I had formulated. In April, I would be back with the children. Until then, I would hold them in my heart and write to them daily but remain here, where I had real business to attend to.

I resolved to approach another man of letters. Hyacinthe Thabaud de Latouche, called Henri, had been a friend of my father's. He had just taken over as publisher of a satiric journal called *Le Figaro.* He was forty-five years old, quite overweight, and arrogant, I was told; and he had a reputation for being very difficult. But he was a great admirer of Rossini, and the first Frenchman to embrace the genius of Beethoven and Berlioz. In addition, he had introduced Goethe to French readers, which in itself was enough for me to overlook the criticisms I had heard.

I sent him my manuscript, asking him to read it and let me know if there was any way he could help me.

The next morning, I got a note from him, inviting me to meet with him in his office in Montmartre that very afternoon.

September 1808

NOHANT

My parents and I had been back at Nohant for several weeks, and the three of us had regained our health. But my baby brother, Louis, continued to decline. For weeks, my mother had tried valiantly to nurse her son back to health. She ate so well she embarrassed herself, but my grandmother seemed to understand the reason for Sophie's apparent greed and often put more on my mother's plate without her asking. My mother ate between meals, as well: thick slabs of bread spread with pale yellow butter and red jam, raw vegetables she pilfered from the kitchen when the cook's back was turned, fruit she pulled from the branches of trees, pastries she kept wrapped in hankies in her pockets. She ate and ate and ate, and all of it was an apology to her son for the neglect he had suffered on our wartime travels—my mother feared her inadequate diet then had affected her milk—and all of it, too, was a prayer for him not to leave her.

She took walks and she spent long stretches of time working on a children's garden she was cultivating beneath a pear tree. Nearby, Louis lay in a basket silently staring up, his tiny hands motionless. I used to kneel beside him and stare at him, trying to will him back to good health.

At night, my mother held Louis close and rocked him and rubbed his back and sang to him, but as he continued to lose weight and decline, she stopped doing that. It was as though just being held required more energy than he had to give, as though he were too fragile to bear any touch at all. Once I came upon her tenderly bathing him as he lay in her lap, and the sight of his prominent rib cage made for a stab of pity in my heart. I saw what my mother had not yet accepted: Louis was not going to recover. He was going to die.

Finally, on September 8, came the awful moment when Louis started growing cold and mottled before my mother's eyes. It was just after dinner; she had been on her way upstairs to nurse him to sleep. Instead, she rushed back to the dining room and sat by the fireplace, imploring my father to build a fire as quickly as he could. This he did, and then he kept stoking the flames as the baby grew colder and colder to the touch. My mother moved as close to the fire as she safely could and wrapped Louis in more and more blankets. She was wild-eyed with panic; she kept calling his name, kissing the top of his head, massaging him through the blankets, rocking him faster and faster. My father knelt beside his wife and son, trying to comfort both of them, wiping at his tears. My grandmother and I stood silently a fair distance away, and I remember that she wrapped part of her long skirt around me in a way of which she seemed unaware.

After a short while, Louis stopped breathing. My mother cried out, one sharp cry, and then began to keen. My grandmother ran for Deschartres, to see if there was anything to be done.

There was nothing he could suggest. Not yet three months old, the baby was dead. Deschartres lifted him from my mother's arms, gave him the briefest of examinations, and nodded at her. "My condolences," he said.

"No!" my mother screamed, lunging for Deschartres in a violent way, as though he were the cause of Louis's death.

My father reached for her, and she turned to sob in his arms. I crept closer but did not attempt to touch either of my parents.

"I have killed him," my mother sobbed. "I have killed our son!"

"No, Sophie. Shhhhh," my father said. I saw him squeeze his own eyes shut, and I saw the resolve pass over his face. He would comfort my mother now; later, he would tend to his own wounds.

My mother wept, the sounds so loud and heartrending it seemed to me that the house would collapse around us. Finally, my grandmother convinced us all to sit again at the table, where the remains of dinner still were; the servants had not dared to enter the room.

My mother had stopped crying by then, but every breath she took was a shudder. She sat blankly staring, her hands open in her lap as though something had just flown out of them. Finally she looked at my grandmother and asked dully, "Where is he?"

"He is dead, my dear," my grandmother said, her usually clear voice thick with pain.

"But where is he?"

"Deschartres has buried him," she said. "And now we must endeavor to move forward."

My mother rose so abruptly she knocked over several glasses. "Buried him! So soon? But I have not prepared him!" She meant washing him, perfuming him, then binding him, as was the custom.

"It is best this way," my grandmother said.

My mother looked quickly over at my father, who only stared into his plate. Then she ran upstairs to their bedroom and slammed the door. My father followed her.

"Come to me," my grandmother said, patting her lap, and I went to sit with her. "Shall I sing you a little song? Are you still hungry?"

I said nothing. A song, a bite of food, the moon and the stars—what difference did it make what she offered me? But she sang. And eventually, I closed my eyes and leaned back against her. From upstairs came the voices of my parents: my mother screaming, raging, weeping; my father calmly responding.

When I was put to bed, I had no thought to give my parents privacy. I went to them as usual; as usual, they let me in.

In the middle of the night, I was awakened by the sounds of my parents arguing in loud whispers. My mother was pacing back and forth, gesturing wildly. My father sat at the side of the bed, his head hanging low. "But we didn't see him before Deschartres took him away!" she said. "How can we be sure? Ah, Maurice, he was persecuted from the moment he was born. I swear to you I saw that Spanish doctor press hard against Louis's eyes with his thumbs, I heard him say, 'Here's one who will never see the Spanish sun.' I heard it, I tell you! And now he has been taken from his mother's arms and put in the cold ground, and we are not even sure he is dead!"

"I am sure!" my father said. "It wounds me as it does you to think that we have lost our son, but he is dead! There is no doubt! You saw it yourself, Sophie, you saw him grow cold, you saw him stop breathing. He is dead! Do not make me say it again and again; each time I do, he dies once more."

She wept, with the smallest of sounds now, and my father went to her and knelt on the floor before her. I kept my eyes mostly closed so that they would not see that I was awake.

"Sophie," my father said, weeping himself, pushing his face into her legs.

My mother abruptly stopped crying. "I want to see him. You must bring him to me. I must be certain he is dead. He might merely have lapsed into a coma. As you well know, people have been buried alive! What if he is out there in the blackness and the cold, all alone and still alive?"

My father started to speak, but she said, "And in any case, I am his mother, and if it is true he is dead, then I shall prepare him for his grave as he deserves. He had no baptism, no graveside service, no chance for the life he deserved—at least let him have a last kiss. Maurice, you must indulge me in this or I will lose my senses! Please, please, I beg of you, bring him to me for one last time!"

Finally, my father agreed to exhume their son. "Keep watch to make sure I am not discovered," he whispered to my mother. Then he dressed and went outside.

After what seemed like a very long time, he returned. He had the little coffin in his arms, and it pained me to see smears of dirt on it.

"Is she asleep?" my father asked, about me.

"Yes, thank God," my mother said, and she went to join my father, who had put the coffin on the floor and was prying open the lid. She knelt beside him, her hands squeezed together in her lap.

"Something very strange happened out there," my father said.

"Really? What?" They might have been at breakfast, having a gossipy conversation over their coffees.

"I first uncovered the coffin of some poor villager. I accidentally stepped on the corner of it, causing it to rise up and hit me in the head, whereupon *I* fell into the grave! I tell you, my blood ran cold; it was as though an icy finger tapped my shoulder. You never saw a man leap so quickly to his feet. And then I felt my forehead break out in a sweat, as though this was an omen of some kind!"

"No, Maurice. It was not an omen. No."

They fell silent, and then I heard a little creaking sound as the coffin lid was raised, and my mother gasped. I saw her lift my brother's body out, then hold him close to her breast. She began to rock side to side. My father leaned over to kiss the baby's head.

"I shall prepare him," my mother said, quietly weeping. "But just for tonight, may we have him back in his little cradle? May we look upon him as though he is only sleeping?"

My father said nothing. Yes, then.

The next day, after I had left their room, my mother prepared Louis's body in the accustomed way. She washed him, perfumed him, wrapped him in linen, and then sprinkled rose petals in his coffin. Just before he was to be put back in the grave, my mother asked if my father would instead bury Louis by the pear tree in the children's garden. It would be a secret, shared only by them.

Louis was buried by that pear tree, and I was told about it only many years later, by my mother, prompted by something I can no longer recall. What I can recall, though, is the pain in my mother's eyes when she told me. I do not believe the loss of a child is something one ever overcomes. One puts on the faces one needs, but inside, one bleeds and bleeds.

February 1831

OFFICE OF *LE FIGARO*

MONTMARTRE

"PLEASE, SIT DOWN," HENRI LATOUCHE SAID, GESTURING AT A CHAIR set close to his own.

I had come to his office with high hopes about my novel, *Aimée.* Almost immediately, I saw why I had heard another rumor about him, that he had a way with women. This was in spite of—or perhaps because of—a childhood injury to an eye that created a sort of red gleam. His face glowed with intelligence, and he had beautiful manners; and if his voice had a kind of muted quality that made one sometimes strain to hear him, the words he spoke were eloquent. He evinced a dry wit and a gift for self-mockery, but I suspected that his was a tender and generous heart.

He himself wrote novels and poetry and plays, but he was best known for his work at *Le Figaro.* He published the four-page daily paper out of the spacious drawing room of his Italianate villa in Montmartre. He loved to lampoon King Louis-Philippe and his ministers; and he did not shy away from reporting gossip, either.

His writers—eaglets, he called them, for the way he regarded them as just now learning to fly—all had their own tables on which to work in the drawing room. Latouche would give them a topic and a piece of paper cut to fit the space where it would go in the tabloid.

He was brilliant at finding raw talent. He taught a writer how to improve and then promoted him vigorously. He had discovered Balzac! I thought that if he liked my novel, he might do for me what he had done for others.

But after we had dispensed with the pleasantries, he leaned forward to look into my eyes. "About *Aimée,* I am afraid I have little to say. It is not in its present form anywhere near publishable."

Very well, then. I had tried. I mumbled a thanks and stood to leave.

But Latouche laughed and put his hand on my arm. "Wait one moment! I did not say you were without talent, did I?"

I sat down again, wary, and waited for more.

He leaned back in his chair, pursed his lips, and stroked his chin in an absentminded way. Then he said, "Tell me, Aurore. Would you be willing to work like a demon to improve yourself? You are gifted, but raw. There are many things for you to learn. But if you do learn them, I believe you can be a great success."

I assured him that I was willing to work hard indeed, that it was my nature to work hard. And then, just like that, he offered me a job on the staff of *Le Figaro.* It was all I could do not to shout out with joy. Instead I offered as dignified a thanks as I could muster.

Among other things, Latouche said, I would be reviewing plays, and I would be obliged to buy my own tickets to see the performances. Box seats, where women had to sit, were expensive. It cost much less to stand or sit on benches under the gaslights, where only men could go. Latouche said that if I went to plays dressed as a man, I would save a great deal of money.

I remembered my mother telling me that she had done this, in the early days with my father; they'd not had the money for box seats, either. She told me she had found disguising herself this way to be great fun.

So it was that I began going out on the town and passing as a man. It wasn't difficult to do, and I found that I very much enjoyed it. There was an expansive freedom, not to say power, in wearing men's clothes. And it was a relief to dress in this far simpler way. I had never liked the fuss involved in deciding which earrings to wear, what kind of nosegay to tuck into my bosom, what color might best complement my complexion.

The style then was for men to wear "proprietor's coats." They were long—down to the heel—and square, so that a woman's form could be easily obscured. They were quite comfortable. I had one made of gray cloth, as well as matching trousers and a vest. With them, I wore a gray hat and a wide cravat. I pinned my thick black hair up and covered it with a hat.

My voice was naturally low, and I had always kept it neutral, absent the fluttery tones and frequent exclamations most women used. In addition, I had never developed the coquettish behavior second nature to most women. Nor did I enter into the tittering kind of gossip over teacups that seemed to pass for conversation at the expense of talking about politics, or art, or literature.

I took to going out with groups of men after the plays were over, and in keeping with my disguise, I put my iron-heeled boots up on the small tables of the clubs where we went. Jules had introduced me to smoking, and I puffed on cigars, and talked about the world, and enjoyed a wide sense of groundedness and belonging.

Sometimes we stayed out all night. Then, in the leached light of the very early morning, I would make my way to *Le Figaro*'s office. I always sat by the fireplace there, the most desirable spot. It was difficult for me to write in the economical way that was necessary. I was used to going on at great length, to luxuriating in digression, and so at first I spent a lot of time on things that ended up in the fireplace.

I reviewed plays, but I also covered politics. I wrote straightforward copy or satire, but privately I wondered what was in a rebel's heart and soul that gave him such courage—for whatever one's political persuasion, one has to admit a rebel's courage. What did those ill-equipped fighters, bricks in their hands, long for most? Were they fighting for themselves or for something larger, and if it was something larger, what kind of value did they assign to their individual lives? Which sentiments bore them most fiercely into battle?

I also wrote short fiction and fillers, sometimes bucolic pieces about the Berry countryside I came from. When Latouche liked what I did, I was deeply pleased, but he just as often called my little pieces too sentimental. In those instances, I set my jaw and resolved to learn from his criticism, not suffer from it.

Things began to move quickly for me in establishing myself as a writer. I had a story accepted by the *Revue de Paris.* I had introduced Latouche to Jules, and he and I were collaborating on articles for the paper as well as on a novel, for which we had found a publisher. I was starting to see that I really could make my living writing, perhaps eventually a very good living.

Everything about Paris fascinated me, including the politics. After the revolution, things were unstable but hopeful: new movements were springing up everywhere. One of them embraced the socialist ideal that property should be shared; another proposed that God was not a paternalistic figure but, rather, an androgynous one. There was communal living, and communal loving, as well.

Things long taken for granted were held up for a new kind of scrutiny, not only in society but in the church. In February, thousands of artisans and workers—carpenters, blacksmiths, cobblers—ousted the *comte* de Quélen, the archbishop. Then they took to the streets wearing chasubles and miters, sprinkling onlookers with "holy water" that they carried in chamber pots.

In my articles, I maintained a skeptical view of politics and lampooned the Chamber of Deputies, where I'd obtained a seat in the visitors' gallery. But I also offered a literary raised eyebrow at Saint-Simonianism. This was the protosocialist movement named after Henri de Saint-Simon that was against inherited wealth and in favor of shared property. It also espoused a belief in equality between the sexes. Easy to put forth that idea, I thought; much harder to achieve. A real equality would require as much respect given to the natural ways of women as that currently afforded men. I did not see it happening soon.

There came a day when the office of *Le Figaro* was seized by the king for its "seditious tendencies." I thought I might go to jail, for from my little desk by the fire, I had written a piece about how recent street fighting had been incited not by the guerrilla fighters, whose only defense was a wall of chairs, but by the well-armed National Guard, whose soldiers' interest was in provocation so that they could have an excuse to fire their weapons and murder with impunity. Then they would go home for dinner and regale their wives with stories of their bravery while they picked chicken from their teeth.

I had also written a parody that ridiculed a panicked government's efforts to keep the peace. I'd said, "All citizens capable of bearing arms must convene from seven in the morning until eleven at night to guard the Palais Royal. And seven-foot ditches must be dug around every house, and every window fitted with bars, to keep away evil-doers."

After the raid of *Le Figaro,* I sat at the kitchen table in the mornings with Jules, telling him excitedly that if I was arrested, it could greatly advance my career. I saw myself holding on to the bars of some dank cell in La Force, where political prisoners went, shouting out demands for my freedom while someone retched in the corner. I saw myself listening to the loud complaints of people caged like animals, of songs of revolution being defiantly sung. I decided I would strike up conversations with everyone around me, gathering material to write an exposé on oppression—and censorship!—in the language of the people of the streets.

When I was freed, I would emerge from prison, blinking in the light. My hair and clothes would be mussed and there would be dirt on my cheeks, but I would hold my head high. My soul would be burning with conviction. I would go straight to the office to write about all I had seen and understood.

Then the government dropped the case. "Ah well," said Jules, and he kissed my forehead. Later we went out for dinner with our friends. As usual, I was the only woman among our group of journalists and artists, and they soon had me laughing again.

I embraced this life, so different from the one I had been living. At Nohant, I had fussed over a failed soufflé and begged friends to visit and write more often so as to alleviate my boredom. I had organized parties as relief from the silent evenings spent with Casimir in the drawing room, him falling asleep over books I had asked him to read, me doing needlework and puncturing the cloth with the needle with far more energy than was required. Now my life seemed rich beyond measure.

How beautiful to rush home to make love with someone who

paid attention to what he was doing, who attempted to include his partner in the act and not just satisfy himself. I was not able to achieve the ultimate climactic experience that Jules did; I still had difficulty translating a passion that burned in my brain into my body; I still could not take leave of myself the way I so desperately wanted to. But I told Jules I was content nonetheless, and it was true. His deep kisses thrilled me. So, too, the slow wandering of his hands and the poetic murmurings of love he whispered to me in the darkness. And when we curled around each other for sleep, I felt a completeness, a *home,* something I had longed for all my life.

Now that we had secured a publisher for our first novel together, I told Jules about an idea I had for another novel, thinking that he could join me in writing it and we would again publish under the pen name we and our publisher had picked together: J. Sand. But he said, "Why don't you do that one alone?"

I was relieved, actually. I was finding Jules too slow a writer, a great procrastinator. Despite the fact that *Rose et Blanche,* our novel about an actress and a nun, was meant to be co-written, it was I who was doing most of the work. I put in strong characterizations, descriptions of the countryside and of the Pyrénées, and scenes of backstage life as well as convent life. Jules spent more time talking about work than doing it, in spite of my constant efforts to champion him, to tell him again and again that I knew he would someday create a work of genius.

"But if I write it alone, shall I use our pen name?" I asked.

"Why not use your own?"

I laughed. Soon after my arrival in Paris, I had been visited by my sour-faced mother-in-law, who, when she ascertained that I meant to make my living as a writer, implored me not to use my married name, Dudevant, and thereby scandalize their family. "I have no intention of doing so," I had told her. I did not add that so far as I was concerned, Madame Aurore Dudevant had died.

September 1808

NOHANT

THOSE WHO SAY LIFE IS A GLORIOUS BLESSING ARE RIGHT. THOSE who say it is endlessly cruel are also right.

A little over a week after my baby brother, Louis, died, on the rainy night of September 16, my father paced through the rooms of Nohant. He could not comfort his wife. She and my father spent their days tending to the garden by little Louis's grave. They planted flowers there, including China asters, because those flowers would bloom for at least a month, and they built up a small mound at the base of the pear tree, where I often sat. They made pretty winding paths and set out benches, creating a place of peace and beauty and charm.

But at night, my mother lay silently on the bed, staring up at the ceiling. My parents had begun to argue over what had caused Louis's death; and my father made my mother cry by suggesting that it was jealousy that caused her to undertake the difficult journey from Paris to Madrid when she was so greatly pregnant, and that if only she had trusted her husband, their son would be alive. Then my mother lashed out bitterly against my father, mostly because she shared that same dark suspicion.

My father was not comforted in his grief by my grandmother; she had become a faint version of herself, afraid of overstepping her bounds by trying to comfort her son. The servants did not speak except when necessary, even among themselves. All was silence and gloom; even I, picking up on the mood of the household in general and my mother in particular, could not be made to smile. My father decided to go out, to dine with some friends in nearby La Châtre; he felt that a little time apart might help him and his wife regard each other with tenderness once more.

My mother and I were in my parents' bedroom, where she had

given me a book to look at while she sat in a chair by the window and gazed out at the rain. Deschartres had begun teaching me to read, and I was catching on quickly. Even in that time of weighty sorrow, I wanted to show off to my mother, whose approval I always desired.

When my father told my mother of his intention to go out, she was furious. She leapt to her feet and began to upbraid him. "How can you leave me at such a time? And here, besides, where I have no friends, where the only company is that lunatic Deschartres and your mother, cold as fish on ice?" This was not quite fair, as my grandmother had traveled a far distance from her complete disregard of my mother. But her overtures were not wholly loving, mixed as they were with a kind of begrudging necessity.

My father tried to take my mother into his arms, but she spun out of them. "To say nothing of the weather, and you on that wild horse, which was not so much a gift as an attempt to kill you! That animal does not respect you; you cannot control him!"

This was an insult my father could not bear, and later I thought that if only my mother had risen above her own pain and had tried to gently persuade my father to stay home rather than insult his equestrian skills, he would never have left that night. But after those words, he stepped away from her: I could see the flush that came to his face on those rare occasions when he lost his temper.

"I am going out," he said.

"And when do you intend to come home?"

He did not answer her; instead, he patted me on the head and left the room.

My mother followed him, shouting after him not to go, to stay with her.

After he went out the door, she stood at the window, watching him mount his horse, then gallop away. My grandmother came to her and tried to console her, telling her that men were this way: they could not sit with sorrow; they needed a way out. She told my mother she would serve him and herself best by letting him go, by not making so many demands on him at a time when he too was fragile and full of despair.

My mother wept and railed; she was both furious and heartbroken, and nothing my grandmother said seemed to have any effect on her whatsoever. But then my grandmother began to speak of what happened to a woman's skin when she wept so hard and slept so little, how her looks could be damaged when she did not care for herself in the way a woman was meant to. My mother, who was then thirty-five, was aware of the fact that, beautiful though she still was, she could not return to the life she had been living when she met my father. She needed him. More important, she loved him.

My father was right in thinking that a little separation would make my mother appreciate him again; he had only just left, and it was plain that already she missed him. Add to this the sober reminder from one beautiful woman to another about the need to hold a husband's interest, lest he stray, and a plan was set in motion. My mother decided that she would go to bed early and, in the morning, would meet her husband with a new outlook. They would begin again.

After my mother and I retired, my grandmother stayed up late, playing a card game called piquet with Deschartres. She had not wanted to tell my mother that she, too, was worried about her son riding out on such a night; his wild horse moved in restless caracoles even when he was tightly reined in. She disliked my father's pride in taking what control he could over such a headstrong animal; she thought it foolish to allow ego to overrule common sense.

When my grandmother expressed her fears to Deschartres, he pooh-poohed them. "Maurice is an excellent rider," he said. "And surely he deserves time away from this trial he has chosen as wife; she is enough to make anyone want to go out in a storm. Don't worry, nothing will happen. And even if it does, Maurice has Weber with him."

Weber, my father's valet, was a much-admired man: loyal, strong, and willing to do whatever his master bade him. He had about him a rather awful smell, and his language was a German-accented French that was hard to understand. But my father was fluent in both tongues, thanks to Deschartres, and he and Weber got along famously.

Thus assured, sometime after midnight, my grandmother began her preparations for bed.

Not long afterward, Weber came galloping up to the house, hollering, and was met by the servant Saint-Jean, who had rushed outdoors in his nightwear to see what the commotion was about. Weber told him what had happened: my father had crossed the bridge outside La Châtre at a full gallop, and was rounding a bend onto a dark road lined with poplar trees. Just as his horse made the turn, it stumbled in a pile of stones that had been left at the side of the road. The horse reared, sending my father flying, and the fall broke his neck. Weber raced up behind, leapt off his horse, and ran to my father, whom he heard say, "Come to me; I am dying." While locals helped move my father to a nearby inn, Weber galloped to Nohant. He told Saint-Jean to tell Deschartres what had happened, then raced back to La Châtre.

Deschartres took my grandmother's coach and set out immediately for the inn. My grandmother learned from the servants that Maurice had been seriously injured and was at the Lion d'Argent in La Châtre. She never walked more than a few feet without distress, but on this night, absent transportation, she walked the entire three miles to the inn, wearing her delicate silk shoes and with nary a shawl for protection from the rain. When she got there, she entered the room where her son lay and fell upon his body. She would not allow anyone to separate her from him. She held my father's still form in the carriage all the way home, and if she wept, no one heard it. It was much later that I came to see that as there is a grief for which tears will not stop, there is also a grief for which tears will not come.

A few hours later, at six o'clock in the morning, my mother was awake and performing her toilette, dressed in a white camisole and a long skirt. I was already up; she had helped me get dressed first. Her mood was fine: all would soon be well; she would reconcile with my father, whom she believed to be downstairs. She would also speak to him about going back to our apartment in Paris; they had been here long enough.

Deschartres burst into the room. My mother turned to look at him and understood immediately that something terrible had occurred. "Maurice!" she cried. "What is it, what has happened to him?"

Deschartres stumbled and stuttered, but my mother made out that her husband had had an accident. "Where is he?" she asked.

"No, you cannot go to him now," Deschartres said.

"But is it serious?" my mother asked.

"Yes, it is serious," Deschartres said. "He was thrown, and it is very serious." Then he abruptly shouted, "He is dead!" He began to laugh hysterically and collapsed onto the floor, sobbing.

My mother screamed, then began to sob herself. She fell back into a chair, put her hands over her face, and rocked back and forth, moaning. I ran to her, patted her bare arm and kissed it, saying, "Maman! Maman!" She ignored me. It was as if she could neither hear nor see me. I kissed her arm again and again and tried to get in line with her vision. She only continued to weep.

Deschartres rose and spoke firmly to my mother: "Attend to your daughter! You must live for her now." Then he left the room. My mother kept loudly sobbing, and I tried over and over again to console her. Nothing worked: my stroking and kissing her, my crawling into her lap and holding tightly on to her neck, even, finally, my own terrified sobbing. She wanted only my father.

I wished then with all my heart that I were a boy. I had felt many times before that if I had been born a boy, I would have been just like my father, and I wanted to be like him now more than ever. On and on my mother wept, she who had so recently lost her infant son, and now her husband. Finally I simply sat still at her feet, waiting.

When there are no apparent consolations for certain kinds of grief, the mind can nonetheless create some. What I eventually came to is that the death of my father meant my parents would never come to the end of their love. Circumstances dictated that they would never have to discover if their feelings for each other would wane, if their passion would fade. Despite the hardships thrust upon them or brought about because of disagreements, they had never fallen into despair about being together or even settled into a comfortable ennui. Now they never would. When my father was killed, they were still deeply, romantically, wildly in love. What I witnessed between them seemed a love of epic proportions.

I was grateful for the memory of their love and their relationship. I was happy that my father, once he found the love of his life, never had to live without her. But I was sorry that my mother had to live for so long without him. It was never easy for her, after he died. I do not believe her pain ever went away, or even lessened.

April 1831

NOHANT

HOWEVER MUCH I MISSED MY CHILDREN, IT WAS DIFFICULT TO leave Paris for Nohant for the three months I would be caring for them. I was in thrall to my work, passionate about my nights with Jules, and emerging into the self I wanted to be.

Yet when I arrived, I was overwhelmed with love, both that which I felt for two-year-old Solange and seven-year-old Maurice and that with which they showered me. They scarcely noticed when Casimir left for his family's hunting lodge in Guillery, and his brusque goodbye to me made me not miss him, either. I had expected to be affected greatly in one way or another upon seeing him again, but the experience was oddly empty. His tone of voice when he spoke to me was flat; his eyes were absent of any emotion.

But the children could not get enough of me; it was as though I had grown two new limbs, the way they kept themselves anchored to my sides virtually all day.

I had been away from them for so long, it was a luxury for me not to separate from them at night, either, but rather to look down and see their lashes dark against their cheeks as they slept, their small chests rising and falling, and to hear the sounds they sometimes made: Maurice's emphatic grunts, Solange's mewls and deep sighs. I could see their eyelids flutter with the drama of their dreams, and when they turned onto their sides, I could gently stroke the soft indentation at the base of their skulls.

I reveled again in the company of ones so young. I loved their honesty and inquisitiveness, their spontaneity, their outsized joy at the smallest of things, their sense of wonder and gratitude. I climbed trees with my children, chased them through the woods, supervised their rides on the pony, read them Homer's stories of gods and goddesses made human, which I had loved as a child, and encouraged them to make up their own stories. We put on plays for one another and for any audience we could gather. Sometimes, as evening fell, I sat on the steps at the side of the house and watched them play. I laughed along with their laughter, that purest and most infectious of sounds. I congratulated myself and Casimir for having done a good job thus far in raising them, our problems with each other notwithstanding. At night I lay still and looked out the windows, which I had left uncovered so that I might see the rising of the moon and the humbling grandeur of the stars, and I gave thanks.

And then, just like that, it was over. One night Maurice balked at sleeping with me, saying it was too crowded in the bed. Then Solange said that she didn't want to sleep with me either, because she was not a baby anymore. In the daytime, they began wandering off by themselves, not so eager to involve me in their play. One afternoon, I found Solange sitting in the lap of one of the kitchen maids, a pretty young blond girl named Odette, who was reading to her. "Solange, come with Maman," I said, holding my hand out to her. "I will read to you."

"I don't want you," Solange said, and it was both embarrassing and painful to hear those words of clear dismissal.

Color rose in the maid's face as she rushed to my defense. But I held up my hand and with a nod indicated that she should go on. If one is going to praise children's honesty when their words please, one must tolerate it when the words do not.

I went in search of Maurice and was reminded that my son had gone to La Châtre with one of the servants to help shop for supplies needed by the groundskeepers. Apparently Maurice took seriously the fact that Casimir had told him that he was assistant master of Nohant, the one in charge when his father was away.

I retired to my writing room, but the passion I had felt in Paris for working on the first volume of Jules and my novel eluded me here. I still wrote, but I got only about a third as much done; and the work lacked original turns of phrase as well as the urgency and sense of discovery that had come so easily before.

I spent hours sitting at my desk, trying to think of what I might want to say. Repeatedly, ink dried on the quill before I had written one word. I walked to the window and looked out at the land, but mostly I was dreaming of Jules on the streets of Paris. I wondered whether he missed me, whether he would take good care of himself, for without me he tended not to eat well and to fall into a kind of defeatist mentality. Our friend Émile Regnault had found us a new place to live, something much better than the single room we had been occupying. It was a sixth-floor garret apartment in a large corner house on Quai Saint-Michel, near the Pont Neuf. There were three small rooms and a balcony, from which we would be able to see Notre Dame and Sainte-Chapelle. I loved that part of Paris—not too modern, still picturesque and poetic—and in July, Jules and I would be living there together.

In the meantime, here I was at Nohant, worried about him and worried about myself, too. My time here, which at first had seemed so fleeting, now felt interminable. Nohant began to feel like the prison I had escaped in Paris. I was bored, restless; then, finally, ill. I wrote to friends in Paris, who suggested I simply come back early and bring the children with me. But how could I do that? I had committed to an arrangement I was bound to honor: three months in the city, three months at Nohant. And in any case, how could my children fit into the bohemian lifestyle I had developed for myself there? No, my fate was to be in Paris, wildly alive but missing my children, or at Nohant, nurturing my children the way I wanted and needed to but with a great emptiness gnawing at me until my stomach and my head ached. I wrote to my mother about my conflicted feelings, saying, "The freedom to think and act is the most important right. If one can join with this the little cares of a family, this freedom is infinitely sweeter, but where do you find that? One way of life always undermines the other."

My mother's response was that I was being selfish. She said I was too wild and was not paying attention to my children the way I should, that I was abandoning them. Well. If I were indeed abandoning my children, I had learned how to do so at the hands of a master.

October 1808

NOHANT

IT WAS SEVERAL WEEKS AFTER MY FATHER'S DEATH WHEN I WANdered outside and found my mother in the children's garden she and my father had built. She was sitting on the ground with her back to the trunk of the pear tree, her eyes closed. It was an unseasonably warm day, more summer than fall.

I crept closer to my mother, who looked so small beneath the pear tree. "Maman?"

She opened her eyes and smiled at me, then held out her arms, and I went gratefully to her. It felt as though this was the first time she had really seen me since that horrible night of my father's death. All of the household—all of the village, in fact—was still mourning my father; he'd been beloved by so many for his wit and his charm, for the way their love for him was so exuberantly returned.

I lay still in my mother's arms, deeply appreciative of the feel of her arms about me, of the rise and fall of her chest as she breathed. Her comfort had been a long time coming, after our grievous loss; I exulted in it now.

After a while, I asked, "What are you doing?"

She pushed my hair off my forehead and kissed the top of my head. "What am I doing? Well, I am having a little dream of when we were all together."

"When shall we be together again?"

She hesitated, then said, "What do you mean, Aurore?"

"When will they be through being dead, Papa and Louis? When will they come back?"

I could see her struggling to formulate an answer. Whereas my grandmother believed in setting down the unvarnished truth, my mother was more respectful of the vulnerable mind of a child. She had heard the servants talking of seeing my father's ghost sitting at the dining room table with his head in his hands and had admonished them not to speak of it in front of me; she had also forewarned my grandmother not to tell me that death was the absolute end.

At first she attempted diversion, saying, "What about Caroline, whom I am also dreaming of? Is she not part of our family, too? Surely you have not forgotten your sister, Caroline, with her charming smile, she who plays with you and your dolls so nicely when she is home from school—she who, in fact, tries to grant your every wish!"

"Yes, I love Caroline very much. But when will Papa and Louis come back?"

"Ah, Aurore." She sighed and shook her head. "It will be a very long time, and we must be patient. You must be a good girl and please your father. For even though we cannot see him now, he is nonetheless keeping watch over us. Do you agree?"

"Yes, and I have been good, Maman."

She raised an eyebrow. It was true that I had not been perfect, that I had fallen into the habit of demanding that I get my way, and was often given it by people too taken up with mourning to discipline a young child. But there was one area in which I was unfailingly cooperative.

"I do my lessons every day."

"So you do."

There was some bitterness in my mother's tone. Deschartres had begun teaching me Latin, the natural sciences, penmanship, and reading. My grandmother taught me to read music and play the harpsichord, but she also taught me manners and voice modulation, and for those things my mother had a great deal of disdain. Sometimes we giggled together in private over my grandmother's insistence on the proper way to hold a fork, the level at which one's chin should be kept, how to bend to pick up something one dropped, should there be no one there to do it for you.

There was one thing I never told my mother, for even at age

four, I knew it would wound her. That was the way my grandmother spoke disparagingly of my mother's father. We were outside walking one day, and I had stopped in my tracks to listen to birdsong. My grandmother pulled at my hand, but I would not move until the bird had flown away.

"Your grandfather was a bird fancier, was he not?" she asked. "I suppose this accounts for your preoccupation with them."

"Yes," I said, "he sold birds, and he tamed them, too. They would sit on his finger and on his shoulder, and they would come to him right out of the air when he whistled. He knew all the birdcalls, and he taught them to Maman."

"Ah. Well, that's very nice, but no way to distinguish oneself, I think. Isn't it true?"

I didn't answer. My thoughts on this subject were too big for me at the time. I could not then express what I came to articulate later, which is that the most superior creation in all of nature is birds. What human could build something as ingenious and perfect, not to say comfortable, as a nest? Their ability and form in flight are awe-inspiring, and their songs are études of extraordinary clarity and quality. Most impressively, they are able to do what humans cannot: birds make harmonious marriages, where both sexes share equally in family duties. Even at this early age I had begun regarding feathered beings as a kind of patron saint.

But on that day, I could only look at the ground and wish that I could kick my grandmother's finely turned ankle. Finally I reiterated that I wanted to have one of the birds that lived in the woods of Nohant as a pet. My grandmother found the idea preposterous. Later in my life, though, I did just that: I kept birds on branches on my desk. They were free to leave and often did—they would go outside, and then they would come back again. Oftentimes, they would perch upon my pen, and in their insouciance they were so charming I could not bear to brush them off. On more than one occasion, I blamed a failed deadline on a barred warbler.

—

There are times when tragedy can bring about a kind of goodness that would not have occurred otherwise. A few months after my father's death, my two mothers, as I came to regard my mother and grandmother, began to cooperate with each other in ways they had not before. They could easily have blamed each other for his death, but it seemed they did not. They were not friends, but they were not enemies, either. Most evenings after dinner, they played parlor games and took tiny sips of sherry from pastel-colored, etched glasses. They played with Deschartres, who was a most disagreeable loser, especially when he lost to my mother. He had superior skills—at least to hear him tell it—but she had all the luck. One night he reacted so badly upon losing that my grandmother coolly suggested that she would have to slap him hard, and as he sputtered and fussed, I saw an intimate look pass between the women, something friends might share, and then the two of them burst into laughter.

My grandmother had begun to admire my mother. She saw how Sophie made all our clothes, even our hats; and if she was too impatient to always take the tiny stitches one was meant to in embroidery, she was quick and marvelously stylish in what she created. She once embroidered a dress from top to bottom for my grandmother in only two days; and when the old woman broke her sewing box, my mother shut herself away to make her a new one. Even Deschartres expressed his admiration for this latter creation; he bent his heronlike frame over the new sewing box for some time, after which he offered what was for him high praise: "Not bad."

In addition to that, without ever having been taught, my mother could tune the harpsichord by ear, replace its strings, and reglue its keys. "Your mother will attempt anything, with great confidence and verve!" my grandmother told me.

She also came to see that my mother was an artist who had never been given opportunities to develop what were considerable talents in drawing and painting and singing. And she praised the letters my mother wrote, calling them lively and "very pretty."

"However, you must work on your spelling, my dear," she said, and rather than rising up in sharp-tongued affront, which I feared she would, my mother did attempt to improve not only her spelling but her penmanship. She also began to read voraciously, a habit that stayed with her until her death.

Despite her many gifts, my mother's only vanity was about her beauty, but even then she was more matter-of-fact than boastful. She could never recognize her own intelligence, not in small part because she was genuinely unaware of it—here, in fact, is where her insecurity came out for the way she envied the society women their education and mental abilities. I occasionally saw women dismiss her with a glance, and I always thought at those times that they had no idea whom they were silently denigrating. My mother was a true Parisienne with a gift for savage wit and mockery; those haughty women were lucky she did not take them on, for they would have been sorry piles of crinolines and jewels when she finished with them.

She could also be extremely irritable and at those times seem to become emotionally untethered. She was free with slapping, too; but in the end there was in her such poetry and heart that one could never get enough of her, no matter what. There were times when she beat me and sent me to bed, and as soon as I was allowed up again, I would run to her and embrace her. And she would cover me with kisses, as though it were someone else who had effected our separation, someone else who had left red handprints on my bottom or my legs or even my face. I cannot say too many times that my mother was the most emotionally volatile, charismatic woman I have ever known. It was she who first aroused passionate love in me. And so it was soul-ripping when the time came that she abandoned me. Or, more to the point, sold me.

July 1831

25 QUAI SAINT-MICHEL

PARIS

I WAS FINALLY BACK IN PARIS, AND JULES AND I WERE IN OUR NEW apartment. We both loved it and our view of the Seine. On calm days, the river shone like flat metal, but on stormy ones, the restless current made it appear that waves were eating waves. We had rooftop greenery there, and a wonderful sense of airiness. Most important, there were two exits.

My husband still did not know that Jules and I were living together and I saw no reason to tell him. It was, first of all, no longer his business what I did with my life. But I also feared him cutting off funds, even though the allowance I received was from my own fortune. Luckily, I had been granted retention, if not control, of what I had inherited from my grandmother, and that was only because of my mother's intervention at the time of my marriage. Though at the time I had worried that her demands might make a bad impression on my in-laws, now I was very grateful to her.

The interior of the apartment was charming. It came with no furniture, however. Jules had no money, and so I bought everything on credit: rugs, furniture, linens, dishes, draperies. I asked Casimir to secure a loan for me so that I might pay off everything when it came due.

When he failed to act, I wrote to my brother, asking him to get me a loan. When Hippolyte also failed to respond, I sent a nearly hysterical letter, telling them both that if they persisted in punishing me in this way—saying that my children were suffering in my absence, withholding from me the money I needed, refusing to respond even to deny my request—I would kill myself, and my blood would be on their hands. I was so distraught I almost believed I would do this, but in the end I reasoned myself out of guilt and despair and went into action. I borrowed five hundred francs from François Duris-Dufresne, a man for whom I had given parties at Nohant in an effort to help him get elected to a political office in Berry. I got another two hundred as an advance from my editor, Latouche. I signed for the loans myself, then wrote to Casimir, telling him that I expected him to cover the payment. Finally, he sent me a brief note saying that he would comply.

For one moment, when I looked at his familiar script—the *t*'s crossed high up, the slant leaning overly far to the right—I let myself think back to our earlier days, wondering how what had happened to us had. We were once a reasonably content couple. I had touched his shoulder affectionately as I passed behind his chair; we had held each other in the night. But it was pointless to look back. I tore his note in half and threw it away.

September 1831

NOHANT

I RETURNED TO NOHANT FROM PARIS IN THE FALL, FOR ANOTHER three-month stay with the children. When I arrived, Casimir was harvesting grapes and so stayed on for a while. At first, I held out hope that we would finally be civil to each other. My hopes were dashed at our first dinner together, when Casimir pointedly directed his conversation to the children and not to me. When once I asked him a question, he ignored me. Solange didn't notice; she was singing to the peas on her plate. But Maurice, always sensitive to the feelings of others, said, "Papa? Did you hear Maman?"

Casimir looked at him. "No. I no longer hear her."

Maurice turned to me. "You must speak louder, Maman." His eyes were hurt and imploring.

"I shall, from now on," I told him. I raised my voice and said, "I shall speak very loudly! Like a giant!"

Maurice laughed, he and Solange both, and they imitated me in loud voices of their own. The incident was forgotten so far as they were concerned. Not so for me, who sat watching my husband eat, his eyes focused on his plate, chewing, chewing, chewing. The air grew dense around me; I put down my fork.

The next day, I was finishing up some last details on *Rose et Blanche.* I had worked hard and had completed what I needed to in only five days. I had not seen any of my Paris friends who were also in Berry. It seemed odd to be without my comrades, whom I normally saw so often—I felt lonely and disconnected.

There was a knock on my door, and I opened it to my maid, who held a small, cream-colored envelope addressed to Madame Aurore Dudevant. From the handwriting, I knew it was from Jules, and my face must have betrayed me; the maid's bland expression changed: her mouth tightened, and one eyebrow lifted.

"*Merci,*" I said, and she said nothing, just turned on her heel and walked away.

I closed my door and read the brief message; it set my heart racing. Jules, missing me terribly, had made a hasty trip from his parents' home in western France to Château d'Ars, the home of our friend Gustave Papet, which was a mere mile and a half up the road.

Late that night, I sat in the upstairs bedroom I had taken, longing to have an opportunity to see him. As if in answer to a prayer, I heard a light tapping at my window. It was Jules, my own Romeo, standing on a ladder he had carried from the orchard, pleading with me to let him in. He had seen the light in my window, had seen me pacing back and forth.

I let him in, laughing, crying, and covered his face with kisses.

Then: "Are you insane?" I whispered. "Casimir is here! If he finds you, he will fill you with buckshot!"

Jules put his hands to either side of my face and regarded me tenderly. "I would happily die for this moment. Anyway, we are protected: Gustave has volunteered to lie in a ditch in the garden directly beneath your window. He will throw a stone if he sees or hears anything."

As it happened, there was no cause for worry. The whole time Jules was in my bed with me, Casimir lay in his bed, snoring, and there was a nearly comical aspect to it. It also enlivened our lovemaking, the thought that perhaps Casimir might awaken.

We were already in a rush—we had missed each other's minds and bodies—but this secrecy added a kind of wild excitement we had not enjoyed before. We bit and pinched each other, he pulled on my hair until I gasped; and in the pain there was a low-down pleasure. We kept whispering to each other that we must hurry and then must part, poor Gustave out there lying in the dirt; but every time we gave each other a farewell kiss, it led to more and more, until our dear friend ended up spending the entire night outside, relieved of his duty only as dawn broke. I was deeply grateful to Gustave and later sent him a letter saying so, calling our friendship nothing less than holy and imploring him to find a way for Jules and me to repay him.

But first, after Jules had made his escape, I sat at my desk, still tingling, to write a letter to Émile Regnault, a medical student I loved as a brother. I wanted to tell someone of Jules and my adventuresome lovemaking; it had made me feel distinctively alive and powerful—and apparently in need of a bit of braggadocio, as well. I wrote, "I am covered with bites and bruises; so weak I can hardly stand I'm in such a frenzy of joy. If you were only here, I'd bite you too until blood flowed, just so you could share a little of our savage raptures."

Then I began to make edits on the pages Jules had given me for our novel. It was due to be published in December. People were saying that no doubt Jules would contribute next to nothing. I hotly defended my lover but those rumors were true. With the exception of a few bawdy (and, in my opinion, tasteless) scenes that appealed to the juvenile aspects of Jules's character—and apparently to our publisher's as well—the book was mine.

Not for many years did it occur to me that there was another side to that evening of stolen pleasure with Jules, a way of looking at it that revealed me not as an independent and freethinking woman who had the right to live her own life but as one blind to the needs of her children. For my lover and I would be warned in the event that my husband's lamp got lit and he began coming toward Jules and me. But what about Solange and Maurice, who, though they now slept in their own beds, still occasionally came to me? What would I have said to them should they have knocked at my locked door, knowing they had heard the sounds within?

July 1810

NOHANT

It was just after I had turned six years old that I came into my mother's room one afternoon to present her with a bouquet of wildflowers. She was packing; her open suitcase lay upon the bed. I dropped the flowers: the day had come. In the morning, she would go to live in Paris. Now I would only see her when she visited me.

Following my father's death, my grandmother had not gone to Paris for the winter, as usual, but had stayed at Nohant. My half sister, Caroline, my mother's now eleven-year-old daughter, was not received there. My grandmother made a point, with a kind of faux, powdered-bosom generosity, of saying my mother was welcome to see her own daughter, of course she was! Just not there at Nohant. Never mind that my father had embraced Caroline as his own child; such sentiments clearly were not shared by his mother. So if my mother wanted to see her other daughter, she had to take a three- or four-day trip to Paris. Naturally, this began to wear on her.

Around this time, in a way that seemed at the time innocent and even fortuitous but that I later came to regard as calculated, my grandmother received a visitor, her half brother and my great-uncle, an unapologetic ladies' man named Charles-Godefroid-Marie de Beaumont. He was absurdly handsome and had about him an irresistible air of gaiety. He missed my father, as we did, but his nature was such that he would always turn to the sunny side, and with his arrival he lifted the gloom for all of us. Now every evening was filled with laughter and lively conversation.

My mother, used to the attention and admiration of men, was drawn to Beaumont. It was not only because of his appreciation for her beauty and charm; he served, my mother thought, as a steady and objective presence who could help her decide the best thing to do with her life now that Maurice was gone. With my great-uncle she weighed the pros and cons of taking me with her to Paris. If she did, we would be poor again, for with Napoleon's defeat came the end of a pension my mother had expected to receive annually from my father's military service. But she would have both of her daughters with her, and after all, as she told Beaumont, it was not wealth that brought contentment.

Beaumont gained enough of my mother's trust to make her feel that agreeing to the arrangement my grandmother had offered was the right thing to do. My mother would be given a sum that equaled the amount she would have received as a pension, plus an additional one thousand francs annually, which was a generous bonus. In return, she would forsake her rights to me with the exception of visits at her own discretion. In other words, my grandmother would be entirely responsible for my upbringing. I overheard my mother agreeing to sign a contract to make her promise legal and binding. To me, it meant that my mother was trading me for money.

The night that contract was signed, I lay with my mother on her bed, inconsolable, despite her reassurances that I truly would be better off, that she would come and visit me in the summers at Nohant; and that in the winter, when I lived in my grandmother's apartment in Paris, my mother would fetch me to spend time with her and Caroline in our old apartment. But I could only hear that the time would come when she would leave me entirely. And now that time was here. I burst into tears.

My mother pulled me onto her lap and kissed me. "Please take me with you," I said. "Don't leave me here without you."

Her voice was full of pain, but she tried to calmly explain again why I could not come with her. Finally, she said, "If I take you away from your grandmother, she will reduce my income to fifteen hundred francs."

The news, rather than helping me resign myself to the fact that I must stay there, only made me think that there was no reason for me not to come with her. In my child's mind, fifteen hundred was a large number indeed, and I told my mother so. In my head, I was already packing my own things.

"No, Aurore," my mother said. "It would not be enough. Half of that amount goes to pay for Caroline's school. I wouldn't have enough to clothe and feed us. Soon you would be begging me to send you back to the comforts of your life here, and who knows if your grandmother would take you back!"

This was a consideration. My grandmother had suffered some small strokes that had made her personality change; she was no longer as even in temperament as she had been.

"But I don't care!" I said. "I never want to come back anyway! It doesn't matter what we eat, we'll have marrow bone soup every night and I will love it because I will be with you! Maman, we will be happy, and so everything will be all right."

She said nothing, and I pressed her further.

"You know I am right. You always say that love and happiness are not for sale, that what is on your back and on your plate is second to what is in your heart. You believe this, just as Papa did!"

She laughed. "You are too intelligent for your own good."

She grew quiet, thinking. Then she said, "Perhaps I would be happier poor with you than I am here, where I live a life wanting nothing in the way of material goods but where my heart cries out for a freedom and liveliness that will never be here. I suppose you long for the same."

"Yes!" I said. "I am just like you!"

Her face changed. "No." She lifted me off her lap and stood me straight before her. "Aurore, listen to me. You don't fully realize what you would be giving up in terms of education and security and the promise of a good match. I would be remiss as a mother if I did not consider these things for you."

"My education here is not good, it is airless! They want me to be a puppet. As for a good match, I can find that on my own, just as you did! I love my grandmother, I will continue to visit and care for her, I will continue to sing for her and put on my plays, but must I live with her to do that? I tell you, Maman, and you must believe me, I do not care about her money or her house or her fine things."

"You can say that because you have had such things! But I know what it means to be a young girl with no money. Poverty is what shaped my life, and I had to struggle hard to overcome my circumstances. I was forced to do terrible things. I want better for you!"

"I know what is best for me! And that is to live with my mother! Look into my eyes and tell me you do not agree."

For a long time, she did look at me. Then she said, "All right, all right! I have thought of a solution. You know I can make charming hats and that I used to be a milliner. I'm going to save some money and open my own shop. Why not? It will not be in Paris—that would be too expensive. Instead, I'll start my place in Orléans, where I worked before. You and Caroline can help me. We will have many customers; we will make enough money to keep ourselves comfortable. In time, you will have enough of a dowry to marry a worker like yourself, who no doubt will make you happier than the namby-pambies your grandmother would pair you with. You are full of passion, like me; you should marry your equal in that respect."

"A hat shop, yes, the most wonderful hat shop!" I cried, and my mother put her fingers to her lips to silence me.

"You must tell no one," she said. "And you must be patient—can you do that for me? For us!"

"I can. But how long before I can come with you? How many days?"

She frowned. "Is this your display of patience? Starting right now, show me what forbearance is in you. Trust in me. Be a good girl for your grandmama, do all she says, and soon you will no longer have to listen to her at all."

I was enormously relieved and spent the rest of the day happily amusing myself, imagining days at the store, evenings in the small but charming place where my mother, my sister, and I would live.

But that night, while I lay in bed listening to the voices below, doubt crept in. My mother had displayed a great deal of sadness when she'd kissed me good night, and I feared she had changed her mind and would not honor her words; instead, she would go away and gradually forget about me. I rose from bed and by the light of my candle wrote her a letter that was an outpouring of my feelings. I asked her to come to my room and tell me again that she would do all that she had promised.

After I had finished, I crept into the hall and down to her bedroom. Hanging on the wall of that room was a pencil drawing of my grandfather, and as it was not a very flattering portrait (it had been done in his old age, when he was fat and jowly), it had been put in a place where, when the door was open, it was hidden. I put my letter behind it. Included in it was a request that my mother leave her response here as well. Then I found her nightcap, put a note in it telling her to move the portrait to look for a note from me, and put her nightcap on her pillow.

After that, I could not sleep, and when I heard my mother go into her bedroom, I went there. She was sitting at the edge of the bed with my letter in her hands, and her eyes were full of tears. I ran into her arms, fearful of her telling me that my suspicions were correct: she was leaving me forever. It was not as bad as all that, but she did confess to feeling a terrible sense of ambivalence. Once again, I employed all my gifts as an orator—even at six years old, I knew I could be quite persuasive—and begged her to follow through on her plans for taking me with her. Finally, she agreed again to our plan.

"Put it in writing," I said. Not for nothing had I heard the negotiations that had gone on when my mother signed the contract giving up her rights to me. I wanted something binding as well, and I also wanted something I could read and reread to boost my spirits while I waited for her to come for me.

"I shall write it," my mother said, "but not now. It is late—you should be asleep. Come, I will tuck you in and kiss you good night and you will have beautiful dreams."

When she tucked me in, she sat for longer than usual at the side of my bed. She was quiet, holding my hands in hers.

"Don't forget to write the letter," I said.

"Yes, yes, in the morning."

"Promise me with all your heart."

"I promise," she said and kissed me once more, then crept out of my room. I lay awake for some time, then closed my eyes, certain I had done all I could.

In the morning, I missed her leave-taking; I had slept through it. I ran to her room, where there was still the indentation of her head on the pillow of her unmade bed. I lay down and put my head where hers had been, my heart aching. Then I remembered the letter she had promised to write: there would be her words, her inviolable promise.

I went to the portrait and, with my heart banging in my chest, moved it slightly to the side. Nothing there. Perhaps it had fallen? I looked on the floor: nothing. I looked everywhere in the room, but there was no letter.

Rose, my mother's maid, came in to clean the room. I sat dry-eyed in a chair and watched her strip the bed, air out the mattress, and then close the shutters.

I dressed and had breakfast, and then I heard my grandmother in the parlor, clapping her hands, which is how she signaled to me that it was time for my lessons. I turned to go to her obediently but with a heart full of bitterness.

January 1832

PARIS

IN WINTER, WHEN I RETURNED AGAIN TO PARIS, IT WAS WITH THE novel I had produced without Jules while I was at Nohant. I wrote *Indiana* all of a piece, in a kind of trance, from a place deep within me. I had no outline; I had no idea where I was going. It was only when I was finished that I saw what I had been about: I wanted to speak of my horror of enslavement, and the way I chose to do it was to write a domestic novel, a novel of manners.

The story centers on Indiana, a woman who is sold into marriage, and her unhappiness with a husband who essentially uses and then ignores her, then a lover she takes who does the same. It featured passionate encounters and suicidal pacts and a woman who drowns herself in her despair after a love affair gone wrong. The material was weighted with feelings I had about love and marriage—and Casimir—that I had been loath or unable to articulate. But in the form of fiction, those feelings revealed themselves clearly.

Characters who had been vague suggestions before I began writing—who had revealed themselves only as shadows behind a screen, whose voices were indistinct murmurs in my ears—came alive upon the page. Contrary to accusations that were leveled against me after the book's publication, however, those characters were not anyone I knew. Parts of Indiana were like me; other parts were not. Some of the other characters were inspired by people I knew but were filled out in ways that were not like people I knew at all. The story had gone its own way.

Once I began opening myself to the truth of one idea through the steady stream of ink upon the page, there was nothing for it but to open myself to all the secrets of my unconscious. Night after night, I wrote steadily for long hours; pages fell to the floor and covered the carpet like snow. It was typical for me to write twenty pages at a session.

When at last I finished the book, I gathered up the pages and stacked them into a neat pile whose height surprised me. Outside, the sun shone and the birds were singing; I had written all night. My fingers were stiff, my back ached, my shoulders, too. Yet I felt awakened from a deep sleep, energized, right with the world, and fully birthed into the proper profession. It might have pleased me if I had known at that time that, between the years of 1832 and 1835, I would have ten novels published, and in my lifetime, more than eighty.

But that day I left my study and called for my children, and when they came running to me, they embraced me with joy. I bent to kiss the tops of their heads and thought, *There, you see? You make yourself happy, and they are happy, too.*

April 1832

OFFICES OF J.-P. RORET ET H. DUPUY

PARIS

I HAD SOLD *INDIANA* TO THE PUBLISHER HENRI DUPUY, AND IT WAS soon to be released. I needed a new pen name, and now I sat with Dupuy to talk about what that name should be.

I could not use my married name, but neither could I use my maiden name. My mother feared shame coming to the family if I did so, and to herself in particular. It was very common for women who were relaxed about their own morals to want the heroines in their novels to cleave to another standard. My mother, the former courtesan, wanted the books she read to be "clean." I had shown her the manuscript, and she had taken dramatic exception to the risqué passages. "Of course you must not entertain any thought of using the name Dupin!" she said, and I did not argue.

I sat in my publisher's office trying to think of possibilities, all men's names. I knew full well the value of not using a woman's name—the work would not be taken seriously, for one.

"The name Sand is recognizable now," Dupuy said, "because of the success of your *Rose et Blanche.* You would do well to keep it; it could help sales. Why not simply change the first initial?"

My editor at the paper, Henri Latouche, had suggested the same thing.

I got up and moved to the window to look out at the busy street below. The sound of English rose up; a man was speaking rather loudly to the woman on his arm. I turned around suddenly with an idea.

"*G,*" I said.

"*G* for . . . ?"

"George."

"Good. Georges it is."

"No, *George.* The English spelling."

"Why English?"

"I like it." In truth, it was a nod toward the English spoken in the convent school my grandmother had sent me to, hoping for a refinement of my manners. George was also the name of my favorite poet, George Gordon, called Lord Byron. And *george* was the Greek word for "farmer," and so in that way I could honor Nohant.

"Very well: *Indiana,* by G. Sand." He looked over at me, squinting. "George. It suits you."

I bowed. "I agree."

When the first copy of the book arrived at my apartment, Latouche happened to be there. We were out on my balcony, appreciating the unusually warm day. There was a knock on the door. I answered and found a package tied with string.

I tore the paper off the book and, breathless with joy, examined it: the front, the back, the spine, the endpapers, the even lines of print upon the pages. Then I inscribed it to Latouche and went out to the balcony to hand it to him with a flourish.

"What's this?" he asked.

"My novel!"

He flipped through a few pages, then a few more. He read with his eyebrows furrowed, a scowl on his face. "But this is nothing more than a pastiche!" he said. "I must say, you owe a great deal to Balzac."

His words stung, but I said nothing. I appreciated the fact that he was always honest.

The next day, however, he sent a note telling me something altogether different. He had stayed up all night to read my book. He praised my originality and even went so far as to say that Mérimée and Balzac suffered in comparison to the author of *Indiana.*

As for Balzac, he had become a friend to Jules and me; and after I mailed him a copy of the book, he sent a note saying he had read the preface and found it "well written and full of sense, but as I had to work, I wanted to hold out against my pleasure, and to judge by the samples I have read, I considered it very dangerous for my imagination."

This ran counter to his behavior when he came huffing and puffing up the stairs to see us. He would boldly pick up pages of whatever Jules and I were working on and, without asking permission, read them. Then he would launch into a long-winded discussion of whatever he was writing. But he ended his note by adding, "It has given me great pleasure to see my friend G. Sand launched, and I shall give him my opinion about the book once read." I knew Balzac read very few other books because he was so busy with his own, and so I found this very flattering.

The arrival of the book into stores brought me overwhelming success literally overnight. It was astonishing. For several weeks, I could barely take in all that had happened—one critic called my book "the masterpiece of the century," which prompted none other than a jealous Victor Hugo to ask, if my book was a masterpiece, "what did that make his *Notre-Dame de Paris,* a whore?" Hugo was a god to me; to be noticed by him even to be insulted was more than I ever could have hoped for.

No matter that we were in the midst of a cholera epidemic; people flocked to bookstores to buy *Indiana.* It sold out time and again, even after multiple printings.

The critics (all male) gave me favorable reviews. Gustave Planche, who was called Gustave the Cruel for the contempt with which he treated writers, praised my "eloquence of the heart," my limpid style. Some critics took exception to my portrayal of marriage as a union that turned women into "domestic animals," but I was also compared to Balzac, for my unstinting way of showing the reality behind the illusion. And to think that before we became friends and colleagues, I had once said that I would walk ten miles just to see Balzac pass by!

There was a kind of androgynous quality in my work that was commented upon: it was said that I had feminized the hero but that certain harsh passages revealed a masculine mind at work. At first, I took umbrage; then I laughed at this observation. It was, after all, not so surprising that when a woman had written a book completely by herself, men were still given credit for it.

For the most part, women were galvanized by reading the book. They seemed to intuit what a man's intellect could not let them fully understand, something I had tried to explain in the preface:

> Indiana is a type. She is woman, the weak creature who is given the task of portraying passions repressed, or, if you prefer, suppressed by the law. She is desire at grips with necessity; she is love dashing her blind head against all the obstacles of civilization. But the serpent wears out his teeth and breaks them when he tries to gnaw a file. The powers of the soul become exhausted when they try to struggle against the realities of life.

Naturally, I was grateful for my success. But aspects of it were strange and uncomfortable. I did not like the reporters who sought me out and often came to my door—I could not speak the way I could write, and to be peppered with questions made me wish I were a tortoise who could withdraw into a built-in hiding place. And it was not just reporters but admirers who came as well. One woman asked what I thought about as I wrote the novel. I said that I thought about *it*. "Ah," she said. "So you cannot think when you are writing?"

Anyone in Paris who achieved a great deal of success could not maintain their privacy. Many people knocked on my door asking for money, and some of them came up with stories far better than I ever could for why they needed it. At first, I fell for many of the ruses; later I learned to be more discerning. But I would often worry that I had missed one who legitimately deserved my help.

It was also discomfiting to be approached on the street by a stranger as though he or she were a friend. When I had read the philosophers and poets who seemed to have a clear sight line into my heart and soul, I used to think that if I could meet them, we would admire each other; we would be companions, we would want to spend time together.

Now I saw the error of that kind of thinking. Now I understood that a poet whose words sent me into a kind of rapture was also a man whose soup dripped from his beard. A human being writes the book, but what writes *for* him or her is more spirit than physical being, and that spirit lives only in solitude.

There was nothing I wanted to say about *Indiana;* I had already said it in the book. But in keeping with my publisher's wishes, I did speak about it, to the best of my ability.

I was able to parlay my success with my first novel into a contract with another publisher, François Buloz, which would oblige me to make a contribution every six weeks to his *Revue des Deux Mondes*. This was originally a travel and foreign affairs journal with a mild and inoffensive tone. With Buloz in charge, though, it was to become a link between France and the United States, and it would now focus on culture, politics, and economics. I would earn four thousand francs a year, and I could continue to write novels, as well. In fact, I had a contract for my as yet unfinished second novel, one of many books I would set in the Berry countryside, to which I gave the fictional name Black Valley. I negotiated it myself, and it gave me twice the amount I had received for *Indiana*—three thousand francs. I was suddenly wealthy from money I had earned myself, and it was exhilarating. I decided that, henceforth, I would use my full pen name on my books: George Sand. And I would use it not only for my books but in my personal life.

With a guaranteed salary, I could now afford to bring my children to live with me in Paris. Casimir had decided upon military school for Maurice, who would soon be turning nine. I didn't like the idea; I wept until my eyes were red over it because I did not believe that a boy as sensitive as Maurice belonged there. But even though Maurice begged to live with me, Casimir exercised his legal authority and said no; it was military school for our son. My rage was buried beneath the dull weight of helplessness. What could I do? It was only three-year-old Solange who would be joining me.

Though I was happy to have her, I knew that my life would change when she was there. I knew it might be difficult to give her the attention she was entitled to and do my work as well. But it had taken hold of me now, the trade of authorship; there was no going back. I hoped both my children would come to understand what I was doing—if not now, in time.

LIVING WITH ME IN PARIS, Solange, I had thought, might become someone my artist and journalist friends would find enchanting, amusing, someone they might help me raise. Jules did help raise her: he adored Solange and delighted in telling me stories about what she had said and done. Once, when he took her on a walk to the Jardin des Plantes to see the giraffe, she told him straight-faced that there were many giraffes at Nohant and that they ate from her hand. He found that fabrication utterly charming. Other friends played children's games with Solange, coddled her, spoiled her with treats of one sort or another.

She was a very different child from Maurice. Already I could see how they would develop: Maurice would be like a strong woman, resembling me much more than Solange did; she would be like an unsuccessful man. She did not have the sensitivity of Maurice, nor did she profit from his powers of observation or his natural tendencies toward kindness and patience. She was extremely willful and seemed to take a perverse delight in hurting people's feelings. No matter our love for each other, no matter the times I missed her only moments after she had gone out with Jules or another friend; from a very early age Solange was a child at war within herself and with me.

I worried sometimes that she was reacting to the turbulence in her environment, that it unsettled her to be yanked from place to place. I had hoped that someone so young would readily adapt to what I thought of as an ideal lifestyle. Casimir loved Solange, I loved her, and Jules did, too. Working together, could we adults not make for seamless transitions? Could we not all share in her upbringing in ways that would enhance rather than detract from her life?

One night, shortly after we'd arrived in Paris and I had tucked her in for sleep on the sofa, I asked her, "Are you happy, my sweet?"

She nodded.

"I am as well. I have dreamed for so long of having you here with me. And you know that Jules loves you too, don't you?"

A smile, and then another nod.

"Is it not wonderful that we all are friends: Papa, me, Jules, and you?"

"Yes," she said. "But when will Papa come to live here, too?"

It was a three-year-old who revealed my faulty thinking, who exposed my hypocrisy and naïveté, though I could not quite so easily admit to that at the time. The mind has a way of protecting the heart, of turning one's gaze in a certain direction, away from what it should focus on. One resists admitting to a failure when the consequences of doing so can be so devastating. My only certainty was that I had gone ahead with my plan to leave my husband and to have my daughter with me, and now here we all were.

Eventually it was clear that my dream of having Solange with me was not working out. I endeavored to entertain her, I took her daily for walks in the park and played games with her, but she was bored and restless and, finally, whiny and complaining and insolent nearly all the time.

She liked the bouquets I kept on my desk, and when I once presented her with the same flowers to keep at her bedside, she immediately pulled every petal off every stem. When I took her out for walks, she would often refuse to walk home, and I had to carry her for long distances while she kicked her feet hard against me.

I was finally rescued by a neighbor woman, who brought Solange over to play with other children in her apartment every day and returned her to me in late afternoon. This neighbor reluctantly confided that Solange did not do well playing with others. She would not share toys, and she seemed to delight in making the other children cry. Embarrassed, I said that I would keep her at home, but the neighbor, who was extremely kind and loved children, said no, she would continue to take her. Solange would get better, she said, though I never saw evidence of that.

Then problems with Jules began. He went from affectionate lover to uncommunicative depressive. All my efforts to ferret out the reason were rebuffed. Concerned, I met with some of his friends at a café to talk about it. "What ever do you think is wrong?" I asked. One of them looked level-eyed at me to say, "Can you not see it? Your success has emasculated him."

That night, as we lay together in bed, I said, "Jules, is this not what we wanted, a literary life for both of us? We had success together for *Rose et Blanche;* now I have successfully published my own novel. We should both be grateful for how well it has done. You should be not mired in despair but eagerly working on your own book, which has every chance of doing just as well!"

Privately, I doubted that his work would enjoy as much success as mine had, but then I also doubted that my next book would be as successful as *Indiana* had been. That novel had been a kind of miracle. Sometimes, sitting alone and trying to realize all that had happened, I saw my good fortune as a benevolent gesture from above, proof that God approved of the choices I had made and was aiding me in my quest to realize my potential. No matter what others might say about my mannerisms or morals, I had my own idea of and relationship to God, and it offered me both peace and direction.

I asked Jules, "Can you tell me why my success has made you doubt your own abilities? What do they have to do with one another?"

He sat up in bed and exploded: "Anyone but you would understand this! You, who claim such sensitivity and perceptive abilities, how can you not recognize the way all of this has been a blow to my ability to work? People constantly coming to the door, and when they are not coming, the relentless scritch, scritch, scritch of your quill! You never stop! You are a writing machine!"

He lay back down, exhausted.

A few leaden moments passed. Then I said, "I shall rent you a room. You can write there. Would that suffice?" I did not remind him that he had had difficulties with his job at *Le Figaro* long before my success. Nor did I remind him that the article for which he'd been most highly praised was in fact a collaboration between the two of us. Jules was a good enough writer, but he was perceived by many as a peevish sort of fellow, one given to a great deal of self-pity. Our friend Duvernet said that he was "a dry creature, eaten up by petty vanities and foolish ambitions."

But I still very much loved Jules. I was still grateful to him for having changed me from someone who dreaded the future to someone who looked forward to it. And however tangential his help and influence were on my career, he had been part of my becoming the author I now was. One had to forgive him his moods for the times when he was loving and generous and gay. In this, he was much like my mother.

After a long moment of silence, Jules spoke, in a voice devoid of the high emotion he had just displayed. He said quietly, "George, I need to go away. While you are at Nohant, I shall go to visit my parents. As for a room for me . . . yes. I think it would help. And after I have finished my own novel and received the advance, I shall pay you back whatever you have spent on my behalf."

After he fell asleep, I lay awake beside him. Then I went to the living room, where Solange lay sleeping on the sofa. I rested my hand upon her small back. I thought about how, lately, Casimir had been so pleasant to me. I thought of how, when he came to Paris when I was there, he took me to dinner and to the theater. I thought of how he did not resent my success at all. Why was that? Because he was not with me any longer?

Solange awakened. "Maman?"

"Yes," I answered. "I am here." I sat beside her until her breathing grew deep and even. And then I tiptoed back to the bedroom. A headache was beginning; I hoped it would be gone by morning.

Winter 1813

RUE NEUVE-DES-MATHURINS

PARIS

By the time I was nine years old, my grandmother and I had returned to living in her apartment in Paris for the winter. My mother would come to fetch me and we would go on outings: to the Chinese Baths, for walks along the Seine, to select a sweet from a store where condensation clouded the glass. On Sundays, she brought me to the tiny, low-ceilinged apartment where she and my half sister, Caroline, now lived. The place reminded me of our old garret apartment, where I'd recited my first stories to my mother.

I was struck, particularly as I grew older, by the disparity between the two environments where I spent my time as a child in Paris. In my grandmother's spacious and exquisitely appointed apartment, one might enjoy a game of catch, should one be permitted such a thing in a place with silk damask wall coverings, crystal and silver at the table, and antiques—which, though much admired, did not invite touch or provide comfort the way my mother's much humbler furnishings did. The truth is, I preferred my mother's home always, though its cramped quarters meant that one scarcely had to rise from one's seat at the kitchen table to help oneself to the rabbit stew on the stove.

My mother did not have the means for the elaborate bouquets that graced the homes of the rich, and so she made cunning paper-flower bouquets, complete with stamens so delicate that they trembled in the heat waves from the fireplace. The dishes we ate from were not translucent china but, rather, the heavy white plates common in less expensive cafés. Still, the food served on them was prepared by my mother, and I believed then, as I do now, that it makes a difference in taste when one's thoughts and feelings and hands are employed in what one serves.

One relaxed at my mother's table. One shared stories, one laughed helplessly, one was entertained in a satisfying way that lifted one's spirits. Most important, my mother welcomed friends and strangers alike to her table. If you came home with someone you had just met on the street, she would share what she had with them, showing them the same face no matter who they were or where they came from. Her belief was this: No matter their station in life, people were united by virtue of their humanity. "We all rise to the same sun and sleep beneath the same moon," she often told me. Only if someone was false or haughty or superior did she display her caustic side to them.

A belief in everyone's equality may have been held in theory by my grandmother, but she failed to demonstrate any adherence in practice. Caroline was still never allowed at Nohant. And then came the day when, at fourteen years old, she tried to visit me at my grandmother's apartment in Paris.

I was in my room when I heard a knock at the door, then a girl's voice speaking. I recognized my sister, I heard my name, but I could not make out the rest of what she was saying.

But the response of my grandmother's maid was all too clear: "That may be so, but I cannot permit you to come in. Run along now."

Again my sister's voice, quieter now, pleading.

"I have told you, you are not allowed in here! Go home! And do not return! If you want to see your sister, it will have to be elsewhere. You are not welcome here!"

Then I heard the sound of the door slamming and the maid's rapid footsteps down the hall.

I saw Caroline infrequently enough that I did not really know her; but that day, when I heard her heart-rending sobs on the way down the stairs from my grandmother's apartment, I became very distraught. I thought of her pretty face and of her sweetness and her patience with me. We played string games and dolls and hide-and-seek, and we often locked arms and sat back to back, rocking faster and faster until we tumbled over, laughing.

I relished the feeling of a special inclusion I felt around Caroline, knowing that she had the same mother and had known my father. It was sisterhood, that was all—a common enough feeling but one that was offered and then taken away from me so often that it had become rarefied in my eyes. Our lives meant that we usually lived in separate places, but Caroline always did her part to try to stay close.

I thought about how she must have made the journey to see me with such high hopes, only to be humiliated. I wept so hard I vomited, and I vomited so much I began to cough up blood. My grandmother's reaction to all this was to blame poor Caroline for upsetting our home's peace and quiet with her unnecessary "demands" to see me. Sorrow and fury vied for the upper hand in me that night, as I thought about how my mother would have embraced Caroline when she heard the story, and that into her eyes would have come a steely hatred. I feared that her disdain would not be for my grandmother alone but would transfer over to me as well, for how was she to know that I was not a willing participant in this awful rejection of her older daughter?

The millinery shop my mother had envisioned as a way to keep us together had not yet come into being, and I feared it never would. I had not become resigned to living apart from my mother, as she had hoped I would; rather, I missed her continuously. Now I vowed to do my part to make it possible for us to live together again.

At Nohant, in my mother's bedroom, was a corner cabinet. Shortly after she left, I had begun collecting things I thought I could sell in order to pay my way from Nohant to Paris. I intended to walk to the city, but I would need money for food and lodging along the way. At first I collected quite avidly: into a far corner of the cabinet I put a yellow amber necklace my mother had given me—a gift from my father to her when he had been stationed in

Italy. I had also hidden a comb decorated with coral, and a ring with a very small diamond, from my grandmother.

After my mother left for good and her visits, then even her letters, began to taper off, I had stopped collecting. I did check often on my holdings, though, fearful that someone might stumble upon them and realize I had plans to run away. Now I resolved to begin my collecting again, as soon as we returned to Nohant.

We had been back in the country just a little more than a week when my grandmother fell seriously ill. We were sitting at dinner when she had an episode involving a kind of paralysis that lasted in excess of an hour. Deschartres was greatly alarmed and carried her to her bed, where he sat beside her all night.

The next morning, I saw her lying there, pale and silent. My heart opened to the old woman, and I abandoned my plans to leave Nohant, at least for now.

I knew that my grandmother had tried hard to offer me what she thought were the best things, both in the way of material goods and in my education. She had never spoken rudely to me, and she had made a great fuss over my talents and my precocity. My mother, on the other hand, seemed to have become less and less interested in me. My grandmother's illness served as a catalyst for my looking at things in the cold light of reason, and I had to admit it made no sense for me to run from the one who cared most for me.

Life went on for me there. And on.

August 1832

NOHANT

SOLANGE AND I LEFT PARIS TO RETURN TO NOHANT. MAURICE STAYED in the city with his father so that he could visit Henri IV military academy in advance of his attending that fall. Though my daughter seemed to have no difficulty transitioning back to life in the country, it took me a couple of weeks to settle into the routine at Nohant, to calm myself from the chaotic pace I was used to.

As ever, I found the estate to be full of delights. In the morning, larks awakened me with their cascading songs, and swallows swooped dramatically in their aerial feeding. In the afternoon, I made picnic lunches for Solange and me to eat on the stone bench outside. We watched the bees gathering nectar from a garden full of flowers whose scent filled the air. There were beautiful yellow-and-black-striped butterflies that often alighted on Solange's knee or hand, and I had to watch her lest she try to pull their wings off.

Each evening after I put my daughter to bed, I took walks outside alone and beheld the glittering stars, which were mostly obscured in the city. I listened to the sounds of the animals moving about in the underbrush of the forest, and to the hooting of the owls. On hot nights, I went to the river to bathe in the dark water.

Every few days, I took Solange out for expeditions to the woods and along the banks of the river to show her the pink and white stars of anemones amid the blue periwinkles. We stood together before berry bushes, plucking off the warm fruit and eating it. I taught her the names of the birds that came to Nohant and told her about her great-grandfather, how he had also loved birds, and how I believed he had passed on to me the ability to charm them onto my finger.

There was more to Nohant than bucolic pleasure, however. There were servants to mind, and many details I didn't want to attend to regarding things I didn't care about. When would madame like her breakfast served? Her dinner? There were menus to be approved, selections of linens, the placements of bouquets, guest lists to be made for obligatory dinners, accounting to be dealt with in my husband's absence. Finally, though, all was peaceful. Solange seemed content, and the house was running on its own.

I began working in earnest on my second novel, *Valentine.* I wrote even more feverishly than I had in Paris; oftentimes, I awakened with my head on my desk, the quill in my hand. The work was thrilling, all-consuming.

"Maman, stop working!" Solange would say sometimes, bursting into my room and pulling me out of the drama of a female aristocrat in love with a peasant, and into the world of a little girl. But I enjoyed that, too. If my vivid imagination served me well on the page, it also helped me become a most excellent partner in games with Solange. She remained difficult, in her way, but we often laughed ourselves breathless, and she would pat my arm and say, "You are a good *maman.*"

When Casimir brought Maurice back to Nohant, I exulted in the presence of my little man. I was also grateful for the fact that now that Casimir was here, I could work all through the night. I started at seven in the evening and wrote until six in the morning. I went to sleep when Casimir awakened; and this seemed to suit both of us.

I received letters from Jules, back again in Paris and, in my absence, living in the room I had rented for him. In one letter, he told me how much he missed me, how anxious he was for my return to our cozy garret in the fall, where I would once again cook for him the rich stews he favored. Reading the letter made me miss Paris: the theater and the opera, the cafés, even the pigeons who huddled together under the arches of the Pont Neuf. And Jules himself, of course: I missed him most of all. I thought of him arguing playfully with our friends, standing there in his tattered frock coat, his cravat so far off to the side it was nearly under his ear. I thought of our coupling at night, how I would run my hands up and down the long line of his back, how he sometimes kissed me so deeply it felt as though he were transferring the essence of himself into me. I thought of how I watched him in sleep, the beating of his heart steady in his throat. I saw us at breakfast with our bowl-sized cups of coffee, talking excitedly about all we meant to do that day.

I decided to take a spontaneous trip to Paris by myself, telling Casimir that I needed to attend to some details for *Le Figaro.* Jules and I would have some time together, and the visit would hold us until we could be together again.

When I arrived in Paris, I went to Jules's room, and had hardly set my valise down before we enjoyed an intense session of love-making. The next day, I went out so as to give Jules time alone to write. I came back earlier than we had agreed upon, thinking that I could quietly read the book I'd just purchased and then, when he had finished work for the day, we would go to a restaurant for dinner.

I let myself in quietly and found Jules in bed with his laundress, a young blond-haired, blue-eyed girl with a mole situated just so at the corner of her mouth. When I'd first met her, I had remarked on how pretty she was. "Her?" Jules had asked.

Now I stood frozen in place, the key in my hand.

The girl pulled the covers up over herself and stared.

Jules leapt to his feet. "Aurore! This means nothing!"

"To whom?" I asked, and then, before walking out, I turned to him to say, "And my name is George." My heart was breaking, but by the next day I had traded despair for resolve. I would find a place to live alone. I had the means, now, to make a decision about where I wanted to be without having to ask anyone's permission. It was something I had aspired to, but how ironic that now that I had such freedom, it felt more sorrowful than anything else.

November 1832

QUAI MALAQUAIS

PARIS

LATOUCHE HAD BEGUN SPENDING ALL OF HIS TIME IN A LITTLE country house he had purchased, and so I asked him if I might take over the rental of his apartment. He agreed gladly. We had become very good friends; in fact, there were rumors that we were lovers. One is helpless in the face of such idle gossip. If one denies the charge, one fans the flames; if one ignores it, one is complicit in suggesting it is so. Well, now that I was to be a woman on my own, I supposed the rumors would fly more furiously than ever before.

In my new place, there were fewer stairs to climb, which meant that it was not light and airy. Nor did it have the views I had enjoyed in the apartment I had shared with Jules. But it was peaceful there. Below were the gardens of the École des Beaux-Arts; across the river was the Louvre.

After a time, I saw Jules again; I never was one to hold grudges. But he was only a friend. My true love became my pen, my beautiful apartment, and the pages I stacked up on my desk each night. If I could not fill my days with the kind of affection I still longed for, I would fill them with another, more reliable kind of love, one that engaged my heart, my mind, and my spirit completely, and one that did not betray me.

October 1817

NOHANT

I WAS THIRTEEN YEARS OLD WHEN THERE BEGAN TO BE EPISODES of violence that escalated among the household staff at Nohant. My grandmother, who had suffered damage from the last stroke she had had and who, in any case, had never excelled in management, deferred more and more to Deschartres, essentially assigning him care of the entire estate. She turned a blind eye and a deaf ear to the arguments and flung plates in the kitchen, even to the abuse that an aging Deschartres suffered at the hands of the cook, who would try to beat him with a broom while poor Deschartres held his arms crisscrossed before him in outraged defense. As for me, I was ignored by the servants, with whom I'd formerly been friendly, for soon after my mother's departure, my grandmother forbade me to talk with them or to spend time lingering in the kitchen. And I was actively despised by Julie, my grandmother's maid.

When my mother was at Nohant, I could see that Julie's hostilities toward both of us burned in her breast; now, whenever I was not with my grandmother, she released the venom she felt—she thought I was fair game. Sometimes she told me that things at the estate had been spoiled since the moment my mother and I arrived; other times she allowed that it had been all right until my father's death. My mother and I were never meant to be there long-term, I understood. Now my mother had been gotten rid of, but I lingered, like a burr stuck in the hem of her petticoat. I began to take solace in the out-of-doors; I was inside only when I had to be. With this I established a pattern that stayed with me all my life: whenever unhappy circumstances unraveled me, nature knit me back up.

In 1816, Hippolyte had joined the army, and so I was the only child living with Grandmama, Deschartres, and the servants. Julie's animosity toward me I have described; but then my own maid,

Rose, began displaying moments of great cruelty toward me as well. I was no longer the little girl she had coddled; now I was older and more complicated. I was not often overtly willful, but there was a reason I was called stubborn: if my obstinacy did not show in complete noncompliance, it certainly did in the disdainful expression on my face and in the halfhearted way I did certain things I knew full well how to do better. Rose would beat me for this as well as for the most minor infringements: forgetting my hankie, dirtying my dresses, smacking my lips at the dinner table. But she never hit me in front of my grandmother or my mother, when she was visiting.

If I had reported Rose, she would have been punished, yet I did not tell either my mother or my grandmother how her behavior toward me had changed. It was by then a deeply ingrained habit to tolerate such behavior, and even to be comforted by its familiarity.

One cold day, when a slate-gray sky hung oppressively low, I went out for a walk in the nearby village. In the street, I saw a small family walking along, handsome parents and their two young daughters talking and laughing. They were carrying parcels and hurrying toward home, I imagined, where they would soon be warm and together for the evening. They would enjoy supper and the companionship of one another, and at night they would go to bed full of a kind of assurance that tomorrow they would all be together again. As I stood watching them go, heavy drops of rain began to fall.

I hoped it would not turn into a storm, for then I would be trapped inside with old people who had no tolerance for the restlessness of the young. I occasionally lost myself in reading, but there was otherwise little joy for me in that house. The studies I'd initially found so stimulating now bored me; the only pleasure I took in the writing assignments I was given was when I padded the narrative with my own fiction. Music had been ruined for me when my grandmother's arthritic fingers prevented her from teaching and she turned those duties over to the greasy-lipped organist from the church at La Châtre. He had technical ability but no feeling for the music; we could not communicate, and I began playing without passion or nuance as he did, just to get the lesson over with.

I walked in the rain toward the woods, remembering the gaiety and romance of my parents together, their and my happiness. Everything had been spoiled, first by my baby brother's death and then my father's; and now I felt effectively orphaned. I gave myself over to what I saw as my own personal tragedy, to the sort of melancholy adolescents are so good at submerging themselves in.

At only thirteen years of age, I had lost so much! And to whom could I turn for comfort? My mother, so many miles away in Paris? My father, deep in the ground? My grandmother, who understood very little about me at all and, in any case, was fading away? God, when I had so little of the faith that seemed to sustain others?

When my mother and I had first lived in Paris, I had gone to Mass with her. She believed in a child's way: she embraced her religion without questions. But my grandmother, who, in my mother's absence, was becoming more and more influential to me, taught me that Jesus was an admirable historical figure, nothing more. The villagers, who also influenced me, were more pagans than Christians; they brought out modern religion only on certain occasions, as if it were party clothes or their best dishes. Day to day, they were governed by superstition and belief in things like werewolves, witches, and humans possessed by demons. This was their religion, something from the Middle Ages, where mythology was vividly personified. I had heard that they had visions and hallucinations, too, and a strong belief in previous lives. So when I had first met Hippolyte and he'd told me he had been a dog in a previous life, he had been serious.

It was greatly confusing, trying to adopt a theology. But finally my own version of God came to me in a dream, complete with a name: Corambe. He was a warm and compassionate being with a tender and unwavering regard for me. He had the humanity of Jesus and the radiant beauty of the angel Gabriel. He was graceful and poetic and ever attentive to my feelings. And though he was a male, he nonetheless dressed oftentimes in women's clothes.

In the woods near my grandmother's house, I created an altar to Corambe. I built it in a clearing gotten to by going deep through young trees that had at their bases hawthorn and privet, and whose denseness prohibited much traffic. There was moss covering the ground in the clearing that both looked and felt like lush carpeting. Long shafts of light fell through breaks in the foliage to dapple the earth.

At the base of three joined maples, I made an altar, using pebbles, rocks, and leaves. I made wreaths from ivy and other natural materials and placed them here and there. I hung small pink-and-white shells from the boughs of the trees; in a breeze, they made a sound that reminded me of the castanets I had heard dancers use in Spain.

I would often go and kneel before Corambe's altar in the dim light, with my hands in the prayer position and my eyes closed. Though no words came to me, a rich feeling of peace did.

Sometimes, the best times, I would feel removed from the aching, lonely side of myself and instead part of a greater whole. I was equal to, related to everything around me: the ground I lay on, the animals rustling in the woods, the leaves stirring in the breeze, the sky high above me.

But on this cold and bleak day, I found no comfort in the idea of going to the altar. I had no idea where to go, what to do. I heard owls asking the same question I was: *Who? Who? Who?*

When I arrived home, I sat outside the front door. I was cold and wanted to go in; but I was loath to give up the freedom I felt outdoors. I put my forehead to my knees and began to weep, releasing long, wailing sobs, and I spoke to the dirt below me, saying the words I longed to say to my grandmother: "You chide me for failing in my studies. I want to fail! You have no idea how I feel or what I have planned, which does not in any way have to do with the ridiculous, old-fashioned things you try to force upon me. Soon enough I shall show you why I have no need of you or of what you teach. I shall be rid of all of you forever!"

I spoke with a passion and fury that contained in it a great deal of truth but mostly reflected my loneliness, confusion, and despair. I was like anyone who seeks a place to put his pain; I blamed my grandmother for all that ailed me. I also spoke as one who believed no one could hear, but in fact Julie was standing just inside the door, in the hallway, and she heard every word.

She jerked open the door and spit out, "You ingrate! How dare you speak this way about the woman who has done so much for you! You would deserve her sending you back to your mother!"

"I *want* to go back to my mother!" I said. "It is all I dream of, to escape this place and live where I belong!"

Julie's eyes narrowed. She stepped forward and leaned down to hiss into my ear, "Quiet yourself! You are having a tantrum, and the truth is, you don't know what you want. I only hope for your sake that your grandmama has not heard your diatribe, for she might just take you at your word and send you away!"

"She need not have heard me, Julie. You know full well you will tell her what I said."

At this, Julie's mouth dropped, and I stood to face her, my hands clenched at my sides, and let go with all the rage that still burned in me. "Do you think I don't see through you? Do you think I don't know that you are kind to me only to try to ferret out information that you can then use against me? Go and tell my grandmother everything; tell her now! I hope it will make her decide to let me go to my mother at once!"

Julie spun on her heel, and I knew she was going straight to my grandmother. I was filled with a great sense of righteousness and hastened to my bedroom, where I slammed the door and then sat on my bed, reviewing all the reasons why I had been justified in lashing out at what I saw as my keepers. Despite my own clearly expressed wishes, I had been left in the care of an old woman whose methods and predilections were foreign and irksome to me: the way I was made to wear gloves and to curtsy before my grandmother's dour countess friends, the way I had to practically whisper when I was inside. I was made to address my grandmother not even in the formal *vous* but in the third person, as in, "Will Grandmama permit me to go outside now?" My mother may have punished me freely, but she always made up for it afterward; and there was honesty in her behavior. I could be intimate with her, not only calling her *tu,* but easily and quite naturally giving my innermost self to her: my stories, my thoughts, my fears, my dreams. She *asked* me to; and in return, she showed me herself.

It seemed to me that by virtue of her nature, my grandmother had inhibited me from being my true self day after day, year after year. I often thought of the animals that roamed free, wishing I could be one of them rather than a human being subjected to such a dull and regimented environment. No one shushed the birds singing in the trees; no one cautioned the dogs not to run too far from home or the horses not to sleep outside in the sun. The pigs could roll in mud; I could not even remove my shoes and stockings for the feel of green grass beneath my feet.

Whenever we traveled to Paris in the big berlin, the many pockets of the coach would be stuffed with all my grandmother needed, and she needed everything: her perfumes and powders and pillboxes and her maid sitting erectly beside her. She needed coverlets against a draft, parasols against any ray of sun. As I saw it, she did not enjoy life so much as protect herself from it.

When we walked in the garden, I was forced to move slowly, along with her, rather than run down the paths, as I longed to do. Because of her, I had to take my lessons with Deschartres in his overly neat room, which reeked of lavender soap; being there gave me a headache. I felt I needed a younger person to keep up with and inspire me, not an old woman to constrain me and fill me with despair. I needed my mother, whose blood ran hot like my own, whose heart knew my own heart's desires.

Now, with all that I had shouted out, I had made my feelings clear. I was aware that in my pain, I had made no effort to acknowledge the good side of my grandmother: her offerings of praise and sweets when I did well with my lessons; her attempts at affection, stiff-backed though they were; her good-hearted intentions to refine me. No, I had only poured out my frustrations.

Because of my outburst, I would soon be released to live in poverty with my mother, my opportunities for education taken from me. So be it. It was the truer, more honest life! But even as I justified what I had said, I was beginning to feel regret for the pain I would cause the old woman. She had not asked to raise me any more than I had asked that she do it; but here we were, stuck with each other, and she was only trying to make the best of it.

Still! Shouldn't she understand that a daughter would want her mother, first and foremost? And shouldn't she have accepted Caroline as one of her beloved son's children and let us all live happily together here? No! She had insisted upon her own way.

I sat for some time, waiting for Julie to call me to my grandmother's side. I intended to express my appreciation in my leave-taking; and my love as well, for the longer I sat there, the more I realized that I did love the old woman.

When Julie finally came to my room, however, it was to say that I was barred from seeing my grandmother. In a prim and self-righteous way that made me want to strike her, she said, "Knowing now that you are so full of hatred for her, your grandmother has decided that you will not have to see her again. She is letting you go, as you desire. In three days, you will leave for Paris."

"I do not hate my grandmother, as you well know," I said. "I am sorry not to be given the opportunity to say goodbye. But I am glad to be returning to my mother. And so I thank you."

Over the next few days, I was indeed kept from my grandmother. I was given my meals after she had taken hers, and dishes were placed and removed by servants whose steely countenances and absolute silence let me know what they were feeling about me. I was allowed out in the garden only after Grandmama had retired. She was in a weakened condition at that point and had been spending much of her time away from me anyway, but now I noticed her absence more.

I was full of a mix of shame and defiance and confusion. I spoke with Corambe about my feelings and was assured by my personal god that I was indeed in the right and was following a noble course. I looked upon this time of estrangement as my martyrdom, which I suffered sweetly: I all but saw myself with a blood-red banner flying above my head, torn and battered but proudly displayed. But after two days passed and I noticed no preparations being made to send me to Paris, I wondered if my grandmother had changed her mind.

On the third day my maid, Rose, told me to go to my grandmother, who she said was suffering. She assured me that Julie would let me into the old woman's chambers; she had already asked Julie to do so. By then, I had had enough time to realize that I had been strikingly unfair in not assigning any blame at all to my mother for her complicity (if not initiation!) in leaving me behind. I had made her into a hapless victim when she was anything but. Nor had I considered the fact that I, too, had played a role in my own unhappiness.

And Julie was right: I was lucky indeed to be living amid the beauty and privilege and peace of Nohant, taking with both hands the gifts I was offered daily.

I was thoroughly ashamed and remorseful and eager to apologize most profusely. I came into a darkened room, where my grandmother lay in bed under her lacy scented sheets and down-filled coverlets, her eyes closed. "Grandmama?" I said, my voice high and tentative, and then I rushed to her side. I fell to my knees and began crying and kissing her, saying, "Forgive me, I never meant—"

She held up a trembling hand, and I stopped talking. I sat back on my heels and waited. There followed an ominous quiet.

Then she turned to look at me, and the warm light that was always in her eyes was gone. Instead, there was a flatness there, worse than anger. "You have come hoping to fall upon my mercy and by so doing return things to the way they used to be. This is impossible. The things you said have pierced my heart, and there is no snapping one's fingers and undoing the damage. For three days, I have considered your assertions and accusations and the feelings behind them. I have slept little and agonized much over what to do. And now I find that I have some things I want to say to you, Aurore. Some of the things I wanted never to reveal to you but now realize I must; other things I have been meaning to say for some time. I would ask that you listen and not interrupt. May I rely upon you to do me that one favor?"

"Yes, Grandmama."

"Very well, then. Bear in mind that I am telling you this for your own good and not to avenge myself. I offer this to you rather than simply ridding myself of you, which would be the easier thing to do."

I felt an eerie coldness at the back of my head. It was a shock for me to understand that my grandmother had despaired of me, too. I was still enough of a child to think that I would be pardoned for virtually anything.

My grandmother drew in a deep breath. "Now, then. First I shall speak to you about myself and the way I was brought up. Then I shall tell you about my beloved son. I want you to know about the way he was raised and about the relationship we enjoyed, at least until he met your mother. And then I am going to tell you the truth about her."

I sat unmoving, my eyes on the floor.

Almost half an hour later, she said, "You may go now; I am tired."

It was with great difficulty that I rose up from my knees. I felt myself to be a leaden mass, empty of feeling. I curtsied and wordlessly took leave of the woman who had told me things I had not known, and that she never should have told me, at least not without mentioning the desperate measures that are taken by poor people that rich people will never understand. My grandmother had coldly told me that my mother was a whore when my father met her and that she had gone back to her old profession in Paris. That if I intended to resume my relationship with her, I would forfeit any benefits my grandmother had intended to give me, not because of my own merits but on behalf of her son. Worst, my grandmother told me that it was entirely likely that my father was not my father at all. According to calculations my grandmother had made long ago, my father was many miles away from my mother, fighting in the war, at the time she would have been impregnated.

That night, I sat for a long while at the edge of my bed, staring out the window at the darkness and the cold pinpricks of the stars. I was trying to comprehend all I had wrought in my outburst to Julie only a few days ago. Up until now, my mother had never been directly criticized, and there had been moments of accord and what seemed like mutual respect between my grandmother and her. Now, because of what I had said, I had been told things about her I would never be able to forget, including the fact that she may have created me with someone I would never know.

I felt a rush of defiance. I went to the mirror and looked for evidence of my father in my face. There! Did I not have his black eyes, his curly black hair? And then I wept, because I could no longer be sure that those things came from him. I stood trembling, telling myself that whether my father gave my mother his seed to make me or not was irrelevant; he gave her his heart. And he gave it to me, as well. He had been present at my birth and had made his mark upon me in raising me from the very beginning. Even in his absence, I breathed him in and breathed him out; he was my true father.

And then I lay on the bed and wept most disconsolately, for I realized I could not be sure of anything anymore. What I regretted most profoundly was my loss of any vestige of home. I myself was the only home I had.

January 1833

QUAI MALAQUAIS

PARIS

MY NOVELLA *LA MARQUISE* CAME OUT IN SERIAL FORM IN THE *Revue de Paris* just after I returned to the city from another stay at Nohant. It again featured a young woman sold into marriage, but this time, she is an aristocrat, and her husband dies. All around her expect that she will remarry, or at least have lovers. She does neither. Her feeling is that she has had quite enough of men until, at the theater one night, she falls instantly in love with an actor named Lélio. How embarrassing for her, that one of her station should be enamored of one so low! And not even an irresistible specimen but, rather, one frail and weak-seeming. To add to that, his voice is high and screechy, his mannerisms effeminate. But the marquise is besotted by the young man. She confides her feelings for him to a friend, who warns her never to let anyone else know. And so the lovesick woman dresses in men's clothes so as to be unrecognizable and to have the opportunity to go to the theater and see the object of her desire every night. They eventually become lovers, and when they end their relationship, it is because the marquise finds herself unworthy of him.

This novel was inspired by the first time I saw the actress Marie Dorval perform upon the stage, in 1831, not long after I had first arrived in Paris. The play was Victor Hugo's tragedy *Marion de Lorme;* it was based on Alfred de Vigny's novel *Cinq-Mars.* Vigny was currently Marie Dorval's lover. She was rumored to have had many lovers, some of them women, actresses with whom she had worked.

The night I saw her, when I stood beneath the gaslights dressed as a man and watched a performance of such simplicity and grace, I understood immediately why Marie was known as the sensation of the romantic theater, the brightest star of the Comédie-Française. I saw why she was the muse of great playwrights: Hugo and Vigny and Alexandre Dumas.

"Love has given me a new virginity," she said from the stage that night, and the line seemed directed to me.

I more than admired her, I felt irretrievably caught by her. I wanted to know her, to spend time with her, to be a valued friend of hers; but I felt as helpless in that desire as any unknown who longs to make an impression on someone so renowned.

When my own reputation began to grow, I thought perhaps I would write to her and see if anything came of it. I sent her a letter that was lighthearted in tone, yet carefully calculated to impress.

The next morning, Jules came to see me, and we were having coffee. There was a knock on the door, and when I opened it, Marie Dorval catapulted into my life. "It's me; here I am!" she cried, rushing to embrace me. In a brilliant shift all the world became a vessel for her support; all but Marie and her golden curls and her narrow waist and her remarkable lightness in movement dropped away. That throaty voice! Here it was at my table, and those blue eyes, now directed only at me!

"I received your letter, and I came straightaway, as you see." She was out of breath, and she took a moment to remove her ermine muff and heavy mantle. Beneath it, she wore a dark green velvet morning dress accented at the shoulder and down the center by a lighter green silk, and the fichu pelerine draped over her shoulders had the delicacy of a dusting of snow. She sat at the table, placed a hand upon her breast, and smiled radiantly. But then her face changed, and she stared into her lap and spoke in a low, almost tremulous voice: "I will tell you, as an unknown, I myself once wrote to a great actress, my heart in my palm. Her reception was ice. I was full of shame. I pulled at my hair and pounded my bosom, I wanted to reel in time and snatch my letter back. *Fool!* I said to myself, over and over. *Imbecile!* I imagined the pages I had so long deliberated over flung aside, wadded up and thrown in the rubbish. Thus did I vow that if ever it was my turn, I would rush to the one so full of longing, take hold of that hand, and say, *'Yes, I have heard your words! I have taken them with great care into my heart, they are enshrined at my very core!'*"

She looked up at me. "Have you no coffee for me?"

In my haste to accommodate her, I rose too quickly and knocked my own coffee over. My face reddened as I offered an apology, as I moved my napkin quickly to keep the spill from advancing onto her lap, where she had laid a most fetching feather bonnet; the satin ribbon ties hung nearly to the floor. She reached out to grab hold of my wrist and told me with her eyes that it mattered not in the least. With this conspiratorial glance, she confirmed what I'd suspected the first time I'd seen her upon the stage: we knew each other. Even before meeting, we knew each other. At that moment, what little light I had left for Jules went out.

Marie explained that my letter had had a deep effect on her—*Incroyable!* said she—and she said as well that she knew it had been written by someone with the heightened sensibilities she shared. She waved her hands about when she spoke; they flew like little white doves around her face.

Even now, I cannot account for the immediate reaction I had to her. In principle, I sought to gain for women the rights they were due and denied, but in practice I did not want to spend much time with them. I found women too often hysterical, too complaining of things that merited no real complaint, too weighted down by their petty concerns to see, much less engage in, the larger world. For the most part, I felt they did not use their God-given intellect but subjugated it. Probably my infatuation, and then my abiding love for Marie was because of her adherence to her own character: both on and off the stage she projected a burning naturalness, a sense of true and vital self.

I knew the cost of such uncompromising ways. As there were ceaseless rumors about me, there were stories of Marie and the multiple lovers she took without apology, without any effort at disguise—in fact, oftentimes her husband was in the adjoining room. But she walked with her head up, moving at the pace she desired, impervious to the vultures. I very much admired this.

She invited Jules and me to dine with her on Sunday night. I accepted for both of us, but in truth I was speaking purely for myself, imagining only Marie and me at that table, by candlelight, in solidarity, at the precipice. It seemed to me that everything in my life that had preceded her had prepared me for her. And it seemed, too, that everything I had longed for and not yet found was in her.

When Jules and I went to dine with Marie Dorval, her husband, and her lover, Alfred de Vigny, I dressed with some care. I now wore men's clothes almost exclusively, and that night I decided to wear a new single-breasted purple surtout that reached to my ankles, made warm by padding from shoulders to chest. It had black velvet trim and silver buttons. Beneath, I wore my usual close-fitting trousers, my waistcoat, a frilled shirt, and a black silk cravat tied waterfall-style. My boots were high and tasseled.

Marie wore a low-cut silk gown of midnight blue, stiffened blond lace trimming the back as well as the tops of the beribboned beret sleeves. The bodice was draped à la Sévigné, featuring horizontal bands with a boned divider, and so it showed the devastating beauty of her shoulders and bosom. She wore drop pearl earrings and a pendant brooch and had tucked small white silk flowers into her hair, which was parted down the center and fashioned into a version of the Apollo knot. Blue was a color I thought she should always wear, and I told her so.

"Ah, but if I am always in blue, you will never see me in yellow, or pink, or white, which also suit me." The expression on her face when she said this was self-mocking, but she was serious, too: she was ever a woman keenly aware of all of her gifts, and if beauty was among them, so be it.

What we ate I cannot recall. In fact, had you asked me while I was eating what it was, I would have been loath to answer, for it would have taken my attention from the dazzling subject at hand—the only subject, so far as I was concerned, though our lively conversation covered theater, the books of the American James Fenimore Cooper, the subjectivity of memory, and the relative merits of the divas at the Théâtre des Italiens.

I was curious to see if what I remembered about her from our brief earlier visit remained true, if each of her emotions was made physical. It was. She seemed passionate about everything—her opinion, your opinion, the taste of the food, the rush of wind outside the window—and all of it was made manifest by a body that truly was an instrument. I had not known how nuanced the lifting of an eyebrow could be until I met Marie; nor had I realized the many variations of a smile, or the language of fingers, or what invitation or admonishment could be issued by the briefest of looks. The modulations in her speaking voice rivaled those of an opera singer's.

There are people one meets in life whom one wants to please, inadvertent kings and queens in the various societies in which we live. And they do not demand this for themselves; rather, it is we admiring subjects who demand it for them by virtue of who they simply are and cannot help being. I wanted to please Marie Dorval. I wanted to hear every story about herself she deigned to tell, and I wanted her to hear all of mine. I felt a great sense of urgency in her presence, and I was impatient with the other guests, who, to my way of thinking, interfered most annoyingly with what was nascent between us.

It took me a long time to see that there were striking similarities between Marie and my mother, even after she told me the circumstances of her upbringing, which resembled my mother's. I suppose I did not want to recognize the similarities. I suppose I wanted a new start in an old game, no matter the cost to me.

Marie-Thomase-Amélie Delauney, a child of actors, was born out of wedlock in 1798. She was put onto the stage as soon as she could talk; she was a beautiful child and even at that age had a charismatic presence. When she was fifteen, she married an actor named Allan Dorval. He died only a few years later, but by then Marie had three daughters. She then married a man she did not love but liked well enough, and trusted: one Jean-Toussaint Merle, director of the Théâtre de la Porte Saint-Martin. What mattered most about him, she later told me, was that he understood her. Which was to say, he would look the other way when she did what she needed to do. He entered into his relationship with her with his eyes wide open, knowing that she would have lovers of either sex whenever she was moved to.

That night at dinner, I sat like a tightly wound clock, the hours ticking away, hoping for a time when she and I could be alone and without distraction. I sensed this was why she had invited me in the first place.

She was then and always a gracious hostess, dividing her attention among everyone gathered there, even acquiescing to her husband in a way that I thought was beneath her. Weren't the revolutionary times we were living in an imperative to stand up for yourself? Did this not require women to change their attitudes not only toward their husbands but, indeed, all men?

It was only as I was taking my leave that Marie spoke in confidence to me. She gripped my hand tightly and stood so close that I could smell the after-dinner anise on her breath. "To think of all that we shall do!" she said, and before I could answer she drew nearer still to say, "Everything about you is exciting to me. You are what men should be."

Jules came over to me then, flinging his cloak about himself, taking my arm, and we went out the door together. At first, we did not speak, and then Jules laughed and said, "A bit excessive, is she not? Such people are best enjoyed from theater seats."

I stepped away and turned to face him. "Such people," I said, "are luminosities we are privileged to enjoy."

"You exaggerate and romanticize," he said. "As is your habit." To which I responded, "And you see like a blind man. As is yours."

—

I THOUGHT I HAD SEEN Vigny's disapproval of me at dinner. A few days later, thanks to the relentless chain of Paris gossip, my suspicions were confirmed. I learned that this lover of Marie's had told others that what he called my "manlike ways" were very unappealing: my dress, my clumsy gait, my low voice, my forthright manner. I was not so much bothered by this; and it did not keep me from liking him. But I feared that his opinion might change Marie's response to me. And so I sent her a note:

> *Do you really think you can endure me? That is something you cannot know yet, nor I. I am such a bear, so stupid, so slow to put my thoughts to words, so awkward and so dumb just when my heart is fullest. Do not judge me by externals. Wait a little before deciding how much pity and affection you can give me. I feel that I love you with a heart rejuvenated and altogether renewed by you. If that is just a dream, like everything else I have ever wanted in my life, do not wake me from it too soon. It does me so much good. Goodbye, you great and lovely person.*

She never answered that letter, and later I worried at the way I had opened myself to her. But I believed that speaking the truth was more honorable than obfuscating it. I waited with hope and even assurance for our next visit, which came soon.

November 1817

NOHANT

After my grandmother's dark revelations, I lived in a kind of limbo. I was not gone from Nohant, but I was not really there anymore, either. I paid little attention to my studies in favor of running wild with the children of the village, and I spent long hours alone in my room, ignoring the lessons I'd been asked to do. My grandmother's words, so heartlessly delivered, changed my idea of myself. If my mother was contemptible, then I, her daughter, must be as well. I no longer loved life. I cared nothing for myself, and my future seemed bleak. I considered suicide, but it was an adolescent's romantic idea of that desperate act; it did not have the weight or gravity that times of such desperation would assume later in my life. An abiding consolation at this time was my black dog, Phanor. Seeming to sense my despair and wanting to ameliorate it, he did not leave my side. His exuberant acceptance of any attention I showed him was my only joy.

But no matter what pain I endured, it was always my habit to gravitate back to hope, and to the idea that I must live for someone or something. Whatever her wrongdoings, I forgave my mother, and I continued to love her.

The same went for my grandmother, though I had decided that I would passively reject what she desired for me: a formal education followed by a marriage that she would arrange. I had seen enough of society marriages to know that they were nothing I desired.

At thirteen, I had grown enough in size and strength that when I failed in my studies or in my behavior, my maid was no longer able to discipline me with blows. She knew that she would be likely to get back what she gave. She described me as an *enfant terrible,* and I suppose from her point of view, she was right. From my point of view, I was only starting to claim what was my due.

After some time, my grandmother called me to her for another talk, which I'd known in my heart had been coming.

"First," she said, "I shall tell you that I have been increasingly disappointed in you—in your care of yourself, both physically and mentally. Where once you showed yourself to be a charming and clever girl, now you display a kind of dullness and lack of interest in your studies. Deschartres tells me your work is careless and rarely completed; when he asks questions of you, your response is a yawn. You seem unconcerned about becoming attractive, as you could be, if you tried. Your hands are ill cared for, and your gait is clumsy—in part because you persist in wearing peasants' shoes that deform your feet. Your complexion is too dark because you will not stay out of the sun; day after day you come home filthy as a potato digger. You seem uninterested in or unable to learn any social graces; you either speak not at all, as though you are above everyone around you, or you chatter on endlessly, boring everyone and leaving no room for the comments and observations of anyone else. I am exhausted by having to constantly tell you to take your elbows off the table, to eat slowly, to cut your meat into smaller pieces, to arrange your silverware properly to signal to the servants that you have finished your meal. You should by now know how to engage in lively and pleasant conversation, rather than sit silent or, worse, sit staring fixedly at nothing, as though you had half a brain. All of this should be second nature by now! I do believe your heart is good, but you must put time and effort into developing your mind in order to be a person of any worth at all.

"I have given up thinking I am the one who can help you achieve what I believe you are capable of. Therefore, in January, you will go to Paris, to the convent of the Dames Augustines Anglaises. It is a school run by the English, comparable to Sacré-Coeur or Abbaye-aux-Bois. Their students are well taught, and the tutors of the social graces there are renowned. Perhaps they can offer you something I cannot; I pray they can persuade you to use yourself and your gifts in a way that is appropriate."

The community of English Augustines was the only surviving convent of its age, having been established in Paris at the time of Cromwell, and its housing had come through various revolutions without suffering much damage. In fact, during the 1793–94 uprising, the so-called Terror, which had preceded my grandmother's move to Nohant, both she and my mother had coincidentally spent time behind its protective walls. I knew that the school's reputation was excellent. But all I could think of was one thing.

I looked happily into my grandmother's face to say, "I shall see my mother again!"

My grandmother nodded and spoke bitterly: "Yes. You will see your mother again. And then you will be separated from us both."

It grew quiet, each of us caught up, I supposed, with our respective ideas about what my meeting with my mother might bring. I was sure she would immediately take me to live with her, at last.

January 1818

COUVENT DES AUGUSTINES ANGLAISES
RUE DES FOSSÉS-SAINT-VICTOR
PARIS

ON THE DAY AFTER MY ARRIVAL IN THE CONVENT, MY MOTHER CAME to see me. I stood before her, grinning foolishly, waiting for her to tell me to gather my things and come home with her. Instead, she said, rather impatiently, "So, Aurore, now you are here. I suppose it's for the best, though I know you will earnestly be taught ridiculous things by bloodless women who cannot decide for themselves how to dress, much less how to think. Mind you keep your wits about you. This is all part of your grandmother's plan for how to properly educate you. You must endure it for a greater good; you must become in one way or another able to manage the riches you will inherit."

I stared at her. "You are not taking me to live with you?"

She raised her eyes heavenward. "Surely you did not expect that. I agreed with your grandmother that you should be here and, in fact, have also agreed to her request not to take you out for visits, even during vacations. I believe she is right in saying it would interfere with your studies and your character development."

My voice grew small in a way that I detested. "But, Maman, you said . . . I thought—"

Her entire upper torso jerked with impatience. "What did you think? That I would assume care for you when I have all I can do to take care of Caroline and myself?"

"But—"

"Be strong, Aurore. Pay attention to your lessons. And do as they ask of you." She kissed me and turned to go.

I watched her walk away. And in that moment I saw clearly what I had been unable or unwilling to see before: I would never get what I needed from her.

Rather than succumb to the despair I felt mounting in me, I shifted perspective. I turned and walked quickly back into the place I had thought I would be leaving that day. My head was crowded with thoughts. I was to live cloistered in this stone village? Enchanting! I was not to see the people of Nohant, even the villagers of whom I had become so fond? A good opportunity to meet others, to start afresh! I was no longer to see the rolling hills and picturesque views of the countryside? Then I was also rid of Deschartres's galumphing along beside me on my walks and lecturing me to pay attention to things I did not feel were important. Who cared about boundaries and acreage and ownership and which particular bovine disease was of concern at the moment?

Yes, I was here now. And so I would be here now.

Here turned out to be a place behind tall iron gates that shaped my outlook and being in fundamental and irrevocable ways. When children lie on their backs to regard the sky for a long enough period of time, they become the sky. Such was my experience there.

As a romantic, I found the convent a good place to be. It offered solitude and quiet, the scent of incense, candlelight illuminating heads bowed in devotion over rosaries, and the echo of chanting at matins and vespers. Everywhere you looked there were crucifixes that reminded you of a story at once beautiful, tragic, and inspiring.

We were cloistered in a stone labyrinth made up of several buildings, chapels, and courtyards. There was an air of mystery and intrigue to the parts that were hundreds of years old and had passageways that led nowhere. I was fascinated by the fact that the ancient remains of English Catholics rested beneath the flagstone walkways, and I found elegant the epitaphs on the tombs, as well as the religious axioms carved into the walls.

All of the nuns and two-thirds of the students were English, Scottish, or Irish, and most of the girls came from aristocratic backgrounds. There were tenants living on the grounds as well, private citizens who had sought refuge from the world; they lived alongside the staff and students.

English was the language spoken, and all the art and furniture was English, too. I began my habit of drinking tea here, and of speaking English much of the time, even sometimes dreaming in it.

By virtue of the reading I had done under my grandmother's tutelage, I was advanced enough to enter the upper class. But because I could not yet speak a word of English, I was put in the lower class, made up of around thirty girls from ages six to fourteen.

I was relieved. I knew myself to be intelligent enough, but I had a great deal of ignorance about many of the subjects my grandmother believed I had mastered. In history and philosophy, I understood general concepts but was largely unaware of the sequence of events. I had not yet learned the tenets of the faith to which I claimed membership.

It was peaceful in that place where a heavy door at the end of the hall groaned shut every evening and was locked with a long iron key. That event signaled the end of the day as reliably as the setting of the sun. A small lamp burned all night in the cloisters, and it always seemed to signify that a watchful presence was among us. I was happy to be far from the contentious relationships I had with my mother and my grandmother, far from life as I had known it: both at Nohant and in my grandmother's apartment in Paris. I did not miss her afternoon tête-a-têtes with her old-woman friends, they with their fluttering hankies and violet candies. I grew calm there.

But this calm did not come instantly. I had first to pass through my period of purposeful rebellion, when I became a member of a group called the Devils.

ON MY FIRST DAY OF CATECHISM, which was an hour-long class taught by a nun called Mother Alippe, I was asked, in a stultifying manner (for who could fail to know the answer to this most basic of questions?), what happened to babies who were not baptized before death. I did not know about limbo at that point, and so I answered quite naturally with what I thought the only answer could be: those souls were held tenderly in God's bosom. A stunned silence fell in the classroom. Mother Alippe crossed her arms tightly over her bosom. "*Where* are those unfortunate souls?" she asked, and I sat silent until the girl behind me whispered, "Limbo." That was what she said but not what I heard. "In Olympia?" I answered. The class erupted into laughter, and I couldn't help joining in.

Mother Alippe rose up to her full height, her face full of fury, but I was able to convince her that it was an honest mistake, and so she administered a mild punishment: make the sign of the cross in order to calm myself and return to a serious state of mind. This I did, in the way I had been taught, which I soon learned was incorrect: I touched my right shoulder before the left. Mother Alippe sighed and called me a pagan.

This may have been humiliating, but it was nothing compared to what all of us girls endured at the hands of our lay teacher for the rest of the day. That teacher, Mademoiselle D., was a fat and frankly ugly woman with a nearly lipless mouth and soiled petticoats. She acted the saint in front of the nuns, but to us girls she was a cruel taskmaster who delighted in delivering scoldings and administering punishments such as making us kiss the ground. This was a standard punishment at the convent, but the nuns would let us get away with cheating and kissing our hands rather than dirt. Mademoiselle D., on the other hand, all but pressed her boot onto our necks. She was one of those for whom the natural gaiety of childhood is an irritant, one who derived great pleasure from seeing others suffer as penance for her own grievances. She took an instant dislike to me, and the sentiment was returned. I fell in with the Devils because of their boldness and their idea that they belonged first and foremost to themselves, but also because they were unbowed by Mademoiselle D.

There were two other groups in the lower form: the Sages, who tried to be good in all ways, and the Beasts, who kept their own counsel and did not align themselves with anyone. The Devils were my clear choice. They broke rules as a matter of course, shrugging off any punishment. In fact, they often wryly despaired of the lack of creativity shown in attempts to discipline them; and if the teachers had listened to what the Devils discussed among themselves as being worthy retribution, they might well have employed the girls' methods and gotten better results.

Another reason I fit well with the Devils was the fact that I did not fear but, rather, admired their leader, whom everyone else tiptoed around. Her name was Mary Gillibrand, but she was nicknamed "Boy" for her loud voice and physical strength. My first exposure to her came by way of stories about her that neared mythology. By the time we met in person in Mother Alippe's classroom, I was expecting a gargantuan presence who breathed fire. Instead, I came face-to-face with a freckle-faced eleven-year-old girl. Mary's way of introducing herself was to say to me, "Ah, so here we have Aurore Du-pain! Dawn bread! I salute you, you who calls Limbo 'Olympia,' you who will no doubt serve to entertain us all!"

There ensued great laughter, and I was part of it. Mary saw that I was not vain and was unbothered by her attack, and this interested her. She continued to make fun of me, and I continued to enjoy it as much as the other girls. Finally, Mary thwacked me on the shoulder, a blow powerful enough to rock me back on my heels. Straight-faced, I gave one back to her.

"Well, then," she said, smiling, mindlessly rubbing her injury. "Shall we go for a walk, you and I?"

"When?"

"Now!"

"But we have class."

Mother Alippe had just arrived with her pile of books and papers. With her back to us, she began arranging them on her desk.

"Watch!" Mary whispered, and as others bustled to their seats, she walked confidently out of the room as though she were invisible. I followed, biting my lip, holding my breath.

We sat down on a bench in a deserted cloister, and she put her face close to mine. "So you're a Devil, eh?"

"I want to be."

"Then you are; I can see you have the stuff. There were three of us; now there are four, a good round number. And now that I know your intentions, let us go back to class. No reason to waste our efforts on Mother Alippe, who is all right with me. But tonight, during evening recreation with Fatcheeks Mademoiselle D., we'll sneak off and not return until bedtime prayers."

"What happens if we are caught?"

Mary shrugged. "Most of the time she doesn't notice. If she does, you might be made to wear a nightcap all the next day, that's all. I find it quite fashionable, and on a cold day, it's of great comfort."

"Does she ever strike you?"

"She doesn't dare. She doesn't dare strike any of us."

I did join the Devils in their adventure that night and the nights following, for what turned out to be marvelous expeditions along rarely used corridors, dimly lit or not lit at all. We tried to pry open locked doors with a table knife, we went up and down stairs that led to blank walls, and we once tried to dig through a wall using our fingernails—someone was sure she had heard faint wailing behind it. We had stubs of candles we'd stolen to light our way in the darkest places. We made up a mission: we were in search of a young woman who had been imprisoned in the convent and now languished in chains, waiting for the one who might find her.

Winter at the convent was difficult for me. I had always fared better in the country at Nohant; the yellow air in Paris never failed to make me sickly. Add to that the severe cold we had the first year I was there, and it made for a miserable specimen who lay in her cot at night with her teeth chattering like castanets, looking up in the dimness at the low ceiling of the ugly room she shared with about thirty other girls. We had a stove, but it seemed as if its function was to smoke and shimmy rather than provide any significant warmth.

After several months I became quite lively and was known by the nickname "Madcap." I began to write both prose and poetry, for fun at first—to amuse and entertain my classmates and my teachers. Later, I wrote more seriously, even re-creating a play I had read at Nohant.

IN APRIL 1819 I moved from the dormitory to my own private cell at the convent. It measured ten feet long, and its width was six feet. I could touch its sloping ceiling as I lay in my bed, and it gave me a child's thrill to do so. One couldn't open the door without bumping it into the chest of drawers, or close the door without pressing oneself into the window's embrasure. Icicles formed from my leaky ceiling in the winter, and in summer I could scarcely breathe for the closeness in the air. But I loved it.

In addition to my bed, I had a wicker chair, an old rug made only more beautiful to me by its faded pastels, and my grandmother's little Louis XV harp, which seemed to anoint the space with a kind of grace and grandeur. The four-paned window did not offer a lovely view: when I looked down, I saw a drainpipe. But if I looked up, I could see parts of Paris.

The church bell was near my cell, and it took some time to get used to its tolling, but I came to love that sound. Rather than keep me from sleep, it lulled me into it. And then I would be awakened by the bells ringing matins, and by the chanting of the nuns, and by the songbirds, who always seemed to welcome the promise of a new day.

It had been a long time since I had sat alone in contemplation. Living in close proximity to the other girls offered many pleasures and comforts, not least among them the giggling fits that young women are prone to at the slightest provocation. But I paid a price as well: the constant presence of others meant that I could not have the kind of solitude my nature required.

Now I could lie in my bed at night and speak aloud to various people: my long dead father, whose warm hand I could still feel holding mine; my fickle mother, whom I still loved; and my grandmother, who, despite my complaints, I knew loved me. I spoke to Corambe, and I said prayers to the Virgin Mary in English—not only to attempt to master the language but to enjoy the lyricism of the words.

Then, when I was fifteen years old, it happened that I suddenly became very religious.

One evening, I was looking out the window of my cell, and I saw one of the tenants of the convent walking slowly toward the chapel. She was old and bent over, and I watched with a kind of detached pity as she made her way to say her evening prayers with great difficulty. What drew people to such faith? How, lacking any evidence, could they so wholeheartedly accept the precepts handed to them as irrefutable truth? I decided to follow the old woman and take note of all that she did.

By the time I arrived in the chapel, the old woman was nowhere to be seen. There were the dim forms of a few nuns and tenants kneeling in prayer, but gradually they all left. The last to go was a nun who came to the altar and prostrated herself before she went out. All the nuns did this when they came to the altar; I had seen it many times and was always faintly amused by it. It seemed as though they had been shot down from where they had been flying about in the air.

But this time, I was profoundly moved by the gesture, by the wholehearted willingness to submit to such humiliation. And, in fact, I saw it now less as humiliation than as a gesture that one was privileged to feel compelled to make.

We students were not allowed to enter the chapel without permission at that hour, and in any case, the chapel would soon close.

But I stayed there anyway. I moved into one of the polished wooden pews at the front of the chapel and sat very still.

It had grown dark inside; but the silver sanctuary light burned with a soft glow. I could make out the candles on the altar and the gold of the tabernacle, a bit of the whitewashed walls around me. Outside, the stars hung in their places in the sky, and I had the sense that I was being watched by them.

I knelt, bowed my head, and closed my eyes. And then I suddenly felt an immense pressure in my chest and did not know whether it was joy or sadness. I kept quiet, breathing in and out, trying not to move in any other way, giving myself over to whatever mysterious force was upon me as the feeling grew and grew and I began to tremble.

In the chapel was a painting by Titian that was very hard to see at any time of day. It was hung in the darkness of the back of the nave and was itself a dark painting. But I had had occasions to sit near it and look at it and had learned what was depicted there. It was Jesus in the Garden of Gethsemane, on his knees, having fainted into the arms of an angel. The angel holds Christ's head against his breast, against his heart. The image came to me now, and I began to weep.

Then I thought of the patron saint of the convent, Saint Augustine, who for a long time struggled with whether or not to accept Christ. On a day when he was full of despair at the weakness of his will, he threw himself beneath a fig tree in a garden, where he said, "How long, O Lord, how long? Is it to be tomorrow and tomorrow? Why not now?" It was then that a voice came to him, saying, "*Tolle, lege!*" (Take it, read it), referring to the Bible, and he had his conversion experience. In his *Confessions,* he wrote about his long-lasting struggle to accept Christ:

> Too late have I loved you, O Beauty so ancient and so new, too late have I loved Thee. Thou wast with me and I was not

with you. Thou hast called, Thou hast cried out, and hast pierced my deafness. Thou hast enlightened, Thou has shone forth, and my blindness is dispelled.

I sat gripped by my emotions; then I, too, heard plainly spoken aloud the same words that had been said to Saint Augustine: *Tolle, lege!* I turned, expecting to see a nun who, having intuited the experience I was undergoing, wanted to urge me on. But there was no one: I was alone in the chapel.

Then a bright light surrounded me, and an incredible sweetness flooded my soul.

I could feel that my body was distinctly my own but temporary, and that my soul was eternal. I could feel that there was no need for fearing death. I could feel the place of abiding love and peace from which I had come, and to which I would return.

Tears ran down my face, and I felt an overwhelming sense of gratitude and joy.

I wanted to confess all of my sins and begin a new life. I fell to the floor, sobbing, and wept on and on until I heard a nun coming in the door to close the church for the night. I quickly ran out, went back to my cell, and, full of a feeling I could only call ecstasy, slept.

The next Saturday, just after lunch, I sought out a meeting in the sacristy with my confessor, Abbé de Prémord. I told him that whereas before I had offered up only an anemic recitation of "sins" that were copies of what the other girls said, now I wanted to make a sincere and thorough listing of my wrongdoings, and this I did, to the best of my ability.

When I had finished, the abbé spoke quietly: "I most sincerely grant you absolution, and you may receive communion tomorrow. Do not carry remorse for anything in the past; in the end, it is only prideful. Let peace dwell inside you, live your life in joy, and give thanks that God has come to you in this way."

I received communion the next day—I held the host in my mouth and felt light fill my soul—and in the days that followed, I burned with my newfound passion. For many months, all through that summer and beyond, I attended Mass with newfound appreciation and understanding. In addition to that, I prayed constantly: on my knees in my cell, sometimes in class, even walking about in the recreation yard, when I pretended to be watching the various games the other girls played. I ate and slept little. I became, to the extent that I could, a mystic, one for whom a scratchy filigree rosary worn around the neck served as a hair shirt. The nuns treated me with great affection, and I felt myself blessed.

One day, talking with Madame Alicia, a nun I particularly liked, I told her about my plans to take the veil.

She listened somber-faced to my words, nodding slowly. Then she said, "You are in no way ready to make such a commitment. I fear that your tendency to overdramatize has come into play, here, and you have—"

"It is not overdramatization!" I said. I could feel the heat rising up into my cheeks, blood throbbing at my temples. "I assure you that I am utterly sincere in my desires."

"I know you believe that with all your heart," Madame Alicia said. "But you must at least consider the fact that you might have taken a notion to an extreme.

"Let us examine what has happened. You believe you have suddenly stepped into a luminous maturity, that you have heard a calling; and now you cannot act quickly enough to put things into place. You feel you are reborn into a place you have sought all your life, that you have found your true home."

She put a hand on my shoulder and looked into my eyes. "Now I must tell you what I see from my side. I see a baby grasping at a sunbeam; I believe you are full more of appreciation and desire than understanding.

"For example, you speak of the value of suffering. Look at the lives of the poor that go on outside our walls. They are the ones who suffer nobly and endure. They shiver in the cold, they go hungry, they bury the small bodies of the children they could not keep alive. They dream of things they know full well they will never have. Of what value is suffering that is self-inflicted? Believe me, life makes for suffering, no matter who you are. But do you not think that God wants us to feel joy as well?

"This is the counsel I would offer you: Live more with this feeling. See how it grows or changes. Then decide what to do. You may find that your gifts are better used elsewhere. Trust in God. He will continue to show you the way. You must not rush ahead of His plan for you nor attempt to predict it; to do so is to dishonor Him. Patience is not only a virtue; it is a form of grace."

Despite those words, or perhaps because of them (for the devil in me never completely died), I continued to believe I would sign the contract that would make me a nun. I gave up my recreation time entirely in order to have time to help with various chores in the convent, in order to have more time to pray. People later told me that I became stupid during that time, and they were right. I did not care any longer for history or languages or the fine arts; I wanted only to move toward the single-mindedness I saw in people who devoted themselves to their faith.

Then my grandmother heard about my plans.

She made arrangements to abruptly withdraw me from the convent. She cited as a reason her failing health, and it was true that there was a noticeable weakness in her, a fading of the essential qualities that made her who she was. She told me she could not ever forgive herself if she left me unsupported after she was gone. I would, after all, inherit Nohant. Someone would need to help me run it. Therefore, it was time for me to start my search for a husband. Introductions must be made, parties and dinners attended; I would need a new wardrobe.

So it was that I gathered up my few things, said goodbye to my friends, and walked out of my beloved cell for the last time. I abandoned the work to which I had dedicated myself and rode blank-eyed with my grandmother to her Paris apartment to begin another life entirely. I was not yet sixteen.

February 1833

DRESSING ROOM OF MARIE DORVAL

PARIS

"So. My darling George. Tell me a story about yourself." Marie's speech was rapid, her eyes wide and shiny bright. In her head, I was sure, were still the sounds of the applause and cheering that had met her performance. Minutes ago, she had burst in the door, downed the glass of champagne I had waiting for her, and disappeared behind her screen to change into one of her lacy silk dressing gowns. She was now sitting at her vanity, taking off her stage makeup.

I sat almost shyly at the edge of her chaise longue, holding my top hat, turning it around and around by the brim. "A story," I said. "What kind of story?"

"Tell me how you came to wear men's clothes."

"Ah. A story about that! But surely you have seen other women wearing men's clothes."

"Yes. But not like you do. There is more in it for you. So tell me. And make it a long story. My throat aches; I want someone else to talk." She wiped under one eye with her finger, removing a bit of kohl she had missed. Bare of makeup, she was even more beautiful.

"All right, then." I stretched my legs out and rested my hat beside me. "Well, I first wore men's clothing when I was a girl, out of sheer practicality. Deschartres, my tutor, worried about my ability to ride my horse while wearing the fussy dresses my grandmother preferred for me. He suggested I wear pants so that I would have a safe seat in the saddle. Of course, I did not go out in society in such clothes; I was not like Honoré de Balzac, parading around Paris in his dressing gowns—many of them none too clean!—as a point of pride."

Marie laughed. "And always with his jeweled cane! Oh! He is a pig, that one, with his sticky rings on his fat fingers and his many chins!"

"Ah, but he is such a divine writer. And he will tell you that his unkempt appearance is *publicity*! Do you know that once after some friends and I dined with him—he had put on one of his usual dinners of boiled beef and melon and champagne cocktails with the irresistible gaiety of a child—he changed into a new *robe de chambre* about which he was most excited. He proposed that he accompany us to the Luxembourg gate wearing that robe. To light our way, he said he would carry his new candelabra. It was a preposterous idea; the streets were deserted at such a late hour, and I worried that on his return home alone, he would be assaulted by thieves or murderers, which I told him out quite plainly. He laughed and said that if he encountered anyone, either they would think that he was insane and be afraid of him or they would think he was royalty and entitled to such eccentricities, and they would bow down before him. And so we went, Balzac carrying an exquisitely engraved silver candelabra with candles blazing, speaking loudly of the four Arabian horses he did not yet have but would."

"The man has no taste whatsoever," Marie said. "I hear his rooms resemble those of an old marquis—silk walls bordered with lace, and knickknacks everywhere."

"True. But, Marie, you must understand that Balzac is one of those magpie artists, attracted to bright jewels and loud color. He will deprive himself of coffee and bread in favor of ornate silverware and china with which to lay his table. He says that he lacks the discipline for elegance, that he finds it too severe.

"In any case," I said, "I will not speak badly about him; he was for a long time a good friend. He is sincere and generous and a great deal of fun. I always used to accuse him of being an animal; he would accuse me of not being one. And so we went on, enjoying our differences, until I asked Jules to move out, and then Balzac chose to side with the one he deemed the wronged partner. I very much regret the loss of Balzac's company, and I bear him no ill will.

I tell you, Marie, there are those who deny his genius, but I believe he is destined for a great and influential career."

"Enough of Balzac. Let us talk about you. You and your men's clothing."

I lay back on the chaise. "As you wish. Well, to continue the story, when I became a theater critic here in Paris, I dressed in men's clothes because my disguise got me into the cheaper seats."

"But does it not feel strange to wear such things?"

"Why should it feel strange? Does a fox feel strange wearing his black stockings?"

Marie laughed.

"Anyway, when I moved here and began to dress as a man regularly, I became transformed more on the inside than on the outside. I experienced an elevation in society, simply because I was thought to be of the opposite sex. The favors I was given as a matter of course! I was lent a kind of gravitas, given respect and inclusion that I had heretofore not experienced. This brought with it a new way of seeing and feeling, and the feeling was . . ."

She leaned forward, her elbows on her knees, her hair now loose around her shoulders, shining and fragrant. "What was the feeling? Tell me."

"To be very frank, it was grounded in something that was sexual in nature. I tell you, Marie, I felt it between my legs, that power, that confidence, that sense of entitlement; and I liked it. Once I had it, I did not want to put it away for stiff crinolines and whalebone stays and gigot sleeves, all of which prevent free movement. Men wear clothes; women are captured by them. I have lost altogether my desire for ruffles and bows, for silk flowers anchored in my hair."

"But these things add such beauty!"

"Perhaps. But I trade that for something that matters far more to me. A feeling that my voice is heard."

"But . . . all this conferred by clothing?"

"Seemingly so. Or maybe such clothing serves as a catalyst to unleash things that have always been in me, among them a desire for independence and for fairness. Whatever the case may be, after the success of *Indiana,* I cast off the secondhand clothes I'd scavenged in haste and began to buy elegant redingotes, waistcoats, cashmere trousers. I bought pantaloons and silk cravats, too, mostly from Buisson."

"Ah, the wonderful tailor on Rue de Richelieu."

"The same."

She nodded slowly, and her eyes moved over my face. "How interesting you are. How bold. And with what delight do I hear your stories!"

"Shall I tell you one more?"

She clapped her hands. "You must! And then we shall order up more champagne, and you must tell me others. You must tell me stories all night!"

"If that is what you want, then that is what you will have."

"You are the most gentlemanly gentleman, and I adore you."

She said it too easily for it to hold the meaning I wanted, but I flushed with pleasure nonetheless.

She got up and came over to the chaise, straightened the shoulders of her ruffled white dressing gown, gathered the train of it about her. "Let us lie down together; I shall rest beside you and listen like a contented child to your every word. What pleasure to have someone transport *me,* for a change."

I lay on my side, and she lay on her back close beside me. The scent of her perfume rose up; I could feel the heat of her flesh. She closed her eyes and sighed. "I am ready; you may begin now."

I began to speak, falling very nearly into the same kind of trance in talking to her that I fell under when I wrote. This had never before happened. I often said that the reason I wrote things was because I couldn't say them. But with Marie, I was able to speak directly from my imagination.

I told her, "One day when I was thirteen years old and dressed in my riding clothes of trousers and shirt and boots, I went walking deep into the forest near Nohant. Suddenly, I came face-to-face with a wolf."

Marie gasped, and her eyes flew open. "A live wolf? With his long red tongue and his stealthy gait? And his sharp teeth?" Her voice broke; soon it would be gone altogether.

I held my finger to her lips. "Listen. Rest your voice. Close your eyes. Obviously, the story ends well enough."

She closed her eyes and moved nearly imperceptibly closer to me.

"Yes, the woods were full of wolves, and I had been warned against them, but I had also convinced myself that I would never have trouble with anything in the natural world—a naïve position that could not be supported by anyone with half a brain, only I was as stubborn then as I am now. At any rate, I was standing near a pond in deep contemplation when the wolf came suddenly out of the underbrush. He held up abruptly at the sight of me. I saw the hair along his back rise slightly; I saw his breath quicken, as did my own, naturally. He was beautiful, colored silver and brown and black, and very thin."

"And did he growl most fiercely?" Marie whispered.

"He did not, actually."

"How did he smell?"

"How did he *smell*?"

"Yes."

"He smelled . . . of wild onion and earth and cold. His eyes were a soulful and limpid brown, possessed of a keen intelligence. I stood unmoving, and then a conversation ensued. I shall report it to you here as it happened, as I *felt* it, so help me God. Perhaps I shall act it out in a little play for you—would you like that?"

"Of course!"

I made my voice gruff to be the wolf.

—Ah. A human. Good evening.

And then I made my voice unnaturally high to be my girl self.

—Mon Dieu, a wolf! Help, help!

—A shameful response to my affable greeting.

—I fear you will harm me; I fear you will eat me!

—That remains to be seen. Permit me to sniff your ankle.

He approached, slowly, and I stood stone still. He sniffed, then drew back in surprise.

—I see you are a female human. Yet you wear the garb of the male.

—Today I do.

—What ever for?

—It allows me certain rights that only males enjoy.

—But the female is the superior sex.

—Not in the world of humans.

—A pity. But humans are in any case perplexing and we in the animal world frustrate ourselves trying to make any sense of you at all. You are good for eating, though.

—So this is my fate, to die by mauling at the edge of the pond.

—Perhaps not. I have only just finished eating a hapless rabbit. Moreover, I like you, for I sense in you a high regard for the natural world, even including wolves.

—Including wolves most sincerely! For I much admire your beauty, cunning, and strength.

—Now she flatters in order to survive.

—I merely speak the truth.

—I think I shall let you live. But do let me pass by for a drink of water. I must insist on a wide berth, for as kindly as we may regard each other at the moment, any wild animal knows to regard your species with great mistrust.

I let him pass, he drank deeply—though with one eye on me—then trotted into the forest and disappeared.

Silence.

"Marie?" I said.

Her eyes opened, and she smiled at me.

"I have bored you," I said. I feared it was so.

"You have done anything but." She went over to the window

and opened it. She leaned out and, in her broken voice, howled. When she turned back, her eyes were full of excitement, and she said, "We are both of us wild like the wolf! How glad I am that we found each other!"

I stood. "Come with me to Nohant!"

"Now?"

"Right now. Your run has ended; you have a little time, and I shall take some. Come with me. You can rest, and you can see the very spot where I encountered the wolf."

She laughed.

"Will you come?"

"Ah, George."

No, then. Not yet.

March 1820

RUE NEUVE-DES-MATHURINS

PARIS

AFTER MY GRANDMOTHER WITHDREW ME FROM THE CONVENT, she set about trying to find me a husband. It was a dreary process; I was paraded before boors, then made to endure the equally boring process of evaluation.

"Did you not find him handsome?" one of my grandmother's dowager countess friends breathlessly asked me, of a man I had met the night before.

"To tell the truth, I found him quite ugly."

The old woman's hand flew to her breast, her fingers spread out like a fan. "No! It is not true! You cannot have felt that way! He is very handsome, and besides that, he is kind and charming. It is not every day one finds such a prize."

"If only it were you in need of a companion," I said, and the woman's face drew into itself, and she returned to her tea and her cakes.

Eventually, I overhead my grandmother telling someone, "There is no more we can do now. She is, after all, still so young. I shall take her back to Nohant and give her some time. She needs six months, a year."

Immediately, I felt better, and I met with my mother the next day to talk to her about accompanying us there. "I need your guidance and support in finding a husband," I told her.

"I need not go with you to Nohant for that," she said. "It is my right to approve of anyone you are to marry. And whoever it is will need to pass my test, not your grandmother's. Let me know when you find someone. And then we shall see."

May 1820

NOHANT

When my grandmother and I returned to Nohant, her condition began to deteriorate. Eventually, she was very weak and oftentimes confused, and I began spending many hours as nursemaid to her.

One night when it was quite late, she asked me to open the shutters to let in the sunshine. "It is nighttime, Grandmama," I said.

"It is not. Open the shutters."

"It is nighttime," I said again, and at this she became nearly hysterical. "Why do you lie to me? I want to see the daylight! Open the shutters at once!"

I stood and said impatiently, "I tell you again it is the middle of the night! I shall prove it to you!" I marched over to the window, flung open the shutters, and stood back triumphantly. For a moment, she lay still, and then she began weeping. She said, "Ah, I am going blind. My God, my God, now I have lost my vision!"

"It is nighttime! Look at the stars!" I said, practically shouting, and then Deschartres came into the room. He had begun sleeping at the house so that he could be on hand if needed. Now he rushed to my grandmother's side, took her hand, and bent to speak to her in low, soothing tones. He listened intently while she responded to him, words I could not make out as they were so mixed with her sobs, and slurred besides. But he understood her.

"Your grandmother is upset that you have told her it is night, when it is day."

When I opened my mouth to argue, he said firmly, "Not a word. Bring me candles."

I gathered together a great number of candles, and he lit them all behind her. The dimness in the room transformed itself into a semblance of daylight.

"Better?" he asked my grandmother.

"Yes, of course. Thank you."

Deschartres looked at me. I nodded, then took my place back at my grandmother's bedside.

THAT YEAR AT NOHANT, I spent a great deal of time in my room reading whatever I liked. I chose the poets, the moralists, and the philosophers: La Bruyère, Pope, Milton, Dante, Virgil, and Shakespeare. By opening my mind to these many influences, I found myself moving away from some of the convictions I had held at the convent.

As my mind reawakened to the challenges put before me by this reading, Deschartres and I began to have long, philosophical conversations, as well as games of logic that I enjoyed very much. I began to respect him in ways I had not before. As he did me.

Almost as soon as I'd returned to Nohant, Deschartres acted as though I'd already inherited it. He put me in charge of all matters relating to running the house. He kept doing his work on our land and in our gardens, and I was extremely grateful, for despite his ongoing efforts, I had never learned the first thing about husbandry, nor did I want to.

Aware of a new kind of restlessness, though, I added a new routine. Early every morning, dressed in trousers and a white, loose-fitting man's shirt, I mounted my mare and rode at breakneck speed into the Berry countryside, alone and free. I loved the way the limitless sky opened something in me; I loved the rhythmic sounds of Colette's hoofs hitting the earth, the short huffs of her breathing. We ran through open fields, and the ground birds rose up before us with a great rustle of flapping wings and high cries.

People in the village began to talk about me in unflattering ways: I rode without a chaperone in men's clothes; I behaved in unladylike ways, visiting childhood friends and shaking hands boldly with men—no shying away from the press of flesh on flesh. Eventually the rumors fed on themselves and grew into outrageous lies: I had ridden right into the church and up to the altar before turning around and galloping out; I never slept; I was a ghoul who delighted in making medical rounds with Deschartres, where I watched gleefully as he bled people. I was up to no good with a young man Deschartres had employed to help me with my scientific studies. In this last, I must confess that the wagging tongues told the truth.

Not long after I had come back to Nohant, I'd become reacquainted with a friend named Stéphane Ajasson de Grandsagne, who lived nearby. He was very handsome and came from a very good family—not wealthy, because of the great number of children in the family, whose care depleted resources, but aristocratic and very well regarded.

Stéphane was now studying to become a doctor, and I was referred to him to learn something about anatomy and physiology. This was because I wanted to be more active in assisting Deschartres as the town's de facto surgeon.

So it was that Stéphane began coming regularly to my room to instruct me in the wonders of the human body. Eventually, we moved on to an appreciation of our own structure and function.

Once, I pulled Stéphane onto my bed with me, then on top of me.

"No, Aurore," he said. "If we were married . . ." But he knew as well as I that we would never be a sanctioned match. Neither my grandmother nor my mother would ever accept a man as poor as he; and his father would never accept me, because he knew that my mother had been a courtesan.

Then Julie, my grandmother's maid, told my grandmother that I was behaving inappropriately, and the lessons with Stéphane stopped. I could not bear Julie any malice. She had only told the truth.

February 1833

PARIS

When I told Marie Dorval about Balzac cutting me out of his life, I did not add that I was as dumbfounded as I was hurt. He had befriended Jules and me at the same time, and at first, Jules had not embraced him. He'd shown reservations about the oddities of Balzac's personality, saying, "He is awfully impulsive!" And I had responded, "One of the reasons I adore him!"

I had loved to listen to Balzac talk with almost sputtering enthusiasm about all the novels he meant to write. I had found him brilliant and very amusing. He had seemed equally enamored of me.

But when Jules and I parted, Balzac slandered me, telling everyone that I was a hypocrite, saying I had lived happily enough in my little love nest with Solange present but that when I broke with Jules, I said it was for the sake of my child. The real reason I left, he said, was because of my love for my editor, Henri Latouche. Of all things! In fact, I had suddenly lost Latouche's friendship, as well. That man was telling everyone that all of my success had gone to my head. Balzac had warned me that Latouche might drop me if I became what Latouche thought of as too successful, even as had happened with Balzac—and this after Latouche had been Balzac's biggest champion.

The final insult is that both of them accused *me* of spreading lies about *them*.

I took to staying in more and more. For one thing, I did not want to hear whispers as I passed by. But another reason was that I was offered far fewer invitations. I had to develop a new set of friends, and it was slow going.

One who insinuated himself in my life at this time, and whose attentions I gratefully received, was a critic, a twenty-nine-year-old man named Charles-Augustin Sainte-Beuve. He was one of those judges who lamented the fact that he was unable to produce a novel and so called himself without talent, not recognizing that it takes a special talent indeed to be a good critic.

Sainte-Beuve was an appreciator of female sensibilities, and he soon became a close friend. I spoke to him about matters of the heart as much as, if not more than, literature and publishing. Sometimes when he came to dine with me, he brought along Hortense Allart, who was the mistress of René Chateaubriand; and both the critic and I ferreted out details about the old master from one who suffered no compunction about revealing all. Hortense once brought along with her, as if he were an offering to me, Charles Didier, an intelligent and virile man who had been her lover in Florence. I found him attractive, but I saw that he was not at all interested in me. He suggested to Sainte-Beuve, who soon afterward shared it with me, that I would probably be a disappointment in bed, since my demeanor suggested that I was incapable of passion.

Ironically, I was writing about a kind of sexual paralysis in the novel I was working on, called *Lélia.*

Sainte-Beuve had listened to a number of pages from it, and at hearing one passage had sat in stunned silence. It was this I read him:

> Desire, in my case, was an ardor of the spirit which paralyzed the power of the senses even before they had been awakened, a savage ecstasy which took possession of my brain, and became exclusively concentrated there. My blood remained frozen, impotent, and poor, while my will took flight. I had as yet drawn no satisfaction. I fought against these lying urgencies of my suffering, knowing full well that it was not in his power to calm them.

When I finished reading that passage to Sainte-Beuve and he finally opened his mouth to speak, I was afraid he would ask if it was myself I was speaking of. And so I cut him off, saying, "Enough of reading for tonight. Let us turn our conversation to something gay. Have you any gossip for me?"

He raised an eyebrow. Then: "Well, since you ask . . ." He sat back in his chair, as satisfied as a fat man being served supper, and began.

The next day, though, he sent a note telling me how powerful he had found my reading, and how listening to it had increased his admiration as well as his feelings of friendship for me. He suggested that when *Lélia* was published, the general public would balk at it, but that "it will raise you high in the estimation of those who see in fiction only a more vivid form of the eternal verities of the human mind. Yours, Madame, is a rare and powerful temperament." I read his note many times over and kept it in my desk drawer, where it often served to lift me out of a failure of confidence. But as much as I admired, enjoyed, and depended upon Sainte-Beuve, my heart still ached for the loss of my old Berry gang. One night I saw several of them out at Vendanges de Bourgogne, a restaurant where our friend Gustave Papet (whom we had called the "rich mi'lord") used to treat three or four of us at a time. They were talking and laughing, enjoying themselves immensely over platters of mussels. They did not see me pass by, and I was grateful. Grateful and full of a burning shame.

I buried myself in continuing to work on *Lélia,* whose heroine went from man to man, because none of them could give her pleasure.

MARIE HAD RUSHED TO meet me at the Café de Foy; her face was flushed, her bosom heaving as she sat across from me. I did not speak at first, taken up, as I was, in admiration of her hectic beauty. But then, seeing that something was upsetting her, I asked what it was.

She began speaking rapidly: "I tell you, I will never understand the mystery of love. A woman comes to a man because she wants only him; then she cannot bear the sound of air moving in and out of his nostrils. She cannot bear the sight of his shadow upon the pavement!"

The waiter approached us, and Marie ordered coffee, falling into her coquettish ways for the benefit of the man, who obviously knew who she was. Instead of the nearly sullen indifference he had shown me, he now adopted the fluttery mannerisms of a nervous old woman taking pills with her tea.

When he finally left to fill her order, I said, "You know, Marie, when Balzac was not exhausting himself speaking about his writing or his decorating, he used to go on about how he was an expert in matters of love. And he always said it is easier to be a lover than a husband, because it is harder to be witty every day than to say pretty things from time to time."

"My distaste is *for* my lover!" she said, and we both began to laugh loudly, causing many heads to turn in our direction. Marie lifted her chin higher, enjoying the attention.

When her coffee arrived, she stirred sugar into it, staring into my eyes in the wistful way of a little girl. "Tell me, George. Do you think love is only an illusion?"

I hesitated, then said, "I think it is our highest calling. And I think you have perhaps simply not found the right person to whom to give your heart." My own heart beat like a metronome, as though repeating over and over what I could not say: *Choose me, choose me, choose me.*

"I don't mean only romantic love," she said. "I mean any kind of love. Even love for our children."

She lowered her voice to a near whisper. "I'm sure you know that rumors are flying around about my daughter, Gabrielle, and me; people are saying that all the while she was growing up, I beat her."

I nodded. I had heard these rumors, spread by Gabrielle herself, of how abused she had been by her mother, and how Marie was now refusing to give a sou to help Gabrielle's fiancé, who was very ill. I had heard the rumors, but I knew the truth.

Very soon after meeting Marie, I'd had occasion to spend time alone with her daughter. We'd run into each other on the street in front of a café, and I'd invited Gabrielle to have a coffee with me. I found her to be a very spoiled sixteen-year-old who was extremely jealous of her mother. It is said that a daughter can forgive her mother anything but beauty, and such seemed to be the case. Never mind that Gabrielle herself was beautiful; she preferred to ignore her own gifts in favor of bitterness and blame against the one who wanted only what was best for her.

"My mother would not let me enter the theater, because she was afraid I would outshine her," Gabrielle told me that day. "And now she won't give permission for me to marry Antoine Fontaney, because she wants him for herself."

If Marie did not want her daughter in theater, I thought, it was to spare her the ugly side of being an actress. And I knew that Marie did not want her daughter to marry Fontaney—who used the pen name "Lord Feeling" for the few articles he had published in the *Revue des Deux Mondes*—because he was actively consumptive. He was very thin, mournful of countenance, and he coughed constantly. Apparently, this was seen by Gabrielle as romantic. He had about him a certain kindness, but his intellect was not great. In addition, the man sought to be an actor when he had no talent whatsoever. Marie could not imagine having to help him get roles just because he was a member of the family, and she was sure that he would ask her to do so—in fact, he had already begun to do so.

So the marriage prospect that Gabrielle brought to her mother was a man incapable of making money to support himself, never mind a family. He owned nothing, and he would be yet another mouth that Marie would have to feed. But I had to tread carefully with Gabrielle, so in response to her telling me that her mother wanted Fontaney for herself, I only said, "Do you really think so?"

"Of course. It is apparent to him and to me, both. You have only just met my mother; you haven't seen how selfish she is, how she thinks only of herself. Why, when I was a very little girl, I was backstage when a piece of scenery fell and broke my leg. My mother did not stop the play. No, she cannot be without the adulation of her fans, and so she continued performing—not only that night, but for the entire run—and she came to see me only between scenes!"

"I wonder if it was because she had to go on working in order to make the money to pay for your care," I said, knowing that this was true. At the time I met her, Marie Dorval was enjoying a great deal of fame, but she was never wealthy. Always, she struggled to pay the bills; and more than once she had creditors threatening to take her furniture.

"She is not what you think," Gabrielle said. "You will find out soon enough what an indifferent and careless personality she is."

I found out precisely the opposite.

Marie flung her cloak back from her shoulders. Beneath it, she was wearing a burgundy silk dress with ruching down the center, and its color was so deep it appeared black at the folds. It made the whiteness of her skin glow like alabaster, like the moon. Her bonnet, gay as always, was burgundy silk, and the crown was decorated with a profusion of flowers. She wore garnet-and-pearl earrings, with a matching necklace. I wondered which man had presented her with these; she had told me she had yet to buy herself jewels.

"I beat her, my daughter says! By God, maybe I should have beaten her! I tell you, Gabrielle wounds me more than any man ever has. What am I meant to feel for her when she treats me this way? Must I love her no matter the cost? I want only to stop her from ruining her life, and she breaks my heart by circulating these vile rumors. And then she accuses *me* of being vicious!"

She leaned her head in closer, and lowered her voice. "Look how people are staring at me here. Look at the way my fans throw flowers at my feet with every performance I give. You and I met because of the brilliant letter you sent, praising not only my talent but the soul you saw inside my person. I have the admiration of thousands, and cannot garner so much as a civil word from my own flesh and blood."

"Young women can be like that sometimes," I said, thinking of the way my own daughter could wound me.

"Gabrielle went to Spain to get married," Marie said.

I put down my cup and looked over at her, surprised.

"Yes, she went and she tried to get married, but she could not do it there, either, without my permission. And so I gave it." She shrugged, but she was tearful, and I saw for the first time the darkness beneath her eyes.

"You must endeavor to stop thinking about it, Marie. There is nothing you can do. You must get some rest."

"Rest! I never rest. I cannot rest. My art is a great stimulant that only makes me need more stimulation. I am perpetually half satisfied. And I have feelings of pain, I have frightful memories that never let up, and I struggle with great difficulty to overcome them. How can rest figure in here?

"Anyway, to tell the truth, if I rest, I get bored. Or, more precisely, I experience boredom without cause. If I knew the cause, I could find the cure.

"I tell myself that what I call boredom is lack of a certain kind of passion. Yet I fear finding that passion too much to look for it; I fear it would overwhelm me. Ah, George, I wish I were like you!"

"I would never wish that on you," I said, laughing. "But, Marie, we are more alike than you know. I too have been 'bored' like you, and not just lately but all my life. Since I was born! And—"

"Only you control it! You approach it as a pragmatist, saying, 'Well, if that's the way it is, then that's the way it is.' And you write to find truth and justice and happiness! You are as noble as Joan of Arc!

"But enough of sadness. Enough, I will speak of it no more! Let us be happy. Tell me, George, are you wearing something new yet again? Show me!"

I rose and then stood back a bit to show her my double-breasted, green-striped tailcoat and yellow silk brocade waistcoat, with its lively pattern of leaves and red berries. Also new were my goffered shirt, with its low cravat, and my stirrup pants, which had leather straps. I had been hoping she would notice; I had bought these clothes for her as much as for myself.

She rested her chin in her hands and gazed up at me, and I stood like a dandy on display for a moment longer.

When I sat down, she said, "Tell me, George. Do you wish you'd been born a man?"

I thought for a moment, then said, "In my youth, I wished that. I very much admired my father and I wanted to be just like him. And I was always very interested in the games and adventures of boys, most of which took place in the out-of-doors, where I always wanted to be. But now I find I don't wish to be either man or woman. I wish to be myself. Why should men serve as judge and jury, deciding for us what can and cannot be done, what is our due? Why should they decide in advance of our deciding for ourselves what is best for us; why should they decide what *is* us?"

"But then you do wish to be a man!"

"Perhaps I wish to be a woman with a man's privileges."

"I must ask you something more intriguing. Do you love women as a man does?"

The noise of the café fell away; all the world fell away. I answered carefully and as truly as I knew how, looking directly into her eyes. "When I love, Marie, it is because of a person's heart and mind and soul, none of which has a sex. It is not the body that attracts me; it is the spirit that dwells within. Once I love the spirit, I come to love the body, even as, if I come upon my beloved's gloves, I love them. Is it the gloves I love? Of course not. It is that they belong to the person who has captured my heart."

She was quiet for a moment, staring into my eyes. Then she said, "Let us walk out. We shall walk arm in arm, and you must tell me everything you see and feel. We shall walk forever, to the end of the earth, and then we shall walk back and have supper in my dressing room. I shall have brought to us every good thing we desire, escargots to pastries, and many bottles of champagne, and we shall charge it all to Vigny as punishment for him having become so dull. And when we are full, we shall eat more, until we are made breathless. And then we shall go out and eat the night. What a tonic you are for me, George; you bring my blood to life; you excite me to the soles of my feet; I thank God for the day I met you!"

"I thank God for that day as well." I lifted a finger to signal the waiter, who bounded forth with the enthusiasm of a puppy, that he might stand once more at the side of Marie Dorval.

After a few weeks, I learned that Marie's son-in-law, Fontaney, had died, followed soon afterward by his wife, Marie's Gabrielle, who had caught consumption from him.

September 1821

NOHANT

THE FALL I WAS SEVENTEEN, MY GRANDMOTHER SEEMED FOR A short time to come back to her old self. I felt sure that many people were privately offering thanks that their prayers had wrought a miracle. Friends came to call, and my grandmother conducted herself with her former charm and intelligence. She ate and slept better. She was no longer confused. But in fact she was still dying, and she knew it. She spoke to me about my guardianship, saying that she wanted to add a clause to her will that would put me in the care of my cousin René de Villeneuve and his wife. "You love your mother very much, I know," she said. "But you do not see her for what she is. I would like you to live with your father's family, but I shan't force you. I would like your approval."

By December, my grandmother no longer got out of bed and rarely spoke. One day after I had left her bedside, Deschartres answered my unasked question, saying, "It could go on for a long time." But on Christmas night, at the age of seventy-five, she died peacefully. Her maid, Julie, tears rolling down her face, attended to my grandmother's last toilette, washing her and then putting on her lace bonnet and her rings. I offered my prayer book and crucifix from the convent for her to be buried with. When she was ready, she looked so calm and beautiful, I could not be sad. I saw that she had passed over in great peace, and it was only given to me to wonder where she had gone. I sat by her bed for a long time, late into the night, reviewing my life with her, hoping that she had felt my love for her despite our differences of opinion.

March 1833

PARIS

THE SPRING I WAS TWENTY-EIGHT WAS A TIME OF GREAT UNHAPPINESS and frustration in my life. It was work on my novel *Lélia* that sustained me, as did the friendship of Marie Dorval. She had become my truest confidante. One evening, I was reading to her from my pages, and she stopped me after this line: "How shall I free myself from this marble envelope which grips me round the knees, and holds me as totally imprisoned as a corpse by the tomb?" When Marie heard that, she put her hand on my arm to stop me from going on. I looked up to see tears in her eyes. "Ah, George. A woman who denies love. It is you whom you write about. It is you, a powerful woman powerless to get what you most need. You seem to have no idea how to achieve it. And yet you have one of your own characters say of Lélia that she is not a complete human being. You have him say that where love is absent, there can be no woman. This is you speaking of yourself!"

"It is a story," I said.

"It is you," she insisted.

I changed the subject. It was painful for me to address what I perceived as a fatal flaw in myself: I did not know how to account for the way my passion sputtered and stalled, for the way what I had felt for Jules had deteriorated into something resembling the feelings of a mother for a child.

Perhaps a week later, dizzy from many hours of writing, I felt I needed a night out. I sent a note to Marie, asking to see her current play. When she received my message, she responded immediately by sending me a ticket to that evening's performance, and she included with it a note of her own: "I shall be gratified to have in the audience one who loves me as you do! Come to see me afterward. I die until then."

After the performance, I sat in her dressing room, waiting for her. She burst in the door practically vibrating, as usual.

"George! How happy I am to see you!" She kissed me, a brief touch to my lips, and then began changing out of her clothes. She no longer hid herself behind the screen, as she had the first time I'd visited her here.

Once wrapped in her dressing gown, she lay on the chaise and crossed her delicate ankles one over the other, folding her arms behind her head. She was a perfect subject for a painter, and I wished then that I were one. I wished I could command her to hold the pose, so that I could examine at length every part of her.

"Now, then," she said. "What have you heard from Mérimée? You must tell me everything; don't leave a single detail out!"

"How do you know about Mérimée?"

She didn't bother dignifying such a stupid question with an answer. No doubt all of Paris knew.

Prosper Mérimée, an esteemed playwright and novelist, was a friend of Sainte-Beuve's, and it was at his urging that I had finally agreed to let Mérimée come to visit me. I had found excuses to put him off many times, pleading illness or my husband unexpectedly making an appearance. Finally he'd sent me an exasperated note that said:

> *I should be much obliged if you would tell me if you are now recovered, and whether your husband sometimes goes out alone; in short, whether there is any chance of my seeing you without making a nuisance of myself.*

And so I saw him. He came to the Opéra with me and Solange, and when she fell asleep there, he carried her home. I found his intellect powerful, and I luxuriated in his strong and calm nature. I saw that he was a cynic with a sometimes careless manner, and that he felt contempt for many of the things I loved—when I described for him the plot of *Lélia,* he laughed! But beneath that exterior, I was sure, was a heart capable of great tenderness. We saw each other again, and that night, as we walked arm in arm along the Seine, I told him, "I want you to know that I have come to care for you, and I offer my love in friendship. I hope you feel the same."

He stopped walking and put his hands on my shoulders, turning me to face him. "Hear me, George. There is only one way for a man to love a woman, and that is in bed. Any talk of anything else—a meeting of the minds, a soulful bonding—is rubbish. Poetic rubbish, perhaps, but rubbish nonetheless. Don't be such a child. Let the right man come to you and you will see you are no Lélia. The right man will inflame your senses and your heart and thrill your body."

"And I suppose that you are that 'right man.'"

"Shall we find out?"

Now it was my turn to laugh.

I told all this to Marie, and she sat up at the edge of the chaise in excitement. "But you must receive him!"

I laughed.

"George, you must! This may very well be exactly what you need. It is all but a gift from God, a sign of compassionate intervention. Don't you see? You have spent all your time with pale poets or with mindless brutes. Here is a man who can offer you an intellect and a body that knows how to please a woman. He has quite a reputation for . . . shall we say . . . technical excellence."

"So I have heard."

"Well, what harm can it do to audition him? Truly, what harm, George? He obviously is very fond of you. He challenges you intellectually. He makes you laugh. He appreciates your great mind. Let him show you what else is up his sleeve."

"I doubt it is up his sleeve," I said. "Unless he is particularly well endowed."

She smiled. "Champagne?"

"Yes."

"First promise me you will receive him."

I sighed. "I promise."

"When?"

"As soon as possible."

"And then you must immediately report to me all that transpires."

I nodded, and she handed me my glass of champagne. I drank it down. Perhaps I could prove to myself that I was not Lélia after all.

I INVITED MÉRIMÉE TO DINE with me. When he arrived, he found me with my black hair wound into jeweled Spanish netting. I was dressed in a yellow silk wrapper and red slippers, and I was smoking a pipe. I wanted not to look or be anything like his other conquests.

We ate a light supper, and then, putting down my wineglass, I said, "Shall we?"

He followed me to the bedroom, and I could feel my heart racing. He sat in the armchair in the corner while the maid and I made ready the bed. My mouth was dry and growing drier, and there was an odd heaviness to my limbs.

Bed prepared, maid dismissed, I looked over at Mérimée, sitting calmly, staring directly at me. I felt nothing but unease. In my mind, I listed his various attributes: He was a handsome man. He could speak Greek, Spanish, Russian, and English. His *Carmen* was the basis for Bizet's opera. His shoes were made of finest leather. . . .

Moments passed that felt like days. I could not think of how I should proceed. I knew nothing more about being the coquette than I ever had. And so I tried to assume the brazenness of the woman I most admired: Marie Dorval. Leaving the lamp blazing, I moved to stand directly before Mérimée and removed my clothes. I was amused to see that this seemed to alarm him. His eyes widened, and his usual sardonic smile disappeared.

Naked before him, I crossed my arms. "Well?"

He rose without speaking, moved to the side of the bed, and began to take off his clothes. He kept his face turned from me, but

I could see that he was blushing. He quickly got under the covers and then nodded at me. I moved slowly, deliberately across the room to climb into bed beside him.

After I lay down, he kissed me, and I kept still, waiting for him to do more. He kissed me again and then, exasperated, pulled my arms up to encircle his neck. I felt as though some dance instructor had positioned our limbs. In a manner reminiscent of times I had spent in bed with Casimir, I made a mighty effort to hold back laughter.

He moved to my breasts, and while he amused himself there, I stared up at the ceiling, waiting for his legendary skill to transport me.

No such thing happened. I felt his flaccid member against my thigh. Finally, he lifted himself to stare down at me and said, "Is it possible that you could *help*?"

I had no idea what he meant. Finally he got out of bed, dressed quickly, and, without a word, started toward the bedroom door.

"But . . . where are you going?"

I began to weep, embarrassing myself. I had been false to myself, I had attempted to be someone I was not; and this was the result.

He shook his head. "This has been a fiasco. You behave like a young girl when you have none of her charms; and you put on the arrogance of a marquise without her elegance." With that, he marched out of the room and then out of the apartment, slamming the door behind him.

I did not sleep that night, and in the morning I sent over a note asking for another chance; I asked him to come and see me at nine o'clock. He did not come.

"MY DEAR, MY DEAR, what a catastrophe, I am so sorry for you!" Marie said.

It was two days later; she had come to my apartment and I had told her the whole story. I was weeping, nearly hysterical. "I had such hope. I thought he might come to love me, and if he came to love me, I would be saved from this ennui, from this pain. Ah, Marie, I must tell you, I no longer relish the freedom I demanded. It is only another kind of jail. I am full of regret. I have made decisions that have changed so many lives for the worse, and I cannot take them back. I cannot do anything but suffer. Last night, I longed to throw myself in the Seine and be done with it. It was only the thought of Maurice and Solange that stopped me."

"This will pass," Marie said. "All things do."

I suppose it might have passed, except that Marie told her lover, Vigny, about what had happened. Then, to make matters even worse, she told her neighbor Alexandre Dumas, gossip extraordinaire, who, with great glee, exaggerated what had happened, saying that I had made fun of Mérimée for being unable to "raise the flag" but that in any case there wasn't much of a flag to unfurl. I thought that for a man like Mérimée to catch wind of this would seal my fate in terms of ever having another opportunity to be his lover. We could not even be friends any longer.

Marie came to my door in tears, begging to be forgiven, saying she never expected such repercussions—though she should have, knowing Dumas. She said that she meant, in relaying the story to both Dumas and Vigny, to obtain for me some measure of sympathy, to cast Mérimée in an unfavorable light. But of course no such thing had happened. I was seen as the groveling fool, begging someone who had rejected me to come back. Mérimée was seen as the man who had been wrongly slandered.

Now Marie fell to her knees, saying, "Forgive me, please forgive me," and I knelt beside her and embraced her. With great weariness and an abiding affection that had not changed, I told her I did forgive her.

After she left, I sat still before the fire, recalling an incident from my childhood.

Madame de Pardaillan was a friend of my grandmother's, and when I was a very young girl, she was in the habit of calling me "poor little one." I always wondered why. One day when I was alone with her, I worked up the courage to ask her. She drew me close and, her voice quivering with great feeling, said, "Always be kind and comport yourself well, my child, for that will be your only happiness in life."

"You mean that I will otherwise be unhappy?"

"Yes," she said, "everyone has times of sorrow, but you will have more than most. And also you will have much to forgive."

"But why?"

"Because it will happen that you will have to forgive the only source of happiness you will know."

I could not have articulated the exact meaning of her words, yet I felt the truth of them. I recalled her arm about my waist, the way she laid her cheek on top of my head after she made her sad pronouncement, and how, in spite of the great number of years separating us, I had felt a bond with her.

Souls are ageless and care nothing for external circumstances. There are times in life when one soul recognizes something in another, and they touch. This is something beyond the boundaries of normal human discourse, something nearly beyond our understanding, but it is a true phenomenon. That is what happened to me that day; I saw that Madame de Pardaillan had endured terrible heartbreak; and she saw that heartbreak would be my fate as well. Our souls touched, and I knew.

Later on the day of Marie's visit, I received a note from a friend who no doubt thought herself helpful in telling me about Marie Dorval's betrayal. I responded to her in this way:

> *You say she has betrayed me. I am well aware of that, but which of you, my dear friends, have not done as much? She has betrayed me once only, but you do it every day. She passed on something I told her, but every one of my friends has put into my mouth words I never uttered. Leave me the freedom to love her still. I know her, and what she is worth.*

A few days later, when I tried to contact Marie, I learned that she had gone on tour without telling me. I had no idea where she was. In desperation, I sent a friend to get her address from Vigny. I wrote to her, asking why she had not told me where she was going. I would have gone with her, to be her dresser. I told her I had wept after hearing she had gone. I told her my heart belonged to her:

> *Nowhere can I find a nature so frank, true, strong, supple, good, generous, great, odd, excellent, and, in a word, so complete as yours. I want to love you always, to cry with you, to laugh with you. If you are sad, I will be sad, too. If you are gay, then long live gaiety! Send me a line and I will come to you at once. Should occasions arise when I might be in the way, you can pack me off to work in another room. No matter where I am, I can always find something to occupy my mind. I have been told more than once to beware of you, and no doubt you have been similarly warned against me. Let the prattlers prattle, you and I are the only persons concerned.*
>
> *Answer soon. You need send only the single word "come" and I shall set off at once.*

She did not answer soon, or at all.

January 1822

NOHANT

BEFORE MY GRANDMOTHER DIED, WHEN I WAS SEVENTEEN, MY cousin René de Villeneuve had come to spend a fortnight with me. It was in an effort for us to get to know each other better, as he had learned of my grandmother's desire for him to be my guardian. I had always liked him, but being alone with him in this way made us like each other even more. He found me interesting where others found me odd: we shot pistols together and stayed up until the early hours of morning, as had become my preference. We galloped through the countryside on horseback, and he did not chastise but instead applauded me for jumping over ditches. We took long walks and discussed politics and philosophy in ways even more satisfying than when I had had such discussions with Deschartres. He sincerely praised my writing abilities.

When it was time for my grandmother's will to be read, René came to Nohant, followed soon afterward by my mother, who arrived with her sister, my aunt Lucie Maréchal, and her husband.

My mother was overly rouged and rough in her behavior, yet I nonetheless felt a lurching in my heart, a reflexive movement toward her. She descended from the carriage with her chin held high and quickly embraced me. "Now, at long last, we shall see what we shall see."

The reading of the will did not go smoothly. For one thing, my mother's allowance was to be cut by one-third. Then, when she heard that I had agreed to live with my father's family, she became incensed and carried on hysterically, rising up to shout that my grandmother's wishes did not supersede her rights as my mother, that she would go to court if necessary. With this last, she looked over at me. "Must I remind you of the countless entreaties you made to live with me? How you wept when I left Nohant, how you begged to leave the convent to be with me?"

I spoke quietly, directly to her. "You hurt me when you did not take me to live with you. Now you go against what my grandmother thought so carefully about and believed to be in my best interests? Can you not see that you are hurting me again by not letting me do what I, too, feel is best?"

She narrowed her eyes. "You have been manipulated by your grandmother and by Deschartres into this way of thinking. You believe yourself too good for me and my way of life—a life, by the way, that your father believed in and adored."

My parents had been happy together, it was true. But it was always my father's wish that his wife and mother would get along, and he struggled mightily to accommodate both of them in his life; even as a young child I could see that. But I knew, as well, that if he had had to choose between them, he would have picked his wife.

And so in honor of my father and because, despite everything, I still loved my mother, who had collapsed into her chair and covered her face with her small hands to weep, I agreed to do as she wanted and place myself under her authority. However, rather than live with her, I asked if I might live at the convent as a boarder. My mother seemed amenable to this, and I could tell that my father's family saw it as a reasonable compromise. René left me with words of comfort, saying that he himself would see about finding me lodging there.

In the end, though, my mother disallowed my living at the convent or at Nohant. My distress at this decision did not make my mother reconsider.

Instead, we left immediately for Paris, where we planned to stay with my aunt Lucie, until such time as legal matters were settled and we could move into my grandmother's apartment.

So it was that I abruptly left the house and the gardens and the fields, the wildlife, and my excellent horse. I left my room, with its comfortable bed and afternoon sun and books and papers and guitar and harp. And I left my dear, bereft Deschartres, who watched the carriage drive off with his hands empty at his sides, his hair disheveled, his body leaning to the left, as though he no longer knew how to balance himself.

When my mother and I lived with her sister, I was reunited with Aunt Lucie's daughter, my cousin Clotilde. She reminded me that one's life is meant to be full of much more gaiety than I had experienced. She loved me as I was, oddities and all, and I was heartened by her cheerful nature and by her belief that matters of the human heart always take precedence over teachings in a book. With her, I was not so studious, and although I missed the richness of contemplation and serious dialogue, I enjoyed the relief of plain fun and girlish laughter, which I had last experienced what seemed like a very long time ago, in the convent. And I enjoyed Aunt Lucie, as I always had: I liked her plainspoken ways and forthrightness, her habit of indulging and praising. And I liked the way she handled my mother: she was not at all intimidated by her, as so many others, myself included, were.

One day when my mother was out, I sat at the kitchen table peeling potatoes with Aunt Lucie; she was making her delicious potato leek soup. "So, Aurore," she said, "is it not wonderful that you are back with your mother at last?"

I smiled but said nothing.

She leaned in so close to me our foreheads nearly touched. "You know, your approach to her is all wrong. Shall I tell you how to handle her?"

I put down my knife and sat up straighter. "Yes."

She looked briefly at me and smiled, then resumed peeling. "First of all, it is your nature to be calm and reasonable, which only serves to feed the flames when she goes off on one of her tirades. Instead, scream back at her! It is only in raising her ire to the maximum that you force her to dispel it; once she is at the top, there is nowhere for her to go but down. Serve her up the same drama she offers you, but do her one better. If she yells, yell louder. If she tears up, then you must sob loudly—pretend you are an actress at the theater. Believe me, if you respond to her in this way, she will quickly exhaust herself, and then you can carry on normally."

I saw the reason in my aunt's words, but I knew I could never behave like that. It was not in me; nor did I want it to be. As my mother had influenced me, so had my father. And he was, after all, the man who, rather than face up to my mother, rode away from her histrionics on that fateful rainy night, looking for peace—and got more peace than he'd bargained for. I appreciated my aunt's advice, and I told her so; but I think she, too, knew that I could never do as she suggested. I would have to find another way to escape my mother's rages and cruelty. Easier to say than to do, when the one who is cruel to you is the one lodged permanently in your heart.

March 1833

QUAI MALAQUAIS

PARIS

My fever was raging; when I coughed, it seemed I rattled the walls. I knew no one would want to be around me, and I did not blame them.

Still, at such times one longs for the comfort of another presence. And so when I heard the door open, I rejoiced to think that one of my neighbors had come by for a visit. But it was not a neighbor; instead, it was Marie Dorval, bright as the sun on this stormy day, stomping the wet off her little boots, dropping her coat to the floor and rushing to my side, never mind my disheveled appearance or flushed face.

"But what have we here?" she said. "Ah, *petite,* I heard you were ill. But look at you, it is worse than I thought. Well, I shall attend to this. But first, a kiss—I must offer a greeting for my wild darling, laid so low!" Not a word from her about her abrupt disappearance, and, as grateful beneficiary of her attentions now, I did not want to bring it up.

I held up my hand in a weak effort to keep her away, but she would have none of it. She kissed my cheeks, my forehead, the angle of my jaw, cooing in sympathy like a turtle dove. She pressed me to her bosom and rocked me back and forth.

"*Oh là là là,* how warm you are. I shall prepare a cool compress for you. Have you eaten? Where is the soup? Has no one brought you soup?"

"There is bread and cheese," I said.

"Bread and cheese! Might as well say nails and bricks! You need soup! After I have made you more comfortable, I shall go out and get what I need to make it for you. But first I shall bathe you and refresh your linens."

"No, Marie."

She ignored me; instead, she bustled about, gathering a basin, towels, sheets, and pillowcases.

"You have rehearsal," I said, and she looked over her shoulder at me, so bright and beautiful, the color high in her cheeks, her dangling earrings catching and then refracting the light.

"I have canceled rehearsal. What need have I of rehearsal when I already know my lines perfectly? And in any case, my audience will forgive me everything. You know that!"

"But—"

"And now you are to say no more about anything. Instead, you will only listen to me tell you of the scandal I witnessed last night. It concerns Victoire Adeaux. Perhaps I need say no more than that! You know her name; you know she has earned her reputation. And I shall also need to talk at length about the entertainment I enjoyed last night with a most lavish suitor to the melody of my husband passing gas in the next room over. Oh! And I am having made a dress that is a dream, a confection, one I will wear for my next play; the dressmaker came this morning with thousands of yards of silk as blue as the deepest sea—I shall be remarkable in it. Are you awake? Stay awake. Later you can sleep, after I have . . ."

She clasped her hands beneath her chin, sighing dramatically. "But *mon Dieu,* look at you! You must not have slept in days! I shudder on your behalf. And you haven't even a single rose beside you!"

I began to cough violently, and she widened her eyes and watched me until I finally stopped and fell back against the pillow, exhausted. "Oh, poor George. Yes, close your eyes, dear one, but listen to me, are you listening? I shall make you well, I shall make you soup with the sweetest carrots and onions and potatoes. And when you have eaten and are bathed, I shall sit beside you and read to you from whatever book you choose. Poetry, perhaps, short bits?

"And you will wear my new necklace as I read to you—look what the gentleman last night pressed into my hand upon arrival!

Emeralds are not my favorite, but this is an exceptional cut, and I think it will look well on you; I will give it to you if you promise to keep it and not hand it over to some suffering soul.

"No, you will not be alone in misery, I shall see to that; we will make your illness a little holiday, we will travel together through this day, and when tomorrow comes you will be much improved—I must insist upon it, for I cannot be distracted from my performance tonight because of worries about you!" At last, she drew a breath. "Have you at least one lovely plate on which I may serve you one perfect slice of fruit?"

"Marie," I said. "Where have you been?"

A miracle: quiet from Marie Dorval. Then: "George," she said softly. "Here I am."

Easy to comprehend that when I was ill, I was helpless before her. But even when I was not ill, such was always the case. She swept me away from my woes and reminded me of my capacity for joy. She seemed to work miracles that were personal and intricate in nature, and that were a testimony to her understanding and generosity. She ridiculed me for my automatic defense of anyone who suffered, but her sentiments in that regard were the same as mine. Beneath the glitter and the gaiety and the fame and the storms of temperament and the constant hyperbole and the demands and the wants and the waste was a truly compassionate being. When I was with her, I brought her most fully to herself. She did the same for me. I thought we held true mirrors to each other's souls.

MARIE'S SOUP HAD THE curative powers she had said it would. Three days after her visit, I was back to myself. I worked well during the day, and that night I went to Marie's show and then let myself into her dressing room. I wanted to surprise her. I lit a fire and sat before it, watching as the flames leapt up, separated, met again.

I sensed her coming before she arrived; I smelled her perfume before she turned the knob on the door. She entered like a glittering whirlwind, her voice hoarse, but speaking rapidly. "At long last, to be finished with a night that I thought would never end! My God, my feet, my throat! They use me up, they grind me out, they can never get enough! Oh, look, my husband has made a fire for me!" I started to answer, then saw that she was not speaking to me at all. Behind her was a tall, strikingly handsome young blond man, someone I did not know; nor, apparently, did Marie.

"Tell me your name again, my darling, and then help me out of my dress," she said. "I am looking forward to—" She stopped then, having seen me standing quietly in the shadows.

"Forgive me," I said. "I wanted to surprise you."

She laughed. "Well, you have succeeded! I am surprised."

The young man cleared his throat, and I picked up my coat.

"Where are you going?" Marie asked.

I pointed to the door. "Call on me tomorrow."

"Stay," she told me.

She took hold of the young man's arm and looked up at him. "You, I shall see on another occasion, perhaps?"

The man started to speak, and she stood on her toes to kiss him quickly, multiple times. "Ah, you are delicious, you turn my bones into water. But run along now and find someone else to play with."

He stood crushed, unmoving, and she laughed and shooed him out the door.

Then she came to kiss me.

"A bit cruel, no?" I said.

She shrugged. "By now, he is telling all his friends that he had me. Ah, let them talk; I appreciate the worth of gossip in keeping alive a reputation I no longer have the energy to maintain."

She flung her fur-trimmed cloak to the floor, along with a huge bouquet, then stepped out of her dress, her petticoats, and her undergarments. The dress, lavender in color, had a pelerine *en ailes d'oiseau,* "wings of a bird," a look of which I was particularly fond. She wrapped herself in the dressing gown she kept draped over her

Oriental screen, then sat at her dressing table to rub cream over her face. By now, her post-performance routine was familiar to me, and I loved watching it.

"Thank heaven you are here, George! Now that I see you, I realize again how much I need you! You always have such a wonderful effect on me. Come and sit by me, take down my hair." I went to her, put my hands in her silken mass of curls, and began removing pins.

She sighed deeply, then cocked her head. "And how are you, my darling, did you love my performance?"

"Of course I loved your performance. There is no one like you. You devastate us. We all were on the edges of our seats every time you spoke. How fully you become your characters!"

"Yes. As do you! We are both instruments of our art—we give ourselves completely to it. And yet is it not completely exhausting? I often wonder if it is wrong to have such passion for one's work. Or even a sin! Why are we so utterly devoted? Tell me, do you think it is a curse?"

I began to massage her shoulders, and she closed her eyes and leaned her head back; her throat was white as a swan's, her lashes a black filigree. I felt a rising up of a strong desire and had to struggle to keep my voice level as I answered her question.

"I think it is our nature, not our decision," I told her. "And I think, furthermore, that it is a blessing and not a curse. Our work sustains us, rewards us, and it endures. It does not attempt to contain us or call us names or try to make us suffer for what we cannot help being. It is how we go to bed satisfied, and why we get up in the morning."

She opened her eyes and sought out mine in the mirror as she spoke. "It is true, all that you say. Yet is there not in you a longing for a deeper connection to something else, something more?" She sighed. "Always, always, something more?"

I spoke carefully. "Are those your feelings, Marie?"

She laughed and spun around on her bench, took my hands in

hers, and kissed them, knuckle by knuckle. "I tell you this truly, George, to be near you is to be reborn. Look at me, I am suddenly wide awake! Let us take off our shoes and stockings and dance barefoot down the streets, let us pull down the stars from the heavens—I will gather them in my skirt for us to have as our own. Let us lie down and ravage each other all night, and then breakfast on champagne and oysters!"

"Shall we?" I asked quietly, my heart racing. Could I at last act on my desires? Marie had just opened her mouth to answer me when we heard a knock on the door. And then her husband came into the room.

"Marie?" he said, and just before her face changed into one of domestic compliance, she glanced over at me, and we shared a look that we had shared before, one that could be translated into a single word that meant many things: *Men.*

I nodded to her husband and took my leave. Outside, the clouds had lifted, and the stars shone brilliantly. Mercilessly. I stood still looking up at them, my hands in my pockets. I ached for her then. Then and always.

All the way home, I made love to her in my imagination, as I thought I could if only she would let me. I would kiss those lips, that neck, that bosom: pink and white, roses and cream.

March 1822

RUE NEUVE-DES-MATHURINS

PARIS

My mother and I had moved into my grandmother's apartment. Rather than the two of us enjoying each other, which I confess I still hoped for, there was cold silence and an ongoing disapproval. My mother seemed to want to punish me for the life I had lived with my grandmother. She seemed intent on breaking my spirit, on taking away from me the things I loved most. She ripped books from my hand, telling me that since she found them incomprehensible, they were no good. She got rid of my maid, saying she did not like her, and even sent back to Nohant my dog, Phanor, whose imploring look when he departed nearly broke my heart.

I felt I had no allies. My cousin René de Villeneuve, once my champion, stopped coming to visit. When his brother, Auguste, came once to call on me, I expressed my dismay about no longer seeing René. Auguste, who was no diplomat, said, "With a mother like yours, what do you expect? She is always rude to René. And besides that, you did not adhere to the plan we all had agreed to. You did not go to live in the convent. Rather, you choose to live here with your mother, and you even show yourself on the street with her and her people. I myself don't mind such a thing, but for my sister-in-law and other important people in society, it is quite impossible to think of getting you married off when you are seen with such types."

However challenging my mother was for me, this made me angry. "First of all," I told Auguste, "my mother would not permit me to live at the convent. I am seventeen years old, not of age, and therefore am obliged to do as she says. What recourse did I have? Secondly, you suggest that it is wrong for me to keep company with my mother and her family and friends. As long as you are taking moral inventory, you might want to ponder this: What kind of virtue would be shown by my abandoning my own flesh and blood? Shall I blatantly disobey my mother? Threaten and insult her? Shall I run away and abandon her as she abandoned me, throwing bad after bad?

"What, after all, Auguste, makes you a nobleman but the circumstances of your birth? It is no credit to you that you sprang from your mother's limbs; you had nothing to do with it. Is it not one's character and actions that make him what he truly is?"

Auguste bristled. "If so, take care to recall the actions of your mother, who before she married your father was—"

"I know what she was! She did what she had to do! Her choices were limited; they were not those of a man!"

He sighed. "Aurore. There are ideals, and then there is the world we live in. You must be realistic. You must be practical. Surely you see our predicament. Our society is not welcoming of women like your mother. As her daughter, if you expect to marry well—"

"The world we live in is the way it is because of the decisions people make. Or do not make, but instead blindly follow behind those who went before, never questioning their motives or reasoning, never thinking for themselves!"

He shook his head. "Aurore—"

"And as for you dangling the prospect of my marriage to a nobleman, what makes you think I want such a marriage? The idea of the convent is more appealing to me than marriage!"

He laughed heartily. "Come, come, let us not pretend that every woman does not dream of getting married! What we hoped for was for you to find a good match, by which I mean a man of wealth and good breeding. But all right, then, marry a commoner, if that is your desire. It makes no difference to me." He raised a shoulder in a lazy shrug.

My heart was racing so fast it was making me dizzy, but I spoke calmly: "If you want to speak in absolutes, then I shall answer you this way. Every man thinks he can speak for any woman. But he would do better to let her speak for herself, and then consider the worth of her words!"

"Bah!" He stood, pulled out his pocket watch, and looked at it. "I must take my leave. But before I go, I should like to tell you something, Aurore. I know that René finds many of your odd ideas charming. I confess I do not share his enthusiasm. Your outrage about such matters only bores me. Men and women live in this society in the way that makes the most sense; we have evolved quite naturally to operate in a way that is best for all of us. That includes recognizing men as the superior sex, though of course women do have their charming contributions to make. I believe that when you mature somewhat, you will come to understand this. And I hope that, despite your feelings toward me now, you will think about our conversation and understand my family's concern for you. I speak for all of us, I know, when I say that I wish you well."

He left, closing the door quietly, and I went to the window to watch him walk away.

June 1833

NOHANT

In early June, when it was my time to be at Nohant for three months, Casimir took the children to see his family for a few weeks. In his absence, I inspected the place thoroughly. My husband had not been tending to the estate the way I would have liked; things looked poor both inside and out.

Ever since I had left to live part-time in Paris, I had made an effort never to criticize anything that went on at Nohant. But this time, as soon as I kissed the children goodbye and watched them and their father disappear down the driveway, I set the entire staff to work. The reward for their efforts, I told them, was that they would all receive two weeks of vacation; I could manage the place alone.

On the last day of the servants' being there (how high their spirits were, every one, from housemaid to stable boy!), I received a note. My pulse quickened; I thought it was Marie sending me details about her arrival; I had implored her to visit me here.

But instead of an excited acceptance from Marie, I found a vitriolic message from her lover, Vigny, calling me a Sappho and telling me that Marie wanted nothing more to do with me. "I ask you on her behalf to refrain from any more attempts to contact her," he wrote. I sat stunned, the letter in my hand. I could not believe this was Marie's doing. But when I thought about how easily she had abandoned me before, I could not entirely doubt it, either. I sat unmoving until the moon began to rise, and then I went to bed, the cold supper of sausage, bread, and cheese that the cook had left for me untouched.

—

THE NEXT DAY, I received a letter from Marie, informing me that she had been outraged to learn of the note Vigny had sent. He had admitted to having done so during an argument they had had, "the most violent yet," she wrote. I confess I felt a rush of satisfaction on reading this. She said she hoped I was faring all right and that she would see me when I came back to Paris, if not before. For despite a terrible exhaustion, she thought she might just take the time she had been given off between shows not to rest, as she really ought, but instead to come to Nohant to visit me.

I closed my eyes at the thought of it. To have her here alone with me! But in matters of great longing, one must tread carefully. Especially with one who liked to be a bit contrary, as Marie did. She never wanted anything more than when she thought she might not be able to have it; she was a woman so used to getting her way that any resistance intrigued and engaged her.

I went to my desk to write her back immediately, saying: "However lightly you may have suggested it, do not think of coming to see me here. I have come for solitude; I have even dismissed the servants. I want to hear only the birds and the wind in the grass, the running of the river. To be frank, I need to clear my head of you, Marie. Anyway, I am writing well, engaged in a major project, and there is no one with charms enough to pull me from it."

Naturally, she came. In late afternoon, four days later, I heard the creak of the carriage wheels, the clip-clop of the horses' feet. I came to the front door and saw her descending from the coach, her parasol raised against the sun.

"You see that I have come despite your letter to me!" she said, after the driver brought her luggage inside. "Surely you could not have expected me to wait for you in the stifling city, wondering if you were truly as well as you suggested. Tell me you are happy I am here, show me!"

She ran into my arms, and I embraced her. She stepped back

and regarded me, tears in her eyes, "So! There! I knew it! I knew you would be glad; I knew you told me to stay away only because you longed for me! Alfred was the devil himself, telling me I must have no more dealings with you, that you were intent only on exploiting me. I am exhausted more by him than anything else in my life. He is jealous of anyone who takes a moment of my time. Men are such infants, so frightened of being pulled from the tit! Except for the pleasures they provide us, which we most assuredly *earn,* they are worthless."

Here before me was Marie Dorval, her body and her mind and her spirit. I wanted to speak lofty words of love to her, to bedazzle her. And so what did I do? I told her I had been on my way to the kitchen to make a little dinner. Would she care to join me there? I had had a sudden attack of shyness, and I feared, too, that moving too quickly on my desires might frighten her off. When birds came to me, after all, it was when I was holding still.

Marie's face brightened. "Ah, George, it is with great eagerness that I accept your invitation. What rarity for me to enjoy the simple pleasures of cooking. No one knows it, but I *adore* cooking! I am not so good at it as most; you will have to forgive my clumsiness if I—"

"As surely you know by now," I said, "I forgive you everything. Even the things you have not yet done."

She looked tenderly at me. "Well, then, my dear. Let us feed ourselves."

We donned cook's aprons and worked side by side in the kitchen. We talked nonstop, sometimes about serious things, but just as often we were silly, welcoming the release of laughter.

We talked about men, too—she was still smarting from her terrible argument with Vigny. "I tell you," she said, "he is enough to make me want to be faithful to my husband, who is a dullard, but who at least asks nothing of me!"

I chopped chives to sprinkle over our omelettes. "As far as I am concerned, the balance between men and women is all wrong, and there seems little interest on the part of men for changing that.

Men know that women need them, and because of that, they acquire an elevated self-confidence. Women, rather than acknowledging their own importance in a relationship, focus instead on their need for it, and in the process they lose their self-confidence. I search in vain for equality in a relationship, and for someone who will want all that I have to give. What is the answer, do you think?"

"I think," Marie said, "that the answer is an omelette."

I laughed, and she said, "I wonder, George, if you have ever in your life been properly treated by a man."

I gave no answer, which was of course an answer.

"I see I must teach you some things." She gestured toward the dining room. "After you."

She loaded up plates on her arm like a tavern keeper. I rushed to help her, and she said, "No. Proceed."

And so I did. In the dining room, she set the plates on the table, then pulled my chair out for me. After I sat, she brushed her lips against the back of my neck and murmured, "I adore you."

She did not let me pour myself wine, and she watched carefully to be sure my glass was never empty. At dinner's conclusion, she cleared the table while I sat idle. Then she came back to the room and announced that it was now time for after-dinner entertainment.

"Ah, good," I said. "I want to take a walk outside to show you the stars."

"No need, for I have seen them in your eyes."

I laughed; she did not. She was firmly ensconced in her role as *séducteur.*

"To the drawing room, then, to play the piano?"

"Your voice is the only music I care to hear."

"What shall we do, then?"

She took me by the hand and led me toward the bedroom.

I giggled like a schoolgirl all the way there, but when we arrived, it grew suddenly silent but for the sound of the frogs singing in the pond.

We disrobed, our eyes on each other, and lay down on the cool white sheets. She turned onto her side, her back to me, and I rested my cheek against the flat space between her shoulder blades, then kissed each knob of the drop necklace of bone that made up her spine. I caressed her bottom, the backs of her thighs, and in her silence I felt her pleasure. Next I turned her over and put my mouth to one of her breasts, sucked gently, then moved to the other. She moaned, low, and I slid down to put my mouth at her center and I tasted her. Then I tasted her more deeply and finally devoured her, until she cried out and her hands, tangled in my hair, pulled up hard, then let go.

We lay still for some time, and then, in a voice not quite her own, I heard her say, "George?" It was not the voice of a prima donna, of the absurdly confident actress who enjoyed the adulation of thousands.

"Yes?" I whispered.

"I am . . . *frightened*."

I pulled myself up to look into her eyes, smoothed her hair back from her forehead. "I am as well."

We were quiet. Then she asked, "Have you yourself experienced what you just gave to me?"

I shook my head no.

"Ah, you must have it, then." She turned me onto my back, regarded me tenderly, and began. I closed my eyes. After a moment, my senses and thoughts began to blur together and I felt a lifting away of self from self. She touched me with her mouth, then with her fingers in a way that made me gasp, and my eyes flew open. Outside, I could hear rain falling, lightly at first; then it pounded down. I closed my eyes again, my heartbeat escalating, my breathing soft grunts. And then I cried out in astonishment at the rippling feeling I was experiencing. My back arched in exquisite tension. It lasted for a long, glorious moment, after which I collapsed onto the bed.

She pulled me to her in a tight embrace and whispered to me, and I felt tears trickle down my face to pool at the edges of my smile.

She slept then, her body pressed to mine. I lay awake, listening as the rain stopped as suddenly as it had begun. I got out of bed and tiptoed over to the window to open the shutters. Moonlight spilled in to softly illuminate the room, and then, carried in by a breeze, there came the perfume of jasmine and the fecund scent of the earth, renewed.

I returned to bed and then I, too, slept. I entered that place we must all go to alone, with another.

We swam in the river upon awakening; we bathed together in the cool waters, from which Monsieur Pistolet, my newest dog, a soulful-eyed spaniel, was cruelly and unusually barred. He was used to diving in from some great height, then swimming to shore with a sapling firmly gripped between his teeth. Or he collected rocks from the silty bottom and laid them in a pile like a stonemason, intent on a project of his own design. As lighthearted as his antics always made me, I did not want him with me now. I left him to pace in circles and whine at the door, and I was entertained instead by the disrobing of my magnificent mistress.

She stood naked in the knee-high grass of the banks and stretched her arms up over her head, her fingers interlaced. Sunlight outlined her body, infused her hair. She smiled at me, and in it I read her pleasure in last night's lovemaking. I still could not fathom what had passed between us; never had I experienced such feelings. My pleasure was my great surprise; my surprise was her great pleasure. There was no discordance, no doubt. There was no separation of anything. We were part of a glorious whole that made up the summer night: a sudden rising up of wind and the rattle of shutters, a pouring-down rain followed by an aromatic and moonlit calm, black chiffon clouds drifting by, and clusters of stars like ornamentation worn at the shoulders of the firmament. Her crinolines were piled on the floor on top of my clothes, her blond hair unloosened and intertwined with my own black tresses.

We had eaten and drunk again afterward. We had left berry-stained meringues on pink glass plates in order to dance together to the music in our minds. Then we had fallen again upon the bed, our mouths pressed together. Kissing her, I felt kissed myself; it was my breasts that were caressed as I touched hers. I knew her body because I knew my own; I touched her in my own deepest place of pleasure and felt what she felt in soulful reverberation.

Before she left, she sat me at my dressing table and arranged my hair in an elaborate style. It took a very long time, and when she had finished, black ropes of braid hung on either side of my face in a fanciful and alluring way. "See how beautiful you are!" she said. "You must re-create this style every day."

"I very much admire it, but I would never take the time."

"But you look so lovely!"

I repeated: "I would never take the time."

She shrugged. "As you like. As an actress, I must take time to make myself beautiful every day, at every hour. There is nothing more dangerous and unreliable than an adoring public. They will turn on you in an instant if you do not meet their expectations, for they depend on you to lift them from their tedium." She sighed and gazed at herself in the mirror. "It requires such effort. It is exhausting. If I did not enjoy looking at myself so much, I would find it intolerable."

I started to laugh, but she turned me around and took my face in her hands and regarded me seriously. "George. Before the carriage arrives, I want to tell you something you will not like to hear. But I believe the source of your unhappiness is that you have an expectation of something that cannot occur."

I pulled away from her and walked over to sit on a chair in the corner of the room.

"You spoke last night of giving all to a man who does not want it. He is right not to. We cannot any of us accept all of another person. No one is equipped for or desirous of such a thing. It may seem so at first, but it . . ."

She began suddenly to sing. It was a child's verse, and I knew it well; my mother used to sing it to me.

> Let us go to the henhouse
> To see the white hen
> A handsome silver egg she'll lay
> For this dear little child today.

"Do you know this song?" Marie asked.

I nodded.

"I bring it up now because when you talk of love, you are talking of the silver egg. Which of us children was not enchanted by the idea of this magical egg that was promised to us in song but never delivered to us? And we *liked* that it was not delivered, did we not? For if it had been, poof! There went the magic and the mystery—and the *story,* the one we loved to hear over and over for the way it continually held out hope. We would have tired of such an egg, no matter how magnificent it would have seemed to us at first, is that not true? So it is with love. You cannot ask for something that is not possible, then regret the fact—even punish yourself for the fact—that you cannot have it. We live not to *have,* George. What we want is not the object of our desire but desire itself."

I wanted to disagree with her. I wanted to point to our night of rapture, our unique way of understanding each other. I wanted to tell her that I knew she longed for the same thing as I; she had told me so in many ways, over and over again, not only with her words but with her sighs; with the beseeching look in her eyes; with the way she laid a hand over her heart. I wanted to ask her to abandon her notions of love and fall in with my own, to suggest that we pledge ourselves to each other and prove to ourselves that what we wanted *was* possible. For she had shown me that I was no Lélia after all.

But I said nothing. Her carriage came, and I escorted her to it, and grasped her hand through the window before it drove away. She was in a different mood by then; she laughed gaily and said, "Do you know, your diatribe against men has made me in the mood for them! I shall forgive Vigny and then persuade him to take me out for an extremely expensive dinner!"

I smiled, never mind that it was the last thing I felt like doing.

She squeezed my hand. "George. We are lucky. We shall have last night forever, our own silver egg. We shan't forget."

"Never."

"I love you!" she called, letting go of my hand as the driver signaled for the horses to pull the carriage away.

I headed back toward the house. I would turn to my work. I would turn to my flowered china inkwell and my quill, my cup of tea and my bouquet of pink roses at the corner of my desk. I would finish *Lélia*. It was Sainte-Beuve who'd convinced me that I should publish it, after I'd shown him fragments that I had loosely put together into the shape of a novel. He was also the one who told the editor of the *Revue des Deux Mondes* to ask me for a chapter for publication in the magazine.

I worried that *Lélia* was too close to the most sacrosanct part of my own soul. It addressed itself to the notion that both prostitutes and married women were slaves to men, yes; it advocated for equality between the sexes, including in sexual fulfillment, yes; but most important, it dealt with the battle of the intellect against faith, with the struggle to believe in a God whose actions did not make sense, and with the need to find the meaning in life. It was a spiritual novel, a mystical one, I thought.

Or I could work on *Pauline,* a light novella I had begun sometime earlier when I was in high spirits, about two women friends. One, Pauline, is bound by the rules of the bourgeoisie; the other, an actress named Laurence, is free in thought and behavior. In these two characters, I conflated characteristics of Marie's and mine: I put some of me in her, some of her in me.

But when I sat at my desk, my mind fixed on one thing only.

When I was a child growing up at Nohant, there had lived, in nearby La Châtre, a man who was called crazy. His name was Monsieur Demai. A young man, he was reasonably attractive—his untrimmed beard gave one pause, but he was otherwise appropriately dressed and always polite and well behaved. He used to appear almost as a ghost might, silent and unexpected, never speaking unless you spoke to him. He had an air of impenetrable sadness. Many people tolerated him without a word; he was harmless enough, but he could begin to irritate after a while for the way he stood silently nearby, observing. He would also walk into people's houses unannounced and had been known to come often into my grandmother's house. She had a tolerance for certain things that could be surprising. When it came to Monsieur Demai, she would never speak harshly to him or ill of him. If he stood mournfully observing past the point of her endurance, she would simply ask him, as did others, "What are you looking for?"

And he would answer in the way he always did: "I am looking for affection."

I once stood beside my grandmother in the parlor, where she had been giving me music lessons, studying this strange man's features as she continued the conversation with him.

"Ah, yes, affection," my grandmother said. "You've still not found it, then."

"No," he said, with the embarrassed demeanor of one who has dropped his dinner roll under the table.

"And where have you looked?" my grandmother asked gently.

"I have looked everywhere."

"Perhaps the garden—have you tried there?"

"I haven't," he said, and into his eyes came a look of bright possibility. He put his hat back on his head, touched his fingers to the brim, and turned to go back outside.

"One has to let him believe he will find it somewhere," my

grandmother said. But Monsieur Demai was destined, in his melancholy madness, to search for what he would never find.

We children never made fun of him. We felt sorry for him, and we liked him in the marginal way the dogs did: we did not want him with us, but we sensed his gentle nature, and we knew he would never hurt us. When I heard the news that he had committed suicide, I mourned not only his erratic presence but the fact that for most of his life, he had been called mad. By then, I was a bit older, and I thought that his ailment was not madness at all but, instead, a desperate honesty; I thought he had lived a life more bold and true than most dare to live. The majority of us venture only so far in our quest for an affection that can still the voice of longing at our deepest center; we grow out of the hope that we will find the perfect and all-encompassing love that Monsieur Demai called "affection." He never lost that hope. Nor, I confess, did I.

Ah, Marie! One night! One night of our entire lifetimes that you said would last undiminished forever, and so it has. Marie, Marie, lost angel, so it has.

THAT NIGHT, I TOOK myself outside to walk by the river, and then far beyond, until I was too tired to do anything but come home, put into my mouth food I could not taste, and fall into bed.

Hours later, I started awake. I sat up at the edge of the bed in the darkness, crossed my arms tightly over myself, and rocked slowly side to side. Eventually, I lay back down, but I did not sleep for the rest of the night.

I had vowed that I would stay at Nohant. Now I vowed that in the morning, I would make arrangements to go back to Paris until such time as my children came home to Nohant. I would send a letter to Sainte-Beuve, asking him to make dinner reservations for us the evening after I arrived. He had written to me at Nohant to tell me he had bought me a blood-red bolero jacket, decorated with pom-poms. "Please bring the jacket to me at the restaurant, for I am in desperate need of cheering up," I told him. And then I packed, making sure I had all the pages of both *Lélia* and *Pauline.*

As it happened, I would not return to *Pauline* for years, and when I did, the tone of the book had changed. I had added this scene:

> By evening, Laurence was gone. Pauline had wept as she watched her climb into the carriage, this time with regret. For thirty-six hours, Laurence had made her feel really alive, and the thought of the next day terrified her. Exhausted, she fell into bed and fell asleep, heartbroken, hoping never to wake up again. When she did awake, she cast a dejected and fearful look about the room where no trace could be found of the dream Laurence had evoked. She rose slowly, sat mechanically in front of her mirror and tried to braid her hair the way it had been the day before. Suddenly, called back to reality by the song of her canary waking up in its cage, forever happy and indifferent to its captivity, Pauline got up, opened the cage, then the window, and thrust out the sedentary bird, who had no desire to fly away.
>
> "You don't deserve to be free!" she cried as she watched him fly back inside at once.
>
> She returned to her dressing table, untied her braids in a rage, and buried her face in her hands.

June 1833

MAGNY'S RESTAURANT
PARIS

"YOU MUST NOT BE AFRAID OF *LÉLIA* BEING SEEN AS AUTOBIOGRAPHical," Sainte-Beuve said, lavishly buttering his bread. "You know as well as I that one's work is rarely interpreted the way one means it to be. Did you yourself not tell me that you were 'educated' by the critics who told you what *Indiana* was about?"

"Yourself included!" I said.

He drew his considerable girth back to let the waiter place before him his dinner: a whole chicken, split and roasted to a dark golden color; buttered red potatoes; and haricots verts. He had already ordered dessert: two dishes, as he could not decide between *pot au chocolat* and a selection of cheeses. He tucked his napkin into his collar and commenced eating nearly before the platter was put down before him. "I am famished, nearly faint from hunger," he said, apologizing for the little piece of potato that came flying from his mouth. I merely took a sip of my wine. I had ordered only onion soup and had yet to lift my spoon.

I had complimented Sainte-Beuve on the bolero jacket he'd presented to me when I arrived but had not had the heart to try it on. And so, in an effort to lift my spirits, he had thrown it over himself. He looked absurd, but he was well known and respected enough that no one raised an eyebrow. No one, that is, but he: he lifted one of his great black caterpillars to inspect me closely.

"Tell me. What has happened?"

I stared into my lap.

He waited, and finally, I decided to tell him everything. After all, I had shared with him in a letter the grim details of my failed experiment with Mérimée; surely this was no worse. And if it was, so what? It would be of great help to let Sainte-Beuve serve as father confessor, and to listen to whatever advice he might offer. I needed to unburden myself.

Sainte-Beuve took great pride in the fact that so many women confided in him. He was extremely close to Victor Hugo's wife, Adèle; many said he was in love with her. When I once asked him about this, he laughed and answered quickly: "Who would not love her?"

For me, this nervous response, given with his eyes averted, confirmed what I had long suspected: not only did he love her; they were lovers. Sainte-Beuve was not a handsome man, but there was kindness in his baby face, and a depth to his gaze that conferred upon him a compassionate wisdom.

I told him about Marie, and when at length I had finished speaking, he put down his knife and fork and spoke softly. "My dear," he said, his face full of sorrow. That was all. The great critic, the eloquent Charles-Augustin Sainte-Beuve, was at a loss for words.

Tears filled my eyes, and I hastily wiped them away, embarrassed, because it was at that moment that the waiter reappeared to remove Sainte-Beuve's plate and, after a nod from me, my own. I had eaten nothing; the butter in the soup lay unappetizingly congealed on its surface.

"You must eat, my dear. Even if you have no appetite. I can see the effect that all this has had on you. It worries me. You will heal from the devastation, but not if you starve to death first."

"At times when I feel sad or upset, I cannot eat or sleep," I said. "This has been true of me since I was a child. I must suffer through whatever pain I am having, and then, gradually, I come back to myself. Surely you know me well enough to know that."

He took a bite of his *pot au chocolat,* smacking his lips at its goodness. He loaded up his spoon with another bite and held it out to me.

I shook my head.

"I shall take away your jacket," he said.

Still I demurred.

He wiped his mouth, put his spoon down, and leaned forward. "I once had sex with a young man. Well, to be honest, more than one."

I rolled my eyes.

"Yes, very exciting but not so satisfying as the cries from some fair maiden. And *that* is less exciting than your new work—which, by the way, I predict will be the cure for this particular malaise.

Judging from what you have shared with me so far, it is more than brilliant."

I offered an anemic murmur.

He sighed. "George. This is no good. How can you work in this condition? And you must work! I believe in *Lélia.* It will be your best book yet, perhaps ever. You will astonish people with what you have done. It will not be a novel for casual and nondiscriminating readers who flip pages rapidly and read with the depth of a lamppost. It will not be for people who are uncomfortable being challenged by literature. But those with true intelligence and insight: they will sing your praises, critics and the general public alike. You must hoist yourself up and get back to it; you must be nearly finished by now."

I shrugged.

Sainte-Beuve removed the bolero jacket, folded it neatly, and handed it to me. I laid it in my lap, taking comfort from the warmth of his body that I could feel in it.

"Listen to me. I have two suggestions for you. Or, rather, I have one suggestion and one imperative. The suggestion is that you visit Hugo's physician, who prescribes for him and many others, as well, 'depression pills.'"

"That I cannot do," I said. I knew what my spirit needed: love and time. Not pharmaceuticals.

"Very well. This next, though, I must insist you take advantage of. I have made the acquaintance of Alfred de Musset. Do you know him?"

"I have heard about him. Too much of a dandy for me, I'm afraid. Is he not very young? And greatly troubled? I heard he is addicted to opium. And champagne. And a certain class of women."

"A lover younger than you has never bothered you in the past. He is twenty-three to your twenty-nine, not so vast a difference. As for him being a 'troubled soul,' I look upon that as being your specialty! Besides, this young man with such character faults is capable of writing sublime poetry and is gifted with impressive intelligence.

Truly, George, I believe you would at least find him amusing. Let me bring him round to your apartment so that you can judge for yourself."

I hesitated, then said, "I think not. Not just yet."

Sainte-Beuve scowled. "So the rumors are true."

I looked sharply over at him. "What rumors now?"

"That you are in love with the critic Gustave Planche."

"Don't tell me—"

"It must be true. I heard it from Balzac. He insists that it is true."

"Balzac would insist that the earth was flat if he thought it would hurt me. He has gone from being a dear friend to a bitter enemy, all on account of my break with Jules."

"He has taken Jules in to champion him."

"So I have heard."

"It appears not to be going as smoothly as Balzac thought it might. Jules has a bit of a problem with laziness?"

I looked at my pocket watch. I would not indulge in gossip about someone I once loved so dearly. But it was true that Jules was lazy. I doubted Balzac would tolerate him much longer.

"I know you want to go," Sainte-Beuve said. "I shall release you if you promise me one thing."

"What is it?"

"Finish *Lélia*!"

"I shall." Finally, I smiled.

I resumed working that night with new determination. And as I wrote, I saw how the book was a philosophical undertaking to try to use the mind to bring peace to the heart, and to construct a morality that one could reconcile oneself to. I used aspects of Marie for the character of an actress, Pulchérie, who had become a courtesan in order to support her need for luxury; I put parts of myself in the character who is her sister Lélia, one who refuses to give up her independence for any man. Just before I stopped working for the night, I added a scene of Pulchérie talking to Lélia:

"Oh, my sister, how beautiful you were. I had never found you so before that day. I had preferred myself to you. I had felt that my brilliant cheeks, my rounded shoulders and my golden hair made me more beautiful than you. But at that instant I awakened to the beauty of another creature. I no longer loved only myself. I rose softly and looked at you with singular curiosity and a strange pleasure. Your thick, black hair clung to your face, and the close curls tightened as if a feeling of life had clenched them next to your neck, which was velvet with shadow and sweat. I passed my fingers through your hair. It seemed to squeeze and draw me toward you. Your fine, white blouse pressed against your breasts made your skin, tanned by the sun, still darker than usual. And your long eyelashes, weighted with sleep, stood out against your cheeks. Oh, Lélia, you were so beautiful! Trembling, I kissed your arm. Then you opened your eyes and your gaze penetrated me with shame. I turned away as if I had committed a guilty action. Don't you remember my confusion and my blushing?"

"I even remember something you said," replied Lélia. "You made me lean over the water, and you said, 'Look at yourself. See how beautiful you are.' I replied that I was less so than you. 'Oh, but you are much more beautiful,' you said. 'You look like a man.'"

I held the quill in my hand, motionless, after I wrote these words, and read them again. Then I blew out the candle and went to sleep.

THE NEXT DAY, I awakened at around two in the afternoon. I had coffee, forced myself to eat a bit of fruit and bread, and then went shopping for flowers. At Nohant, nature surrounded and cheered me; in Paris, I had to buy pieces of it to bring it inside.

After I selected the pink and white peonies I wanted, I set out for home. It had rained furiously the night before; around three A.M., while I'd sat writing, I had feared that the windows would give way to the force of the storm. Now, although the rain had stopped, the streets were rivers of mud. Carriage wheels got stuck, and while hack drivers tried to urge the horses on, prostitutes approached the men who were riding inside. When they were refused, they only laughed gaily and moved on to the next carriage. *I could learn from them,* I thought.

I walked past Jovin's, which sold gloves, and stared into the window. I went into the store, harboring a fool's hope that I might find Marie there. Of course she was not inside. Instead, when the bell tinkled merrily, there appeared a pretty young shopgirl whose eyes, with their dreamy gaze, told me she was elsewhere—with her lover, I supposed. In love, your joy is offered to the world and your happiness is reflected back to you; in pain, you suffer alone. Though I held my shoulders back and my head high when I walked into the street again, I felt as though I were cramped into myself, my head tucked between my shoulders, trying to find shelter when there was none to be found. Only one other time in my life had I been this desperate for something to lift me from what was to what might be—which is to say, to leave behind despair for hope.

April 1822

BRIE

ONE DAY, SAYING THAT THE FRESH AIR WOULD DO US GOOD, MY mother brought me to a large villa in the country. It belonged to Monsieur James and Madame Angèle du Plessis, a couple we had recently met at a dinner party and who had invited us to visit them. Restless as always away from the city, my mother left after one day, but she told me to stay longer—the gracious hosts were more than amenable—and she would come to collect me after a week. In fact, she did not take me home for nearly five months, but that was for reasons of my own as well as hers.

It turned out that our hosts were well aware of my family history—James had been acquainted with my father in the army—and on meeting me, he had taken pity on my sorry state. At the dinner party, he had seen me stare into my lap when my mother spoke of my grandmother, criticizing her in her usual sardonic way. But it was hearing me say that I dearly missed living in the country that had prompted him to speak with his wife about inviting my mother and me to their home.

Angèle, a most maternal, kind, and caring person, was glad to have me join their brood: they had five children, all girls younger than my seventeen years, and their household was chaotic but full of cheer. She wrote to my mother asking permission for me to have an extended stay, and my mother agreed, saying she had no objection at all, that it would be a relief to be away from what she described as my constant state of melancholia—never mind that it was she who was most responsible for it. She told James she was weary of trying to get me married off, for, despite the grim prediction of my father's family, I had received several proposals, all of which I'd refused with as much grace as I could muster. For his part,

James said that it appeared that I was the kind of person who would need to choose for herself, and what was the harm in that?

Even after many years, James was very much in love with his wife; and he told my mother that he could understand perfectly well my not wanting to be attached for life to someone I did not know or had not even met. Surely my mother would agree that there was no romance in a marriage arranged solely as a business transaction, and surely she, who had loved her husband so dearly, could not begrudge my yearning for romantic love as well. Given my mother's history with my father, she could not make much of an argument against that.

And so the du Plessis family all but adopted me, and Angèle and James acted so much the part of my parents that I began calling them mother and father. For their part, they referred to me and treated me as their daughter. Angèle bought me new clothes and shoes; and she enjoyed doing it as much as I enjoyed being the beneficiary of such largesse.

I was granted other benefits that I very much appreciated: I was able to use the library and read whatever and as much as I wanted. But eventually I found that I wanted to leave behind the world of the mind and *thinking* for a while. I spent hours walking in the nearby park, where I found acres of tall, mature trees, their wide trunks begging an embrace, their deep grooves suggesting secrets folded therein. There were, as well, willow trees dipping their branches into what looked like mirrored, depthless ponds, deer slicing through shrubbery on their way toward hidden glades, and wildflowers blushing in the grass. In that man-made park was the deep green fecundity of a forest in the wild, and I loved it. I went for glorious rides on fine horses, rekindled my interest in music, gained weight, and finally slept well.

My mother would visit me at Le Plessis occasionally and ask me in confidence if I wanted to stay; and the stiffness in her manner let me know what she was hoping I would say. Each time, I would assure her that I did want to stay. It was hard to say who was more pleased at this.

Staying with the du Plessis family reawakened both the childish and the maternal instincts in myself. I found myself running in the fields and actively playing with the family's children; but I also helped to settle them down when they were too rowdy, when they were hurt, when they were in need of a kind of singling out for the devoted attention that every child occasionally needs. It is not inaccurate to say that I came to the du Plessis household craving death, if not in fact near to it; and they nursed me back to health with a steady, selfless love. They were also responsible for my finding my husband, in a rather unusual way.

I had been to a mime drama with my chosen parents, and we had gone to Tartoni's for lemon ices afterward. Angèle spotted someone across the room and asked James, "Is that not Casimir?"

"I believe it is!" James waved the fellow over. He was a slender, aristocratic-looking young man—he had that air of casual elegance associated with good breeding and a privileged life. He had, as well, the stirring, overly correct posture of the military, and there was in his face a kind of merriment; these things reminded me of my father.

"My dear Monsieur Dudevant!" James said. "Tell me, how is your father?"

Casimir gave them news about his father, a colonel who was apparently very much beloved by the family du Plessis. He then sat close to my adopted mother and whispered something in her ear.

"That one?" Angèle asked. "Oh, she is only my new daughter." She spoke loudly, with mischief in her eyes.

"Your daughter!" Casimir said. "Then she is my wife, as well! You must recall that you promised me your oldest daughter's hand, but this one is far more suited to me by age. And so thank you very much indeed; I shall accept her in Wilfrid's place."

We all laughed, but inside I could feel a small flame ignite. All the misgivings I had expressed about marriage aside, I wondered if I might perhaps be ready after all—in a couple of months I would turn eighteen. Perhaps it was time.

A FEW DAYS LATER, I heard Casimir's voice floating upstairs to where I was in bed, awake but lying idle. I leapt up and performed a hasty toilette, then made my way downstairs.

He smiled upon seeing me and offered a courtly bow. "I see my wife has arisen," he said.

"And what has my husband to report that will make my having left a cozy nest worthwhile?"

Such playful banter soon gave way to our running outside with the du Plessis children. Casimir demonstrated a wonderful sense of playfulness that day, which he exhibited without any self-consciousness or apparent aim, and I liked this about him. I felt that he was not in any way courting me but, rather, was simply being himself.

After more time together, my view of him changed from what it had been at that first meeting, when my romantic fancy had taken flight. I now regarded him in the calmest, most pleasant of ways, as a friend and confidant; and I felt sure he looked upon me the same way. Nonetheless, we continued to call each other "husband" and "wife"; it was simply an extension of that original lightheartedness we'd enjoyed upon our first meeting, nothing more.

Still, people thrust their fantasies upon us and, in one way or another, urged matrimony. Finally, one day I took James aside and said, "I am afraid our little joke must come to an end. I admit that I was at first intrigued by the idea of marrying a man like Casimir, but we have developed a friendship that can never be anything but that. I must ask you to help me put an end to the rumors that suggest otherwise. Anyway, someone told me that his inheritance will be great; there would be no reason for him to marry someone like me."

But James told me I was mistaken in this last. "While it is true that the colonel is very wealthy, Casimir will not inherit all that wealth. Half of the fortune belongs to the colonel's wife. Of the colonel's own half, part is from his pension, which his son will not be given. What is left, Casimir will indeed inherit, but it is less than what your fortune will be. So he would, in fact, do well to marry you, when you look at it that way."

He paused, then went on: "But, Aurore, I think we both agree that there is more to look at than this. My advice to you is to do as you please when it comes to marriage and Casimir. But keep in mind that you could do far worse. You two do seem to enjoy each other a great deal."

Not long afterward, Casimir proposed. There was nothing very romantic in it. It amounted to him saying that he wanted to ask me first if I would consider marrying him; if so, he would have his father take it up with my mother. This was the reverse order of what was usually done, but I liked the notion of him leaving it solely up to me. He told me to take a few days to think about it—or, for that matter, as long as I needed. If I found the idea of him as a husband not repugnant (and this he said in such a way as to make us both laugh), then I could let him know, and he would set things in motion.

"I will think about it," I said.

That evening after I retired, I lay awake in bed, wondering if I should accept him. It meant a great deal to me that James and Angèle liked him and his family so much. It was good that I could be relaxed around Casimir, and, on further thought, I realized that I had come to regard him as my best friend. He had not said he loved me, but I felt this not as a slight to me but, rather, proof of a rare kind of honesty.

He had said that even though he did not find me attractive, that I was not beautiful or even pretty, there was nonetheless something appealing about my matter-of-fact nature, my directness. He told me, "I was, of course, not serious when I first said you should be my wife, but something happened when I said the words—a sudden thought that this really should be so. And then when I came to call on you and found such ease in your company, the idea that we should make a life together only grew stronger."

I thought of how he teased me about what he called my exaggerated reactions to everything, how he said that he had never seen the use for such passion. It was true that my emotions brought me to the highest heights, but they also brought me to my knees in agony. Perhaps Casimir was right in saying that an easy friendship, and not passion, was the way to domestic happiness. James and Angèle seemed to enjoy that kind of friendship, and their marriage was far more harmonious than my parents' stormy relationship, which, while full of romance, had also been full of screaming matches that rattled the skull.

Marrying Casimir would not be the ideal of my girlish daydreams, but it would be better than returning to live with my mother, and I knew I could not stay with James and Angèle forever. And so the next morning, I told Casimir yes, have my mother meet with your father; let us see if she will agree to our marriage.

"It's too bad it's not the old colonel himself who is asking for your hand," my mother said, after she came to Le Plessis and met privately with Casimir's father. "I am impressed by his gentleness and his reputation, and he is, as well, quite handsome. Very handsome, indeed. It's nothing to sneeze at, if your husband is good-looking. It makes a difference in ways you do not yet understand." She and I were ensconced in my room, where she was going to deliver her verdict.

"You do not find Casimir handsome?"

"My dear. First of all, his nose is far too long; it slides down his face as if intent on escaping it. His ears are too womanish, and the flesh on his face has a kind of doughy quality. He will not hold on to his hair. So no, I do not find him good-looking. Ah, Aurore, I had hoped for a handsome son-in-law to take my arm."

"And so you refused him?"

"No, I did not. I accepted because I knew you wanted me to." She looked coyly at me. "But! It was done very cleverly, in such a way as to give me room to change my mind."

My mother stayed for a few days, testing Casimir in various ways, though she called it getting to know him. Finally, she agreed that in two weeks, after Casimir's stepmother, Baroness Dudevant, had returned home from where she had been visiting her family, a date for the wedding would be set. Until then, all of us were to spend more time together. All of us except my mother, who raced back to the noise and the hurry of the Paris streets.

But in a few days, she was back at Le Plessis, screaming at the top of her lungs that she had been deceived. She pointed a finger at Casimir. "You have misrepresented yourself! You are a waiter!"

Casimir was dumbfounded and could not speak. None of us could, at first, and then I finally said, "Maman, have you had a dream?" Her dreams sometimes remained so powerful and realistic that she could not separate them from reality.

She did not answer, only stood glaring at Casimir, awaiting an answer.

Finally he recovered enough to defend himself. "First of all, madame," he said, in a calm voice that I knew would only anger her more, "there is no shame in being a waiter. But I have never been one. I would never have had time! I finished military school, went into the army, and then lived with my father while I got my law degree. I am sorry to disagree with you, but I was never a waiter." He began to laugh, he couldn't help himself, and then we all did. I was relieved that he could laugh rather than be frightened away from me by such behavior.

My mother was enraged; her nostrils flared, and the color rose high on her face. She pulled me aside and spoke from between her teeth: "This household is not what you think! Your precious James arranges marriages only so that he can collect a hefty fee! As for his wife, she has no morals; you see how her household is wild."

There was nothing to do when my mother got like this; reason would not prevail. And so I said I would return to Paris with her, right now; I would go up and pack and we would leave immediately. Together, we would get all the information we could about Casimir.

This calmed her down considerably, and she said, "Oh, never mind—you stay here, since you like it so well. But do nothing until I have done more investigating."

Eventually my mother gave in and designed a marriage contract. The terms stipulated that my husband would control my fortune, which was usual. What was unusual was that I would retain it; it would be legally recognized as mine. The contract also stipulated that I was to have an annual personal allowance of three thousand francs. Casimir agreed to it, and we were married.

Immediately afterward, we left for Nohant. Deschartres was overjoyed to see me, and I him. *Finally,* I thought, *my happiness begins.*

June 1833

LOINTIER'S RESTAURANT

104 RUE RICHELIEU

PARIS

LÉLIA WAS IN PROOFS WHEN GUSTAVE PLANCHE INVITED ME TO A dinner that François Buloz, the editor of the *Revue des Deux Mondes,* was giving for regular contributors. In an amusing turn of events, I was seated next to Alfred de Musset, the man Sainte-Beuve had wanted me to meet but whose introduction I had declined.

After we introduced ourselves to each other, he said, "Ah, George Sand! I know of you, of course, but I have not yet had the pleasure of reading your work."

"Nor I yours," I said and took a sip of wine.

He stared into his own glass, and I was glad for the opportunity to look closely at him. He was very handsome, possessed of a high forehead, thick and curly brown hair with hints of blond that made it seem lit from within, a well-formed nose and mouth, and light blue eyes that one had difficulty looking away from. He had a habit of lowering his lids when he looked at you, which made for a simultaneous disquieting and hypnotic effect. He wore a swallowtail coat with a high velvet collar and pearl-gray pants that did not require one to use any imagination to picture what lay beneath. He carried a swagger stick and wore his top hat at a rakish angle over one ear. A dandy, indeed. As for me, I had worn a black silk skirt and jacket, a plain outfit offset by a small jeweled dagger in a gold sheath, which I had tied at my waist and believed to be very stylish.

Alfred, *vicomte* de Musset, was charming. He was also polite, an interested listener who gave way for opinions beyond his own, and he had a great wit. He told me he called Sainte-Beuve "Madame Pernelle," and in spite of my fondness for my old friend, I had to laugh, for when he wasn't looking like a child trapped in a man's body, Sainte-Beuve did rather resemble the silly old lady in Molière's *Tartuffe.*

Mostly, though, Musset and I spoke seriously and most sincerely, and he refrained from the profanities he was known to lace his speech with. We discussed politics, various pieces that had lately appeared in the *Revue,* and then moved on to relationships, though in a largely superficial way. Each of us was asking, I suppose, if we were committed to anyone else. I told him I had gotten off on the wrong foot with men and preferred to live my life as an independent woman, offering only friendship to men; he told me that he had sought pleasure over love.

"If it would please you, I could send you a copy of *Contes d'Espagne et d'Italie,*" he said, in a shy way that endeared him to me. I had heard of his book, a collection of poems and sketches that had been very well reviewed.

"I would welcome the opportunity to read it," I said, and it was true. I could never get enough of good poetry, and Sainte-Beuve was not the only one who thought Musset divine.

I gave him my address, and each line I wrote set my heart to beating faster.

"Perhaps I shall deliver it myself," he said. "Tomorrow evening?"

"I work in the evenings."

"In the morning, then."

"I'm afraid I sleep quite late, as I often work through the night."

"I see." He was embarrassed now, and a silence fell between us.

Finally: "Come at one in the afternoon," I said.

"There, you see? I knew you would let me come!"

I laughed. "How did you know?"

"Ah, George," he said, leaning nearly imperceptibly toward me. "Your eyes are portals."

THE NEXT DAY, I awakened early: around noontime. After breakfast, I inspected my wardrobe to see what might be interesting to wear. I settled on a pair of harem pants and a loose-fitting red silk robe that had a habit of falling open. With this I wore a pair of backless slippers that were considered very daring. Never mind that my heart was not fully repaired from the devastation I'd suffered at the hands of Marie; I was still a passionate woman whose soul thrived on a certain kind of stimulation. Besides, Marie and I had resumed enough of a friendship that I was not entirely without her; in fact, I had every intention of telling her every detail about this meeting with Musset.

He arrived promptly at one. He had wrapped his book in beautiful marbled paper and anchored upon it a single red rose.

I thanked him, then ushered him in. I could see that he was very much intrigued by my outfit—not to say stimulated, if his widened eyes and sudden nervousness were any indication. I saw, too, a fine trembling in his hands.

I asked if he would like to smoke some Egyptian tobacco with me. He declined but said he would be happy to sit with me while I enjoyed it. And so I gave him a chair, then sat at his feet with my hookah, drawing in smoke and blowing it up toward the ceiling.

I said nothing, nor did he, for long moments at a time. When we did talk, we spoke of last night's dinner, of the various people who had attended it with us. We talked, as well, about the beauty of the chestnut trees, which were flowering, and I told him that at Nohant I loved to lie beneath those trees and think. On the pretext of deciding that he would like to try the tobacco after all, he came to sit on the floor beside me. I offered him my pipe, he took a puff, and pronounced the tobacco very good indeed. Then, expressing keen interest in my Oriental slippers, he reached out a finger to trace the raised design on the fabric. Ever so slowly, with his eyes locked on mine, he slid a finger in to stroke the arch of my foot. I felt a rush of longing that, were I not seated, might have knocked me over.

And then: a rapping on the door. Surprised, I went to open it and found Gustave Planche, who had come to call on me, as he often did. We would sometimes lunch together in a café, fueling rumors that we were lovers, though in all candor Planche's problems with hygiene would never have allowed me to be intimate with him. Still, one had to give him his due: he was a genius not only as a critic, but as a person with the perceptive skills of an artist. He had remarkable insight into a number of things, including the look on Musset's face when he came to the door behind me. "I was just leaving," Musset said, and Planche stepped quickly aside, so that he might pass.

After he had gone, I glared at Planche.

"Come, now, you can't be serious," he said.

I said nothing.

"You? He can even have *you*? George, I beg you, do not be so stupid as to join that bunch of vapid and immoral women who fall mewling at his feet."

"I have work to do," I told Planche, pushing him out the door.

Later that day, a note was delivered to me from Musset. He had read *Indiana* and said he must have more of me as soon as possible. I made arrangements for him to receive the proofs of *Lélia,* which would be published in a few days, though I knew full well that what he wanted more of was not just my words. But Planche's reaction had given me pause. I would wait awhile to see Musset again.

A week later, I received a note from Musset praising *Lélia* to the skies. He also added this:

> *You have nothing to offer but a chaste love, and that is something I can give to no one. But I can, if you think me worthy, be to you—perhaps not a friend, for even that sounds too chastely in my ears—but an inconsequent comrade, who makes no claims and will therefore be neither jealous nor quarrelsome, but will smoke your tobacco, crumple your négligées, and catch a cold in the head as a result of philosophizing with you under all the chestnut trees of contemporary Europe.*

I wrote back that I would receive him that evening at eight for dinner, so long as he departed by ten, when I would begin work.

That night, when he arrived, I escorted him to my table, where candles burned in spite of the still-light summer sky. We started to sit down, and then he cried out, "I cannot continue with . . . I must tell you all that is in my heart."

He stood trembling while I stared at him, astonished but, it must be admitted, flattered as well.

I took him by the hand, led him to the living room, sat in a chair, and gestured for him to sit opposite me. But he remained standing before me, his hands clenched at his sides. "I cannot work. I think of nothing but you!" Then, startling me, he fell to his knees and began weeping. I reached out to touch his shoulder, and he put his head on my lap, his arms around my waist, and sobbed.

I thought about what I might say to him. I knew his father had died in last year's cholera epidemic and that he and his older brother were dependent on their mother for an income that had been substantially reduced. I was sympathetic to the kind of pressure he must be under to make his writing pay. I decided to tell him that the best thing to do was to try to not think about it, to make his writing a kind of chapel, a sacred place to which he did not admit anything but his imagination. I wanted to soothe him into a calmer state, to offer again to be his friend, even a kind of mother substitute who could give him comfort, advice, companionship, and the occasional roasted chicken. For as much as I enjoyed the eroticism I had felt with him so far, I thought it best to go no further.

Before I could speak, however, he leapt to his feet and rushed out of the apartment.

I sat stunned for a while, then ate dinner alone, thinking about what had transpired. Then I changed into my dressing gown and wrote until night gave way to the rose gold of morning. I moved to the window to regard the street below: still quiet, but with signs of life stirring: a merchant washing down the sidewalk outside his store; a man setting up to show off his performing dogs, an artist at his easel. I stretched, yawned, arched and massaged my back. Then I performed a sleepy toilette and climbed between lavender-scented sheets to enjoy a sweet release. I hoped for dreams I would remember, and could use.

It seemed there was something to using material from the unconscious: *Lélia* had enjoyed a first print run of fifteen hundred, an inordinately large number for the time, and it had sold out immediately. This was in spite of the fact that it garnered several bad reviews—one source called it "dangerous, teaching skepticism." But that review served only to make it sell better. Gustave Planche had said in the *Revue des Deux Mondes* that women would understand *Lélia:*

> They will underline those passages in which they have found, set down in words, the memories they harbor of their own past lives, the record of their own unpublished miseries. With tears in their eyes and veneration in their hearts, they will acknowledge the impotence which here proclaims itself and reveals its torments. They will stand amazed at the courage of such an avowal. Some will blush to think their secrets have been fathomed, but in the privacy of their own minds, they will admit that *Lélia* is a speech not for the prosecution, but for the defense.

It had become the book one had to have, even if one did not read it.

The day after Musset fled from my apartment, there came a knock at the door and I was handed a note by a messenger. It was from Musset, and I sat down to read it, not having any idea what to expect. These are the words he wrote:

> *I have something stupid and ridiculous to say to you. You will laugh in my face, and hold that, in all I have said to you so far, I*

was a mere maker of phrases. You will show me the door, and you will believe that I am lying.

I am in love with you. I have been in love with you since the day when I came to see you for the first time. I thought I could cure myself by continuing with you on the level of friendship. There is much in your character that might bring about a cure and I have tried hard to persuade myself of this: but I pay too high a price for the moments which I spend with you. And now, George, you will say—'Just another importunate bore!' (to use your own words). I know precisely how you regard me, and, in speaking as I have done, delude myself with no false hopes. The only result will be that I shall lose a dear companion. But in truth, I lack the strength of mind to keep silent.

I read the note again. I kissed it.

And then I did nothing. I did not write back to him. I tried to will him away from my thoughts. If what so many people said about him was true, he was dangerous, making women fall in love with him and then discarding them with impunity; and in any case, I was not ready to enter into another love affair. Deep in my heart, I still burned for Marie.

But the next day, another note from Alfred arrived:

I was a fool to show you more than one side of myself. You should love only those who know how to love. I know only how to suffer. Adieu, George; I love you like a child.

I sent a note back immediately: "Come to me." And he did.

A FEW DAYS LATER, I had dinner with a group of my Berry friends, all of whom had renewed their friendships with me after my break with Jules. They had heard about my goings-on with

Musset, and rather than be happy about our finding the joy we both deserved, they looked like they were gathered around my casket for a final goodbye. Gustave Planche said, "To put it bluntly, my dear, I fear you have taken leave of your senses." I told him I appreciated his concern, then stopped seeing him.

If I could not have Marie, at least I could have this besotted young poet who called me—the pants-wearing, cigar-smoking, low-voiced independent—the most feminine woman he had ever known. On more than one occasion I found myself dizzy with the delights he offered me. I did not experience that release I had found with Marie, but I loved loving Musset. Never mind Mérimée—here was the skillful lover!

Musset began our lovemaking with poetic praises of my body, with caresses so soft I could barely perceive them, and ended with the headboard banging into the wall so hard I finally had to move it out several inches. He covered me with kisses from the top of my head to the soles of my feet, he entered me from on top, from behind, from the side. He put his fists in my hair and pulled until I gasped in pleasure, he called out my name over and over as he thrust himself inside me. We made love on the floor of the bedroom before the fireplace, on a settee in the parlor, and once on the dining room table in a frenzy that was like nothing we had known previously. No china was lost, but some silver made a magnificent clatter as it fell to the floor. I arose from that session with candle wax in my hair, with my lips swollen and bruised.

We were happy outside the bedroom, too. Our politics aligned: we looked with nostalgic favor on the old days of the empire, which had at least been run with precision, as opposed to the present government, which often seemed full of confusion and at odds with itself. As advocates of civil liberty, we were sympathetic to the effects of the 1830–31 November Uprising in Warsaw, and we made friends with many Polish expatriates.

In addition, we both adored music, though he bowed to my superiority in both knowledge and practice. And he liked practical jokes as much as I. Once, when I gave a dinner for friends, he dressed as a girl to serve us our food and "accidentally" stumbled, dumping a water pitcher on the head of the philosopher Eugène Lerminier, who for once lost his overbearing and stuffy manner: he giggled like a madman as he wrung out his hair.

THAT SUMMER, THE HEAT in the city was unbearable. I got up early one morning to meet Marie Dorval for a walk at the Jardin des Plantes, but neither of us could find relief there. At one point Marie looked around, then raised her skirts high and called out loudly, "Come, breeze, to explore the place that everyone longs to visit! I invite you to come and take your pleasure, and in so doing cool my flesh!" But the air remained still, and finally Marie gave up and let her skirt fall and resettle itself. She was dressed all in white but for the blue satin ribbon around her waist and in the trim of her wide-brimmed hat. We walked slowly on, and I told her about Alfred. Only the night before, I had invited him to come to me at midnight, when I could be sure the children, who were staying with me, were sleeping. It had been a monumental effort to keep quiet.

"Well," she said, "now that you are married, you must have a honeymoon."

"It would be bliss to go away with him," I said. "I long to be with him uninterrupted, day and night! But my resources are running low; it would be difficult to fund a vacation."

Marie sighed, exasperated. "Someday you must endeavor to find a lover who has money!"

I didn't bother to disagree; it was too hot to argue. But my belief was that a rich man only feels he has more license to control his woman—as well as everything else. There may have been some frustration in making more money than the man I was with, but there was power in it, too, and a strange satisfaction that I did not feel I could easily explain to anyone else.

Anyway, the success of *Lélia* meant that I would be paid more by my publisher as an advance against the next book, negotiations for which I had begun. In matters involving romance, I might not negotiate wisely; but when it came to business, I had become clever.

"Fontainebleau is not far," Marie said. "You should go there. Take a riverboat; it is very pleasant. The forest there is romantic, so deep and dark and wild. And it will be cool!"

It did sound like wonderful relief. The sun was beating down so hard that my clothes burned my skin, and the heaviness of the air made it an effort to breathe. I thought of the oak trees and the Scotch pines and European beeches I knew to be in Fontainebleau, and I had heard praised the violet-colored orchids, the wild madder and cranesbill and peach-leaved bellflowers. There were imposing rock formations and gorges that invited exploration on foot, and I was an enthusiastic hiker. I had heard, too, about the great variety of birds there: woodpeckers, whose industrious rhythms never failed to amuse me, and blackcaps and tits.

I decided to propose a trip to Fontainebleau to Alfred that evening. I thought I knew what his answer would be. He would welcome the opportunity for our having more time in bed as much as I. It still astounded me, sometimes, where I had gotten to in matters of sex, considering where I had started out. It astounded me, too, that I had moved from such wariness of an individual to such love for him. But one can never untangle the intricacies of and motivation for love; one does best to simply enjoy the flowering of two hearts.

September 1822

NOHANT

"WHY DO YOU LAUGH?" CASIMIR ASKED, LIFTING HIMSELF OFF ME and rolling away.

"I can't help it," I said. "It is comical, is it not?"

"Rather than satisfy you, your husband amuses you, is that it?" Casimir sat up at the side of the bed, and I heard a kind of hurt in his voice that I regretted causing. I put my hand to his back, but he pulled away from me and got up. "As for me, I find that sex with you is like lying on a board. Next time, should there be one, I shall give you a book to keep you occupied, so that you needn't study the ceiling so intently, trying to find something to interest yourself."

"Casimir," I said, but it was too late. He was putting on his clothes.

"You should have told me of your frigid nature. After all, there are only so many ways for a man to check a horse's teeth."

"But I—"

He slammed the door, and I pulled my nightdress down and lay still in the bed. I stayed awake, waiting for him to come back and lie beside me, but he did not return. In the morning, he was cheerful at the breakfast table, and we planned our day as if nothing at all had happened.

CASIMIR AND I WERE never compatible in *actes intimes.* Most of the time, I continued to alternate between hilarity and confusion as a reaction to his lovemaking. But sometimes his brusqueness hurt me, and on one occasion when I cried out, he put his hand over my mouth to silence me, then proceeded.

Still, we were successful enough that I was enjoying my first pregnancy in the winter of 1822–23. I learned that when a woman is with child, her focus shifts dramatically: she cares for the one inside her with a single-mindedness, if not ferocity, that she is incapable of resisting. All her hope rests on what will be; all her efforts go toward preparation. Even when I was engaged with other pursuits, gauzy thoughts of the baby floated in and out of my brain; everything I did in caring for myself was an act for the protection and provision of my unborn child.

I was left alone often, for Casimir loved to hunt, and in long hours that might previously have been given over to reading and study and thought, I now became interested in and appreciative of the domestic arts. Much can be made of public speeches, political movements, and the might and right of various armies who take up arms in support of their ideals—or in blind allegiance to another's will and ego—but in the end we are all human beings who long for our basic needs to be satisfied in the way that only home and hearth can.

In later years, I came to believe that this inclination toward nurturing is one of the main reasons that the female is the superior sex. I saw quite clearly that if our humanistic abilities were given the worth they deserved, the world would be a far better place. But women are not naturally self-promoting; most of us quietly put ourselves last. It seems it is our nature to compromise and not make a fuss. Some think these qualities are instinctive and, therefore, inescapable. I certainly always recognized that I was as much a victim of my heart and my womb as any other female. And in spite of persistent misperceptions of me regarding my views on feminism, I never advocated for women choosing work over family, never advocated for taking women away from their homes and their children.

Did I love being an artist? Yes. But I worked because I had to, and not for one instant did I ever underestimate the importance of what a mother can do for her children. Or fail to do.

For six weeks that winter when I was pregnant, I was ordered to bed by Deschartres, after an episode of spotting early in my pregnancy, the news of which I had shared with him. I was only mildly concerned and was seeking reassurance from him in his role of village doctor, but he became so alarmed, I did as he said, even though I did not really believe it necessary.

I spent that time in drowsy contemplation of what life as a mother would be, sewing various things for the layette. And then, as fate would have it, I began practicing mothering skills with my favorite species.

It was an unusually cold winter that year. The snow was high and did not melt, and birds were dying of hunger. They were so weak and desperate, they put aside all fear of humans and allowed themselves to be taken in hand. Deschartres first brought in a blue-hooded chaffinch so weak he appeared dead. I believed he brought him to me so that we might mourn together, despite the fact that Deschartres would never admit to any sentimental or anthropomorphic feelings. But we soon noticed a bit of movement, a flicker of the bird's eyelid, a jerking in the legs. I took him gently under the covers with me to warm him, laid him on my breast so that he might feel my heartbeat, and hoped that something about that universal rhythm could comfort him. He soon revived, and we gave him some crumbs and water. Then he hopped across the bedcovers, took off for a brief tour of the room, and came back to me to rest.

In a matter of hours, the bird's movements were confident, then a bit anxious, for he wanted back outside. And so we raised the window to let him go.

After that, there was nothing for it but that I must care for all the birds in distress that anyone came across. I asked for a green coverlet that might seem like grass to the birds, and had boughs of evergreen wrapped around the bed's four posters. The sound of birdsong is always sweet, but when, by your ministrations, you believe you have saved a free and glorious creature from an early death, your pleasure knows no bounds.

Those birds served another purpose, too, which was to give Casimir and me our first experience as caretakers together. Casimir would come in from the outdoors with his cheeks ruddy with cold, his nose hairs stiff and frosted white. He would remove his gloves and rub his hands together, bringing back warmth and feeling, before he ventured to gently touch our charges. "And how are our children today?" he would ask.

"See for yourself," I would tell him, pointing to the coverlet, where there might be up to six birds nestled, these in addition to the several who had warmed up enough to investigate the room. Those perched on the canopy of the bed, on the tops of the portraits hung on the walls, and on the windowsills; and they hopped across the floor and the rugs, pecking at bits of food we put out in little saucers for them. It seemed an absurdity, a dream, this impromptu bird sanctuary, but to my delight it was altogether real.

"They are happy, are they not?" Casimir would ask, in a schoolboy's shy yet prideful way, and I would agree that they were happy indeed.

I knew that Casimir was speaking not only of the birds, for despite our difficulties in bed, we were content in those days. Part of the reason was that I thought I had uncovered the secret to a successful marriage.

Many new brides carry with them a certain smugness. They look with pity upon the bitter or strained relationships of the long-married, vowing that they will never be in that position. They believe themselves to be in possession of a superior way of thinking and of behaving.

Here is proof.

I received at that time a letter from a friend I had met at the convent who was experiencing a great deal of anguish in her marriage. She confided in me quite trustingly and openly and asked me what I thought she should do. This was the advice I gave her:

It is essential, I believe, that one of the two, in marrying, should practice self-abnegation, should renounce not only his will but even his opinion, should firmly strive to see through the other's eyes, to like what he likes, etc. The only question is if it's up to the man or the woman to remake himself thus on the model of the other, and since all power is on the side of the beard, and since, besides, men are incapable of such a degree of attachment, it is necessarily up to us to bend in obedience.

I often reread the copy I kept of that letter, at first flattering myself that I had dispensed such good advice but later astonished at my naïveté, and regretful of passing on advice that, if held to, would lead to the death of a soul. Those words were very far away from a time that came in my later years, when I wrote a letter to a young woman telling her that love was "a bad thing, or at least a dangerous trial." I went on to say, "Maternity procures ineffable delights; but, either through love or marriage, we must pay such a price for it that I would never advise anybody to incur the cost."

Strange are the vicissitudes of a normal life. Strange and unpredictable.

TOWARD THE END OF JUNE, it was time to travel to Paris, where my child would be born. It was also time for Deschartres's lease at Nohant to come to an end. I had spoken privately with Casimir, urging him to allow Deschartres to live out his remaining years with us. I was worried about him. While he excelled in overseeing Nohant, I knew that he often fumbled in other endeavors. More than one person had told the old tutor that he must never attempt to have a business of his own, for he would soon be ruined. In Deschartres's practice as a doctor, he would never take payment and, in fact, become enraged by those who attempted to pay him. One patient who tried to leave a rabbit at the doctor's doorstep was met with loud remonstrations and a shaking fist and had the rabbit flung back in his face.

Casimir offered no resistance to my request to have Deschartres stay with us. But Deschartres himself would have no part of it.

"Your husband has been kind not to interfere with my long-standing authority here, though you and I both know he is eager to take up his rightful place. But I could not make the same promise to him. For forty years I have been lord and master at Nohant. You women never got in my way, and your father always gave me total freedom. If I stay here now, I would be constantly critical and trying to be involved in matters I am no longer part of. No, it is time for me to set off on my own. You know that I have desired this for a long time."

Deschartres's last day at Nohant would be June 24, 1823. In advance of that time, Casimir and I left Nohant for Paris. But first we spent a few days at the country estate of James and Angèle du Plessis, where I was always glad to stay: the house was full of visitors and boarders. My choice for company was always children, for their honesty and high spirits and for the way they entered into a game for the sake of the game alone—they were not interested in impressing anyone, or holding forth, or enlisting someone to come over to their point of view. Whereas adults often became wearying to me, children were endlessly interesting, enlivening, and quick to forgive. I could feel that they cared for me, too; we were kindred spirits in our need for heedless gaiety.

Casimir was surprised by the joy they never failed to inspire in me; he had seen, by now, that I had difficulty with times of despair, the cause for which I could not usually articulate. It would not have mattered if I could have told him the reason; his response to melancholy in me was to get as far away from it as he could. But it was an unalterable part of me, a darkness that came sometimes and made me pine, as if for a lover, for the blankness of death.

I would eventually see that certain kinds of melancholia are natural for many artists, and not only melancholia but strange kinds of behavior that are difficult for anyone who is not an artist to understand, let alone embrace.

July 1833

PARIS

When Alfred de Musset and I went on vacation, I left the children with my maid and was given a promise from Gustave Planche that he would stop in and check on them. I did not see Planche the way I used to, but our friendship had been too deep for me to deny us altogether. I was touched by his offer to help me, for I knew he still did not approve of Musset.

Alfred and I took the riverboat down the Seine to Fontainebleau and settled ourselves into a charming country inn. We were eager to get out and explore: Alfred had been there before and wanted to show me a certain place where echoes reverberated off the canyon walls. And so after an early dinner, we hired a driver to take us into the woods, saying that we would walk back.

At dusk, Alfred found the place he was looking for and bade me to sit at the edge of one cliff while he traveled to the top of the one opposite it. The light had not yet left the sky, and there would be a full moon; nonetheless, Alfred bent toward me solicitously to ask, "Will you be all right here alone?"

I laughed. "Do you mean, will I be frightened?"

He nodded.

"Of course not. I have never been afraid of the dark!"

Not so for him, apparently, for soon after he left me, I heard a bone-chilling cry. I leapt up and began moving down the hill, half running, half falling, regretting the fact that I had not worn pants. Thorns on the bushes I passed tangled in my dress, but I had not time to stop and release the fabric, and so I let it tear: I feared for what had happened to Alfred.

I found him huddled on the ground, shaking, crying, nearly delirious. I approached him slowly, put my hand on his shoulder, and spoke softly: "Alfred?"

He spun around and grasped my knees so tightly he nearly knocked me off my feet.

"Alfred! What is it?"

He stopped sobbing and looked up into my face. "I saw . . . Oh, George, I saw a horrible sight. Some *being* appeared and assaulted me with his speech; he said terrible things. And when he turned to look directly at me, I saw that it was myself I was seeing—my own face on that terrible specter!"

I sat beside him as he began to weep again. He apologized, and I murmured assurances and rubbed his back until he calmed down, and then we walked together back to the inn.

I felt for him nothing but compassion, a loving pity. I wanted only to go back to our room, where I would care for him further. And that is exactly what I did. I soothed him, held him to my breast and stroked his beautiful hair, telling him over and over that it was all right, it was over, everything would be fine, we were together. At last, he looked up at me and the boy in his face disappeared. He took me nearly savagely into his arms.

In the morning, he awakened before me, and when I sat up in bed, he presented me with a drawing he had done of last night's terror, him wide-eyed and quaking in my arms, me with my dress shredded, my face full of its own kind of alarm. He had meant it to be amusing, but I did not want to revisit in any form something that had hurt him so; nor did I want him to belittle the tender ministrations I had offered him, those things that had let him recover from whatever had upset him. What had happened to him was real. For him to make a joke of it was to deny a part of himself, and I did not want him to think he had to hide any part of himself from me. I told him so.

"Never mind all that," he said. "Get dressed; we will have a hearty breakfast and hike the day away. Would you like that?"

I hesitated. He came over and kissed me, and every concern I might have had about his breakdown disappeared. I transformed it into an event that served only to demonstrate his great sensitivity and imagination. I did not know then, as I would come to find out later, that he suffered from a particular kind of mental disorder that would bring great distress to us both.

June 30, 1823

HÔTEL DE FLORENCE

PARIS

When Maurice was born, early in the morning on June 30, I was rendered not only speechless but incapable of any movement for hours, save to hold him in my arms and regard him. I watched every flicker of his eyelids, every movement of his arms and legs, the rise and fall of an abdomen I found heartbreakingly fragile-looking, with its one blue vein running close to the surface. His hair was black and plentiful, silky and fine and curly, like mine. Casimir could claim as much responsibility as he liked; in my mind, the child who lay staring up at me, the cosmos in his eyes, belonged solely to me.

There was one other who seemed as besotted as I by the tiny individual who lay with his hands resting on his belly like a satisfied diner, his fingernails tiny chips of pearlescence. That person was not his father, whose admiration for his child seemed but ill-disguised admiration of himself. No, the one who regarded the baby with a tenderness equal to mine was Deschartres.

Here came the old curmudgeon, striding regally through the streets of Paris in some outdated frock coat he had had stored away for who knew how many years, the ill-cut, bright blue garment adorned with brass buttons. He cared nothing for the disapproving or haughty looks he encountered on the streets of Paris; his focus was on one thing: finding his way to his beloved Maurice's namesake.

When Deschartres arrived at my bedside, he unwrapped the blanket in which Maurice was swaddled and inspected with grim solemnity every part of him. Then, satisfied, he wrapped him up again and held him for a long time. He did not kiss him, except soul to soul. He did not offer me every good wish, except by quick glance. He did not speak of my father, except to take one last lingering look into the face of this new Maurice; and I believed his brow was wrinkled with the weight of all that he was remembering, and all that he was hoping for. The tears that stood in my eyes attested to the same feelings.

In the first months after I gave birth, Deschartres had a great deal of contact with baby Maurice and spoiled him as much as I would permit. And since I, too, spoiled the child, I permitted a great deal of it from others. I did not believe one so young could really be spoiled, anyway; I felt that all the attentions paid Maurice now would only be to his advantage later. And if his character as the man he became is any example, I was correct in my thinking.

IN AUGUST, SEEKING RELIEF from the heat, Casimir, Maurice, and I went to stay with James and Angèle du Plessis. Then, in October, we went on to Nohant. The stillness there, in comparison to Le Plessis—which, at one point, had accommodated forty guests—was astonishing. I did not want such extreme numbers of people about me at all times, but I did wish for occasional visits from two or three friends who might want to talk about more than hunting and local politics, or how best to run Nohant, or how one's bunions ached.

Almost every evening after dinner, Hippolyte (who, with his sickly wife, was staying with us) and Casimir would have conversations that never rose to a level above this. They would share snippets of gossip in the way of old women at the market, then tell crass barroom jokes that no one but they found amusing. They would often drink themselves into sickness and pronounce it a perfect evening before they fell into bed. When I compared these evenings with the noble and enlightening ones I'd witnessed when my grandmother was alive, my heart ached. I felt full of shame to have let slip her dignified traditions; I saw clearly, now, the value in such things.

Oftentimes, on those nights that degenerated in such a fashion,

I would slip away to go into the little room on the ground floor that I had created for myself for times when I wanted to be alone. It was there that I had my books and my herbals, my butterflies and my small collection of rocks. There was no bed, but I hung a hammock in which I could rest and dream.

In that little room, on the drop leaf of a little chiffonier that had belonged to my grandmother, I began writing again, too. What I produced was ill-formed and undisciplined and usually quite sentimental. But it showed me that writing could lift me out of my surroundings entirely and into a rarefied place of peace, one that was not subject to the weather in another's soul.

On the whole, things were going very badly between Casimir and me. One rainy afternoon, full of despair, I had tried writing to a friend about Casimir's and my problems. "Lately," I confided, "his affections, such as they are, are wasted on me. So early in our marriage, it seems too late for everything. It is as if we are two vessels in a sea of fog, not sure if its lifting would reveal anything more promising than the gray we have grown accustomed to."

But, afraid that if I sent that letter, the sentiments expressed therein would become realer and more constant, I burned it. Then I proceeded to the garden, where Casimir was brusquely ordering workmen about. I stood beside him for some time before he turned and asked me what I wanted. The words were in my mouth: *To find you. To share again the simple joy we knew.* But when I spoke, it was only to say, "Luncheon is served." And he refused me, saying he was not hungry. Not at all.

I sat alone at the table and was offered food by servants whose pity for me was nearly palpable. I spooned in mouthfuls of a soup I could not taste, feeling a terrible erosion of confidence, then pushed myself away from my meal to go to Casimir's and my bedroom. There, sitting in a chair by the window and watching my husband outside, I did the only thing I thought I could do: I made a pledge to try harder. I couldn't be sure that most—if not all—of our problems weren't my fault. It was true I had endured some cruelty from my husband, but I had also conveniently overlooked my bad behavior toward him. For I was my mother's daughter, and when I wanted to, I could use my intellect and sharp tongue to cut Casimir; and at such times I did so with a devil's pleasure.

Spring 1824

NOHANT

EARLY ON IN THE MARRIAGE, CASIMIR HAD PROCURED FOR ME A new piano, which we could ill afford, and I had looked upon it as a great act of love. I loved music, and thanks to my grandmother's tutelage, I played well. I also knew a great deal about harmony and theory. I played regularly in the evenings, and I thought that my husband enjoyed it. When I played for friends who visited, they complimented me enhusiastically.

But then, in an odd turn, Casimir began abruptly leaving the room whenever I began playing the piano. I knew that his turning away from me then had to do with something other than notes upon the page. Nonetheless, for him and for the sake of our marriage, I gave up my music, which caused me great pain.

And that was not the only thing troubling me. Under Casimir's direction, that spring Nohant underwent a number of changes that others would call improvements but that I saw as a removal of the rustic things that had made it so charming. The serpentine garden paths, so lovely and wandering, were straightened. Dogs and horses who had gotten old were put to death; no more was I calmed by the sight of old Phanor at the fireside, his graying muzzle resting on his paws. There was a peacock at Nohant, a rascal who raided the strawberries, but he also ate most gently from my hand. When I mentioned to Casimir one evening that I had not seen the peacock that day, he looked up from his soup and with some irritation said, "I told you I was getting rid of him." He also got rid of dead trees and enlarged the courtyard. In so doing, he destroyed the dark alcoves that had so enchanted me in my youth.

Gradually, Casimir, flexing invisible muscles, renovated virtually everything, most often changing things simply for the sake of change. For me, it was not much different from dogs marking territory. I could not argue with him; he was my husband and so, by law, the care of Nohant was up to him. But after he had finished his "improvements," I walked outside not with familiar pleasure but with a sense of disorientation and deepest sorrow.

One morning, I sat down at the breakfast table and burst into tears. It surprised me as much as it did Casimir. "What ever is the matter now?" he asked, and I saw that the patience he had shown for me and what he called my moodiness had come to an end.

I calmed myself and tried to speak reasonably: "I think it is probably only springtime and the way it affects me sometimes. I am often made melancholy at this time of year."

Casimir sighed and shook his head, then resumed eating.

I straightened in my chair and spoke louder: "But also, I am no longer happy living here. Nohant no longer feels like home."

Casimir put down his fork and leapt up in exuberance. "Thank God you feel this way, for I would live anywhere but here!"

If our reasons for wanting to leave Nohant were not the same, we could at least agree that we wanted to find another place to live; and having that goal in common helped us get along better than we had been. In later years, when I thought of how content other couples were to stay at home with each other, I realized I should have known that our constant moving here and there was only a way of distracting us from what neither of us wanted to face.

It was a life of constant deception that we had come to. When Casimir left me alone for his various excursions into Paris or to other places, I wrote him letters telling him how much I missed him and longed for him to come home. Then, when he came home, I wished that he would go away. For his part, it was the same: in letters, he called me his angel; in person, he scorned my company.

We had not gotten, either of us, what we had bargained for, and our only true affection was for a false persona that each of us created on paper.

When we changed residences, we became busy with the myriad details that moving always involves, and we did not have to think about all that was wrong between us. And so we frequently changed residences.

CASIMIR WANTED TO GO TO LE PLESSIS, but I was reluctant to wear out our welcome there. And so we arranged with our hosts to contribute to the household costs and stayed with that delightful family for four months.

As always, I loved playing with the children, all kinds of organized games that even included young Maurice, who was still crawling. We marched around the gardens and the immense grounds and chased each other across the lawn. Such simple and pure antics revived my spirit.

Casimir did not see it that way, however. I believe that for him, the children were competition, and his ego was already challenged by my inability to respond to his brusque advances at night. Unable to confess to a jealousy of rosy-cheeked innocents, he converted his feelings to rage and aimed it at me.

One morning, as I was playing with the children on the terrace, I accidentally got sand in Casimir's coffee cup. "Do that again, and I shall slap you," he said.

"No, you won't," I said, and, in a way I blush now to say I thought was charming, I dropped a few more grains in. He reached over and slapped my cheek, never mind the presence of others—adults as well as children.

Everyone fell silent, embarrassed. I put my hand over the stinging redness and walked away. I was sure that Casimir would follow me, and I did not want him to. I vowed that if he did, I would slap him back and admonish him for his treatment of me.

Yet when he did not follow me, I sat forlorn at the base of a tree and bawled like a calf. I wept because I missed the Nohant of my youth. I wept because of my naïveté in getting married, at the ideas I'd had about the lovely life I would lead. And I wept because I had been taught to hold my tongue and not challenge authority and because Casimir, as my husband, had authority over me. There was nothing for me to do in retaliation except what I did do: that night, when we went to bed, I completely rejected Casimir's advances. I told him I was in the bed with him only because I had to be. "If we were at Nohant," I said, "I would be in my little room, in my hammock, and all the better for it."

"Be my guest," said my husband. "Go to your hammock."

I laughed. "And how would I get there?"

"For all I care, you can walk." He turned away from me. In a few moments, he began to snore. I lay wide awake, thinking of the rumor I had heard that he had a mistress in Paris, and how I had offered only the mildest of reproaches. In a letter, I'd told him to sleep well but *alone,* in a nearly jocular way. I wanted to let him know that I knew and did not approve. That was as far as I could go. I couldn't divorce him for adultery—the law was infuriating and unfair for the way it permitted a man to divorce his wife for infidelity, but not the other way around.

And so I lay there and listened to him snore.

August 1833

PARIS

ALFRED DE MUSSET AND I RETURNED FROM FONTAINEBLEAU TO Paris happy and well rested. The day after, I met Marie for coffee and told her that she had been right to suggest a getaway for Alfred and me. "What did I tell you?" she said. "It is refreshing to have a different view out your window, and of your beloved." She leaned forward, her eyes flashing. "And it spices things up, am I right?"

I looked down into my cup.

"Yes, I can see that I am right. I am happy for you, my darling. And what welcome news for Alfred to come back to!"

The August 15 issue of the *Revue des Deux Mondes* had just been published. In it was a long poem of Alfred's that took up twenty-five pages and had been wonderfully well received. His public acclaim spread far and wide. One night, as we went up the steps to the Opéra, Alfred flung aside an unfinished cigar he had been smoking, and it was eagerly snatched up by a young woman, who wrapped it in her handkerchief and then called out to him. He ignored her, blushing; I gave her a little wave and playfully chided Alfred for his coolness toward his adoring fan.

At the end of August, the children left for Nohant, and Alfred moved into my apartment with me. I relished the presence of him there, as well as the routine we developed: I worked all night while he slept; then, in the morning, when I slept, he worked until I arose. We would spend the late afternoons and evenings together: walk out, dine, read aloud to each other, make love; and then I would all but tuck him into our bed and go to the desk in my dressing gown.

There was no more coming home to a darkened room with a ticking clock the only sound therein, a single cigarette put out in a saucer the only evidence of someone having been there. Alfred loved me. And being loved let me breathe, let me work, let me live.

December 1833

PARIS

ALFRED AND I DECIDED TO GO TO ITALY FOR THE WINTER. HE had not been working well, and he hoped that a place so inspiring to other poets would reawaken his creativity.

I was extremely disciplined, and I knew I would have no trouble taking up my pen every night, no matter where I was. I got an advance from Buloz for what was to be my "Italian novel," which I was certain would be inspired by our trip, and I promised to deliver it by June.

I had Solange with me at that time, and I made arrangements for my maid to bring her back to her father at Nohant. Maurice was in school in Paris and would be able to go to my mother's for his days off. There was one last thing to do before we left, a visit I felt compelled to make.

Alfred's mother, the *vicomtesse* de Musset, had reportedly rather coldly tolerated our living together. Then, when Alfred told her of our plans to travel to Italy for such a long time, she became greatly agitated.

It had not bothered Alfred or me when his friends protested our going. They predicted our trip would be a disaster. But then they would: his friends had never embraced me. For one thing, I was an impediment for him living the kind of wild life he had enjoyed with them before he moved in with me: the drinking, the opium, the prostitutes.

His mother's protests were another story. He was very close to her, and whatever grief she suffered tore at his own heart. As a mother myself, I understood the nervous concerns of a woman who had lost two of her children in infancy; and there was the added sorrow of having lost her husband so recently. Alfred, her youngest child and reportedly her favorite, suffered frequent bouts of ill health. I could imagine what might be going through her head: *What if something happens when he is so far away from me? Who will care for him?* I knew from experience that one worried about one's children as a matter of course, but when one was separated from them, the worries became magnified.

On the day of our departure, I told Alfred I would go to see his mother in order to reassure her face-to-face that he would be well looked after.

"It isn't necessary," Alfred said.

But I told him, "I shall be back shortly," and went downstairs to secure a carriage. I soon arrived at the townhouse at 59 Rue de Grenelle and asked the driver to go to the door and request that madame come out to speak with me briefly. After several minutes, Alfred's mother exited the house and climbed into the carriage to sit opposite me.

"Thank you for seeing me," I said.

She merely nodded. Her mouth was set, her chin trembling.

"I want to assure you that I love your son with all my heart and I will look after him while we are away."

"He is often not well," she said, and her eyes filled with tears.

My heart opened to her. "Yes, I know that, but I know, too, what seems to make him recover."

There was a long silence. The horse stomped its hooves and shook its head, pulling restlessly at the reins. The driver spoke sharply to it, and it stilled.

Finally, the *vicomtesse* sighed and took my hands into hers. "I feel I have no choice, for if he is not with you, he will fall into his old ways, which nearly killed him. I wish he would not go so far from his mother, who adores him, but I can see by your coming here that your affection and concern for him are real. Therefore, I give you reluctant permission. Please remind him to write to me as often as he can."

"I shall have no need to remind him; he adores you."

We embraced each other, and then she climbed out of the cab.

All the way back to my apartment, I smiled. I was about to embark on a romantic voyage with the man I loved, and the news I would share with him now would make him able to enjoy it as much as I. Solange was being delivered safely back to Nohant; Maurice was safely ensconced in school. I leaned back against the carriage seat and thought, *All will be well.* There was no other time in my life where expectation was such an ill fit against reality.

Spring 1825

NOHANT

In the fall, Casimir and I had left Le Plessis and moved to a small apartment on Rue du Faubourg Saint-Honoré. I thought it would do me good to be near friends and family, but in the spring I fell into a deep depression. At my wit's end, I sought out my old confessor at the convent, and he suggested that a little retreat there could do me good.

What a tonic, at first, was that dearly familiar place. I had once been so sure I wanted to live out my days in that convent, whether as a nun or a boarder. I had relished the communal living, where one was simultaneously alone but with others; now I wondered if I had made the right decision in leaving. It seemed that I had allowed myself to be dissuaded from what had been a true calling, that I had abandoned sublimity for practicality.

Lying once again in a narrow bed and hearing the locks click at night, I felt the calm that came with the implied imperative to pray and to meditate. All around me were minds engaged in the same gentle, soundless practice; all around me was peace. That feeling stood in stark contrast to the doubts and furies and sadness of my marriage.

In confusion, I sought out the nun we had called Madame Alicia, whom I had much admired. After listening to me talk about how I felt I might have made a mistake in leaving the convent, she told me I was blessed to be living the life I was. "Were you really so happy here before?" she asked. "I recall the despair you felt from time to time. I recall your frustration at not being able to achieve what you wanted here. You must remember that the turtle carries his house with him wherever he goes. If you were to return to the convent, if you were to abandon the life you have made for yourself outside these walls, I believe you would soon regret it. You are not a fickle child any longer, Aurore, with the luxury of being able to run here and there and everywhere, claiming each time that *this* is where you want to be forever. No, you must choose a place to be, and commit fully to it."

"But how do I discover which place that should be?" I asked.

She put her hand to my cheek. "I believe you know already. It is a matter of admitting to yourself what you love most. And that has less to do with love than with courage."

I realized I was not fit any longer for the convent. I was a mother, first and foremost; I would stay in my marriage and raise my son.

At one point, I realized I had not heard from or about Deschartres for some time. After making inquiries at the place where he lived, I learned that he was dead. He had taken a business risk and lost all of his fortune. Not long afterward, he had died.

I heard no fond words about him from anyone. My half brother, Hippolyte, mourned him the way one mourns the passing of anyone who loomed large in one's youth (which is to say that Hippolyte mourned not Deschartres but the loss of his own youth), but he had never liked our tutor, not as a child and not as an adult. My mother's eulogy was to write in a letter to me, "Finally he is gone!" The people in the Berry countryside had respected him, but they'd also feared and ridiculed him.

It was true that he'd been short-tempered and eccentric, and one could easily tire of his dogma. But he'd also been an honest and charitable and trustworthy man.

It was ironic. For all his intelligence, he had failed to grasp a simple truth: he needed some form of love, and he had found it at Nohant. Leaving that place, he lost it. It was my belief that because of the mistakes he had made, he took his own life—stoically, of course. Neatly.

I had always known that I would miss him when he was gone; I had not foreseen how much.

With his death went one who had known my father and who adored my child as I did, one with whom I could still have spirited academic discussions, one whom I might ask questions of and receive an unfiltered answer with no regard as to how I might feel about that answer; and this, it turns out, is more valuable than it might seem.

After my father died, I felt that Deschartres always looked out for me. He might not have felt it his place to comment directly upon the events and people and decisions in my life, but he was a vital witness, one on whom I had depended in many ways since I'd been that wide-eyed four-year-old who had arrived rather unceremoniously at Nohant.

When I learned of his passing, I took a long walk through the grounds that he had so carefully tended. Despite the changes Casimir had wrought, I saw my old friend's hand everywhere. I prayed for a heaven in which he would sit once more playing parlor games with my grandmother, who had loved him best of all.

June 1825

THE SOUTH OF FRANCE

THOUGH I TRIED NOT TO SHOW IT, I WAS NOW DESPERATELY UNhappy with Casimir. And I had no one in whom I could confide and be comforted by. My mother was increasingly a stranger to me. In the letters she sent, she made fun of the ones I had sent to her, telling me I was putting on airs with my language and saying that she prayed I did not begin speaking as I wrote. Yet this woman of the people had adopted a name similar to those of the old countesses she used to make fun of: she asked me to address her letters to "Madame de Nohant-Dupin."

I did find solace in my child. I read to Maurice. I took walks outside with him and watched him crouch down with his hands on his knees to gravely inspect grass and rocks and insects. I played hide-and-seek with him, and whenever I found him in his hiding place, he would laugh himself breathless. After I laid him down to sleep, I would stand watching him, full of love.

But the nights came. Or times of idleness in midday, when I pressed my hands and forehead against the windowpanes as if seeking a way out. Or times when Casimir and I sat silently in the parlor together after dinner because he had rebuffed all my efforts at conversation, letting me know by his sour or vacant expression that he preferred not to weary or bore himself by responding to anything I said. At these times, which happened with more and more frequency, I felt a shredding despair so acute I wondered that I did not begin to bleed.

And then I did begin to bleed. I developed a respiratory ailment, a cough that would not go away, and oftentimes I coughed so hard that I brought up blood. I feared I was consumptive, and when I confided this to Casimir, he dismissed me with a laugh. "When will you stop being so dramatic?" he asked.

In late June, we were paid a visit by two young women with whom I had gone to school at the convent. It was a tonic to see Jane and Aimée Bazouin, even though their normal gaiety was dimmed from their having lost their oldest sister to an early death. In order to get all of their minds off that sadness, their father was taking them to the hot springs at Cauterets, in the middle of the Pyrénées Mountains in the south of France. People went there to heal not only physical ailments but spiritual ones as well.

Maurice's birthday was on June 30, and my twenty-first birthday would follow on July 5. It was decided that afterward, Casimir, Maurice, and I would join my friends at Cauterets, then journey on to the Dudevant country house in Gascony. "Perhaps the change in scenery will do something for you," Casimir said.

It did indeed, though not in a way either of us expected.

When the coach pulled up to Nohant, ready to transport Casimir, Maurice, and me to the mountains, I was alone in my room. I made a note in my journal bidding goodbye to Nohant, for I feared that I might never see it again if I was, in fact, consumptive. But then, smiling in the false manner to which I had become accustomed, I climbed in for the four-hundred-mile-long journey, which would take several days.

On the first day, I tried reading the poetry of Ossian, but darkness soon overcame us, and I was resigned to sitting with my thoughts. I closed my book and looked out at nothing, trying to block out the ceaseless complaints of my husband, who found no joy in the journey and could focus only on when we were going to arrive.

When we traveled through Châlus and Périgueux, my heart was aching. But by the time we passed Tarbes, I felt a change in my mood. When we got closer to the mountains, I moved to the top of the coach, where Casimir was, to ride with him and the driver. Casimir was still irritable at how long the trip was taking, and asking imperious questions of the driver, as if the man were trying to deceive him, or as if the trip would be cut in half if only *he* could take the reins.

As for me, I wanted to better see the breathtaking scenery: the poetic undulation of the land and the majestic rise of the snow-capped mountains in the distance, never mind the heat and dust of where we presently were. Those mountains were awe-inspiring not only in their breadth and height and beauty but by the plain fact of them being there, by the mystery of their creation.

After we reached the foothills and began our steep climb up, both Casimir and I were often overcome with fits of a nervous laughter. In those instances, I felt closer to him and began to think perhaps we could find our way back into the kind of happiness we had once enjoyed. I looked forward to our having a relaxing vacation together.

Outside of Cauterets, we were met by Jane and Aimée, and then we went on to our hotel, where we had a furnished apartment. I felt greatly content to be there.

When I awakened the next morning, we were surrounded by fog. Then, little by little, the landscape began to reveal itself. It seemed an apt metaphor for what I was experiencing, for the way I felt Casimir and I were coming back to life. But then I realized I was to be left alone: Casimir was going hunting; he would be gone until nightfall. "But what am I to do all day?" I asked.

"We are here for your health, are we not? I suggest therefore that you attend to it." The door closed behind him. He was off to the out-of-doors and to adventure, where he would see the wondrous things we had been told about: waterfalls coming from rock walls that rose straight up several thousand feet and bridges made of snow, crafted by nature, though they looked like the handiwork of skilled stonemasons. Casimir let me know that he meant to go hunting often, if not every day. And starting tomorrow, he would leave at the proper time: so early in the morning that it would still be night.

As for me, I was meant to stay in the hotel and take the cure, which required the charming activity of being doused with water and then wrapped in a blanket for hours. Then I would be surrounded by society people whose attempts at conversation, I knew, would be anything but stimulating to me. They would be an imitation of the many dinners I had been made to endure in Paris. Those people may have been fine for Jane and Aimée, but I was incensed. I soon found a more like-minded friend with whom I could escape, and escape with her I did.

Her name was Zoé Leroy, and she was the twenty-eight-year-old redheaded daughter of a well-to-do wine merchant. She was staying with her family across the street from me. The streets were so narrow in that town that one could carry on a conversation across them, and that is how Zoé and I began our friendship, each of us looking out our windows one morning, exchanging pleasantries at first about the beauty of our surroundings. But then one day Zoé said, "I must confess that I find it a bit dull here." With that admission, with which I robustly agreed, we were soon taking excursions on horseback by ourselves, galloping along the narrow mountain roads and, when they got too narrow, walking on them. Rather than lying pale and wan beneath my blanket at the hotel, I was outside, leaping from boulder to boulder in clean air under a turquoise sky, hoping to encounter a bear. My companion had no husband ordering her about or restraining her, and I relished the freedom I, too, enjoyed by being with her.

One day, Zoé and I were joined by a friend of hers, a twenty-six-year-old man named Aurélien de Sèze. He came from a long line of prominent jurists and was himself distinguished as a junior at the Bordeaux Bar. With his thick, dark, curly hair, large black eyes, and oval face, he rather resembled me, I thought. I had no belief in love at first sight, yet upon meeting him I felt an undeniable visceral stirring; and I believed Aurélien when he later told me that love at first sight is precisely what he felt for me. We discovered early on that we were true soul mates, despite the fact that he was a monarchist and a devout Catholic, whereas my beliefs—political and religious—bordered on or were frankly heretical.

Zoé was only too happy to help facilitate Aurélien's and my relationship. In one of our confidential chats, I had told her, "I may have married too soon."

"What you did, my dear, was to marry the wrong man," she said. "He is all dullness to your effervescence. He is crippling you."

She had had enough of Casimir even before the day he chastised her and me for "making ourselves conspicuous." This is what he called it when, on a trip from Cauterets to Gavarnie, Zoé and I rode ahead of our party in order to escape their empty chatter and constant complaints.

"What a relief to be without those citizens from the land of banality," she told me as we waited for them to catch up. "Let us enjoy ourselves before they get here. Let us take in this extraordinary beauty in a *conspicuous* way!" I laughed, but her face grew serious and she said, "Aurore, you must never apologize for your superior intelligence and your insight. You have so much more to offer than those others who spend their entire lives never having one serious thought! And you deserve so much more than you have!"

I knew exactly whom she thought I deserved.

Aurélien was rich, he was handsome, he was an aristocrat; but what drew me to him was his facility with language and his natural wit. He was the most well-spoken person I had ever known and, like me, adored poetry. He was able to converse with ease and insight on many subjects, including philosophy and religion and literature, subjects that Casimir had no interest in.

Aurélien was engaged to a beautiful young woman named Laure Le Hoult, whom, he soon confided, he had discovered to be uninteresting and cold, with a flatness to her personality that her dazzling good looks had at first obscured. This he told me on a day when Casimir again went hunting and left me to seek my own pleasure, and my pleasure that day was a horseback ride with Aurélien. We had stopped by a stream to let the horses drink when he walked over to stand close to me, a warm light in his eyes. "I hope I will not offend you by telling you that meeting you has convinced me that I have made a mistake in proposing to Laure. Had I known that there was a woman such as you—"

"I am married, Aurélien."

"As I am aware. And in sharing this with you, I mean only to . . ."

He sighed and looked into my eyes, and I felt a yearning to step closer that was so strong I had to move away.

But I was pleased by the admission; I could not hide it. After so long a time of feeling unwanted and unloved by Casimir, I found Aurélien's words wonderfully uplifting. But when he put his arm around me, I gave him a look that made him rapidly remove it.

"Aurélien," I said, "I believe you may have been as deceived by me as much as by your fiancée. I am not always the gay adventuress you have been spending time with these last few days. I am oftentimes melancholy, full of an unhappiness I cannot explain, and in that state I am seemingly unreachable. So far as I can tell, my future is one of sadness; I have no hope that things can change. I cannot leave my husband, nor do I believe that I will ever achieve any sense of joy with him. I have chosen badly, but I have chosen. And miserable though I may occasionally be, I would feel worse if I were to betray my morals."

"Then I will console you in your misery," he said. He moved closer to me and pressed his lips to my neck.

It burned me. Literally. I jumped away from him and chided him, but my words could not convey an anger I did not feel, and he understood me to be glad of his affections. And there we were. Powerless to move forward or back, suspended in a way both agonizing and delicious.

He apologized, shamefaced. "It is exceedingly difficult to keep my ardor in check around you, Aurore. Yet my morals are the same as yours. And so at times when my will is weak and I attempt to make advances, I must ask you to resist me."

We made a pact, then, to embrace our platonic romance, to find and enjoy in each other the pleasures we could not find in the people we were bound to.

When a tragedy occurs, one has a moment of innocence upon awakening the day after; one has forgotten the sadness of the day before. But then sorrow lands heavily at the center of the breast and all but steals the breath away. So it is with joy; one awakens having forgotten a happy event, and then remembers, and experiences a feeling like being shot through with light.

The day after Aurélien's admission to me, I awakened, lay still in the bed, and then laughed aloud. I put my hand over my mouth to muffle the sound, but I had no need for doing so: Casimir was long gone, as usual, and rather than feel abandoned, I was relieved.

It was a very different feeling than when I had first been left to my own devices. Then, I had made a melancholy entry in my diary that spoke of how, when a husband took himself from his wife's side because of duty, it was a sadness shared and tolerated by the two of them, the sadness mitigated by the expectation of the pleasure they would enjoy when they were reunited. But if a husband needed to be away from his wife in order to live his life more fully, the wife experienced a loneliness made worse by humiliation.

It was not humiliation I was feeling now but a galvanizing excitement. I rose to tend to my toilette, to dress and breakfast, to spend time with Maurice before turning him over to the nursemaid, and then to go outside to find Aurélien.

Cauterets was a small town, and it was easy, not to say inevitable, to run into people again and again. I saw Aurélien often: with his fiancée, with Zoé, and, for brief, exhilarating periods of time, alone.

At one point, we went on a boat ride, and he carved the first three letters of our names into the boat. I had watched him doing it, but when he finished, I looked off into the distance, as if I had been unaware. "Look," he said. "Even our names begin the same way."

I made a face that suggested a kind of indifference I did not feel, and it hurt him. This spontaneous and joyful act, inspired by love, he now saw as juvenile and overly revealing; and he probably wished he could snatch the moment back for the sake of his dignity. The color rose in his face, he pocketed his knife, and we spoke very little until we reached the shore again, where we parted ways.

For the next three days, Aurélien did not speak to me. I suffered more in those three days than I ever had with Casimir; I wanted to die. Even the darling antics of little Maurice did not lift my spirits:

those times I took him from his nursemaid, I felt I had nothing to offer him. Having enjoyed with Aurélien the brightness of an engaged and loving presence who aroused a sensuality in me that I had despaired of ever finding, now I could not—or at least did not want to—be without it.

The next evening, the sky was dramatically streaked with violet and rose, and I went outside alone to enjoy it. I was walking in the street when I saw Aurélien coming toward me. I went quickly to him and asked if I might have a word.

"I am on my way to meet my fiancée and her family," he said, in a way so pointed I felt sure it was designed to hurt me. But then, seeing the pain in my eyes, Aurélien took my arm and led me into the shadows. "What is it?"

I stood straight before him, my hands clasped tightly together. "I want to tell you that I did not respond to your romantic and endearing gesture of carving our initials on the boat because I'd promised to resist you. If I had shown you what it meant to me, one thing would have led to another, and we would be engaged in something we would end up regretting. Acting on our love would put an end to it, because we would not survive the pain we would cause innocent others. I must ask again: Given our circumstances, would it not be best for us to be chaste lovers, sharing of each other's minds and hearts alone? Might we in this way honor our obligations and yet satisfy our deepest desires?"

I knew, asking him this, that men were unlike women, that it was much more difficult for them to be without some sort of physical expression of their ardor. But Aurélien said, "Aurore, I love you for your mind and your soul, your superior intellect. It is not now nor has it ever been my intention to cause you any pain. I am sorry if you suffered on my account, thinking that I would ever ask you to do otherwise. I am, my dearest, quite simply yours; and obliging you is my best happiness."

I could not speak for joy, and his face was radiant. He took my hand, kissed it, and we walked our separate ways. I felt my life had tipped on its axis toward the proper angle. Even the prospect of Casimir coming home and regaling me for hours with what he believed were scintillating tales of shooting eagles did not mitigate my joy.

AURÉLIEN HAD MADE PLANS to take an excursion with Laure and her family to Gavarnie. I asked Casimir innocently if we might join them, and he agreed. On the way there, Aurélien managed to find a way to ride beside me.

"Thank God you have come," he said. "Behave as though I am extolling the beauty of these cliffs and let me say instead how enchanting I find you, how perfect your exotic eyes, your supple waist. But know, too, that I would love you if you were ugly."

I laughed, as did he. Then he said, "Soon we will have to part, but I will write to you and in this way attempt to preserve every tender feeling we have. I hope that you will answer me. Zoé has agreed to be our courier."

The notion was thrilling. "How can you think I would not answer you? You suit me so perfectly. No matter what we are talking about, I find your words delightful."

"I feel the same. And though I respect the wisdom of keeping our relationship to our minds and hearts, know that I nonetheless do indulge my imagination from time to time." His eyes did not move from mine, yet I felt them travel the length of my body. "Please understand that I say this not to embarrass or dishonor you but to touch you in the only way I can—or will. I mean to find a way to sing the praises of an irresistible woman; being with you, one is helpless not to."

"Where are you?" Laure called from up ahead, her voice thin and peevish. Aurélien gave me a burning glance before he spurred his horse forward. I watched him go, thinking it did not matter any longer where he was, when his heart belonged to me. I flashed a smile to Casimir, because love from another had made me generous toward him.

Soon it was August, and time to go home. Casimir and I felt that an abrupt descent from the mountains might be difficult for Maurice, so we decided to stop for several days at Bagnères-de-Bigorre. This was a fashionable spa, pleasant enough, with its cheerful clientele and the colorful carriages being pulled through the streets by handsome horses whose high stepping and prancing made Maurice clap and point. Its location in a wide depression in the land made one feel held in the palm of a gigantic hand. But then the heat began to take hold. I looked at the Pyrénées in the distance with longing, but of course it was not just the comfortable climate I missed.

On our last night there, Casimir and I were having dinner when I saw what I thought at first might be a hallucination. Aurélien was approaching our table. And then there he was, as real as my racing heart.

Hearty greetings were exchanged between him and Casimir, while I had all I could do just to speak. "Join us for dinner!" Casimir said, and Aurélien agreed, pulling up a chair and stationing himself at a safe distance from me. Everything about him had grown dear and familiar to me; I watched him cut his meat with an odd kind of proprietary pride. The very way he sat in the chair seemed perfect, artful; and I resonated to the intelligence and charm he displayed in talking about the most minor things.

Later, when Casimir left the table for a moment, Aurélien leaned in close to me and spoke urgently: "I could not go on to Bordeaux with my fiancée and her family; I had to come here and find you. I had to know if what I felt for you was true. Seeing you now only confirms it: you ravish my senses, you have my heart and my very soul."

I flushed with pleasure; I wanted to leap into his arms and tell him to forget my words advocating moral responsibility and restraint. But here came Casimir back to the table. He put his arm about me and said it was time for bed.

I said a prim good night to Aurélien, but then I added brightly, as though it had only now occurred to me, "Aurélien, on your way home tomorrow, would you like to ride over to Lourdes with Casimir and me, to see the grotto of the wolf? It is a unique experience, quite stimulating to the senses, I'm told." I could feel Casimir's eyes boring into me, his discomfort at my inviting Aurélien on our expedition without asking his permission first. He no doubt took umbrage at the sexual undertone in my description of the place, as well. I didn't care. I felt a sense of desperation at the idea of leaving Aurélien again, so soon; and I knew that at least some of the time during the eighteen-mile journey, I could ride side by side with him without raising Casimir's suspicions. And indeed that is what happened: several times, for a few minutes each, I rode nearly knee to knee with Aurélien, grateful for the opportunity.

At the Grotte du Loup, we joined other tourists in crawling on our bellies into the cave. Then, as we progressed farther and could stand, we entered into a darkness so deep we could not see our hands before our faces. Our only source of light was the flickering torch the guide at the head of the party held, and we were bringing up the rear. At one point, I felt arms encircle me from behind, I felt someone pulling me against him and pressing his slightly opened lips to the nape of my neck. I did not scold Aurélien, I did not move away from him; rather, I leaned back for a moment, wishing that we could spend days in that forgiving and obscuring blackness.

All too soon the expedition ended, and Aurélien and I were again saying goodbye. I was relieved that Casimir's attention was diverted long enough that Aurélien could add one final thing to his otherwise formal farewell: "Hold in your heart what I said: from now on, I live to please you."

I watched him ride away from Lourdes and felt as though he were taking my vitality with him. That night in bed, Casimir made amorous advances that I did not think I should resist. But as he drove himself into me, I imagined it was instead Aurélien. Afterward, overwhelmed with guilt, I lay there listening to the sounds of my husband breathing, full of shame at the notion that though I had not betrayed him in the flesh, I had in spirit.

The first betrayal is the hardest. It is also the one that helps facilitate the second, and the one after that, and the one after that. And so it goes, until it is seemingly effortless to transfer from one set of arms into the other. Yet it is anything but effortless. Rather, it is the most arduous and soul-wrenching thing one can do, to search endlessly for a way to stop searching.

December 1833

VENICE, ITALY

When Alfred de Musset and I traveled from Paris to Italy, I was well until we reached Genoa. There, I became aware of feeling feverish. I also had stomach pains but did not want to mention them to Alfred. But that night, there was no hiding the fact that I had dysentery. Alfred had wanted to see the ballet and did nothing to hide his disappointment that we could not go. I told him to go alone, that I would be all right without him. I made that selfless offer hoping he would refuse it, but he took me up on it and returned at such a late hour that I was sure he had done more than watch women dance. I was too sick to care.

In the morning, I was far from recovered, but well enough to travel. We were driven down the coast to Pisa, which I saw through a kind of fog. By evening, when we were in the hotel and Alfred asked whether I would prefer next to go to Rome or to Venice, I no longer cared. "Flip a coin," I told him, feeling as though I were speaking from the bottom of a barrel.

He did flip a coin: heads for Rome, tails for Venice, and it came up tails. Then he flipped it again, for good measure: Venice. He flipped it seven times in all, and it came up Venice every time. He lay on the bed beside me and kissed my forehead. "It seems it is our destiny to go to Venice! That means we can visit Florence on the way." He began to list all the sites we would visit in that historic city. I did not hear them all; I fell into a sound sleep, from which I hoped to awaken refreshed and well.

In the morning, I felt better, although weak and a bit unsteady on my feet. When we arrived in Florence, we saw far too many museums and churches for the state of my health, but I did not want to complain.

When we finally arrived at Mestre, that mainland part of Venice on the Adriatic, it was ten o'clock at night, and I nearly wept with relief to learn that we were one gondola ride away from the Albergo Reale. This was a beautiful hotel that had once been a palazzo, and I had booked us a two-bedroom apartment there. We climbed into the hooded black gondola, which in my state reminded me of nothing so much as a coffin. There were curtains that provided privacy to riders, and were I feeling better, I would have covered my lover with kisses. As it was, Alfred drew the curtains aside and I lay against the colorful eiderdown cushions, watching the world glide by. Even in my condition, I was dazzled by the sight of the city: the rising of the moon over the still waters, the domes and terraces and the intricate fretwork. In the darkness there, the sky held on to blue, and the stars shone down with a different kind of luster.

Our rooms at the hotel were magnificent. We had our own ornate balcony, high Gothic windows looking out over the quay and the lagoon, and a blue-wallpapered drawing room complete with piano. I fell gratefully into bed and prayed for a complete recovery so that we could enjoy this place together.

FOR SEVERAL DAYS, I felt well and we enjoyed exploring the sites. The city, though toned down from its previous independent status and Byronic lasciviousness by the straitlaced Austrian government, was still a delight. It was like a Turner painting come to life; and the changing colors of the sky alone were enough to provide ample entertainment. Add to that the delicious character of the Venetians (what joy to hear the gondoliers exchange insults about each other's circumstances of birth and then, once safely separated by a significant distance, vow to murder one another using their oars as weapons!), the sumptuousness of the food, the muted roar of the Adriatic crashing onto the shores of the Lido, the cannon shot that announced a new day, followed by the tolling of the church bells, and one felt that one did not want ever to leave.

At night, I lay in the arms of my lover, soothed into sleep by recalling the wheeling seagulls I had seen against a cobalt-blue sky, or the towers and domes of the city whose silhouette at night suggested a kind of magical forest, or the little lights that beckoned at the end of the canalettos.

Then I woke with a crippling migraine, which plagued me off and on for days. A physician named Pietro Pagello was called to bleed me, which offered some relief. But the bleeding did nothing to affect the attitude of my lover, who had become distinctly unloving. He sat slouched in a chair and pouted one evening as I lay resting on the bed before dinner, saying it was frustrating and dispiriting traveling with someone who was sick all the time. My response was an aggrieved silence. Had I not given him permission to go out alone and enjoy himself? All I had asked was that he stay away from gambling at the Lido. But did he honor that request? No, and then I had to beg Buloz to send me money to cover his debts.

He stood abruptly. "Let us at least go to La Fenice tonight," he said. "All you will have to do is sit up straight in a chair and listen to music. Do you think you can manage that?"

"I have no desire to see opera that will pale next to that which I see regularly in Paris," I said. "What I can *manage,* as you put it, is dinner in the hotel, which I would hope to enjoy with the man who purports to love me—the same man who is traipsing around Venice in the footsteps of his heroes, Byron and Shelley, in search of inspiration, which has so far eluded him, and whose efforts—or lack thereof—are being financed by me! We've been gone for over a month, and you have produced nothing!"

His face turned bitter. "I wondered how long it would take for your anger to show. Well then, as long as you have seen fit to speak your mind, I shall do the same. Let me bare my soul to you, as you are always insisting you want me to do.

"I feel I have made a mistake, George, and that I do not love you after all. What I have experienced with you on this trip would make anyone understand why I have come to this conclusion. Rooms reeking from gastric assaults and a woman who cannot bear the unearthly beautiful light of this place because her *head* hurts and, when she does feel marginally well, holds back in love because of some prudish nature she heretofore had not revealed. I want spicy, wild sex, not this! The only thing you are passionate about is locking yourself up at night and writing your precious fiction, ignoring all that is before you here, which, if you would pay attention to it, would make your stories infinitely richer! You write on demand, like a parlor trick, and expect me to do the same. But I require inspiration to write, and inspiration comes from living *life*!" He took a breath after this long-winded barrage, then spoke quietly: "No, I do not think I am made for this."

It was as if I had been shot in the chest. I sat wide-eyed, unmoving.

"I'm going out," he said, and he left. I did not see him for days. I waited, and I worked. Parlor trick! No, it was survival.

When Alfred finally appeared again one morning, he looked terrible. He was feverish and pale and said that he believed he had contracted a social disease. No doubt he had, but this was more than that. Any anger I held toward him fell away; he was the man I loved and the precious son of the woman to whom I had made a promise to care for him. He and I were stranded here together. In his gay times, he belonged to all; in illness, he had only me.

I sat him on the balcony in the sun and covered him with a blanket. I arranged for food to be sent up, but he could eat nothing. That night, he was delirious, sweating, occasionally leaping out of bed and moving monsterlike about the room, naked and yelling at the top of his lungs. He was a small man, not much taller than I, but when I tried to restrain him, I failed. All I could do was hang back in fright and wait for the episode to pass.

The next day was even worse; his skin burned to the touch, and he was barely responsive. I called upon the hotel staff to help me, to once more send a doctor to our apartment. Pagello came again and diagnosed typhoid fever. "He is dangerously ill, madame," he said. "I feel I must stay here with him."

And so Pagello and I together stayed at Musset's bedside for eight days and nights. I did not leave him even to change my clothes. I kept close to him, alert to his every move.

When Musset slept, Pagello and I often talked in whispers; we had need of passing the time in some way other than regarding the rise and fall of our patient's chest.

Musset was ill for weeks. After the critical first week, Pagello began coming only twice a day, in the morning and in the evening. I began to look forward to these visits very much. I knew he found me attractive: in one of our low-voiced conversations, he had told me he had seen me the first day I was there, sitting out on the balcony with Alfred, smoking. "You were wearing a scarlet turban, and that is what at first attracted my attention. But then I saw your eyes, and I could not move. I asked my companion, 'Who is that woman?' When I learned you were the great writer, I was further impressed."

I looked away and did not respond, but I confess that his words felt comforting, in the wake of the tongue-lashing I had been given by Alfred. In addition to that, Pagello was a very handsome man, with wavy hair and large, expressive eyes and a gentle voice. He was rumored to be much in demand by the women of the city.

Once when Musset lay sleeping, Pagello pulled me gently onto his lap and kissed me. I did not resist him. It was such pleasant relief from my role as nursemaid, and in any case, Musset and I were through—had he not told me as much? Eventually, the handsome doctor and I began spending time together in the room adjoining Alfred's, each of us attuned to any sound that might come from our patient. I luxuriated in the attentions of a stable, even-tempered, and practical man who was a gifted healer in more ways than one.

One night, as Pagello and I sat talking in low tones, we heard Alfred raging, making accusations about Pagello seducing me. I rushed to his bedside and told him that the doctor and I were just talking—about him! Alfred was right in what he suspected, of course. But I did not feel I could admit to these altogether justified transgressions when he was still so ill.

By the time Alfred fully recovered, in mid-March, I was convinced that I was in love with Pagello. And so when my old lover attempted to renew our physical relationship, I wanted no part of it. I would not then or ever be involved with more than one man at a time.

Alfred and I made plans for him to go back to Paris. I told him I would accompany him to Mestre, then bid him adieu. I would stay on in Venice another few months, to finish my novel.

Now the shoe was on the other foot. Alfred said he was resigned to my decision, but with his wounded eyes, his sorrowful smiles and his frequent sighs, he seemed devastated. In a letter he sent me first thing upon arriving in Paris, he told me he had gone to my apartment and put to his lips a cigarette that, on the evening of our departure, I had smoked half of, then stubbed out in a flowered saucer. He had smoked the rest of it, and he told me it was because he had wanted to feel what I had felt; he had wanted, in this strange and long-distance way, to have the feel of my lips on his.

He wrote that he had been wrong to say he did not love me, for he did; and he ached in his despair at having lost me. But because he loved me, he said, he would wish me well in my new relationship. He knew I would not be returning to Paris until August, and he hoped he might see me then, even if it was in the company of my new lover. He thanked me for finding him a child and making him a man.

When his letter arrived at the hotel, I read it on the balcony and then bowed my head and wept. For from the moment he departed, I had missed him. It came to me that I was able to love Pagello only as counterpoint to Musset.

But when I looked up, I was soothed by the beauty around me. In late afternoon, the light turned the lagoon into liquid copper. Every day, I could hear the songs of the gondoliers and the cries of the fishermen and the good-natured arguing by housewives over the price of melons. There were beautiful gowns and exotic masks worn at balls, lavender clouds at sunset. I could take walks in narrow alleys or lie back in a gondola for an evening ride that passed beneath the Bridge of Sighs. From the window behind the desk where I wrote at night, I could see lambent lights reflected in the dark waters, the luminescence seeming to ride the waves; and on foggy nights, veils of mist rose and swirled on journeys of their own. Spring was coming soon, and Pagello had said the moss would turn emerald green, flowers would overflow from the balconies, and the caged nightingales people kept there would sing.

IN JUNE, I DELIVERED my latest novel, *Jacques,* to Buloz. I also penned an essay, "A Letter from Venice," to be published in the *Revue.* Then, in fourteen days, I wrote a novella called *Leone Leoni.* It featured a character based on Musset who was extremely complicated, to put it kindly, but also divine, and another character based on Pagello, whom I described as a simple savior. Buloz, particularly captivated by the character based on Musset, said it was the "strongest and most vigorous" character I had ever written. The praise sat uneasily in me, for I had drawn more heavily on a real person for that character's portrayal than I ever had before. What would all of my readers in Paris make of this thinly disguised Musset?

I considered not publishing the book after all. But then I decided that, like it or not, this was unalterably my profession. Love, hate, betrayal, adoration, deceit, truth, lies—it was all grist for the mill. It took many years for me to learn that all need not be—indeed should not be—said. But by then, of course, much ink was out of the bottle, and one could not pour published lines back into it.

At the end of July, I made my way back to Paris. But I was miserable there. Without a love relationship, I found the city cold, even mocking. I could find no comfort, even in my work. In desperation, I decided to go to Nohant.

It was not my turn to be at the estate, and so Casimir would be there as well. Ironic, I thought, to be fleeing Paris and going back to the husband I had so decisively left on that January day three years ago.

All the way back to Nohant, I stared out the window at the landscape, taking the most private of inventories, wondering if I should have done anything differently, reviewing again the slow fall that had led Casimir and me to the place we found ourselves in now. I thought of Aurélien and Cauterets, and all that had come to pass in Casimir's family's home afterward.

September 1825

GUILLERY, NEAR NÉRAC
GASCONY

AFTER THE GLORIES OF CAUTERETS, THE COUNTRY HOUSE OF THE Dudevants had, in my opinion, little to recommend it. It was dark, furnished roughly, and the quarters were cramped: Casimir, Maurice, and I were given two rooms on the main floor where we were always in one another's way. It rained ferociously, causing both the river and its tributaries to overflow. Fog enshrouded the woods we bordered, where wild pigs ran over the mossy earth. At night, the wolves howled, and I never got used to it; each time, the sound made for a sensation like needles pricking my backbone. Sometimes they were right outside our bedroom window, gnawing at the wooden shutters.

The meals were heavy and greasy, the sauces too rich for my constitution. There is little more tedious than sitting for hours at a table and eating virtually nothing, while those around you grunt in satisfaction.

While I adored my father-in-law as much now as when I'd first met him, the baroness, my mother-in-law, was a different story. Without saying a word, she made it clear that she believed Casimir needed to do more to take his wife in hand. I knew she found me demanding and moody, unwilling to graciously play the proper submissive role. My heart aching with missing Aurélien, I would not accommodate her: I gave her cold remark for cold remark, silence for silence.

I was restless, stuck there for many long hours without the company of my husband, unless I chose to accompany him on hunting expeditions. Though the hunts alleviated the boredom, they were not something I wanted to devote my life to, and Casimir never seemed happy that I was along, anyway. I was without my books, without my harp or piano or guitar, without friends. The people in the area, though kind in many respects, were uncultured, and I found no one with whom I could engage in conversation. I would often sit alone at the edge of the bed, holding back tears. "Casimir hunts, and I age," I wrote to Zoé. I wrote to Aurélien, as well, through Zoé, and it was through her that he wrote back to me. This epistolary relationship made survival in that bleak place possible.

One day I received a letter from Zoé inviting me to visit her in La Brède, where her family had a house. She suggested that Casimir and I pick her up in Bordeaux, and we could travel together from there. I was anxious to accept, because Aurélien was in Bordeaux.

I convinced Casimir that we should go because of the number of his relatives living in Bordeaux. We could stay there for a few days before continuing on to La Brède, I told him, giving him plenty of time to visit all of them.

Despite the letters that had flown back and forth between Aurélien and me, I had been worrying about losing the love I was suddenly so dependent upon. Aurélien had vowed that our relationship could remain platonic, but I feared that if I did not eventually submit to him, I would lose him entirely. And if I submitted to him, I believed I would not be able to live with myself. How to embrace my child, Maurice, who every day came running into my arms, when those arms had held a man other than his father? I wanted to see Aurélien and talk openly to him about this dilemma.

Casimir agreed to this visit, in part, I'm sure, because of my flagging spirits. I believed he looked at me as he might a problematic wheel on a carriage: something that he would rather not spend time on but that needed to be fixed in order that he could go on with his life. So it was that in early October, we left Maurice with my in-laws and journeyed to Bordeaux. With every mile that brought us closer to Aurélien, I felt better.

Yet it was with a mix of joy and despair that I first saw him. Zoé had told him where I was staying, and on the second day, when

Casimir had gone out to visit an uncle, Aurélien came to the hotel room.

When I opened the door to him, all my plans for how to receive him—gladly, but with restraint—fell away. I burst into tears. He rushed to me and took me into his arms, and I leaned into him for support, my head on his shoulder. And then I closed my eyes and stayed there, because the feel of him was so wondrous and so welcome. When I at last opened my eyes, I saw Casimir standing at the threshold. On his face was a look of incredulity that rapidly turned to rage.

"Leave this place immediately!" he told Aurélien, who started to speak but was quickly silenced by Casimir repeating the command, much louder. I feared that all the guests in the hotel would hear. Aurélien gave me a helpless glance, then quickly strode off.

Now Casimir turned to me.

I backed away from him. "No, you misunderstand. I have not . . . we have not . . ."

"You will never see him again. Ever!"

I fell to my knees, sobbing. I could find no measure of control. I wept so hard, I could scarcely breathe.

"Please, please," I said. "I have not dishonored you. He is only . . . It is an innocent . . ." Again, I began to sob. I tried to get up to make my way over to my husband, who stood a few feet away with his arms crossed, his eyes narrowed, but I fell again, and then lay still on the floor. "What have I done?" I moaned, and I meant losing Aurélien, for I thought I surely had.

Casimir took my words as a confession and an apology to him. He crouched down and patted my shoulder and spoke with a gruff tenderness: "Now, now. We shall overcome this. There are troubles that come in the course of a marriage; we shall be strong and carry on."

I had thought, when he came over to me, that he was going to strike me, and I had turned my face away and covered it with my hands.

He did not strike me this time, but I wept on and on. Finally, from what seemed like a faraway place, I heard Casimir say, "Enough. Let me help you up, Aurore." There was some fear in his voice.

Then Aurélien appeared again at the still-open door, and Casimir moved toward him, his hands balled into fists. I was too hysterical to hear what the two men said to each other. But in a few minutes, Casimir closed the door, then came to sit in a chair near me. I sat up, but did not yet trust myself to stand.

Casimir spoke quietly, calmly: "I understand now what has transpired between the two of you, and I forgive you, Aurore. I forgive you both, and I grant you the same freedom you had before. It will be upon your head if you choose to deceive me; but I know you as an honorable woman, and I believe you will uphold your true values. Come now, stop crying; it is over. We shall carry on as before, all three of us."

"Thank you, Casimir," I said, over and over. I moved to sit on the floor beside him and gingerly laid my hand upon his knee. After a while, he put his hand over mine. I thought, *I will give Aurélien up, I will not see him again.*

By morning, though, my feelings had changed. When Aurélien had first come to the room, he had given me two letters, which I had stuffed into my bodice before I fell into his arms. That night, when I changed clothes before bed, I hid the letters in a book I had brought along. At dawn, I tiptoed to the window and read the letters, standing with my back to Casimir, who lay sleeping.

What Aurélien told me in those pages made it clear that he neither expected nor desired a consummation of our relationship. Out of his great respect for me and my morals, he was prepared to continue with what we had: a chaste and, as he and I both saw it, a superior love. I cherished the idea that I could still have him.

Thus it was that, astonishingly, the four us—Zoé, Aurélien, Casimir, and I—set out for La Brède the next day. We chatted pleasantly, enjoying the beautiful fall day, and when my husband took my hand in front of Aurélien, he and I only stared levelly at each other.

When we arrived at La Brède, Zoé and I went upstairs to refresh ourselves. There, I told her all that had happened the previous day.

"Ah! It will be all the more interesting, then, to see what is written here," Zoé said, pulling from her bag a letter that Aurélien had given to her that morning to pass on to me.

I read it immediately, my hands trembling. Then, with tears in my eyes, I told Zoé that Aurélien said he had stood outside the whole night, looking up at my hotel room window to see if a light came on, worrying about whether or not I was all right. He said that he would do anything he needed to in order to take all the blame for what had passed between us. He would allow himself to be called or would call himself a rebuffed seducer, he would sacrifice anything for my safety, he loved me, adored me, now and forever. Our relationship was the centerpiece of his life, but if I wanted him to, he would let me go; he would always sacrifice his happiness for mine. Only tell him what I wanted; he would do it.

I looked at Zoé, who shrugged. "Well, what *do* you want?"

The truth sprang from my mouth: "To give myself to him."

"Tomorrow, then," Zoé said, as blithely as if I had requested to take a leisurely stroll on the grounds. "After Casimir goes hunting. He will go hunting, will he not?"

I nodded.

"I'll tell Aurélien. I am glad for the two of you."

Leaving me to dress for dinner, she turned suddenly at the threshold, grinning. "Alert me when you awaken; I will help you prepare."

I WORE WHITE. ZOÉ LAUGHED, calling it overly obvious, but I liked the way I looked in that dress. She had come to my room before the sun was up and had helped me with my hair, with the selection of my undergarments.

"Do you suppose he is being as meticulous?" I asked Zoé.

"Of course! Just now, I imagine he's looking into the mirror, saying, 'Top hat or not? Pearl stickpin or . . . oh no, look, a nose hair gone wild!'"

We laughed, but I was nervous; my mouth was sticking to itself, and one hand continually massaged the other. Zoé poured me water and cautioned me not to drink all of it. She stood back and regarded me when I had finished dressing. My dress was ankle-length and had a pleated bodice. A black velvet belt accentuated my small waist, and a round neckline showed off my bosom. The sleeves were puffed and ended with a frill at the wrist. I wore the double-stranded pearls my grandmother had given me, trying not to think of what she might say about what was going to occur. My shoes were black and dainty, and I reminded myself to take small steps and not go running to Aurélien the moment I saw him. Zoé dabbed perfume at the back of my neck, straightened a ringlet at the side of my head. She handed me a beautiful silk shawl, something she had recently purchased and had yet to wear herself.

"Are you ready?" she asked.

"Yes."

She kissed my cheek. "He awaits you in the garden, beneath the oak closest to the back of the house."

I descended the staircase quietly, aware that with each step I was getting closer to something I could never undo and might profoundly regret. I kept on.

Once outside, despite the dimness, I saw him immediately. He stood with his back to me, and I could tell by his complete immobility, his overly correct posture, that he was nervous, as well.

When I got closer, he spun around. "Aurore. My God, how beautiful you are!" He held his arms out, and I stepped into them. I closed my eyes and luxuriated in the scent of him.

He said my name again, softly.

I stepped back and looked up into his face. He smiled tenderly. "I have worried so about you. Tell me what happened after I left you in Bordeaux. He didn't hurt you, did he?"

"No. He forgave me. He forgave us both."

His face was uncomprehending.

"He has left it to us to behave in a way that will not dishonor us. He says he trusts us."

As soon as I said the words, I knew I should not have. Aurélien stepped back, away from me, and hung his head. "I did not sleep last night, for worrying about the pain we might cause if we were found out. But now . . . Ah, Aurore, what nobility he has shown, in leaving it to us to decide whether or not to betray him! What a great heart we would wound if we were to go forward with what we long to do! And however much pleasure we would enjoy, what agitated guilt we would harbor afterward!"

"But then . . . what shall we do?"

He sighed. "There is no answer. I cannot have you; I cannot be without you."

"Aurélien," I began, in the calmest, most reasonable voice I could muster, but he seemed not to hear.

"In giving us our freedom, your husband has made us prisoners of our conscience. Aurore, we cannot go on with this. We must cease even from exchanging letters."

"But then you love him more than me!"

"No, no, my darling, of course not. But surely you see what an impossible situation we find ourselves in. Let us live in the memory of our love, but also in peace. In time . . ."

I knew there was no persuading him away from his decision. He looked deeply into my eyes, then motioned for me to go back to the house.

When I climbed the stairs to my room, I encountered Zoé in the hallway. "Aurore! What has happened?"

I offered the smallest movement of my hand.

"Shall I come with you?"

"Not just now," I said, surprised by the calmness of my voice.

I wanted to sit by myself for a while. Then I would change out of my white dress and black shoes and into the simple blue dress Casimir favored. I would fold the beautiful shawl so that I might return it to Zoé.

Soon, though, I heard a light tapping at my door, and when I opened it I found Zoé and Aurélien standing there. I ushered them in, and all three of us wept, then laughed together. Aurélien said we would maintain an innocent correspondence and, in that way, our platonic love; Zoé had persuaded him to do so.

When Casimir and I departed to go back to my in-laws', I left the white dress hanging in the armoire. I vowed to make every attempt to change my attitude toward what I saw as my fate, to live out my life with a man I did not love.

BACK IN GUILLERY, I endeavored with all my heart to love my child and my husband and married life, even the little hunting lodge in which we were living. It was not the kind of countryside I was used to, with its sandy soil and dark woods of evergreens and cork trees, their deep shadows unrelieved by shafts of light. But the weather had warmed, and I followed winding paths beneath the saplings and found small streams running alongside gigantic ferns. The babbling sound of the water delighted both Maurice and me. Occasionally, when the air was right, one caught sight of the Pyrénées, which lay ninety miles away. They presented themselves in a kind of pink haze with a silver overlay, and whenever I saw them I had to steel myself against a kind of crushing melancholy. But I did that. I also made efforts to get along better with my mother-in-law, and Casimir and I went to parties and visited people who lived in the grand manors nearby. I did not turn away from my husband in bed. Still in all, it is a lie for me to say I truly cared for anything there but Maurice.

To Zoé, I wrote of my frustration at not being able to say in letters to Aurélien all that was in my heart, to find a place for passion at least upon the page. I had made a promise to Casimir that he was free to read the letters that passed between Aurélien and me, and so I was careful to keep them neutral in tone. Zoé, ever practical, and ever on the side of true love, freed me with a single question: *Did you promise Casimir that you would let him read your journal?*

Delighted, relieved, I began pouring my heart and soul onto the pages of a journal that I would eventually pass on to Zoé to give to Aurélien. It was a perfect way to honor my promise and still express to Aurélien everything I wanted to. I wanted him to know me as completely as possible, and so I shared with him memories of growing up at Nohant as well as things about my day-to-day life in Guillery. I took particular pains to describe the way my flesh longed for the touch of his.

On the rainy morning of November 6, Casimir was on his way to Nohant, where he was going to check on things. He was looking for some papers regarding our property in the desk in our room, and he found my journal pages, meant for Aurélien. From the tone of his voice when he called me into our bedroom, I suspected what had happened.

"Sit down," he told me, and I sat at the edge of the bed, trying to keep my face impassive, though my heart was racing. I laced my fingers together to keep my hands from shaking. He reached into a drawer, pulled out the pages, and waved them before me.

"What are these?" His face was florid; he struggled to keep his voice low.

"I gather you already know," I said. What defense could I offer? I waited for him to mete out some sort of punishment.

But he only flung the papers to the floor and left the room, then the house. He was off to Nohant as planned, and I sat in a hunting lodge where I did not want to be, the pages in disarray at my feet.

After a while, I picked the pages up and put them in order. I would not destroy them. They were only the truth. I put them back in the desk drawer and left the bedroom to tend to my son.

I found him sitting with his grandfather, who was regaling him with a story about when he'd gone out riding through the woods to visit a friend, and by the time he arrived at the gate of the house, fourteen wolves surrounded him. Fourteen! Yes, he counted all the tails, and that's how many there were. Fourteen. This was a story I had heard many times, and I was glad to see my father-in-law was telling it in a way that served to amuse and not frighten my son.

I sat down a distance away and listened to the ending, the part where one of the wolves leapt up and snapped at the hem of my father-in-law's cloak. There was nowhere to run. So my father-in-law coolly confronted the danger head-on. He dismounted, removed his cloak, and snapped it in the faces of the wolves, scaring them all away. "A mere waving of a cloth, and they ran home to their mothers, their tails between their legs," he said. "They climbed into their beds and pulled the covers over their heads. 'Oh, I am so frightened, wee wee wee!' So you see? Sometimes the things we fear are as afraid of us as we are of them!"

Maurice beamed, then said, "Again!"

My father-in-law smiled at me over the top of Maurice's head, and I smiled back.

Then the sun suddenly pushed through the windows, a welcome bit of warmth and light. The rain had stopped, and my father-in-law told Maurice to come with him; they would go outside for a bit of roughhousing. I was very glad of this, for I had just gotten an idea for something I wanted to do, and I did not want to be interrupted.

In the bedroom, I laid out paper on the desk and began a letter to my husband. I would not offer my throat to the wolf. I would stand up and defend myself.

Soon afterward, I received a letter back from Casimir, one full of love and hope. He had read certain demands I had made and found them fair. He had wandered about at Nohant, and when he stood in the library, he was full of regret for the way he had never made any real attempt to read the books there. He saw that he had taken me for granted and had not ever really understood who I was. But he would no longer be so blind; he would cooperate with me in trying to revitalize our marriage.

I recall reading that letter, my head bowed over the page, my heart full of hope. Easy to say I should have known better.

Fall 1826

NOHANT

LESS THAN ONE YEAR AFTER WE HAD VOWED TO REPAIR OUR MARriage, I sat with Casimir in the parlor after dinner, trying not to let anger overtake reason. I had just learned that he had lost thirty thousand francs of my marriage settlement by investing it in a nonexistent merchant ship; he had been swindled. Casimir's father had died the past winter, and his stepmother had not seen fit to give my husband anything. He was totally reliant on my fortune, and now he had lost a significant amount of it.

A number of things came to my mind, but in the end I elected to say only this: "We are finished with you running this place. Starting now, I will take over."

I expected an argument, but I did not get one. Instead, Casimir rose heavily from his chair and walked out of the room. Then I heard the front door slam, followed by the pounding of his horse's hooves. He would be going to Château de Montgivray to see my brother, I was sure of it, and he and Hippolyte would drink themselves into oblivion. Or at least that is what he would tell me. In fact, it was more likely that he would be going to see Hippolyte's wife's maid, a young and beautiful Spanish woman who had once worked at Nohant, and with whom I knew Casimir was intimate. I had found her in bed with him on a day when I returned home earlier than expected from one of my shopping trips to Paris. I fired her immediately, fired her as she stood in the middle of the room weeping, a sheet wrapped hastily around herself. Later that night, Casimir tried to persuade me to take her back. "Be reasonable," he said. "You know these things happen." I would not take her back, and so Hippolyte hired her.

Most of the time, my marriage felt like trying to hold on to fog. Worse, at least so far as I was concerned, there was little to Aurélien and me any longer, either. His letters had cooled markedly in tone; I felt sure that he had found someone with whom his passions need not be sanitized or relegated to black lines on a white page.

A year passed this way. My health began to suffer; I had frequent chest pains and migraines. I resolved to go to Paris for medical consultations and found someone willing to accompany me there. That was Jules de Grandsagne, the brother of Stéphane, the young man with whom, as a girl, I had delved into the mysteries and glories of the body when he had instructed me in my room at Nohant. I would go in late December, and Jules said he was sure Stéphane would like to see me. As I would him.

December 27, 1827

PARIS

"Aurore!" Stéphane de Grandsagne stepped aside from the door and gestured to the interior of his apartment. I came in and moved a pile of books from a tattered gold velvet settee so that I could sit there. Then I took full measure of a man who had lost none of his attractiveness, despite his gauntness and the dark circles beneath his eyes. His muttonchops made still more pronounced the height of his cheekbones. His dark hair was still thick and curly, his nose straight, and his lower lip full. Nor had he lost a way of looking at me that was thrilling.

"How goes the collection?" I asked. On the way to Paris, his brother had told me of the efforts Stéphane was making toward building a people's library. "He's working himself to death!" Jules had said. Stéphane wanted to provide at least two hundred books, on every subject, so that working men and women who were otherwise denied access to advanced schooling could educate themselves. I had come to visit Stéphane to congratulate him on his enterprise and to see if there was anything I might do to help. But I also came because I remembered him as someone to whom I could speak intimately and openly, a true friend.

"We have made great progress, and I am pleased," Stéphane said. "But you, Aurore, I see that you are . . . Are you unwell?"

To my chagrin, tears began to stream down my face.

He pulled me up from the settee and into his arms, and kissed me.

I protested not at all. Not in the slightest. And a full hour later, when I arose from his bed, I observed with wonder that nothing in my body or soul hurt; it was as though Asclepius had laid his hand upon my brow and offered me his mythical cure.

But the next day, on the way back to Nohant, I stared out the window of the coach and was overwhelmed with remorse. I knew immediately, as I had known with Maurice: I was pregnant.

When Solange was born, I saw that Stéphane's features were unmistakably in her face: she looked nothing like Casimir and not even like me. Yet the only one who directly questioned me about this was Aurélien de Sèze, who happened to visit us at the time of Solange's birth. Casimir bore him no jealous grudges any longer.

As Aurélien sat alone with me in my room and Solange lay sleeping on my breast, he gently laid his hand on the top of the baby's head and stroked her hair with his little finger. I was reminded of the softness of his touch.

"She is beautiful," he said. Then he sat back in his chair and regarded me seriously. "Behind your back, people are saying that the child is Stéphane de Grandsagne's."

"Yes. I know they are."

"Is it true?"

I didn't answer.

"Do you love him?" he asked, and I heard the pain in his voice.

My eyes filled. "It's you I love," I whispered. "Still."

Now it was his turn to be silent. I didn't know if it was because his own feelings had changed or if he simply had not heard me. I did not repeat myself. He stood, started to speak, but then did not. He kissed my forehead gently and left the room. I continued to stare at the chair where he had been sitting and quietly wept, until Solange awakened and I turned all of my attention to her. Never mind that it was someone else who had conceived her with me; Casimir was her father and my husband. I would persevere. I would overcome. This deception would be woven into Casimir's and my life together; after a while, we would not notice it. We were civil enough. But from now on, Casimir and I would have separate bedrooms. That much truth I had to allow.

December 1830

NOHANT

THE WRITING I DID IN MY LITTLE ROOM AT NOHANT WAS PROGRESSING. What once had been random observations and journal entries were becoming pieces of fiction that took on a kind of authority of their own. I learned that wind informed, that memory informed, that hopes and dreams did. So, too, a fork on a plate, an unopened letter, the shine of wet on cobblestoned streets—all of these could help shape a story.

Solange was now two, an imperious toddler who at bathtime inspected her belly button with the gravitas of a field marshal sizing up his troops. She offered me toys with an emphatic thrust that on occasion nearly knocked me down.

Maurice was a young philosopher who told me on his seventh birthday, "Now I have entered my first old age."

Together, they ran and shouted and played all day; at night, when I tucked them into bed, I was grateful for the fact that they had both a mother and a father here with them.

Sometimes, when there was peace between Casimir and me—if, say, we sat together in the parlor while the wind lashed the trees and rain drummed hard on the roof and thunder boomed and lightning lit up the sky so brightly one needed to close one's eyes against it, or if one of our children did something that made us smile at each other—at such times, I would chastise myself for ever wanting anything more, or for having made declarations and demands one moment that I only regretted making the next. From the time I'd been a child, I had wanted to probe and comprehend the mysteries of life. I had wanted an elemental loneliness to be taken away by an abiding and comprehensive love; I had wanted, too, to know an ecstasy that would last forever.

But perhaps I needed to think about what I had. And perhaps I needed to understand that one could not look for a constant when life—and people—were ever changing.

January 1831

NOHANT

ONE MORNING WHEN I WAS ON MY WAY TO PARIS TO VISIT MY MOTHER, I went into Casimir's study to tell him goodbye. He was not there, but on his desk was an envelope with my name on it, with instructions not to open it until his death. It was his will, I was sure, and for a moment my heart was full of tenderness for him. I was moved as one always is when considering the death of someone near. Casimir had told me he was writing a new will, so as to include certain provisions for the children.

I opened the envelope, feeling that, since it was addressed to me, it was my privilege. But when I saw what he had written, the blood left my head. It was not a will at all. Rather, it was a letter to be given to me after his death, and it was full of vitriol. He had detailed transgressions fueled by my "perversity." He had expressed his disgust and total disregard for my person.

I had brought myself to a kind of peace in our marriage. But now I had to admit the truth: we were a couple ill-bound by strained tolerance on one side and hatred on the other. Casimir did not occasionally find me disappointing or irritating or vexing and then return to an abiding affection for me. I saw now that he had stayed with me for my fortune, nothing more.

He lacked the courage to speak the truth to me in life, but he had no compunction about saying it after his death, when his letter, so full of rage and maledictions, would hurt me more—and when he would not have to defend himself against any response of mine. He was cruel, and he was a coward.

It was enough. I thought, *I will leave him.* Whatever sorrow or defeat may have been in that decision, it was overshadowed by relief.

I considered my options. If I told Casimir I wanted the children half of the time, he would fight me. So as a ruse, I would tell him I was going to live full-time in Paris, without the children. This would frighten him into some sort of compromise I would not be able to effect otherwise.

My old habit of optimism took over: I moved quickly to the door and out, the letter in my hand. In the hallway, I came upon Casimir, his cheeks red from the cold, his spirit jaunty. When he saw what I was holding, he stopped in his tracks. "Aurore," he began, his tone split between reprimand and apology.

I handed him the letter and said calmly, "I'm leaving you and the children to go and live alone in Paris."

So it was that the day came when I heard the sound of the carriage wheels crunching on the gravel, and I walked out of the house at Nohant to start a new life, to start living.

September 1834

NOHANT

HAVING LEFT MY LIFE IN PARIS TO COME TO NOHANT, I LAY BY the river, very near the place where Marie and I had bathed the summer when she'd visited. The children were playing in the woods. I had kissed them many times before I'd separated from them that morning, until they'd finally pulled away from me in exasperation. Maurice was eleven, and outgrowing his tolerance for what he saw as excessive maternal affection, and six-year-old Solange was ever in the habit of pulling away from me.

I had kissed my children so earnestly because I was saying goodbye. A melancholy more extreme than any I had ever felt had come upon me. I could find no relief even in writing. The fantasies that had flowed effortlessly from me from the time I sat in my improvised playpen were coming to me no longer. I sat at night before the white pages I used to fill with stories, and nothing came. Nothing.

I was thirty years old and felt old as time. I had failed in every love relationship I had attempted: with my mother, with God, with marriage, with Aurélien, with lovers, with my children. And with Marie, whose light still shone brightest for me, who still seemed the one with whom I might have been enduringly happy. These days, I enjoyed her company in friendship and no longer aspired to anything beyond it; I would have embarrassed myself in attempting it, and I had no doubt that any attempt at rekindling romantic love would have turned her away from me entirely. She had finished with that the day she'd left Nohant, and I knew perhaps better than anyone that it was always easy for Marie to leave behind what no longer engaged or amused her.

Marie was gone. Musset was gone. One is not living when one does not use the parts of oneself that are most vital, most especially the need to love and be loved. In that respect, I was already dead.

I stood and watched the river run past, imagining lying on the silty bottom and letting my lungs fill with water. I imagined the peace of nothingness, a lifting of the weight I found lying across my chest when I awakened every day. I took a step closer to the water's edge.

And then something happened that was as startling as what I experienced in the convent chapel. I heard above me a great and sudden rising up of sound, a euphoric trilling of what must have been one hundred birds in the tree beneath which I had lain. I watched them fly away as though on cue, and the despair I had been feeling seemed to fly off with them. At first I stood immobile, afraid to believe that this had happened. But then I became full of an invigorating resolve and walked quickly back to the house.

At the beginning of October, I would return to Paris and put Maurice back in school. I would enroll Solange at a boarding school I knew of where the classes were small, and where I hoped she would profit from the discipline and the structure. I saw that I had been making that most common mistake of a parent who feels unappreciated: that of being lax and indulgent in an effort to be loved, when it is the opposite behavior that encourages a child's adulation.

That morning, I had received a letter Musset had sent me a few days ago from Baden, where he was trying to cure himself from the effects of his hard living. Over and over again, I had read his grieving lines:

> *Tell me that you give to me your lips, your teeth, your hair yes, all of them, and that head which I have held between my hands. Say, oh say, that you embrace me—you—me. Oh God! When I think of these things a lump comes into my throat, my eyes grow dim, my knees tremble. It is horrible to love as I love! How thirsty, George, how thirsty I am for you!*

I had felt it best not to encourage him and, nearly numb, had written that we must never meet again. Now I would tell him otherwise.

October 1834

PARIS

ALFRED AND I MET AGAIN AND VERY SOON AFTERWARD RESUMED our physical relationship. But then he began drinking in excess, and he told me it was because he had learned—from Pagello telling everyone—that the good doctor and I had been intimate before Musset left Italy, not only afterward; I had lied to Alfred. And so I admitted it, thinking that this would be the end of it. Instead, it started a new cycle of abuse.

Without warning, Alfred would go into a sulk and at those times pepper me with questions about the lovemaking between Pagello and me. At first, I tried to remain calm, but then I grew angry. What right, I asked, had he to chastise me about being with another after he had rejected me?

We had been back together for only a few days when I hurled this question to him, and he erupted into one of his famous rages and stood nose to nose with me to scream, "You will never understand me or, indeed, any man! My God, George, your naïveté astounds me! How I regret my time with you—all of it! Again we are come to this: I no longer love you. Who could love such an unfaithful and selfish being whose only thought is for herself and her desires? At least the other whores I see admit to their true natures and professions! I am finished with you. Do not attempt to contact me."

He slammed out of the apartment. For weeks, I stayed in Paris, hoping we would resolve things. After all, he had done this before: denounced me and then rushed back to me to proclaim his love. I thought Musset did love me, and it was the devils in his nature (and of his acquaintance) who sometimes talked him into pushing me away. I sent him notes of love, then of anguish, to which he made no reply.

For diversion and to lift my spirits, I agreed to sit for the artist

Eugène Delacroix, who had been commissioned to paint my portrait for the *Revue.* I felt an instant bond with that great and handsome man. He seemed leonine to me, with his overhang of brow, his great head of tousled black hair, and the narrow strip of beard he wore directly down the line of the deep dimple in his chin. There was wisdom and compassion in his dark eyes, as well as a kind of knowingness that made one feel seen to one's core. It was a disquieting ability he had. Marie once said of him, "Most men look at me clothed and imagine my body naked; he looks past my body straight to my naked soul."

Although Delacroix was inordinately perceptive, he had the strength of character not to use what he saw in any sort of manipulative way. I trusted him from the moment I laid eyes upon him, and when I sat for him that first time I began to pour my heart out to him about Alfred. But I had hardly begun my story when he exclaimed, "Ah, yes, Alfred Musset, the poet. An extraordinarily gifted young man, not only in literature but in art. He could make his living as an artist, I have no doubt. Did he ever mention wanting to do so to you? For if he would like, I could take him under my wing."

"No, he only amuses himself with drawing. He does not want to commit himself to it. His first love . . ." My throat tightened, and Delacroix looked up from his easel.

"His first love is poetry." And then, to save myself, I changed the subject: "I should like to invite you to come sometime to my country home at Nohant. I believe you would enjoy painting there in any season."

"Perhaps this winter, I shall."

"Do; I shall set up studio space for you."

I made sure we avoided the subject of Alfred for the rest of our visits, and at the last sitting I secured Delacroix's address so that I could write to him when I was back at Nohant.

A few nights later, I visited Marie in her dressing room. We spoke about Alfred and me. As jilted lovers do, I looked for my mistakes, wondered aloud about how things might have gone in a different direction *if only,* examined aspects of the relationship from every side.

How many broken women, I wonder, begin sentences with, "But he said . . ."

When I said that to Marie, she burst out loudly, "'But he *said,*' 'But he *said,*' 'But he *said*!' When did he say it? In your arms! Or seeking to be in your arms!

"Ah, George. In this state of arousal men are as wild-eyed as a dog with a steak over his head, and as the dog will do any trick he knows to get his meat, so will a man. He will tell you anything. And when he has spilled himself inside you, you will swear it was his brains that were left there, for he will have little or no memory of the amorous words that sprang forth from him. Or if he does remember, it will be because he has memorized them to use on such occasions." She laughed. "I tell you, their acting ability at such times makes me look like an amateur! If only I could watch them and take notes. See how he lowers his lids to murmur these words of love! See how he runs his fingers through her hair! And this *growl,* emanating from deep within; how he has perfected the tone so as not to be frightening but exciting! *Regard le tigre!* And now cue the trumpets, here comes the charge of the penis, the wild clenching and unclenching of the buttocks! What exhilaration in the rhythm of the ride, what calculated intensity, how this maestro conducts his little orchestra of body parts!"

I said nothing. She knew what I was thinking; she knew the way a woman in love wants to believe that her man is not anything like the others.

She spoke quietly then: "George. When it comes to the treatment of women, one man is like any other. You don't want to believe it. I don't want to believe it. But it's true. Your poets answer to the call of their groins even as do the peasants in the fields. Women long for words to sear their souls; men offer them the best they can do in that regard and then immediately forget what they have said.

They have their way and then go out to piss against a wall and think about what they might have to eat."

I sat still, thinking that Alfred did not forget his words of love; he was in thrall to his own utterings at least as much as I was. Then Marie said, "What you must do is ignore him. For another well-known fact is that men want what they cannot have. We have talked about this before, George. My advice to you is that you do not endeavor to see him. Do not write him. Ignore him! Then see how fast he comes scratching at your door." She yawned and apologized for doing so.

"It is I who should apologize," I said. "I forget that people do not stay up all night as I do." I hoped she would beg me to stay; but she did not. Instead, she sleepily escorted me to the door.

I walked out into the empty streets, where the fog lay in a thin blanket over the Seine. I walked with my head down, my hands in my pockets.

Marie had tried to help me, but the only friend's words I had heard and resonated to lately were those of Sainte-Beuve. I had passed him recently on the street on a rainy day, and we had sought warmth and shelter in a café. Over steaming cups of café au lait, we began talking about the break between Alfred and me. "Poor George," he said. "I must tell you: in some ways, I feel responsible. I should never have arranged for the two of you to meet."

I shook my head. "Even in pain, I feel grateful that Alfred and I shared our love, though it was so full of strife it makes me wonder if it really was love. I confess that oftentimes I don't think I understand love. How would you define it?"

He stared out the window at the rain sluicing down from the awning. Then he smiled sadly and looked over at me. "Tears. If you weep, you love."

Well, then, I thought, *I have loved a great deal.*

I ignored Marie's advice to ignore Alfred. I wrote to him again, telling him that he could spurn me as often as he liked but begging him to say that he was not forever closed to the idea of us seeing each other again, if only sometimes, if only on occasion and with no conditions attached. I begged him to say that he had not really meant "never again."

Again, my note went unanswered. And then I heard he was out in the bars, laughing, carrying on, and often saying spiteful things about me. Finally, in deepest despair, I again returned to Nohant, but not before again inviting Delacroix to visit me there.

December 1834

NOHANT

I WAS NOT A WEEK AT NOHANT WHEN I RECEIVED A NOTE FROM ALFRED, a sincere and naked apology for his outbursts, his temper, his cruelty. He included a lock of his hair, something I had asked him for long ago.

I sent him back a leaf from my garden and nothing else. It was all I wanted to say: once alive, now dead, still beautiful.

And then I received news in a letter from one of my Berry friends that Musset was telling everyone that the breach was final: he and I were never to be together again. He had been seen in the company of the same woman several times, a petite blonde, quite beautiful and apparently also well bred.

Delacroix was outside painting the day I got that letter; I read it sitting on a bench in the garden near the place where he was capturing the deep gold of late-afternoon light through the naked boughs of the trees.

I felt a great surge of emotion and longed to speak with him, but I did not want to disturb him. I would tell him at dinner what had transpired. Quietly, I took my leave and went off to my bedroom. I sat holding Musset's lock of hair and then went to the gardener's shed for a pair of shears.

Back in my room, staring into the mirror without really seeing myself, I chopped a great hunk from my black hair, which Musset had so loved and praised, which he had gathered it into his hands to kiss. I cut another piece, then another, then another still, until I looked like an ill-kempt peasant boy; my shorn locks fell unevenly around my face and stuck up in the back. I bundled the hair I had cut off in a package. I addressed it to Musset and laid it on a table in the hallway. Tomorrow it would be posted.

In the hall, I passed a maid, who tried not to show her shock at my appearance but failed. Her eyes widened, and I heard the sharp intake of her breath. I stood my ground until she curtsied and moved on. Then I went back to my room, sat at the edge of my bed, and sobbed, my hand pressed hard into my chest.

We are all fools in love, all of us, even the strongest among us. Anyone who claims otherwise is worse than a fool: he is a liar.

"MON DIEU!" DELACROIX SAID as we sat down to dinner that night.

I looked calmly over at him.

"George."

He moved to my chair, tenderly kissed my forehead, and stared into my eyes, reading at once my sorrow. Friend that he was, he did not ask me to explain. He knew that I would tell him what I wanted when I was ready. All he said was "Let me do your portrait. Never have I seen such terrible beauty."

I let him. He captured my pain in the way my eyes stared off at nothing and, somehow, even in the empty space around me. He drew my lips gone thin and pale. He drew the irregular lines of hair that now barely reached the bottom of my neck, framing a woebegone face whose flesh seemed to droop. I had carelessly folded the ascot above my redingote; it almost resembled a hangman's noose. What Delacroix created was a portrait of hopelessness.

Yet it wasn't long after Musset received the package with my hair that we were locked once more in a desperate embrace. "How

I wept that day!" he told me. He had come to see me at Nohant at the end of December, and in January, I had returned with him to Paris.

For six weeks we both enjoyed and suffered through the last gasps of a dying love. Finally, due mostly to his ongoing jealousy and increasingly abusive treatment of me, we really had finished with each other.

In March 1835, I returned to Nohant without telling Musset I was going. I knew if I did tell him, he would come over and create a scene.

My first night back there, in a state of great tranquillity, I produced twenty pages of writing. I had found myself again, and as well my voice on the page. I no longer loved Musset, but I did not hate him. In a letter of farewell I wrote to him, I said:

> *But your heart, your good heart, do not destroy it, I beg of you. Give your whole heart or as much as you can to every love of your life, but let it play its part with dignity, so that you can look back and say as I do, I have often suffered, I have sometimes been deceived, but I have loved. It is I who have loved and not some artificial being driven by ego and ennui.*

I meant to soothe him, to restore some sense of equanimity to both of us. But my words did more than soothe him. Later, in one of his plays, I heard one of his characters say:

> One is often deceived in love, often wounded and often unhappy, but one loves, and when one is on the edge of the grave, one looks back and says: I have often suffered, I have sometimes been deceived, but I have loved. It is I who have loved, and not some artificial being driven by ego and ennui.

When I heard that, I only smiled. My last gift to him. That play by Musset, incidentally, was called *Don't Fool with Love.*

There were times when I wondered what it said of Musset that he so often and easily deserted me, that upon our final break he immediately began a romance with another, while I was for so long unable to recover. But then what did it say of me that it took a young man weeping in my lap, wiping his nose with his fist in the fashion of a schoolboy—what did it say of me that this is what he needed to present to me before I could fall in love with him?

Late March 1835

NOHANT

THAT SPRING, I FOUND MYSELF EXHAUSTED—PHYSICALLY, MENTALLY, spiritually. Even nature did not offer its customary solace. I turned to Plato, to Shakespeare, to the Koran and found no relief. I played the piano, dull-eyed, and ate without tasting. I knelt at my bedside once again, bowed my head, and begged to feel Corambe. I called out in silence to a being who seemed to have abandoned me.

I continued to work, however, filling pages with a tranquil penmanship that belied the tumult inside. But there had been a change in the way that I wrote. My popularity and deadlines and financial obligations meant that I could not take all the time I wanted to finish my stories and novels. Now, as ever, I dismissed the thought of my being a great writer. Nonetheless, I wanted to do my best. But toes tapped, and hands grabbed pages before I was quite ready to let them go. I envied the writers who could let everyday events, random encounters, memories, and dreams weave themselves into their work. I knew I did my best work when I let that second mind, that unconscious force, take over, when it felt as though I were drifting along in a boat that guided itself. But that kind of writing was impossible to do with the pressure I now felt.

I was turning my short story "Mauprat" into a novel. Like my other books, it reflected my life, this time the future as well as the past. For although I wrote about mental anguish and entanglements and a disturbed way of thinking, which reflected aspects of my time with Musset, I also focused on things beyond the individual. I addressed myself to problems in society that prefigured the politics I was soon to be actively engaged in.

Writing served to lift me away from myself and the sadness I was feeling. But when I wasn't at my desk, the pain could be excruciating. Most of my Berry friends seemed to be of one mind, and the advice they gave me was to try to reconcile with Casimir. Wouldn't living in a kind of placid peace with him be better than what I was enduring now? Where had all my lofty ideas about passion and romance gotten me?

Over and over again, I tried to explain my own sense of ethics when it came to love and sex: one needed the former to engage in the latter, or else one was a prostitute. "Then be one!" my friend Alexis Dutheil implored me. "Be Casimir's mistress, for the sake of your children, for the sake of your own mental health!"

He said this even after I told him about an incident when friends were over and Casimir, in a drunken sulk, had ordered me out of the drawing room for the crime of comforting our son, to whom Casimir had spoken cruelly. I did not comply. "I'll box your ears!" he said, and I laughed at him. Bad enough that I reacted this way, but my response prompted the other guests to laugh as well. At that, he catapulted out of his chair and then returned to the room with his hunting rifle. His face was flushed, his eyes wide; I all but expected him to froth at the mouth. He was subdued by one of the guests, and I do not think any among us believed that he would actually shoot me. But he had gone to the gun cabinet. He had had the weapon in his hands.

IN THE YEARS SINCE I had left, Casimir had kept to the same routine: hunting, drunkenness, and women. He managed Nohant poorly, constantly losing money, but erupted in anger if anyone tried to suggest things that might help. He did not care to converse on any topic but local politics and the weather, and the latter only insofar as it pertained to his ability to hunt.

I, on the other hand, had built up a life full of painters and writers and musicians and philosophers and dissidents. Yes, I had been devastated by Musset, but at least it was a poet I had loved, not a man who had no appreciation for the arts.

In Paris, my dinner parties often lasted all night; my guests made their way home at dawn, silly with drink but deeply inspired by all they had shared with one another. There was always much laughter, shouts of appreciation, even applause. Franz Liszt could sometimes be persuaded to play, and when he did, we all felt enraptured and elevated.

It was Alfred who had introduced me to Liszt and his mistress, Marie d'Agoult, whom I nicknamed Arabella. She had left her husband and children to be with Liszt, and she served as inspiration for a very different kind of revolution that was being talked about ceaselessly in the streets of Paris. Bad enough that she had abandoned her husband and family for another man, but to have a child out of wedlock with him and show not a flicker of remorse!

Having children changed everything, but it did not decide everything. And so I vowed that instead of staying with a husband I could not abide for the sake of my children, I would try to teach them to live by their consciences, no matter what the world around them might think, or say, or do. I would teach them by my example.

April 17, 1835

BOURGES

I HAD AT LAST FOUND MYSELF WITHOUT AMBIVALENCE ABOUT THE direction in which I wanted to go. Now I was sitting in a restaurant forty-five miles north of Nohant in Bourges, where I had been brought by my childhood friend Alphonse Fleury. He knew the brilliant lawyer Louis-Chrysostom Michel, known as Michel de Bourges, and had suggested I meet with him here, to see if he would represent me in a process that should have been started long ago.

Divorce had been abolished by Napoleon, but one could secure a formal, legal separation with specific terms; one was barred only from remarriage. I had no interest in remarriage, but the idea of being given an equitable settlement—of having Nohant returned to me as my own and having a fair share of the money that had, after all, been mine in the first place—was greatly appealing. I wanted also a kind of sexual freedom I did not now enjoy: when one was separated from one's husband, one was not condemned for other pursuits.

Fleury thought Michel would be the best person to represent me. "He never loses!" he said. I had heard this. I had also heard that in addition to his eloquence in the courtroom, Michel had a reputation for a fierce intelligence and a charisma that had made this militant republican the much-admired leader of the current government opposition. I very much looked forward to meeting him.

When he walked into the room, I was startled into silence by the size of his head; it was as though he had two brains fused together, fore to aft. He was thirty-seven to my thirty-one, but he looked like an old man: bald, stooping, and myopic.

Michel later told me that for his part, he had expected me to be dressed as a young man. He had thought of me as a child poet whom he had long admired from afar, and that upon meeting me he might offer to make me his "son." Though I did still often dress in men's clothes, I would also, either by whim or necessity, wear dresses and bonnets, and a finely made dress of peacock-blue silk was what I had on that night. There was no mistaking the fact that I was a woman.

He took my hand and bowed. "George Sand. May I tell you first that I am a great admirer of yours. *Lélia* is a work of genius."

"From what I have been told, you are the genius."

Fleury had told me Michel was married to a rich widow. I saw that he dressed like the peasantry he came from, in clogs and a rough greatcoat—though I noticed beneath that a blindingly white shirt made from the finest linen. Upon his head, he wore handkerchiefs fashioned into a kind of cap that would be permissible to wear indoors; it helped to keep him warm, for he was always cold. Something about this humble garb on such a fiery personality made me able to immediately relax. And there was an occasional softness to his eyes that suggested that somewhere inside this radical was a gentle spirit.

"Tell me the purpose of your meeting with me," he said, and I told him far more than that.

I told him about my upbringing, about the relationships I'd had, finally about the way that on the face of it, I lived an aristocratic life, but my heart and my politics were ever on the side of the people. "I am not one of those who look down upon their servants," I said, and he threw back his head and laughed. I recognized the irony and blushed.

"Understand, it is more than that," I said. "I have always tried to see the worth of the individual despite the clothes he wears, the place he resides, or the accent with which he speaks. I grew up playing with peasant children, and I—"

"Bah! Because you drop into their world now and then does not make you one of them. You find them interesting, charming, you pick from what they offer to suit your own needs. Then you go home to a plate full of fine food and sleep in imported linens."

I looked pointedly at his white shirt, and he smiled. "I suppose we can all be caught out in hypocrisy one way or another," he said. "But my wearing a linen shirt is not tantamount to your blowing kisses from the balcony of the privileged to those who suffer below. If you speak kindly to your house staff, if you write a few articles in a newspaper about the rights that should be given to every person, you have not done your duty."

"And what is my duty?"

He studied my face. "Your duty is to use whatever talent you have to make for a kind of equality among people that we are nowhere close to achieving, and that many people do not want to have. Your duty is to persuade those who do not want it to, if not embrace it, at least accept it; and if one method does not work, you must engage fully in another."

"You mean radicalism, fighting in the streets."

"And perhaps more than that." He grabbed hold of my wrist and spoke quietly but with great earnestness: "Life is difficult enough in and of itself, George. Is it not incumbent on us to create a social order where we do not let the weakest fall and the strongest survive?"

I pushed my empty wineglass away from me, staring into the burgundy residue at the bottom. "I listen in shame to your ideas of revolution and reform. You are right to suggest I have led a life of solipsism. Despite my mother's blood, which runs in my veins, I have watched from a distance the people's struggles and have reported their anguish without real understanding. I have allowed romantic passion to rule my life and have committed myself to faithless individuals rather than worthwhile causes."

"Mea culpa, mea culpa, mea culpa. You remain solipsistic in excoriating yourself for your solipsism! Have done with that, George! You are here and alive, are you not?"

I said nothing, full of a rising hope that prevented speech.

"Your life is not over; it is about to begin! You will never be satisfied with the love of an individual; that kind of love will only disappoint. Turn your gaze outward, away from yourself, and toward a noble goal. It is that kind of purpose that brings lasting content, that speaks to the truest desires of the heart and the needs of the soul."

I was galvanized by Michel's words, inspired in a way that seemed superior to the passions I had known before. I committed my writing talents to the cause and then, inevitably perhaps, to Michel himself. For his part, he gave me a ring to serve as a symbol of what we might look forward to when we were both free.

After a few months, though, I began to see that I did not always agree with Michel. I began to think he was similar to those he wished to overthrow: a despot who demanded a slavish loyalty and affection from his followers. It seemed that Michel invoked the name of the people in order to bring glory to himself.

CASIMIR HAD INITIALLY AGREED to our separation. Then he changed his mind and fought against it for over a year. But finally Michel secured for me a legal separation that left me with Nohant, with custody of Solange (later, I also obtained custody of Maurice), and with ninety-four hundred francs annually. Casimir received less. My fiery lawyer argued brilliantly for me, Madame Aurore Dudevant, sitting demurely in the courtroom in a white hood and a white dress with a collar of flowered lace.

Michel addressed himself to Casimir with a kind of deadly irony. He looked at a paper in his hand and said, "You list here Madame Dudevant's many faults. To name a few, you say that she often dressed like a man and smoked cigars. I assume that you found that very . . . Well, I confess I have a hard time guessing. Was it frightening? Dangerous? Did it break a law of which I am unaware?

"Never mind—we shall move on to the next complaint, which is that she had relationships outside the marriage." Here he looked up. "Perhaps in imitation of you, who only weeks into your marriage pursued and easily conquered your wife's maid? Is not imitation the sincerest form of flattery? Or did she perhaps seek comfort with another after episodes such as the time you struck her across the face in full view of others?

"But I digress. We were talking about your wife's many flaws, not yours. So, let us see what other sins she has committed. Ah, here is a brash demand: she asks for money from her own inheritance! A wonder you waited so long to bring her to court!

"Now, here is a vexing problem. Your wife wrote *Lélia,* recognized as a work of genius. You poor fellow, I'm sure it is utterly exasperating to be married to an artist whose income pays the bills when one's own inclination is to not work at all.

"Well. Rather than bore the court with the rest of this long list of grievances, I feel compelled to ask you about something I find very confusing. Perhaps you can enlighten me. With all these faults displayed by that diminutive woman sitting there, why would you go to court to keep her from separating from you?"

He won for me easily, and Casimir moved to his family's hunting cottage in Guillery.

Despite our differences in politics, I still had feelings for Michel. But after I was free, he began to retreat from me. *Mauprat,* which was about a wounded beast of a man being subdued—transformed, really—by a woman's love, after which they marry and live happily ever after, I now saw as the wishful thinking it had been.

I was at odds with myself. On the one hand, I had written to a friend, "I will lift women up from their abject state, both in my life and in my writings." And yet, embarrassingly, I had also written a letter to Michel begging him simply to let me do all that I could to make him happy. I told him in that gushing missive that he would find me much like a faithful dog, a study in devotion.

What drew me to Michel was a passion grounded in politics. But politics will not forgive what love can; nor will politics endure what love will. Politics will not give a close embrace; it will not press upon a mouth a kiss that satisfies the beggar inside. It will not say to another: I will protect you from what frightens you; I will bring wild strawberries to your bedside; I will not betray you. Never mind that those words are often found to be lies; one longs to hear them anyway, one needs to; and one persists in trying to hear them in order to find a certain peace, without which one feels half of something meant to be whole. Even God was lonely: we, His children, are the evidence.

My affair with Michel lasted less than a year. What followed were several halfhearted love affairs with other men that died for lack of fuel to feed the flames. Finally, I told myself and others that I was too old for the ups and downs of romantic relationships and would henceforth devote myself to things that mattered and upon which I could depend. I could not have been more sincere—or relieved. Or wrong.

May 1836

NOHANT

AFTER ALL THE ACRIMONY IN FIGHTING FOR MY SEPARATION FROM Casimir, after all the charges and defenses, all the lies and half-truths—of which, I readily admit, both parties were guilty—I was at last home again, and in rightful possession of the place where I had grown up. I took up permanent residence at Nohant on a day when the bagpipes played and there was dancing under the great elms. This was because it was the feast day of a saint, but I let myself enjoy the fantasy that the celebration was also to welcome me home. Those servants whom I had not fired for their allegiance to Casimir I released to join in the festivities.

I was alone, standing before one of the windows in the dining room. I had toured the great house, I had wandered through every room, and in every room memories had assaulted my senses. I saw myself lying between my parents at night in the bedroom they had shared; I saw my baby brother, Louis, dead in his cradle. I saw Deschartres pacing before me, his hands clasped behind his stooped back; I saw my grandmother dressed in her lace and silk, her cockade trembling upon her head, instructing me on the harpsichord; I smelled her vetiver.

In my old bedroom, I had sat in a chair and spoken to the ghost of my child self, who lay on the floor in her peasant's play clothes, reading books with a great hunger and appreciation, mouthing the words to herself for the pleasure of their cadence. I'd remembered how it had been my habit to gently flick the corners of the pages back and forth as I read them, and how I had sometimes pressed my face into the folds of the books. Julie, my grandmother's maid, had once punished me for this.

Now I pressed my forehead to the glass and, with eyes closed, listened to the music being played here in the place where I most belonged. And then I wept copious tears, for all that had befallen me, and all that had not.

A FEW MONTHS LATER, I received a letter from Maurice that tore at my heart. He had been made fun of by other boys at his school, who told him of stories written about me in the newspaper:

> *They said all sorts of things, because you are a woman who writes, because you are not a prude like most of the other boys' mothers. They call you, I can't tell you the word because it is too wicked. . . . You must know what is happening in the heart of a good son and a true friend.*

Must history always repeat itself, not only in the larger ways of politics but upon the personal playing field of the self? Of course I knew what was happening in Maurice's heart; the same feelings had been in me when my own mother was attacked and derided. I vowed to find a tutor for Maurice and pull him from a school where he did not belong, even before such vicious attacks had befallen him. I knew he would not fight back against such cruelty; he would only bear it in an elegant manner completely foreign to his tormentors. In the morning, I would go to Paris to collect my son.

I went outside and wandered among the trees and the flowers, then went to the cemetery to visit the graves of my father and Louis and my grandmother. I wondered, if my father had lived, what he would have thought of my success, as well as my notoriety. I thought he would have been more understanding, more forgiving, than my mother had been.

My father had defended my mother against her accusers, my grandmother among them. He believed that the moral compass of an individual was the true gauge by which one should measure and live one's life. If that compass was in keeping with what others thought, so be it. But if not, one was meant to answer to oneself: that was the way to come to a true and lasting peace. Perhaps the only way, I thought now.

October 1836

HÔTEL DE FRANCE
RUE LAFFITTE
PARIS

In September, I had taken the children to Switzerland to spend six weeks in the company of Franz Liszt and Arabella and their newly born daughter. I was in high spirits, we all were. In addition to my children, I had brought my maid and some friends; Franz and Arabella had surrounded themselves with a gay coterie as well. We lived in a way that both inflamed my senses and calmed my nerves. I saw how the balance of work, friendship, and family made for a satisfying happiness. Absent the tension caused by my years-long friction with Casimir, I was able to focus on my children in a different way.

Thirteen-year-old Maurice was the soulful artist, the one I found easier to love. A mother wants to love her children equally, but she is human, and she can favor the child who is more like her, or at least who fights less against her.

Solange, now eight years old, had long bedeviled me. Since her birth, there had been a strange kind of dissonance between us. When I smothered her with attention, she pulled away. When I put space between us, she resented me. When I begged for access to her soul, she ignored me. She was rude to my friends. She was unwilling to cooperate with figures of authority, and yet when they became exasperated and used punitive measures, she immediately bent to their will. It was as though she rejected kindness and invited harsh behavior toward herself.

I would have been willing to assume the blame, to think that my temperament and proclivities disallowed my being a good mother, but Maurice dispelled that theory: he adored me, and I him. Being with him was like swimming in a placid pool of water; spending time with Solange was like going over the falls.

There were times when I lay in bed worrying about her, and I would resolve to do all I could to make things better between us. The next day I would approach her with my heart open, and she would hurl insults at me. She would turn her back and walk away, and I would stare after her, my love transformed into a mix of despair and—it must be admitted—a feeling like hatred.

But late that summer, I came to understand something about her. We were out in the mountains climbing one day. I was struck by her beauty: her long blond curls, the pure whiteness of her skin despite the sun. She ran up the steep inclines over and over again, complaining only if any one of us tried to help her. Once she turned to me after I had expressed a great appreciation for everything around us and said, "Don't worry; when I'm queen, I'll give you the whole of Mont Blanc."

I thought, then, that what Solange wanted, what she needed, was to be credited with her own strength and ambition. In this respect, I thought, she was like me. I let go of a kind of wariness and believed that Solange and I would finally be able to love each other openly, freely, lastingly.

—

When I returned to Paris, I gave up my apartment and moved into the hotel where Franz and Arabella lived, to the room below them. We shared a common sitting room, and it was filled with writers and artists and musicians and the wailing of Franz and Arabella's baby. Our regulars included the radical priest Abbé de Lamennais, the poet Heinrich Heine, the novelist Eugène Sue, and the socialist philosopher Pierre Leroux. So many interesting individuals, all of whom offered a kind of nourishment, both individually and collectively.

On November 5, I was invited to a musical soirée at the home of Frédéric Chopin. It was on the fashionable Right Bank, on Rue de la Chaussée-d'Antin. I saw how true the rumors were that he adored the color gray: the wallpaper was a light version of that color, beautiful against the white trim, and the brocade furniture was a shade of oyster. He liked his luxuries: he had a silver tea service displayed against a white silk hanging, and his dinner service was Sèvres, in turquoise and gold. I knew that the fresh flowers he had in abundance were replaced daily. The whole apartment, though small, gave the illusion of airy space and was a study in understated elegance.

That evening was the first time I had heard him play—he almost never gave concerts, preferring instead to earn money by charging outrageous amounts to teach and by selling sheet music of his pieces. That night, I lost my heart to his music before I lost it to the man. He played first a duet with Liszt, a sonata for four hands, then performed an improvisation, something for which he was famous. In its minor chords, I heard what I believed was a mourning for a love that he could not have. I knew about such things, and I understood the lasting melancholy that came with it. My eyes filled with tears. I put down my wineglass, walked over to the piano, and kissed him full on the mouth. *The you that I hear in this music, I understand and love—instantly and wholly.*

His feelings toward me were not precisely the same. They were, in fact, quite the opposite. After we had become lovers, he told me of the letter he had written to his family after he had first made my acquaintance. "I said you were a coarse and ungainly and crude woman who wore men's clothes and smoked cigars in public, then expressed my doubt that you were a woman at all. I said I found distasteful your devouring eyes and deep silences, and your frankness about sex I found absolutely unnerving."

The journey from that point of view to one quite different took two years. In the meantime, my busy life as a free woman went on.

January 1837

NOHANT

ARABELLA, LISZT'S LOVER, CAME TO STAY WITH ME AT NOHANT that winter when Franz was touring. We were not the best of friends. She was under the mistaken assumption, as were so many, that I was ever a fearsomely independent figure who had a well-deserved reputation for bold behavior, the consequences be damned.

I saw Arabella as a person with a cold heart and a suspicious mind who was overly concerned with appearances. She rarely wore the same thing twice, and she spent an inordinate amount of time styling her hair each day. She would mouth the words of others as though they were her own in order to make herself appear intelligent. We tried hard to get along for the sake of Liszt, whom we both loved. But when we embraced, it was with the light of day between us.

One evening, after we had had what I think both of us would have described as a surprisingly pleasant day together, we sat before the fireplace after dinner. The children, exhausted, were in bed. "You know, George, Maurice is a very sensitive young man," Arabella said.

I smiled. "Yes."

"And talented; only thirteen, but he could easily make his living as an artist."

"So I have told him. As has Delacroix."

"A wonder that Casimir so blithely handed him over to you; he is such a devoted son, such a pleasure to be around."

"Casimir is one of those lucky individuals who is rarely bedridden. He has no patience for those who suffer from various illnesses, as Maurice does. He thought Maurice hypochondriacal and all but punished him for his weakness. When he found out his son had an enlarged heart and rheumatism, he took it as an affront to his own masculinity. He was only too happy to give custody of Maurice to me. And I was glad to have it."

"Of course you were."

A silence fell. I waited for Arabella to comment on eight-year-old Solange. It had been a tiring day with my daughter, complete with displays of explosive behavior one might see in a toddler. At one point, Solange had flung her hairbrush across her room, nearly breaking a window. I wasn't sure how much my guest had overheard of all that.

Finally, I said, "I must apologize if you were bothered by any unpleasantness today."

One finely shaped eyebrow raised. She murmured something I could not hear, then turned to face me and said, "May I speak frankly?"

"Please do."

"One hesitates to criticize a friend's child. But I must say that I find Solange to be very difficult. She is a natural and unrepentant rebel, one who seems to delight in extremes of emotions. I doubt that she will ever be able to go along with commonsense rules."

I flushed, then defended my daughter in a mother's automatic way, saying, "I should be happy for her if that is so. A woman in a man's world needs to be rebellious."

Arabella turned her sherry glass slowly in her hand, and I

watched the flames from the fireplace cast colors on the liquid. When she looked back at me, her expression was empty of malice; I saw that she felt genuinely sympathetic. She said, "Perhaps what you say is so. Perhaps what I see as Solange's faults may turn out to be heroic. Please understand that I know she is not without her virtues. She is also unusually beautiful. But . . ." She leaned forward. "There is a kind of manipulation she has already mastered. She has a preternatural ability to spot one's weaknesses. You will have to exercise your own strength against hers.

"Also, if you will permit me to say this, I believe she is jealous. I suppose no one could be the daughter of one so famous and not be resentful of time taken away from her, of attentions shared by others when she wants them for herself alone. Far be it from me to advise you to deny yourself for her sake. But you must be prepared for the revenge she will take on you."

I said nothing. Already I had seen evidence of this. The carefree relationship Solange and I had enjoyed in Switzerland was now only a memory. A few days ago, when I had awakened and begun looking over my work from the night before, I saw that three consecutive pages from the middle of my pile were missing. I looked around my room, under the bed, even on the ground outside the window I had left cracked open. The pages were nowhere to be found. But when I came into the dining room, I saw that they had been thrown into the fireplace and burned: a quarter of one page lay with its charred edges off to one side, in the ashes. I knew who had done it, and I called Solange into my bedroom to account for herself. "Was it you who burned my manuscript pages?" I asked.

She stared at me, her face cold and unyielding.

"Why?"

Again, I was met with silence, and I dismissed her. I knew why she had burned the pages. She craved her mother's love the same way I had craved my own mother's—and still did. And as I was never satisfied, so Solange was destined to be always wanting. My mother was a slave to her need for love and attention. As an artist,

I belonged primarily to my work. But whereas I, for the most part, had suffered in silence from the wrongdoings of my mother, Solange would not. Perhaps could not.

I rewrote the pages and found them better than before.

Living with me that winter, Arabella discovered other things about me. My capriciousness was revealed in all its glory; every day gave her another example of how indecisive I could be; she remarked upon it humorously, but with her brows knit. She came to understand that what many people misinterpreted as coldness or disdain was actually my shyness. She, who outfitted herself in wildly expensive dresses and jewels every morning, whose hair needed to be styled just so, saw that what I preferred most was a peasant's smock.

Most tellingly, though, she saw my weakness and hypocrisy in love. Despite having renounced romantic love in general and Michel de Bourges in particular, I still wrote passionate letters to him, begging to simply cast my eyes upon him. One night, I showed her one in which I had written,

> *The delights of love are to be found not only in those fleeting hours of furious passion which send the soul careening madly to the stars, but also in the innocent and persevering tenderness of intimacy.*

She looked up from reading, and I expected her to express sympathy, or agreement that the best part of love was indeed that gentle intimacy, or at least admiration for the way I had with words. But she only said, "I should have thought you would have preferred Chopin."

She leaned over and touched my hand, and her eyes softened. "Poor George. Such a fire in your soul, and nothing for it to lay hold upon."

It is one thing to keep the shadow of love's humiliation hidden in a corner of one's soul; it is another to have someone bring it out into the open. Being revealed in this way is devastating, but it is a relief, too; one has no choice then but to acknowledge the truth, and begin the process of moving forward.

Liszt came back in May, and the house was full of sublime pleasures. He and Arabella were in the bedroom below me. Near their window, I had stationed a piano for him, and I often wrote to the sounds of his composing. I thought the birds must be in thrall to his music, for they fell silent whenever he played. Sometimes I paused in my storytelling to listen to the broken phrases he began, then left suspended in the air; and it seemed as though the breezes outside carried the music onward, where it brushed against the nodding blossoms in the garden before lifting itself heavenward.

After dinner, we would gather on the patio to talk and smoke, and one evening Arabella, who loved to dress dramatically, came outside in a diaphanous white gown and a long white veil that fell to her heels. She talked with us for a while, then rose to walk around the grounds. She was like a ghost; she would vanish behind the trees and then silently appear again. Franz and I watched her as if in a dream, beneath a rising moon that finally settled, seemingly caught in the branches of the pines. In the stillness, one could almost hear the heartbeat of the earth. I sought out Franz's eyes and understood that he heard music in what we were seeing. As for me, phrases floated into my brain. I believed that the next day each of us would translate some part of the experience into our respective art.

My guests and I had had a very pleasant day. The weather was fine for hiking, and Franz and Arabella had accompanied Maurice, Solange, and me for a long walk. The countryside offered gifts at every step: a slight give to the warm earth, wildflowers grouped like freestanding bouquets, clear running streams, birdsong of every variety, the inviting darkness and spicy pine scent of the woods.

Afterward, we had a dinner of roast chicken stuffed with lemon and garlic, fingerling potatoes, and a mix of lovely vegetables from the garden, followed by an apple tart. Then we adjourned to the drawing room, where we enjoyed piano music from Franz, card games, and charades. Maurice and Solange, who were exhausted, went to bed after that, but Arabella lingered with Franz and me. Then she, too, began to yawn and excused herself.

"I suppose I should try to work a bit," I told Franz, "but I am enjoying your company."

"I have work to do as well," he said. "Why don't we do so together? I shall sit at one end of the dining room table, you at the other."

I was not sure we could work in each other's company, but I agreed to it. Anyway, my work had been going so poorly I doubted I'd get much done no matter where I sat.

We gathered our materials, took our places, and tended to our individual endeavors. Franz worked on a score; I worked on an as yet unnamed novel. There were the sounds of quiet, for quiet is rarely absolute: the clock ticking, the house creaking, the wind rising up now and again, the owls hooting. I tightened my shawl about myself as the night deepened and the air grew cool. Once, I silently brought tea to both of us.

There was in Liszt's company a rare peace. I knew that he would not interrupt me, and I knew, too, that he would not be jealous of work that took me away from paying attention to him. It is to be expected that people who are not artists might not understand the need for one to immerse oneself totally in one's work; but it also sometimes happens that other artists feel no compunctions about interrupting, or in feeling slighted that one's attention is not focused on them first and foremost. What jealousy can be inspired by a person's singular devotion to something the other cannot share! It was a concern for Liszt, I knew, who had once confided to me that it was difficult to play the piano with a woman's arms around his neck.

Just as the sky was beginning to lighten, I wrote a few lines to finish a scene. Then, as quietly as I could, I began to gather my papers so that I might retire.

"Don't go," Franz said.

I looked up at him. "I don't want to disturb your work."

He smiled. "I have been finished with my work for some time. I have been watching you."

I was embarrassed. "I'm afraid there is not much to see."

"Ah, you are wrong. The words you are writing play out upon your brow. It is fascinating to behold."

"As music is represented in your face when you play."

"Without a doubt. But you also sigh quite often."

"Do I?"

He nodded solemnly, then imitated me, arranging his features into what I suppose he thought was a reasonable facsimile of feminine expression and heaving a sigh.

I burst out laughing, quickly covering my mouth; I did not want to wake the others.

Then I said, "Do you know, Franz, some mornings I sit in my room when I awaken, waiting to hear the sounds of your piano. And I often grow quite impatient that you have not yet started when I am ready for you to!"

"I thought you slept the mornings away."

"Only when I am working well. I am not working well lately. Tonight was an exception. When I am happy, my pen can barely keep up with my thoughts. When I am in despair, my imagination is as flat and lifeless as my spirit."

"Tell me, dear friend. What is the sorrow that fills you with such despair?"

"It is simple. I am not loved."

"But your friends, your children, your many admirers! And surely you must know how much I love you!"

"I am grateful for that. But I need romantic love as I need air to breathe. I need someone to offer body, heart, and soul and to accept mine in return."

Franz rose from his chair and came to sit closer to me. He took hold of my hands. "George, the soul of a man belongs only to God. And that is how it should be."

"I know you believe that, Franz. I know that you have not lost the ardor for God that you had as a child."

It was one of the things that made us immediately close, the similarities Franz and I shared with regard to mysticism. Early on, he had confided in me, somewhat shyly, how he used to speak aloud to the statue of the Virgin that was at his bedside as a boy. I had told him about Corambe and even shown him the spot where I had made my altar. He had moved forward into the space and stood quietly, his back to me. Then he had turned around to say, "I can *feel* what this place was to you." I had nodded, my heart full. How glad I had been to have met someone who as a youth had longed for the same transcendence, who had read the same books as I, who had considered devoting his life to the church even as I once had.

"Imagine, Franz," I said now, "if we had followed our earliest longings, you would now be a priest and I a nun!"

Franz smiled wryly. "It seems we have strayed far from that course. I fear you and your bold demands for personal freedom have had a corrupting influence on me!"

"Not fair, for you are your own bad influence! Your mind is divided between aesthetic ideals and lust for women, and your heart cannot choose between the need for freedom and the need for love."

He sighed. "You are right."

We were quiet for a long moment, enjoying the comfortable silence the way good friends can. But then a kind of melancholy came upon me and I said, "We both long for something bigger than ourselves. But whereas you still seek that in God, I now search for it in love. Perhaps we are both irrational and destined always to be disappointed."

Franz began to speak, then stopped himself.

"What is it?" I asked.

"Please understand that I say this with love, George. With love and great concern. I may sometimes be disappointed, but I do not despair as you do. I fear that in your romantic relationships, you tend toward the self-destructive. You choose men because they need you, not because you love them. You begin in passion but move quickly to maternal feelings."

I thought for a moment. "If that is so," I said, "perhaps it is because I feel that if they depend on me, they will not leave me. If they will not leave me, I can open my heart to them."

"But where in this equation is there room for you to be cared for? You give disproportionately, and then you suffer the consequences."

I had heard these words before. I pulled my hands away and sat straighter in my chair. "You have been talking with Arabella. I see that she has shared her conclusions about my heart's concerns with you."

He started to defend her, but I held up my hand. "You are more of a friend to me than she. Had you not been away on tour, I would no doubt have shared my feelings with you rather than her."

"But do you agree with what you call her conclusions?"

"Do you?"

"Ah, George. I am afraid I do."

I wanted to argue vigorously, but the words rang true. How much of the failure of my love affairs lay squarely with me? How much did I contribute to the end of things because of habit, or example, or fear? How much did what I shared with Marie Dorval make the failure of any other relationship a foregone conclusion? I did not know. It is an ongoing and exasperating truth about our species that one can be remarkably astute about others but blind to oneself.

But Franz had problems of his own. I leaned forward and looked directly into his eyes to say, "We both are ill-suited for love. You want a woman to be a golden-haired angel fallen to earth. Then, when your fantasy is inevitably revealed as being all too human, you want to run away."

Franz's stomach growled just then. "The body speaks," he said. "The body begs us to move from anguish to bread."

Over breakfast, we changed our conversation to something less threatening to both of us. I suggested that language was limited for creative expression, but music was not.

"No, music is limited, too: to the power of the instrument, to the power of the musician's imagination, to one's ability to let go of conscious thought in favor of an unseen power."

"It seems we are back to mysticism," I said, and then, hearing rapid footsteps above us, I added, "And to the start of a new day."

"Before you go, if I may be a priest after all, peace be with you," Franz said.

"And with my spirit," I answered. I did wish for it, truly.

August 1837

PARIS

ON A LOVELY SUMMER AFTERNOON, MY MOTHER DIED. SHE WAS UNaware of the seriousness of her condition, a liver that failed her. Her doctors had told my half sister, Caroline, and me that her pain was now over and there was no need to let her know that she had not long for the world. He advised us to let her last days be happy ones, and indeed they had seemed to be. We took her for a carriage ride through Paris, despite her dramatic weakness, and she smiled throughout. Her last words, to Caroline, were "Please tidy my hair." Afterward, she looked at herself in the hand mirror, smiled, and her soul flew away.

She was buried in Montmartre Cemetery. The next day, before I returned to Nohant, I stood by her grave and let wash over me all the memories of her I could recall. Flowers and butterflies were everywhere; it seemed incongruous to have tears on my face and a leaden ache in my heart that made it hard to breathe. My mother had been as difficult in her later years as she ever had been; I never knew, when I visited her, what face I would be met with. But she had been the first one to hear the stories I made up and, when she was in the mood, the one who most ardently praised them. I remembered clearly her pulling me onto her lap and kissing me what seemed like thousands of times, then putting my hands together to make me applaud my own ingenuity. She had taken me to the theater when we had no money for bread. She had instilled in me respect for honesty, and she had been a fierce defender of my actions when I had gone to court to separate from Casimir.

There was a flame in my heart for my mother that burned steadily all my life, regardless of the way she treated me. Overall, I believe that she tried her best. She was a deeply passionate woman, one who in another life would have had her many talents broadened and widely praised. She was broken irretrievably by the death of the truest love she had known, all but mortally wounded; yet she lived on as best she could.

And I was her daughter.

June 1838

PARIS

A KIND OF TURNING POINT CAME BETWEEN ME AND CHOPIN. Though months had gone by without any contact between us, we had long had an interest in each other. But that spring I came to Paris often, and he and I saw each other then. He would play for me, and afterward we would talk long into the night.

It was on one of those evenings that I had come close to achieving the kind of intimacy I sought. We shared a kiss, and afterward I pressed against him, letting him know that I was eager for more. But the mood evaporated when Chopin stepped back from me, flustered, and said, "Certain deeds could spoil the remembrance."

By then I knew the man as tidy, fastidious; he was exacting, with his insistence on lavender kid gloves, silk waistcoats, muted cravats, the finest leather boots, and hats made light so as not to bear down too heavily upon him. When he was out, his shirts were white batiste; when he taught, he wore white muslin blouses with mother-of-pearl buttons. He would not be without his good soaps and his scented water. He was extraordinarily sensitive: a rose petal in a snowstorm. His manners were exquisite; he was a model of discretion and had a truly kind heart. But he was also full of contradictions: he would "fall in love" with three women in one evening and not go home with or even follow up with a single one. He loved his homeland, Poland, passionately; he had relished living in a household where intellectuals connected to the European Enlightenment gathered; but he made himself an exile rather than live under Russian rule. He knew himself to be possessed of frail health because of his numerous respiratory problems (some said he was consumptive), yet he refused to eat well or get enough rest.

Most bafflingly, he seemed to want out of a self-imposed prison regarding the display of his affection, yet he did nothing about it. Liszt said that Chopin gave everything but himself. I knew Chopin had been hurt in love by a young Polish girl whose parents had disallowed their marriage, but that had been long ago.

I wrote for help to Count Albert Grzymala, our mutual friend and Chopin's countryman, asking for guidance. If Chopin's affections were bound up with another, I said, I would desist in my attempts to forge an intimate relationship with him. But otherwise, what would compel him to open himself to me? What lay behind his inability to indulge in the joys of an intimate and exclusive relationship? I wanted to care for him, who needed care; did Grzymala think he would let me?

It was a very long letter, and in it I did a great deal of soul-searching. I wanted to be fair, to be honorable, to be honest. I did not want to force myself upon someone who would rather I not do so. But Chopin's responses to me had varied so much I was lost in confusion.

The letter I got back from Grzymala was nothing less than an exhortation to accelerate my efforts. And so I did. One evening in the summer of 1838, alone with Frédéric in his apartment, I took him by the hand and led him to his bed. I laid him down gently, lay beside him, and kissed him. When I pulled away, I saw in his face a kind of sadness, but then he put his hand to the back of my neck and gently drew me down to him, and one thing—eventually, tenderly—led to the other. Afterward, when I lay beside him, our breathing a melody in counterpoint, he idly ran his fingers through my hair. There was in the gesture a kind of distractedness, and I could sense that there was something he felt unable to say.

I spoke softly: "I know that there is now and will always be something that keeps you from me completely. I will not ask you what it is, but I will tell you that I, too, have a certain inability to offer myself wholly. As I would never ask from you something I am incapable of giving, I suggest that we serve as comfort and shelter for each other, that this be our form of love."

With that, there came from him a great sigh of relief. When I looked up at him, he nodded.

November 1838

MAJORCA, SPAIN

I ONCE WROTE TO A FRIEND THAT MY MOST BEAUTIFUL, MY SWEETest journeys have been made "at my own fireside, my feet in the warm ashes and my elbows pressed on the worn arms of my grandmother's chair." But with winter approaching and my concerns about Maurice developing rheumatism, I decided to take the children away for the season, to a warmer climate. When Chopin heard I was going, he argued jealously that he himself would benefit from such a trip, perhaps more than my son would.

"Come with us, then," I said, pleasantly surprised, for Frédéric found disquieting any disruption of his routine. Still, after some wrist-rubbing thought, he agreed that he would. We considered Italy, but then some Spanish friends enthusiastically recommended Majorca, the largest island in the Mediterranean's Balearic archipelago.

We decided to travel separately to Perpignan. Though my separation from Casimir was legal, Frédéric still feared the gossip that swirled around us at any provocation. And he had not yet met my children. In Spain, he said, we would all be on equal footing, for none of us had been to Majorca before.

We arrived in Palma, the island's capital, in mid-November. It was nearly comical to see aloes and lemon trees when we knew how the wind was whistling through the bare branches lining the boulevards in Paris. The warm air against our exposed skin had us closing our eyes in hedonistic pleasure. The colors were so saturated, so primary, they reminded one of a child's drawing: blue seas, red pomegranates, yellow lemons, green mountains. During the day, one heard the beguiling tinkle of the bells on the donkeys, and at night came the romantic and far-reaching sound of guitars.

My children were immediately charmed by Chopin. He was

kind and gentle and sensitive to the fluctuations in their moods, perhaps because he, too, was victim of such fluctuations. They also very much appreciated his music—Solange, especially; and he promised that once we were settled, he would give her piano lessons. "When I get back to Paris, I shall play just like him," she told me, and I thought she actually believed it. I said nothing to dissuade her from that belief: her behavior had been very agreeable from the outset of this trip, and I did not want to disturb the equilibrium.

Our rooms were not clean or comfortable (our mattresses were slabs of slate), nor was the food delectable—one had a choice of fish and garlic or garlic and fish—and it was cooked in rancid oil. I hastened to find us a house to rent with more forgiving beds, where we might prepare dishes more satisfying and nutritious. I located one soon enough, but then the weather abruptly changed to cold and rain, and Frédéric began coughing in such a violent way that the owner of the house, fearing contagion, not only evicted us but charged us for a new mattress, as he said he would have to burn the old one.

I found us another place, one far out in the country. It was three rooms in an abandoned Carthusian monastery, on a mountain in Valldemosa. The Charterhouse was a collection of well-constructed buildings with a large enclosed area. It overlooked the sea on two sides, and the children and I loved exploring its mysterious passages: it brought me back to my convent days. A sacristan visited daily, and an apothecary-monk rented a cell a long way from ours, but he rarely came out. He sold us marsh mallow herb or couch grass (the only medicines he had) for exorbitant prices.

Otherwise we were alone but for the woman next to us, named Maria-Antonia, who rented a room in the monastery and offered to let us use it for cooking, as she had a stove. She also volunteered to be our housekeeper. She refused compensation, saying that she preferred to help us for the love of God, but she mostly helped herself to our meager supplies. Most of the work she was meant to do fell to me; it was a case of it being easier to do it myself than to explain to Maria-Antonia what I needed done. I would clearly state my objectives, and she would stare at me as if I were a talking portrait.

My days were spent tutoring the children and exploring the monastery and the island with them, cooking, talking with and nursing Frédéric, and fitting in writing when I could—there were, after all, bills to be paid and the publisher's hand reaching across the miles.

As for Frédéric, despite his ill health, he was remarkably prolific in his work, composing, on the piano we had brought in, mazurkas, scherzos, and, most notably, his preludes: he, too, had taken an advance against promised works. In some of those preludes, I thought he evoked the place we were in. The darker ones suggested his terror of phantoms in the cloisters: they conjured long-dead monks and death and funerals and the heavy scent of incense caught in the folds of clothes. The sweeter ones I thought must have been inspired by the high cries of the children playing outside, or by the farmworkers' cantilenas rising up from the foothills, or by the nestling sounds of the birds who sought shelter in the dripping boughs next to our window while thunder rumbled out its long complaints. Once, I remarked on the way that Frédéric had incorporated the patter of rain into a composition and made the mistake of referring to it as imitative harmony.

"Imitative!" he said. "No, it was not *rain* that inspired me; it is the tears of heaven that fall upon my heart!"

"Imitative!" echoed Solange, in her haughtiest tone.

I let it alone. I did not remind Frédéric of the times I had seen his creativity directly influenced by something other than himself. At Nohant one afternoon, we were out walking and I spoke rather poetically about the verdant countryside around us. Frédéric stopped walking. "Do you know how beautiful that is, what you just said?"

"Do you really think so?"

He nodded.

"Well, then. Put it into music."

We went inside, eager as children who have been called to open gifts, and he sat at the piano and immediately began improvising a pastoral symphony. I stood behind him as he played, my hand on his shoulder.

Another time he was sitting at the piano late at night, idly improvising, and he suddenly fell silent. Delacroix, who was visiting us and had been listening to him, said, "Go on! You are not at the end yet."

"Nor even at the beginning!" Frédéric said. "Nothing comes to me. Nothing but shadows. To put it in your terms, I'm trying to find the right color, but I can't get the form."

"Yes, you must have both," Delacroix said, "and usually you find them together."

Frédéric stared out the window, shaking his head. "Suppose I find only . . . moonlight."

Delacroix leaned forward, his eyes shining. "If you find moonlight, you ask it to speak and you play what it says."

I was sitting in a chair doing some needlework, and I smiled, pondering this interesting statement, wondering how such a concept would show itself in my work.

Suddenly Frédéric began to play, nearly formlessly at first, then in a way that had us nearly swooning. Describing it later, I wrote:

> He begins again, without seeming to, so uncertain is the shape. Gradually quiet colors begin to show. Suddenly the blue note sings out, and the night is all around us, azure and transparent. Light clouds take on fantastic shapes and fill the sky. They gather about the moon which casts upon them great opalescent discs, and wakes the sleeping colors. We dream of a summer night, and sit there waiting for the song of the nightingale.

—

THE UNRELENTING RAIN AND cold in Majorca made Frédéric more and more ill and, finally, confined him to his bed. A Frenchwoman on the island gave me goosefeathers so that I could have pillows made for him. I called in three different doctors, none of whom helped him and one of whom, with his wide eyes and nervous manner, had Frédéric convinced he would not make it through the night. He ate very little, and I could not blame him: we were once delivered a skinny cooked chicken that came complete with a flea hopping upon its scorched back. "See how he dances the tarantella!" Solange said, and the children laughed, and I thanked God for their good natures at such a moment. I paid exorbitant prices—well over four times what they were worth—for the fish and vegetables and eggs I was able to procure; the locals laughed behind their hands at me when they departed. I learned early not to haggle; when I did, the offended merchant would pack the merchandise back up and refuse to sell it to me, and the next time the price would be even higher.

From the moment we arrived, we were not well regarded: I with my man's name and men's clothes, and even my daughter in trousers. Worse than that, we did not go to church! No, no favors were forthcoming from the people on whom we so desperately depended. When it rained very hard—which was often—no one would risk coming up the road to deliver anything. At those times, we made do with bread so hard it could have served as a minor weapon of war.

We were stuck there; Frédéric's steadily deteriorating health made it imprudent for us to attempt to return to Paris. But there is something about untoward circumstances that can bind people closely together, and that is what happened to our little group in Majorca. Sometimes things were so bad that we could only laugh helplessly, then wipe our eyes of tears.

We made up stories, we recited poems, we exulted on rare sunny days when the lingering raindrops bejeweled the least blade of grass. But when Frédéric stopped eating altogether, I became fearful that he would die. On the day in February that I arranged for passage on the very next boat out—a boat carrying pigs!—he filled a basin with blood he had coughed up.

After an arduous and anxious journey, we checked into a hotel in Marseilles—Frédéric did not have the strength to make it to Paris.

I directed my attentions to restoring Frédéric's health, and soon he stopped spitting blood and began eating again. I was able to return to producing fifteen or twenty pages of prose a day. I was rewriting *Lélia,* creating the more sanitized version of the novel that my publisher had requested for a reissue, and was working, as well, on a new book, called *Spiridion,* which incorporated elements both mystical and revolutionary. It was not what my publisher had hoped for, but it was what I wanted to write. He sighed and put it into print; my readers waited impatiently for me to return to a form more like my earlier works, ones more romantic and richly detailed, like those written by Balzac. (He, incidentally, had come back into my life after he had suffered his own frustrations in trying to help my fickle former lover Jules.) But I could serve only one master; and it was not my publisher I chose, but myself.

May 1839

NOHANT

FINALLY, CHOPINET, AS WE OFTEN AFFECTIONATELY CALLED HIM, was plump and healthy again, and we and the children were back at Nohant. Life was lovely there, at first. I created an *appartement* for Frédéric next to my bedroom, with his own bedroom and a library.

I wallpapered the space with a gay Chinese print in red and blue, and although at first I could see he was holding his tongue, he came to like it very much—it was, after all, au courant.

Downstairs was a new Pleyel piano I had gotten for him, and while he sat composing, I took the children out for expeditions in a much more forgiving countryside than the one we had just left. Chopin's output was prodigious in those months. Relieved that everyone's health was good—Frédéric's lungs, Maurice's joints, Solange's pulse, which had a tendency to race—I, too, worked well.

It was at that time that I wrote my novel *Gabriel,* and I did it using only dialogue. It concerned a princess who is given a boy's education. As an adult, she dresses as a man except for three months a year, when she dresses as a woman to please her lover. He is named Astolphe, that name borrowed from a man who was openly homosexual and in love with Chopin.

It was ever mysterious to me the ways writing could excavate things from the secret corners of the soul. Oddly, sometimes I could not see what my writing placed directly before me—in this case, a moving back and forth between the sexes. Balzac praised that novel's psychological acuity; most others left it alone as an iconoclastic oddity.

One night I sat writing at my little desk, a candle lit with a high and steady flame. I put down my pen and moved to the window, suffused with a kind of contentment. Outside, clouds floated peacefully past the moon, and I stared up into the firmament with a prayer that this life would continue, that for once I would be able to count on something lasting. The love Frédéric and I enjoyed had moved entirely to the spiritual, and I found I preferred it to the wild fluctuations of the earlier passions I had known. Delacroix had recently done a painting of the two of us, where I was listening to Frédéric play and in my face was a rich contentment. I was looking off to the side, and there was a smile playing about my lips of which I was unaware. I seemed (and was) totally entranced by the music. Long after that painting had been seen by others, it amused me to learn that people said I was sewing. They saw one of my hands holding fabric, another raised in midair to hold something they assumed was a needle. Had they looked more closely, they would have seen the truth: in one hand I held a handkerchief, which I used for tears when the music overcame my emotions. In the other hand was the butt end of the cigar I was smoking.

That night at Nohant, however, I beseeched whatever power might be listening to keep safe these three beings I loved most in the world: Maurice, Solange, Frédéric Chopin. My family. I vowed to devote my life to them, to care solely for them and my art. I commemorated this promise by scratching on my windowsill a line in English from one of my favorite poets, Lord Byron—*All who joy would win must share it*—followed by the date: June 19, 1839.

Those words were a variation of what I was always saying, one way or another. When one takes the long view, one sees that I did not say much else.

September 1839

16 RUE PIGALLE

PARIS

THAT FALL, CHOPIN HAD TO GET BACK TO HIS STUDENTS, AND IT was too expensive for me to stay at Nohant, where uninvited guests came nearly every day to my table—sometimes a dozen at a time!—and I was too softhearted to turn anyone away. We decided to move back to the city.

Frédéric dispatched his friends to find us places to live, and we were lucky enough that they turned up paired pavilions at the back of a garden, offering us the privacy we both longed for. For propriety's sake, now that we were in the crowded city and fodder for the gossipmongers, we did not live together.

Solange stayed with me when she visited from school. My

daughter had once again been sent away to school because shortly after we got back to Nohant from Majorca, she had returned to her exasperating moody and often hostile behavior. Once Chopin's darling, she began making fun of him, insinuating things about his character and sexuality; she called him "Sans Testicules." Such outbursts made no sense to me; my daughter was once again walking through a garden and decapitating flowers. When I tried to give her more attention, thinking that her rude behavior reflected a need for that, she only grew more hostile toward me. I no longer knew what to offer her. The stricter environment at school did not seem to help her, either; but I was hopeful that, in time, it would.

As for Maurice, he was sixteen now and would soon be finished with school and in need of finding a vocation. We were both thrilled when Delacroix took him on as a studio assistant.

Frédéric and I lived a happy lifestyle, with our combined friends. On my side were Delacroix, Balzac, the poet Heine, the actors Bocage and Marie Dorval, and the usual rowdy and unkempt journalists. I had also new friends who visited regularly: a locksmith, a baker, a weaver, a stone carver whose poetry I helped get published, and a cabinet maker. Frédéric's friends were musicians, singers, princesses, countesses, and Polish expatriates.

We often had community dinners together and lingered long at the table discussing again and again how best to approach the "social question." I would be lost in the ideas of Friedrich Engels and Karl Marx, in discussions about how, if one assumed the world was rational, certain principles could be applied to the management of people, no matter what their social standing. I would postulate that the future of the world was in the hands of the working class, that in time the masses would rise up from where the so-called enlightened had chained them down. Frédéric would sit silently with a frozen smile on his face, asleep with his eyes open, and eventually disappear. He tolerated my dissident friends, but at heart he was an unapologetic aristocrat. Still, he relied on me, a woman whose sympathies lay with the people, to help him with his work.

Before Frédéric knew me, he would start things and let them languish; he had a great deal of trouble finishing things. I saw why; sometimes when we were out for a walk, he would hum or whistle a captivating phrase. When we got home and he sat at the piano, he would frustrate himself trying to remember what the notes were. But I remembered. I would stand a distance away, watching, and if he agonized for too long a time, I would walk quietly over to strike the appropriate keys, to unloosen and remind him. "Yes, yes, of course; I know," he would say, shooing my hands from the keyboard.

Chopin composed half of his oeuvre at Nohant. And at the end of 1841, I served as his manager, in spite of his general unwillingness to perform in public. Liszt had just returned from a wildly successful solo tour, and so a jealous Chopin grudgingly allowed me to arrange for a concert for him, albeit with a violinist and a singer to share the bill. From the moment he agreed to do it, he plagued me with doubt and questions and demands I found hard to tolerate. At first, I laughed off his concerns, but then one day I got angry and stood inches from his face to tell him of my frustrations.

"You don't want posters. You don't want programs. You don't want too big an audience. You don't want anyone talking about the concert to you. I suggest when the day comes, you play in total darkness, on a silent keyboard!"

At this, he finally stopped interfering and let me go on with my plans.

The concert was a great success. I arranged for hothouse flowers to bank the double grand staircase of the Salle Pleyel, and it was an illustrious audience that ascended the red carpet up to the concert hall. When Chopin first came out on stage, I could feel his nervousness as though it were my own. But when he began playing, he disappeared into his own genius. He closed his eyes, and I closed mine. Then it felt as though the audience breathed as one. He had chosen an extremely challenging program featuring pieces he had written since we had come together, among them the four mazurkas of Opus 41 and the extremely difficult Third Scherzo, which he played with such force I feared he would break the piano.

His performance was met with calls for encores, with loud bravos, with women actually fainting from appreciation. Liszt published a review in which he spoke politely of the other performers that night, but he called Chopin the king of the evening. (About which my oversensitive Chopinet said, "Yes, I am the king for one night, raising the question of who is the king for all the other days! I am king, but only within his empire!")

The "king" netted six thousand francs from the concert and immediately dispatched orders to his manservant, Jan, asking for suede gloves, two new colognes, a pair of dark gray pants—in the current fashion, but with no stripes!—and two new waistcoats, velvet, with a minute pattern.

IN 1842, FINDING THAT our apartments on Rue Pigalle were cold and damp, and that the climb up to them made Chopin short of breath, we moved to Square d'Orléans. It was just off Rue Saint-Lazare and, to my proletariat heart's delight, was a kind of commune, presided over by Countess Charlotte Marliani and her husband, Emmanuel. There were eight structures built around a central courtyard. Other artists lived here, among them dancers, painters, actors, and musicians. I rented the roomiest place and painted my drawing room walls a coffee brown. Frédéric's quarters, much smaller but quite elegant, were across the courtyard. Maurice had a tiny studio on a high floor, as befitted his bachelor status.

I relished the stimulation of being around like-minded people, and, as I became increasingly politicized, I began spending more and more time away from Frédéric, going to the kinds of meetings that led me to start my own journal, *La Revue Indépendante.*

Most summers, we returned to Nohant, and I worked continuously to make it better for my family and my guests. Chopin devised a tiny puppet theater; I created an art studio for Delacroix, and he and his cat, Cupid (whom I daresay he loved better than any woman), came to stay for ten days. What a joyful time we had then, the house noisy with talk and laughter and the echo of footsteps coming down the stairs. There were hikes around the grounds and through the forests, horseback rides in the fields; there was eating and drinking all hours of the day.

Whenever we were at Nohant, I invited people to visit, lest Chopin become bored. Whereas I could be content for long periods of time in the quiet of nature and was, in fact, restored by it, Frédéric needed constant stimulation. He needed the theater and the opera, the business of the streets. To the extent that I could, I created that for him in the country. He loved it when the famous soprano Pauline Viardot came, as she often did. He would play Mozart's operas and she would stand at the piano and sing, and at those times I thought the angels in heaven envied us mortals who sat transfixed before her.

When Frédéric's father died, he isolated himself in his room and fell into a black despair from which I began to think nothing would lift him. But then I invited his sister Ludwika to come from Poland. During her visit, she and I got on famously, each of us deeply appreciative of the other not only for the ways in which we cared for Chopin but for each other's beings. Something about our mutual regard restored Frédéric's spirits. After Ludwika went back to Poland, our friendship continued—and deepened—in letters.

The years went by, and I breathed easily; I thought I was done with looking for happiness and peace.

July 1844

NOHANT

I TURNED FORTY, THE AGE AT WHICH ONE WAS CONSIDERED OFFICIALLY old. And Maurice turned twenty-one, the age for becoming a man and stepping into his role of master of Nohant. With this he developed a certain animosity toward Frédéric, for it seems men lack the ability to live peacefully side by side when their need to dominate is challenged. Frédéric had a generally kind nature, but he also had his distinct preferences. A kind of tension announced itself: Maurice began to hold his head a different way when he was around Frédéric, and the lift in his chin spoke volumes.

In Maurice's first act as master, he fired Frédéric's manservant. Then he fired the ancient gardener at Nohant, who had been there when my grandmother was in charge, and finally he discharged a housekeeper whom we all knew as lazy but tolerated for her musical laugh and cheerful high coloring.

I understood that Maurice needed to make some dramatic decisions, both to establish his claim and to be financially responsible. I sent away with generous compensation the people he had discharged. I hurt for them, but I had to let my son run Nohant the way he saw fit. He also asked me not to take Frédéric away for the winter; he said he needed my help to complete the transfer of power from me to him.

As for Solange, her animosity toward me grew. This was because I took into my care a distant cousin on my mother's side, a twenty-year-old girl named Augustine Brault whose mother was a prostitute and who I feared was being pressured into becoming the same: I had heard that her mother frequently brought her daughter along on her assignations. I knew the girl to be bright, kind, and talented, with a remarkable singing voice. She had unruly black hair, clear green eyes, and the classical kind of bone structure that would assure her beauty into old age. She was tall for a woman and moved with an easy grace. What I thought best about her was that she was full of energy. I could not help but feel it would be a pleasure to have her in the household, and in any case, I wanted her not to fall to circumstances that would ruin her life.

I spoke to Maurice about taking her in. He, too, cared very much about her and agreed that she would be a welcome addition. And so I offered to pay her parents to allow me to assume her care.

I had often worried that Solange felt alone in the family and that she seemed not to be skilled at making or keeping friends. I hoped that Augustine might serve as an older sister to her, a confidante, but after she arrived, all Solange seemed to feel for her was jealousy and contempt.

Frédéric did not like Titine, as we called her, either. He found her uncouth: too loud, too outspoken, too direct, and he thought she was calculating and scheming. He was openly rude to her. "She is only here because of her desire to marry Maurice," he told me one night as we sat alone in the drawing room after dinner.

"I would welcome it."

"Surely you are not sincere in saying this!"

I kept silent.

He turned in his chair to face me more directly. "You agonize about your relationship with your daughter, and then you do this. Can you not see that she will view this as a threat? She will feel that you prefer this relative stranger to her!"

To be honest, I had to admit that I did prefer someone whose gaze went out into the world rather than focusing relentlessly on herself. Deep in my heart was a stubborn—if battered—love for Solange, but I could not say that I admired her. I attributed her narrow vision, her constant preening, and her self-adulation to her youth, and hoped that she would soon grow into the capable and giving young woman I still believed she could be.

"You may think you are arranging to have two daughters who can help and learn from one another," Frédéric said. "In fact, you are only arranging to lose one. Solange is desperate for your attention, and again and again you turn her away."

It is she who turns from me! I wanted to say, because it was true. It had always been that way between her and me.

Generally speaking, it is the adult's place to side with the child, who is not well equipped with tools for self-defense, and whose needs and vulnerabilities are great. I would do the same myself. But Arabella had been correct in saying that my daughter was highly skilled in manipulation. Frédéric could not see it. And in the end, he sided with an increasingly voluptuous and flirtatious—and, yes, ever more manipulative—Solange against me. Thus were the battle lines drawn for what would prove to be our undoing.

In May of 1846, in what I believed was an effort to get away from me, seventeen-year-old Solange made a rapid match, agreeing to marry the first suitor she had, a Berry man named Fernand de Preaulx. I found him pleasant but nothing more. On the evening she accepted him, Frédéric congratulated her warmly. I asked her to come into my room so that we might have privacy.

There, I sat her on the bed with me and took her hands into mine. I looked directly into her eyes to say, "There is something I must ask you, and I hope that you will answer truthfully. Woman to woman, I will tell you that I married your father without being in love with him, and nothing but trouble followed. Trouble and heartbreak."

"As I very well know."

"I don't want the same for you. And so it is in this spirit that I ask you to tell me truly if you love Fernand."

She pulled her hands from mine and spoke in a flat voice, devoid of warmth or feeling. "Yes. I love him."

"Solange, whatever has been between us . . . it is important that you speak honestly now, that you not betray yourself simply to leave here. Our differences can be resolved, as they have been in the past. Perhaps we are too much alike. Perhaps we have both been too headstrong to—"

"I told you that I love him! Why must you now insinuate that I do not? Does it suit your own peculiar need for drama? I love him and I will marry him!"

I waited, but nothing more was forthcoming. Finally, I said, "Very well. Then I, too, offer you my congratulations. And if you like, I shall take you to Paris for your trousseau."

"Is that all?"

I nodded. She brushed roughly past me and was gone.

I was the first woman to become a bestseller in France and had achieved worldwide fame. My work had been praised to the skies by critics who found fault with Victor Hugo. Almost every day's post brought letters of praise. But my own daughter despised me. What had I done, I wondered. What *had* I done?

Maman! I suddenly heard Solange's child's voice say. *Watch me! Look, Maman, look at me, why aren't you watching?* I pushed my face into my hands and wept.

February 1847

PARIS

SOLANGE WAS SITTING BEFORE HER MIRROR WHEN I ENTERED HER room.

"I have been invited to the studio of the sculptor Auguste Clésinger," I told her. "Why don't you come with me?"

"Why are you visiting him?" she asked my image in the mirror. She finished with her hair and turned around.

"He is an admirer. He has asked to do a bust of me."

Her face filled with scorn. I saw that she was ready to refuse me, so I told her quickly, "But I would like him to do you, instead."

It wasn't true, at least not until that moment. For a year, I had been flattered by this young artist's requests to sculpt me, and finally I had agreed that when I next went to Paris I would accommodate him. He sent a letter expressing what seemed to be sincere gratitude. It was full of misspellings, but it had a rough charm. And it showed the sort of unselfconscious passion I was ever unable to resist.

I had seen the thirty-three-year-old sculptor once in a café with Marie Dorval; she had pointed out the man with the dark good looks and muscular build who was hunched over his coffee, gesturing dramatically to the man with whom he was speaking. "Paris's latest irresistible rogue," Marie said. "He is a sculptor of some distinction, and his most recent work caused a scandal: it was of a writhing nude lying on her back. He called it *Woman Bitten by a Serpent,* but we all know it was more properly *Woman in the Throes of an Orgasm.*" Staring at him and biting into a pastry as though it were his shoulder, she added, "He is a former cavalryman; you can see the evidence. One can forgive a questionable reputation when one can enjoy such a physique."

Bad reputation or not, I had looked forward to seeing how he would sculpt me. But now I seized on another opportunity to try to make Solange shine.

I was trying to bring my daughter back to me somehow. I'd used various methods to downplay myself, including letting myself go in a way that would have horrified my mother. I'd gained weight—my formerly enviable waist was long gone, and I had an extra chin. I did not speak of my work, and I hid away the letters of admiration I received. No matter what I did, though, it was never enough; I seemed ever to be a stone in her shoe. I had wished for shared joy when we selected things for her trousseau, but instead I felt I was along with her only to pay the cost of her expensive selections.

But she took me up on this offer, and we went to the studio together.

I made the introduction and proposed that Clésinger sculpt Solange in my place. I saw his attraction to her immediately: she was, after all, a beautiful, buxom young blonde with smoldering blue eyes and a glowing complexion; one of my radical journalist friends had described her as looking overly ripe for the picking.

"I should be honored if you would accept as my gift my sculpting both of you," Clésinger said with easy gallantry, and both of us agreed. I was asked to leave Solange alone in the studio with him so that he could get started with her right away. I looked over at her—*Are you comfortable with this?*—and she nodded at me, smiling. A few days later, she told me at dinner that she had put her engagement on hold indefinitely.

"Because of Clésinger?" I asked. "Have you fallen in love with him?"

"It is because of you. Because of what you said to me about being sure. I am no longer sure."

"But because of Clésinger?" I persisted.

"I am putting my engagement on hold, and that is all. Stop pestering me."

In April, a week after Solange and I had returned to Nohant, Clésinger showed up at our door, telling me that I had twenty-four hours to agree to him having my daughter's hand in marriage and demanding that I secure her father's permission as well. There was something thrilling about it for both Solange and me. That night, for the first time in a long time, she kissed me before she retired.

I sent a letter to Maurice requesting that he accompany Clésinger to make the request of Casimir, in person, and in it I wrote of the ardent suitor:

> *He will get his way because his mind is set on it. He gets everything he wants by dint of sheer persistence. He seems to be able to go without sleep or food. He was here for three days, and slept no more than two hours. I am amazed, I am even rather pleased by the spectacle of such strength of will. I think he will be the saving of your restless sister.*

I confess that I was more than "rather pleased." This situation seemed to have brought Solange and me together. Both of us knew that Casimir would voice no objection but that Chopin, who was in Paris, would not be happy about this turn of events. It was a breach of good manners, of good taste! Solange would be abandoning an aristocrat for a commoner!

"I think we must not tell Frédéric, yes?" I said to Solange one evening when I sat in her room with her. She was in her nightclothes, her beautiful hair tumbled down upon her shoulders in advance of her braiding it.

"Heavens, no!" She giggled.

I kissed the top of her head. "Our secret, then, yours and mine together."

She nodded almost shyly, and I saw a flash of the little girl she used to be.

Frédéric heard of the upcoming marriage when he read the announcement in the newspaper. He was conspicuously absent at the wedding that followed in May, two weeks later. Although he sent a warm note to Solange, wishing her great happiness, I knew he was furious. As soon as I returned to Paris, he was in my apartment, pacing like a caged animal. I half expected him to pick up a chair and throw it, as he had reportedly done with his students when he was displeased at their efforts and his usual foot stamping would not suffice. "You know of this artist's egregious reputation, do you not?" he asked me.

"I hardly think it is *egregious.*"

"He is a drunkard. He is deeply in debt—he owes hundreds of thousands of francs. He has just abandoned his pregnant mistress—whom he regularly beat!"

"Who told you this?"

"Delacroix. But it is well known, George. You must have heard these things!"

"I have not. And unlike these gossips, I have met the man, and he is charming."

"I won't have it."

I stared at him. "First of all, it is not your place to have or not have the marriage of my daughter to the man she loves."

He opened his mouth to speak.

"No," I said. "I shall not listen to you go on about how to be a good mother, to insinuate, as you always do, that I am anything but.

What do you know about raising a child? It is all well and good for you to play entertaining friend, sympathetic ally, but when you tire of the children, what then? Off you go to one well-appointed place or another, where those who love you will guard your right to be alone so long as you desire.

"And let me say as well that since I have known you, you have never been able to face facts or understand human nature. You are all poetry and music, a child yourself, protected from unpleasantness because of your prodigious talent, yes, but also because of your constant respiratory illnesses, which seem to me at times to be a bit too convenient."

He had fallen into a chair to endure my lambasting, and because he was silent I thought that he might even agree with at least some of what I'd said. But this last was too much. He looked up at me, and in his eyes was such pain, such betrayal, that I fell to the floor and laid my head in his lap, weeping. "Forgive me," I said.

He rested his hand on my head. His breathing slowed, then calmed, and he said simply, "My apologies, Aurore."

June 1847

NOHANT

SEEING SOLANGE MARRIED MADE ME EAGER FOR MAURICE TO TAKE that step as well. For some time, I had hoped that he would marry Augustine. I knew that he found her very attractive for many reasons, and certainly he had advocated with me on her behalf. But then my son seemed abruptly to lose interest in her.

One day I took a walk with him, and after an agreeable silence, I asked about his intentions.

He shrugged in a way that aroused my wrath.

"What do you mean? Do you no longer care for her?"

"I *care* for her. . . ." He kicked a clod of dirt before him, and I grasped him by the arm to stop him, then turned him around to face me.

"I shall not marry her, if that is your question."

I closed my eyes and let go a huge sigh.

Maurice laughed. "Come now, Mother. Are you not the one who argued against Solange marrying Fernand?"

"It is a different situation."

"How is it different? Am I not to save myself for someone I feel passionately about?"

I had no answer. We resumed walking.

"Has she given herself to you?" I asked quietly.

"I was not the first."

"How do you know there have been others?"

He only looked at me.

I turned my gaze forward and walked on.

An artist named Théodore Rousseau, a friend of Maurice's, had recently visited. He was a famous painter of landscapes, and Maurice had told me he was besotted by Augustine.

I felt responsible for Titine's well-being. Indeed, I loved her. I had taken her away from her mother to give her a better life, and I wanted to make sure she would be provided for after I was gone. To that end, I began an exchange of letters with Rousseau, starting by letting him know that Augustine was very much taken with him. He wrote back to me immediately, expressing his ardent feelings for her. I shared the letter with Augustine, who, understanding all too well the change in Maurice, expressed a modest measure of appreciation. I wrote back to Rousseau:

If you could have seen how the color rushed into her cheeks, and the tears into her eyes, when I showed her that beautiful letter, you would be feeling as calm and radiant as she has been. She flung herself into my arms, saying, "Then there really is a man who will love me as you love me!"

A few weeks later, I told Rousseau that if he married Augustine, I would provide a dowry of one hundred thousand francs, to be paid gradually, out of my royalties. When Solange heard about this, she was furious. All her bitter jealousy of Augustine returned. She and Clésinger were living well beyond their means and had run through Solange's dowry in weeks. Now they expected me to finance their hothouse flowers, their hired carriages, their expensive clothing and evenings out.

But Rousseau declined my offer. He had gotten an anonymous letter, he said, that told him that Augustine loved Maurice and that if she married another, it would be her distant second choice.

Knowing full well that "Anonymous" was Solange, I argued for Rousseau to move ahead nonetheless. "One of the joys of marriage, after all, is the way that time together can make love grow," I wrote him. At this, he grew suspicious, wondering why one who so often had objected to matrimony was now trying to push it on him.

He did not understand my feelings in this regard. I did not object to matrimony; I objected to the inequality in it. Let men and women enjoy mutual respect in the institution, and I was all for it!

But it was too late. Exit Rousseau. And enter a furious Solange.

July 1847

NOHANT

MAURICE, SOME FRIENDS, AND I WERE HAVING DINNER ONE EVENING when a carriage pulled up. I went into the front hall to see Solange and Clésinger walking through the door. I was not surprised; I had invited them to spend some time in the country, hoping that the simple beauty of Nohant might remind them that the most lasting joys have nothing to do with purchases. Whatever my failings as a mother, I did always try to impress upon my children the restorative and timeless pleasures of nature, art, and camaraderie.

But now! Clésinger, who appeared drunk, dropped their bags to the floor and began speaking in a loud voice that drew my son out into the hall with us.

"What is the meaning of this?" Maurice asked. "Lower your voice at once!"

"I shall not! Your mother is going to hear us out, one way or another!" He turned to me. "The great George Sand! If anyone knew of the way you treated your own daughter—"

"Auguste—" Solange began, embarrassed, I think, by the way he was acting. However great her ire, her behavior was never this crude.

He turned toward her so menacingly, she fell silent. But then, quietly, she said, "We are in need, Mother."

"I have no more to give you!" I said. "The money that was offered to Augustine was to come from royalties I have not yet received."

"Then mortgage this place!" Clésinger said.

My mouth fell open.

"I ask again that you leave; we shall discuss this later," Maurice said in a low voice, aware, as was I, that our dinner guests had fallen silent.

"I shall not be thrown out!" Clésinger roared.

Then a rapid series of events happened that will never dim in my memory. Maurice took Clésinger's arm to escort him out. Clésinger reached into his bag to pull out a sculptor's mallet, which he raised over Maurice. I stepped between them to slap Clésinger's face once, twice; he punched me so hard in the chest I nearly fell to the floor. Maurice shouted, "I am going for my gun!" at the same time that one of our guests, a priest who was imposing in stature, came to subdue Clésinger, then told him to leave at once. Clésinger grabbed two of his sculptures that I had on tables in the vestibule and walked out. I looked to Solange, but in her face was only bitterness, and she followed her husband out, slamming the door.

The next day, she sent a note from a nearby inn demanding my carriage to take her and her husband back to Paris. I refused her, in part because I hoped she might calm down and we could have a reasonable discussion of her other demands. Instead, I learned that she wrote to Chopin, telling him of the terrible treatment that she had suffered at her mother's hands. And he sent his carriage and his driver to fetch her, offering, as well, his condolences and the promise of his open arms.

Furious, heartbroken, betrayed, I wrote to Frédéric that he need not bother coming to Nohant unless he cut Solange and Auguste Clésinger out of his life. I told him how they had appeared at Nohant, so full of vitriol. I told him that they frequently asked for money that I could not provide and rejected the spiritual things I could give.

I am wild with grief, I told him. I feel as if my daughter is dead. I asked that he not even speak her name to me, that he regard her as a matter of indifference.

There followed days and nights of bitter pain. I could be distracted from it for an hour or so at a time, but then it would return. I waited for the relief of Frédéric arriving from Paris, but he did not come. Then I worried frantically that he was ill and made plans to go to Paris to check on him, though I was ill myself, not only in spirit but in body: I had a fever, and every bone ached.

Finally, I received a letter from Frédéric:

> *Solange will never be a matter of indifference to me. Your pain must be overpowering indeed to harden your heart against your child, to the point of refusing even to hear her name, and this on the threshold of her life as a woman, a time more than any other when her condition requires a mother's care.*

Her condition. So Solange was pregnant. She had not told me, as surely Frédéric must have known; surely he must have known that! I read and reread this cold response, which made no effort to console but only criticized me. Not a word about what it must have been like for me to have been attacked in my own vestibule. No acknowledging the endless times I had tried to reach my daughter, the way I had tried to take care of her.

I wrote him back:

Do as your heart tells you, and take its instinctive promptings for the language of your conscience. I quite understand.

As to my daughter . . . she has the bad taste to say that she needs the love of a mother whom, in fact, she hates and slanders, whose most sacred actions she sullies. You have undertaken to lend a willing ear to her, and perhaps you really do believe what she tells you. I would rather see you go over to the enemy than myself take arms against that same enemy who was born of my body and fed of my milk.

Take good care of her, since you seem to have decided that it is your duty to devote yourself to her. I will not hold it against you, but you will, I hope, understand me if I say that I shall stick to my role of outraged mother. To have been a dupe and a victim is quite enough. I forgive you, and will not, from this day forward, address so much as a single word of reproach to you, since you have confessed frankly what is in your mind.

Goodbye, my friend. May you soon be cured of all your ills, as I hope that now you may be (I have my reasons for thinking so). If you are, I will offer thanks to God for this fantastic ending of a friendship which has, for nine years, absorbed both of us. Send me news of yourself from time to time. It is useless to think that things can ever again be the same between us.

And then, as I have the fragile and contrary heart of a woman, I waited for him to come to me, or to at least respond. He did neither. We marched forward into our separate lives.

March 4, 1848

PARIS

I WAS ON MY WAY TO SEE CHARLOTTE MARLIANI WHEN I RAN INTO Chopin in her anteroom, coming out from having just visited her himself.

"George!" he said.

"Frédéric." I kept my tone neutral, and I tried not to let my eyes devour him in the way he used to make fun of me for. He was pale, thin. I took his hand briefly; it was cold as ice.

"How do you fare?" he asked.

"Well, and you?"

"The same. Have you any news from Solange?" he asked.

"Last week I heard from her."

"Not yesterday or the day before?"

"No."

He smiled: half joy, half sorrow. "Then let me tell you that you are a grandmother. Solange has had a little girl, and I am delighted to think that I am the first to inform you of that fact. Her name is Jeanne-Gabrielle."

"But then she came early!"

"Yes."

I stood still; he bowed and made his way downstairs with his companion, an Abyssinian man named Combes.

I was turning to go into the apartment when I heard Combes calling my name as he bounded up the stairs again. I waited for him to reach me. "Frédéric wanted me to tell you that Solange and the baby are in good health," he said breathlessly and smiled.

"And this he would not tell me himself?"

Combes spoke softly, "He could not climb the stairs again, madame."

I rushed downstairs and asked Frédéric all about Solange,

though I wanted desperately to inquire about him as well. He dutifully answered every question about my daughter, ending by saying that Solange had had a difficult labor but that the sight of her child had made her forget her pain.

I looked into his eyes. "As it ever goes. If given a chance, true love will always vanquish pain."

"So it is said. Well. Good evening." He bowed and started to turn away, and I quickly said, "And you, Frédéric? How is your health?"

"I am well," he said, but he would not meet my eyes and instead bade the porter to open the door to his carriage. He did not turn around. He climbed in, and Combes followed him, the carriage creaking with his greater weight; and then it drove away. I stood at the edge of the street on a clear evening, the stars a rebuke, the memories falling like rain.

I thought, *Love begins as a rhapsody and ends as a dirge.*

I never saw him again. And most unfortunately, Solange's baby died within days.

May 1848

PARIS

MICHEL DE BOURGES AND I MAY HAVE COME TO A BAD END, BUT his political proselytizing was not entirely in vain. After the July Monarchy was overthrown early in '48, it seemed that at last a socialist republic would rise up. Undone by love (though what I declared was that I was through with it), I went to Paris and immersed myself in politics, giving it the same hectic energy and trusting heart I had offered my paramours.

I was called "the mind and the pen of the new regime." I wrote government circulars, and I had access to all members of the provisional government at any time. I was privileged to award friends of mine temporary positions as commissaries of the republic at Châteauroux and La Châtre, and I even appointed my son as mayor of Nohant. What hope I had for the elevation of the masses! What faith I put in the courage of the people! But how far we fell in our efforts to grant freedom, and in such a short length of time. By May, the general elections showed us that the cause of the socialist republic was lost. All our efforts for the creation of a grand republic had failed.

Back at Nohant, I was greeted by men with tipped hats and straight lines for smiles; these same men wanted to burn my house down for my liberal politics. They were not like the protesters in Paris, who had barricaded the streets with everything from chairs and paving stones to broken cups and saucers. The people of Berry were more conservative than I had imagined them to be. The new mayor of Nohant, who was a political adversary but a personal friend, even suggested I leave town for a while. I shared this advice with some friends and received a letter back from Delacroix, in which he wrote:

Liberty purchased at the cost of pitched battles is not liberty at all, seeing that true liberty consists in the freedom to come and go in peace, to think as one will and eat as one likes, and enjoy a great many other advantages to which political upsets pay no attention.

He was right, I thought.

Not long afterward, I was out for a walk in the country one day with my old friend François Rollinat. He reminded me of how, a year ago, we had walked there and I had told him a story called "The Waif." I had told it in the same easy, conversational style as an old village woman had told it to me, so long ago.

"I remember," I said. "And it seems that in one year, we have aged ten. So much has changed from that day when we spoke here."

François nodded sadly and looked out over the land. He drew in a breath, as though pulling the vision of all he was seeing deep into his lungs. Then he said, "Yet the stars shine on and the smell of the air is still sweet. Perhaps that is the only offering we can make. Let us use art again as we once understood it, and treat the anguish of the soul with the balm of the natural world."

"Yes," I said. "Let the cobbler return to his last, and the novelist to her pen."

My next book was *La Petite Fadette,* which was praised for its evocation of the beauty of the rustic life, and it put me back in the good graces of the public, where I stayed.

October 1849

PARIS

OCTOBER 17, 1849, FRÉDÉRIC FRANÇOIS CHOPIN DIED. SOLANGE WAS among those at his bedside; in fact, I heard that he died in her arms.

People said I did not care enough to go to him or to attend his funeral, but I was not told he was dying. I knew he was ill; I had heard that his sister Ludwika had come to care for him. After she arrived in Paris, I wrote to her, inquiring after Frédéric, but heard nothing back. Therefore I assumed it was nothing serious, and that he would recover the way he always had.

He had often said that he wanted to die in my arms; I had responded that if the fates decreed he went first, I would be the one to hold him then. My name may not have crossed his lips as he lay on his deathbed, but I know beyond knowing that I was in his thoughts and deep in his heart, and that if he did not call for me, he wanted to.

In the years that followed, I would be reviled for having caused his death, when in fact I'd extended his life. Without me, the world would have far fewer of his mazurkas, polonaises, preludes, and waltzes. It would be without his ravishing B-flat Minor Sonata, which he completed on a stormy afternoon at Nohant, after which he called me from the kitchen, where I had been putting up plum jam, to hear it. I stood at the piano with my fingers stained blue, with minute blossoms that had fallen in the wind on my walk that morning still dotting my hair. After he lifted his hands from the keys and the room fell abruptly silent, I opened my eyes and smiled at him through tears. And the breath he had been holding came rushing from him.

The world will ever love Chopin's music. I loved not only his music but, to the bones, I loved that shy and private man, he with his constant cough and listless appetite, his nervous complaints and the raised veins in his feet, the tenderest of tributaries. And he loved me. We were not the thing each of us privately longed for; but our understanding of that made it possible for us to be to each other what we were. Our souls met and mingled in our love for music, in the grace and transcendence it provided us both. For all those years we were together, I listened daily as he played out his rapture, his questioning, his suffering; I knew him as well as he knew himself and perhaps better. However unconventional the manifestation of love between us, it was a true love. And even after it was over, it lasted.

It was Chopin who began our ritual of theater: it became incorporated into the house's routine as much as were the lavish breakfasts followed by walks, followed by work, followed by dinner, followed by fun. We might read aloud or play dominoes or cards, but mostly we loved play-acting.

Later, Maurice built a marionette theater and carved from willow wood twenty different characters, including a theater manager, policemen, Bamboula the Negress, and the Comtesse de Bombrecoulant, who made a show of displaying her ample bosom. The puppets' faces were painted by Maurice and his artist friends, and I sewed elaborate costumes for them: silk gowns and little frock coats and waistcoats enhanced with starched ruffs, embroideries, and feathered hats

Two years after Frédéric's death, I combined the billiard room and Solange's former bedroom into a large space that I made into a real theater, complete with a raised stage, proscenium, and benches for the audiences. To the left of that was Maurice's marionette theater, which I made high enough to hide the bodies of the people who animated the puppets.

There was beautiful, hand-painted scenery. I had equipment for sound effects: piano and trumpets and the horns used for hunting; and I had machines for making the sound of rain, wind, thunder, cowbells, ocean waves, carriage wheels, and birdsong. Long after Frédéric had left Nohant and even long after he'd died, I often saw him sitting in the audience watching the shows, erect in posture, the crease lines in his pants legs undisturbed, every soft hair on his head in place, his hands folded lightly in his lap, his lips pursed to let escape a whisper of the music he was putting to the scenes being played out before him, his delight muted but obvious; his love contained, yet given.

FACED WITH GROWING OLDER, one is consoled by things both predictable and surprising. Grandchildren are expected to bring joy, and I lost my heart to all of mine: first to Jeanne, Solange's second daughter, who, to my great sorrow, died young of scarlet fever. But then came Marc-Antoine, Maurice's son, who was born after my son had the good sense to marry Lina Calamatta, who became a true daughter to me. The couple had two more children, Aurore and Gabrielle, and they offered me boundless joy. Those little ones and I made a nest of the wild thyme that came up year after year. They sat in my lap and I rested my chin on their heads, and I taught them to read, and the birds sang, and the wind parted the grasses, and the flowering gorse rose up next to water colored pink by a setting sun. What else better was there? What else better had there ever been?

February 1866

PARIS

"AH! SO TONIGHT WE ARE GRACED WITH GEORGE SAND IN HER peach silk dress, here to rape Flaubert."

This is the comment I overheard as I sat down with a group of men in a private dining room at Magny's restaurant. This group, made up of various artists and writers, had been founded by Sainte-Beuve, and they gathered bimonthly to dine and to enjoy vigorous conversation. After having received many invitations to join them, this was the first time I had come. It was for the express purpose of being with Gustave Flaubert, though not for the reason suggested.

In 1862, I had given Flaubert a good review of his historical novel, *Salammbô*. He had written me to thank me, and I had invited him to visit me at Nohant. At the time of this dinner, he had yet to come, but in the letters we sent back and forth a great friendship developed, in spite of our differences in worldview and character.

Over and over again I invited him to Nohant; over and over again he made his excuses—he was very much a recluse. In one letter, I told him: "You fancy that the work of the spirit is only in the brain, but you are very much mistaken, it is also in the legs. You live in your dressing gown—the great enemy of freedom and the active life."

And he wrote back to me: "I wonder why I am so fond of you. Is it because you are a great man or a charming creature?" (This because I often assumed a male persona in my letters to him, just as I did in my private journals.)

On the night of the dinner, after a few minutes of my sitting silent and stiff-backed at the table, my glass of wine untouched before me, Flaubert finally blew in with the winter wind and came to sit beside me, close enough that I could feel the cold coming off his coat. I was becalmed by his open, handsome face. He was in his mid-forties then, tall, blond, green-eyed, and one of those men who have about them a sense of coiled strength. I was in my early sixties, beginning to show age in my graying hair and in a certain drooping at the jowls, though my energy had not diminished.

He acknowledged the rest of the group, then turned to me with a kind of mischief in his eyes. "George," he said, lifting the lace at my sleeve to kiss my hand.

"Gustave," said I, and kissed his. Because of the warmth and camaraderie we had developed over the last six months through letters, I felt comfortable being playful.

I leaned close to him to whisper into his ear: "You are the only man here who doesn't scare me."

"And you are the only woman who *does* scare me."

"It isn't so," I said, smiling, and began rolling a slim cigarette in my customary pink paper, using the Turkish tobacco I loved.

"It is. I find myself practically tongue-tied."

"You must know that you can say whatever you like. I would welcome your taking chances."

He watched me finish rolling the cigarette and said softly, "Such delicate hands for such a strong woman. They invite a caress."

I held the cigarette out to him and looked directly into his eyes. "Are you so inclined?"

He laughed. "And you say you are not a coquette!"

"I assure you, I am not a coquette! But neither am I the strong woman that people make me out to be."

Gustave signaled for a glass of wine. Then he turned back to me and smiled. "To be with you, and to feel that I am with an old friend! What a pleasure. I find myself exceedingly happy at this moment. And you know from my letters how rare that is!"

"I do indeed. And tonight I hope to lead you to embrace the idea that life is more joyful than you allow it to be."

"Ah, so that I am able to 'let the wind play in my strings a bit,' as you suggested that I do in my work."

"Precisely. Do away with any system for writing. Simply obey your inspiration."

He leaned back as our plates were put before us, then raised his wineglass. "To you, and to your efforts to improve my life, even to making my writing as painless and flowing as it is for you. Though here I very much doubt you will succeed."

It is true that in all our years of friendship, I did not succeed in moving Gustave from one who agonized over every word, who doubted himself at every turn. With his first great success, *Madame Bovary,* he had encountered full force the arbitrary nature of publishing and criticism, and the bewildering frustration that could cause. The novel first came out as a serialization in the *Revue de Paris,* which was at the time being watched by the government for any writing that could be seen as scandalous. It was said that when a friend of Gustave's who was an editor at the magazine told him the publisher wanted cuts, including the scene of Léon and Madame Bovary making love in a closed carriage traveling the streets of Rouen, Gustave gave that friend a message to give to the publisher in return:

> *I don't care. If my novel upsets the bourgeois, I don't care. If we end up in court, I don't care. If they suppress the* Revue de Paris, *I don't care. You had only to reject* Bovary. *You took it on, so much the worse for you. You'll have to publish it as is.*

Naturally, he did not succeed in refusing all cuts, and the novel was not much liked when it came out in serialization. When it became a book, however, with those scenes reinstated, it was, after a few mixed reviews, very highly praised and sold well.

I visited Gustave several times at his mother's house in Croisset, near Rouen. I always found the view from that fine house on the banks of the Seine beautiful, even when the river's waters were a muddy yellow. When I was there, we worked all day and talked much of the night away, usually in his study, with its green leather sofa and bearskin rug before the fire, with its stuffed parrot and gilded statue of Buddha and bowl full of sharpened goose quills. He had floor-to-ceiling bookshelves crammed with volumes he had read—the man devoured books, often reading three in a day, and he took great offense at being interrupted while he did so. Reading was nearly as sacred to him as writing.

We spoke a great deal about our works in progress, which we read aloud to each other. He called me "Dear Master," for the assistance I provided him with his work on *L'Éducation Sentimentale* and *Un Coeur Simple.* In acknowledgment of our friendship, I dedicated my novel *Le Dernier Amour* to him—that one with a theme of adultery not weighted down by guilt!

Whereas work was Gustave's highest priority, I had never attached nearly as much importance to mine, because what consumed me most was the search for the absolute in love. First it was my mother I dedicated myself to, then God, then a series of lovers. In old age, my brain centered more than anything else on the love of my grandchildren. And also, because of Flaubert, on chaste love.

During one of my early visits to him, Gustave and I sat warming ourselves at the fire late into the night, and at my urging we shared many stories about our lives. When I returned home, I had a letter from him that said:

We parted at a moment when many things were about to pass our lips. All the doors between us are not yet open. You inspire a great respect in me, and I do not dare to ask you questions.

I answered:

I was very happy in the week I spent with you. I feel an infinitely kind protectiveness in you. I didn't want to leave, but I was keeping you from your work. From a distance I can tell you how much I love you without overdoing it. You are one of the rare kind, still impressionable, sincere, in love with art, uncorrupted by ambition, not intoxicated by success.

He responded:

They were very fine, our nocturnal chats. There were moments when I had to restrain myself from giving you little kisses as though you were a big child.

Despite rumors that I was out to "rape Flaubert," the love we shared, in which we found an intimacy both of us had long desired, was completely innocent.

Our relationship did suffer somewhat toward the end, as I grew weary of Flaubert's frequent complaining. He was a terrible pessimist, and I had my life's work cut out for me to persuade him that one could hold on to optimism even as one moved toward death. I did not look upon aging as a downward spiral. I did not fear it. I saw it not as movement toward a dark and frightening thing but, rather, as a natural goal. There is a dignity in death; one does well to meet it halfway with calmness and acceptance and, if one can, rest assured in the knowledge that when the veil is lifted one will see that God possesses a caring hand after all.

I still believed in life eternal, though, as ever, my faith was of my own making. I was long done with the way that man attempted to represent what religion should be and to make it in his own image. I knew my time was coming, and I did not despair. Instead, I enjoyed the deepest happiness I had ever known. My mind was active, I was able to go out for long walks, I was even able to stay up for more hours of the day than I had when I was younger.

There was no longing for the days of my youth. I had lost all interest in fame. I wanted money only to secure my ability to leave behind something for the grandchildren. Perhaps most important, I still felt useful—in fact, more useful than I had been in my younger years, because what I offered was more direct: a heartfelt embrace, a pretty blue dress I had made, a winter stew, a story still wet upon the page that I shared with those young ones gathered at my feet, having written it just for them.

All of this I tried to explain to the Old Troubadour, as I called Flaubert—because of his love of Gypsies. But the troubadour also sings of love, and I believe that at heart Gustave was as susceptible to the charms of romance and the quest for joy as the rest of us, no matter what he might have said. How else to explain the apparent hypocrisy he displayed when he finally came for the first time to visit us at Nohant? He took a seven-hour train ride followed by a one-hour carriage ride, no doubt grumbling all the way. Then, when he stepped into the happy cacophony of our house full of people, what a change I witnessed!

The first day, with a grand flourish, he presented the grandchildren with dolls, which were wonderfully well received. The next day he relaxed enough to take a walk outside and look at a ram I wanted him to see.

"His name is Gustave," I said and saw a little smile flicker beneath Flaubert's monstrous mustache.

On his last night there, astonishingly, Flaubert appeared before dinner dressed as a woman and proceeded to dance the cachucha. It was both grotesque and delightful, and we were a most appreciative audience, laughing and applauding until, in splendid falsetto, he bade us stop.

The next day, he went home and returned to his hermitlike ways, and became immediately depressed.

Yes, we all need love, perhaps most especially those who argue against the need for it.

April 1873

NOHANT

INSIDE, THE MUSIC HAS STARTED AND MY GUESTS ARE BECKONING. But I do not go back to the house just yet. For I have found the answer I was seeking, the answer to what was most vital of all the things in my life, and it is the deep love I had for Marie Dorval. Having called her into my consciousness now, I want to stay with her longer.

I saw her many times after she left Nohant that day; we met for coffee and conversation, we went to plays and concerts and had dinners together, she came to my salons in Paris. In the spring of 1840, I wrote a play for her to star in, which closed in a week. She was deemed too old and too fat to play a romantic heroine; she was booed off the stage.

Naturally, this devastated her. And she grew very afraid of what her fate might be. I invited her to live with me; I told her I would always take care of her. I confess I hoped that we could find love again, that what had been snuffed out between us might now, because of this misfortune, resurrect itself. "Come to Nohant," I told her. "We can leave everything in Paris behind."

She smiled. "It is a lovely dream, the two of us together there again. But I must continue to tour to provide for my family. And you know my work is in my blood, as is yours; I cannot separate it from myself."

She played in smaller and smaller towns, in smaller and smaller roles, for sums so minute I wondered that she could feed herself. Despite her objections, I often sent her money, so that she could afford to keep her beloved grandson, Georges, with her when she was in warmer climes. From one such small venue, she sent me a letter that ended this way: "Isn't it curious, all of our lives, we long to know what our future will be. It is a mercy we do not know."

She died on May 20, 1849, at fifty-one years of age, her health ruined from life on the road, her great beauty and fame a distant memory. She died, too, from a broken heart, for she was inconsolable after Georges died, the year before. "I do not expect to recover from seeing one so young die so nobly," she told me. "I do not expect to, nor do I want to." She had always told me that the only love she was helpless against was that she had for children.

I was informed of her death one morning in a letter from René Luguet, her son-in-law. He had invited her to come to Caen, but she wanted first to go to the Français Theater in Paris, in an attempt to find work that might pay her five hundred francs a month and enable her to survive. The director did not mince words: he told her that her request was absurd. He *might* be able to find her something for far less money, he said, but he would have to overcome the resistance of the board. How humiliating for my dear Marie, who once had all of Paris at her feet! I imagined her small person standing before him, her head bent in shame, those little hands holding on to each other for want of anything else to steady her.

She went to Caen after that but had no sooner arrived than she fell seriously ill. A doctor was summoned; her condition was pronounced critical, and it was advised that she not be moved. Luguet reserved a coach nonetheless; Marie wanted to die in Paris. She made it to her beloved city and her familiar bed. She asked for Dumas fils, and he came immediately. He reassured her that she would not lie in a pauper's grave; he would pay for a proper place for her to take her rest. "Even in death, they will flock to see you," he said. She died with a smile on her lips.

"You were her last and latest poet," Luguet wrote. "I read *Fadette* aloud at her bedside, and we had a long talk about all the wonderful books you have written. We wept as we recalled the many moving scenes that they contain. Then she spoke to me of you, of your heart. . . . Ah, dear Madame Sand, how deeply you loved Marie, how truly you understood her spirit."

There was a black cross over her grave, Luguet said. On it were these words: MARIE DORVAL: SHE DIED OF GRIEF.

I secluded myself in my bedroom for the rest of the day. I sat quietly before my window, looking out as day progressed into night, and the terrible pain that lay in my heart refused to lessen. I had promised myself to take care of her family, to bring them to Nohant for every holiday; but this did nothing to help. And so I turned to my imagination.

In my mind, I created a scene of me at her deathbed. I made the room dark, lit with candles that cast a flattering glow on the face of my vain beloved. I put myself bending over her, clutching her hands, as we talked in low voices about the life we might have had together. Marie's face brightened in playfulness at one point. "But tell me, would we have had donkeys? For you know I love donkeys. They are so gay and comical."

"We would have had many donkeys, and in winter I would have made them fat and in summer I would have braided garlands of daisies for them to wear around their necks. I would have used cook's grease to polish their hooves. And we would have ridden them to the river, to that place where we bathed."

"Ah. I was beautiful then."

I leaned closer. "You are more beautiful now than ever, because you are more revealed."

I saw her close her eyes in peace; I saw her soul materialize like a thin white vapor, then rise. I saw myself closing my own eyes, and then opening them to a world that was forevermore without Marie Dorval. I saw myself kiss her forehead, her cheeks, her mouth, each knuckle on each hand. And then I left her to the heavens.

It was this fantasy, finally, that let me breathe.

I would have done anything, if it could have kept her. Then and now. But there was no holding on to her, any more than one can hold on to a setting sun. Yet in my imagination, at least, I was beside her as she left this life, the last thing she saw and touched.

I stood, lit a lamp, and made my way to the kitchen, because I was hungry. I did not want to be, but I was.

A few days later, I was delivered a letter Marie herself had written. She must have known her time was short. The note was brief, and the handwriting labored. It said, "In our time, I gave you all I could, and more than you know. Now the curtain closes. Live with the perfect memory of what we shared and be glad that we suffered no disappointments in each other, that we had only love. My darling, be happy!"

If we are pained by memories of what we have loved and lost, then we are also gifted by them. I think often of how, in the years that followed our night at Nohant, there were times when fire still passed between us. Her eyes beneath her bonnet, a deliberate swish of her skirt, a certain hesitation in her gait when she passed by me. And there is this: Whenever I stand before the Indre, it is not only the river I see. It is Marie Dorval, naked upon the bank, preparing herself to come to me.

Be happy!

I move toward the music and the lights in the house, toward those I love and who love me.

A stitch in my side, a sharp pain. I gasp and hold tightly to the branch of a tree, wait until the pain passes, and go on.

June 8, 1876

NOHANT

It is difficult to speak. For weeks now, something has raked at my insides; sometimes I cannot help but cry out. Last night I said to those gathered round my bedside, "Farewell, I am dying." But here I still am.

It is early morning; outside, the sky is dark and the trees move dramatically in the wind. Soon a storm will come. I want to live to see it. This is the way of nature: to persuade us around one more bend, to beckon us to behold one more vista.

I close my eyes and try to move my thoughts from my pain to the memory of the things I so loved witnessing here: the furrows of turned earth, the sun-shot clearings in the forest, the winding rivers, the canvas of the skies, the minute architecture of the wildflowers. And always the birds. And always the green. Green! It is the color of hope given by God to His children—all of them: the long dead, the living, those yet to be born.

The need to speak rises up so powerfully in me it is as though something has pushed hard against my spine. I feel my midsection rise; my shoulders press back against the pillows.

"It hurts her so!" I hear Solange say, weeping, and I open my eyes to look at her. It is not pain, I want to tell her. It is not pain; I am beyond pain now. I try to speak and fail; only my lips move. I try again, and she leans closer. *"Laissez verdure,"* I whisper. *Keep the greenery.* Incomplete, but all I can manage now. *Laissez verdure:* Let nature inspire and sustain you, and comfort you to the end. It is the truest sacrament, and—I see it now—the only perfect love.

I lean back, and a great peace comes to me. A widening. A settling. And then I am there.

It is Solange who closes my eyes, the bitterness between us at last departed, even as my soul has.

June 10, 1876

NOHANT

THE PEASANT WOMEN HAVE COME TO MY GRAVE SITE, AND THEY kneel in the wet grass. I see their lips moving as they say the rosary, I hear their murmurs and their weeping, their cries of despair. If only I could lift their hearts as mine has been lifted, in my passing. My darling Flaubert, sobbing so he can scarcely breathe, his shoulders hunched, rainwater running down his back. Now comes Paul Meurice, reading the words sent by Victor Hugo:

> I weep for the dead and I salute the deathless. Can it be said that we have lost her? No. Great figures such as she may disappear—they do not vanish. Far from it. One might almost say that they take on a new reality. By becoming invisible in one form, they become visible in another. Sublime transfiguration. The human form eclipses what is within, masking the true, the divine visage, which is the "idea." George Sand was an "idea." She has been released from the flesh, and now is free. She is dead, and now is living.

A nightingale sings. I turn toward the heaven in its breast, and am gone.

And so, what of it all? What of me and my passions and personas, my great loves and failures of love, my writing, my politics? What of the clanging opinions, the endless queries as to the whys and wherefores of how I chose to conduct myself? In the end, there is but one answer to every question, whether it is spit at me or made as gentlest inquiry: I was I.

I step across any reflections that are too dark with great strides, and when I am in my right mind, I find life acceptable because it is eternal. You call that my dreaming. I call it my faith and my strength. No, nothing dies, nothing is lost, nothing ends, whatever you may say.

– George Sand, in a letter to Delacroix

AFTERWORD

WRITERS APPROACH HISTORICAL FICTION IN DIFFERENT WAYS. Many are like Dutch realist painters, exacting in conveying characters' features and personality traits, in detailing dates and sequences of events, and in attempting to paint things exactly as they were. My approach was more that of an Impressionist, someone wanting to get enough of a sense of one reality in order to create another.

When I began doing research for this book, I was struck by the number of inconsistencies I found about the life of George Sand. The image said to be her on more than one cover of a book about her is, in fact, that of her son, Maurice. Amid the many biographies I read I found disagreements about the date of her birth, when events occurred, how and why and when—and even if—she said or did or felt certain things, and when and where her books were written. One scholarly text gave her birthplace as Nohant, when in fact she did not arrive there until she was four years old. I found different orderings and spellings of her given name, which was Amantine-Lucile-Aurore, if you go by her own words and those inscribed on her tombstone. Some writers say it is obvious that George Sand and Marie Dorval were lovers; others categorically deny it. Even things in her autobiography are suspect: about certain facts she presented in *Histoire de Ma Vie* (*Story of My Life*) regarding her grandmother's first marriage, one biographer wrote that there was not a word of truth in it.

Such discrepancies are the bane of the nonfiction writer and bliss for the novelist: they left me free to pick and choose among the delicious "facts" of Sand's life in order to imagine a story, to occasionally make minor modifications in the time line, and to use my own instincts in interpreting the meaning of certain events or statements.

I consulted and am particularly indebted to two excellent books: *Story of My Life: The Autobiography of George Sand,* edited by Thelma Jurgrau, which in 1991 was masterfully translated by a great number of people into a 1,184-page book so that George Sand's own words about her life could at last be available in English; and *Lélia: The Life of George Sand,* by André Maurois, translated by Gerard Hopkins. I am also indebted to George Sand herself, whose beautiful words are woven throughout the manuscript.

Most of the events in this novel are based on those I read about: some are my creation, but all of them serve to support my major premise, which is that George Sand was an extraordinary (in the truest sense of the word) human being whose raison d'être was love, and who loved most deeply—and tragically—another woman.

I suppose anyone who reads in depth about George Sand falls a little in love with her. I certainly did. I hope that in this fictional portrayal—my dream of her, in essence—I have left her her mystery and given her at least part of her due. Readers seeking further information about the "real" George Sand may be interested in reading one of the many biographies about her or, even better, her books.

ACKNOWLEDGMENTS

IT IS OLD NEWS BY NOW TO SAY THAT A BOOK IS NOT BROUGHT FORTH by just one person. Certainly that was the case for *The Dream Lover,* and there are a number of people to whom I would like to offer my heartfelt thanks. First and foremost among these is my editor, Kate Medina, who responded so enthusiastically when I first expressed my interest in writing a novel about George Sand. Many months later, when I was quite certain—*quite* certain—that I wanted to abandon the project, she said exactly the right thing to keep me going. Kate knows books, she knows authors, and she knows how to do her job in the most admirable and elegant way possible. She should wear a crown when she comes to work every day. In my mind, she does.

Kate's assistant Derrill Hagood is unfailingly kind, patient, and perceptive, and she has done me so many favors that were I to list them all, this book would be twice as long. Thank you, Derrill, for the way I can always count on you. Your kind of dependability is a rare and wonderful thing in today's world.

My agent, Suzanne Gluck, sent me emails letting me know exactly how far into the manuscript she was and how she was feeling about it the first time she read it, and she felt no compunction to tone down her positive response. Her energy, intelligence, creativity, and happy nature are appreciated, and I feel lucky indeed to be represented by her. When people ask who my agent is, I lengthen the syllables in her name just to enjoy sharing the information longer.

Early readers included the extremely talented writer and artist Phyllis Florin. Cindy Kline read a chunk at a time when doubts were beginning to occur, and she assured me that the book was alive and well. Nancy Horan, esteemed author of *Loving Frank* and *Under the Wide and Starry Sky,* offered valuable insights about the writing of historical fiction, to say nothing of sisterly support. And, speaking of sisters, my writers' group offered advice, wisdom, and friendship with this book, as they have done so many times before. My thanks yet again to Veronica Chapa, Arlene Malinowsky, Marja Mills, Pam Todd, and Michele Weldon. And welcome to our newest member, Ina Pinkney.

My copy editor, Bonnie Thompson, was a dream to work with. In the margins of the manuscript, she would occasionally make suggestions in the kindest, most respectful, and gentlest of ways, and invariably I would all but smack my forehead, thinking, *Why didn't* I *think of that?* I have such respect for her instincts, knowledge, and sensitivity, and I can hardly wait for her to make better whatever I come up with next.

Associate copy chief Beth Pearson, with whom I have worked since my hair was black, is aware of how much I like, admire, and depend upon her, but let's have it in print once again, shall we, Beth?

Benjamin Dreyer: You know what you did, and I want to express my thanks again for your calm expertise. Thanks to Barbara Bachman for the book's stunning interior design, and to Ruby Levesque and Paolo Pepe for its magnificent cover. And to the many others on the Random House team: Thank you for believing in me, and for doing what you do so well.

Last, but certainly not least, I want to express my deepest thanks to the readers who gladden my heart every day, and permit me to do the work that I love.

THE

The Dream Lover

ELIZABETH
BERG

A
Reader's
Guide

ELIZABETH BERG
ON GEORGE SAND

> To anyone who observes my life superficially, I must seem either a fool or a hypocrite. But whoever looks below the surface must see me as I really am—very impressionable, carried away by my love of beauty, hungry for truth, faulty in judgment, often absurd, and always sincere.
>
> —*George Sand, in a letter to a friend*

EVEN WITHOUT KNOWING MUCH ABOUT HER, MANY PEOPLE ARE fascinated by George Sand. I am one of them, and I was amazed that no one had written a novel about her. I called my friend Nancy Horan (*Loving Frank*) and told her she just had to write a novel about George Sand: her life was so sexy, so *interesting*! Nancy said, "Nah, *you* do it." So I did.

George Sand, whose real name was Aurore Dupin Dudevant, was a nineteenth-century French novelist whose work elucidated the deepest thoughts and feelings and frustrations of the female psyche and, later in her career, illuminated class struggle. In 1831, when she was twenty-six, she left her philandering husband to attempt a literary life in Paris. At twenty-eight, she published her first novel, *Indiana*, and it made her the first woman to become a bestselling novelist in France. It also made her famous internationally. She was prolific: she wrote more than eighty novels, thirty-five plays, and a great deal of nonfiction. Her work has been widely praised by everyone from Fyodor Dostoyevsky to Elizabeth Barrett Browning. Yet she is mostly remembered today for wearing men's clothing (first, so she could get cheap seats at the theater), smoking cigars, and having scandalous love affairs, most notably with composer Frédéric Chopin, with whom she lived for eight years and whose work she helped shape and inspire. She was friends with Franz Liszt, Gustave Flaubert, and Eugene Delacroix, who painted her. But I believe that the greatest love of Sand's life was a woman, a French actress named Marie Dorval, who, at the time George Sand met her, was the toast of Paris. (She was also was a nineteenth-century wild woman, taking lovers of either sex with impunity and with her husband's knowledge.)

I was first attracted to George Sand because of some tantalizing information that I came across about her in *The Writer's Almanac*'s daily newsletter, which offers a poem and snippets of information about things literary. When I began researching Sand by reading her long autobiography, a number of biographies, some of her novels, her letters, and her journal, I saw that she was a woman of great contradiction: her father was an aristocrat and her mother was a courtesan. George Sand was a rebel who was put into a convent to learn the social graces and ended up wanting to become a nun. She adored children and prized the ideal of family but became estranged from her own daughter and husband. She had a great appreciation for life but also frequently contemplated suicide. She loved the peace of her country estate, Nohant, but was equally drawn to the hustle and bustle of Paris. She spoke out against the enslavement of women yet enslaved herself to men. Described by poet Alfred de Musset as the most feminine woman he had ever known, she often called herself a man. Her entire life was full of drama, both by circumstance and by her own hand.

I came to admire George Sand for the beauty, crystalline logic, and easy flow of her prose, for her acute insight into the human psyche, and for her evocation of the loveliness of nature. I admired as well her mysticism and her politics. But mostly I admired her for her essential goodness of heart, her humanity, her vulnerability. She was a political activist who was heavily involved in the 1848 Revolution; an extraordinary intellectual who sat in salons and had long discussions with poets, writers, politicians, and philosophers; and a staunch advocate for women's rights. But as she would be the first to admit—and often did—her raison d'être was love, and in it she was a fool, just like the rest of us. With this novel, I wanted to present an intimate portrait of a highly sensual, brilliant, complicated woman whose ideas are as relevant today as they were more than 150 years ago.

A CONVERSATION BETWEEN ELIZABETH BERG AND NANCY HORAN

NANCY HORAN IS THE BESTSELLING AUTHOR OF *LOVING FRANK* and *Under the Wide and Starry Sky.*

NANCY HORAN: I know you were strongly drawn to George Sand's story but you resisted writing a novel about her at first. What made you jump in and go for it?

ELIZABETH BERG: Well, the real answer, as you may recall, is that you *wouldn't*! One day I read a little about George Sand on *The Writer's Almanac,* and I got very excited about learning more. I especially wanted to know the "good stuff," which is to say, deeply personal things about her character as well as her thoughts and feelings, even if those things were largely conjecture. I thought you would be the perfect person to write a novel about her; I so admired the way you provided intimate access into the character of Mamah Cheney in *Loving Frank.* So I called you to beg you to write about George Sand. I believe when you answered the phone I said, "Nancy! You have to write about George Sand! She's so *interesting*!" You had just finished *Under the Wide and Starry Sky,* and you weren't ready to begin another huge undertaking. And, of course, I assume you are like most writers and want to pick your own subjects, not have them thrust upon you. At any rate, you said, "*You* write it!" I told you I couldn't possibly. But then the idea wouldn't go away, and so I plunged in, buoyed up by the last words you said to me: "Oh, of course you can write it. It will be fabulous!"

NH: I think creating a voice for a real historical figure, particularly for someone who lived nearly two hundred years ago, is rather tricky. How did you arrive at the voice you used for George Sand? Did you pull expressions from her letters to integrate into the dialogue? Did you stick to language as it was used at the time, or did you feel free to use more contemporary expressions?

EB: You know, it *is* a tricky thing, and I did try hard to stay away from contemporary expressions, which, when you're reading historical fiction, can take you right out of the story. In the end, I think the way the language thing worked for me was the way my other books have worked best: the less predetermined—the less *conscious*—things are, the better.

When I was nine years old, my family lived in Texas for a while. It took me about thirty-five seconds to develop a Southern accent, to incorporate "y'all" quite naturally into my speech. I came in one night and told my parents my friend and I had to stop playing because Sherry was "fixing to eat." My parents exchanged amused glances, and I thought, *What? What's funny?*

Anyway, what I mean to say is that things rub off on me. I have a tendency to imitate, to pretend, to dramatize, as I believe many fiction writers do. So when I read (i.e., "listen to") a lot of a person, as I did when I read George Sand's thousand-plus-page autobiography, *Story of My Life,* that person's ways of thinking and speaking rub off. George Sand entered my subconscious. I began to dream of her; then, I thought, to dream *like* her. I know that might sound arrogant or at least unlikely. But I believe she captured me, and I was a most willing prisoner.

NH: I find the foreignness of the past attractive territory to explore. Modern lives seem more daunting to portray in a fresh way, since so much is familiar terrain. Do you agree? Can you talk a bit about the different challenges and attractions of portraying modern lives versus historical lives?

EB: I agree that the past is wonderful to explore: evocative—thrilling, really—and quite necessary, when you're writing historical fiction. But I find it much more difficult to write about the past than the present. I move through pages very quickly and easily when I write about modern times. When I'm trying to re-create something from so long ago, the pressure bears down upon me. So much to find out about, and to be responsible for! Clothes, language, the sounds of the streets, what bathrooms were like, how lamb was served, the tone of the newspapers, where one bought soap, the feel of a carriage ride over cobblestones. I spent a long time with my chin in my hands writing this book, wondering if I really should go on with it.

NH: George was considered a scandalous woman for her time. What do you think was particularly unusual about her? Do you think her reputation affected—helped or hindered—her career as a writer? How did it feel to write a novel about such a controversial figure?

EB: Henry James described coming up with the idea for a novel as creating a big "to do" around a character. When you write about someone real who was so controversial, the "to do" comes built in. But I am always interested in the backstory—when someone is described as being scandalous, or out of order, or different, or demanding, especially when that someone is a woman—and I am full of questions. What made her that way? What kind of vulnerability is behind great strength? What kind of sadness lives inside a person believed to be joyful? Or, conversely, what gaiety is there in someone viewed as being very serious? One of the things I learned in writing this novel is that the esteemed Russian writer Ivan Turgenev loved being silly. He was quite the party animal, as opposed to another of Sand's close friends, Gustave Flaubert, who was like Eeyore the donkey in his depressive outlook.

I think what was unusual about Sand was the way her male and female qualities existed side by side, the way she was fluid about assuming the character of a man or a woman, sometimes simultaneously. Also, she was a mass of contradictions: she advocated strongly for women but didn't like being around them all that much (with one notable exception). She was called bold but in fact was very shy. Her strongest desire was for love, but she had a pattern of having (or making) relationships disintegrate. In her time and even now, she was both reviled and adulated. She created her own god, renouncing the ideas found in organized religion, yet in her youth she wanted to be a nun.

Her reputation may have helped her as a writer, but I think it was mostly her great talent. And in any case, her reputation changed. In her own small hometown of Nohant, she went from being disapproved of—even reviled—to being called "The Good Woman of Nohant," and she was deeply mourned by everyone from peasants to princes after her death.

As to how it felt writing about her, one phrase will do: challenging but exhilarating.

NH: George's relationships with women, especially the women in her family, were very complicated. What connections do you see between George's relationship with her mother, Sophie, and George's subsequent relationship with her own daughter, Solange? With other people? With the actress Marie Dorval? Chopin? What might these relationships say about George herself?

EB: This is a very complicated question with a simple, two-part answer, as I see it. If you do not get the love you so desperately need early in your life, you search for it ever after. And whatever your experience of love was in those young and vulnerable years, you tend to reenact it in future relationships. Sand's mother was by turns loving and cruel, or at least indifferent; so Sand was with her own daughter. In Sand's relationships with men, she tended to go quickly from being passionate to being maternal, because she felt that if men needed her, they would not leave her. For Marie, she served as a man who loved with the intensity and devotion and sensitivity of a woman. I think it takes an enormous amount of insight and hard work to make yourself step out of or away from dangerous patterns that you adopt unconsciously early in life, but it can be done. That George Sand was happy and at peace with herself in her later years (after so many years of experiencing deep depressions and suicidal ideation) attests to that.

NH: Was it daunting to write about another writer? Did you reach any new understandings about the art of writing by studying Sand's works and her comments on the subject? Do you see yourself any differently, as a writer, now that you've written this book?

EB: It wasn't daunting to write about another writer, but it was daunting to write about someone so fiercely intelligent, and whose prose was so startlingly lucid and precise. I didn't reach any new understandings about the writing process; rather, I had my own methods validated. Sand did not plot, she was wildly prolific, and she wrote from the heart. I can, as they say, relate to that.

NH: You re-create so wonderfully life in Paris in the 1820s and '30s, and in the French countryside near Sand's family's estate at Nohant. What did you find about these places, this era, that inspired you? Was it liberating to write about an era different from your own?

EB: It was great fun to imagine how the sights and sounds of the city of nineteenth-century Paris would collide with the pastoral life Sand lived at Nohant. My challenge was to present the charms and allure of both lives. Sand loved and needed the intellectual and artistic and political life she had in Paris, but she needed equally the gifts of nature that she found in Nohant.

I was inspired by all the revolutionary goings-on in Paris at that time, and the way that roles of women were challenged, the way that socialism kept trying to assert itself, the way that artists—writers, musicians, painters, poets—gathered together in salons for entertainment that was the opposite of virtual reality. Would that we had such salons today! I wanted to be there in those salons, and one of the joys in writing this book is that I was.

As for the scenes of nature, I'm a nature and bird lover myself, so all of that came pretty easily.

NH: What do you hope that your readers will take away from this book, and from George herself? What do you feel is most important about her relevance today?

EB: George Sand's struggle to become and stay herself, in all her permutations, was of paramount importance, and that idea is still relevant today, whether you're a man or a woman. How is it that we find our deepest truths? What directions in life serve to move us toward our highest purposes? How do we accommodate and respect changes in ourselves? What do we owe the earth, and each other? How can we focus on appreciating the small gifts we are offered daily, for free, and relieve ourselves of the never-ending quest for more, more, more? How can we honor (and use!) what makes us different from others, rather than be ashamed of it? What is the best way to love and be loved?

All of these questions percolated in me as I wrote about George Sand, and I would be happy to have people who read the book take away the idea that answering such questions is not only our duty but our great pleasure. I would also like readers to consider whether it is true that we owe it to ourselves, and to those we love, to live in truth, even when it's hard—perhaps *especially* when it's hard. If I could wish for one more thing, it would be that George Sand's prose would be appreciated again, and that she would be understood as someone who was a bit more than the ruthless cigar-smoking nymphomaniac she is often portrayed as.

Finally, honestly, I will tell you that I hope readers will finish the last sentence of *The Dream Lover* and think to themselves, *Boy! That was a good read!*

QUESTIONS AND TOPICS FOR DISCUSSION

1. George Sand felt she was abandoned by her mother. Did being left with her grandmother at an early age make her stronger or weaker? In what ways would George's life have been different if her father had lived?

2. George behaved boldly but was at heart very shy. Did you notice any other paradoxes in her character and life?

3. Two very different environments were important to George's life and work: the city of Paris and her country home at Nohant. Which do you think was more important to her? What did each offer her?

4. How do you think George's marriage affected her art? Do you think genetics or life circumstances contribute more strongly to the making of an artist?

5. George fluidly assumed both male and female roles. She often referred to herself as a man, yet Alfred de Musset called her the most feminine woman he had ever known. What was your perception of George?

6. The mother-daughter relationships depicted in *The Dream Lover* are particularly complex. Do you think Sophie was a "bad" mother? What about George herself?

7. What do you think George needed most from a relationship? How is that different from what she believed she needed?

8. George described herself as "very impressionable, carried away by my love of beauty, hungry for truth, faulty in judgment, often absurd, and always sincere." Do you agree?

9. In her quest to live truthfully, George left her husband altogether and was away from her children much of the time. How do you feel about that? Was she motivated by necessity or selfishness?

10. George quickly became maternal with her male lovers. She said at one point that it was so they would become dependent on her and not leave her. What do you think of this statement?

11. One of the great sorrows in George's life was her contentious relationship with her daughter. What might have improved her relationship with Solange?

12. *The Dream Lover* suggests that Marie Dorval was the great love of George's life. How do you feel about Marie's assertion that one seeks not the object of one's desire, but desire itself? Could George have accepted anything but continuous passion in a relationship?

13. Nature and spirituality were important constants in George's life. What were the sources of these affinities? How did they play out in her work and in her life? How did they affect her worldview? If she had been allowed to become a nun, do you think she would have stayed one?

14. Some people say that the hardest sorrow to bear is the idea of what might have been. What do you think?

15. Did you learn anything surprising about George's famous friends, such as Chopin, Flaubert, Balzac, and Liszt?

16. At the end of the novel, George is quoted as saying in a letter to Delacroix that nothing dies, nothing is lost, and nothing ends. What sentiments or experiences do you think fueled that remark? How do you interpret it?

17. Do you think that George and the things she wrote about are still relevant more than 150 years later?

18. *The Dream Lover* invites us into the world of salons. Do you think that book clubs are the same kind of enriching, stimulating environment? Why do we need book clubs? What do they offer our spirits and psyches that reading alone does not? How can they be expanded to provide an even deeper experience?

To plan your own French book club meeting with the Dream Lover Book Club Salon Kit, please visit issuu.com/rhpg/docs/dreamlover-bookclubkit_v7-rgb/1.

PHOTO: © CHRIS POPIO

ELIZABETH BERG is the author of many bestselling novels, including *Tapestry of Fortunes, The Last Time I Saw You, Home Safe, The Year of Pleasures,* and *Dream When You're Feeling Blue,* as well as two collections of short stories and two works of nonfiction. *Open House* was an Oprah's Book Club selection, *Durable Goods* and *Joy School* were selected as ALA Best Books of the Year, *Talk Before Sleep* was short-listed for an Abby Award, and *The Pull of the Moon* was adapted into a play. Berg has been honored by both the Boston Public Library and the Chicago Public Library. She is a popular speaker at venues around the country, and her work has been translated into twenty-seven languages. She is the founder of Writing Matters, a reading series designed to serve author, audience, and community. She divides her time between Chicago and San Francisco.

elizabeth-berg.net

Facebook.com/bergbooks

About the Type

This book was set in Caslon, a typeface first designed in 1722 by William Caslon (1692–1766). Its widespread use by most English printers in the early eighteenth century soon supplanted the Dutch typefaces that had formerly prevailed. The roman is considered a "workhorse" typeface due to its pleasant, open appearance, while the italic is exceedingly decorative.